An
Accidental
Spy

Other Books by Stephenia H. McGee

Ironwood Plantation

The Whistle Walk

Heir of Hope

Missing Mercy

*Ironwood Series Set

*Get the entire series at a discounted price

The Accidental Spy Series
*Previously published as The Liberator Series

An Accidental Spy

A Dangerous Performance

A Daring Pursuit

*Accidental Spy Series Set

*Get the entire series at a discounted price

Stand Alone Titles

In His Eyes

Eternity Between Us

Time Travel

Her Place in Time

(Stand alone, but ties to Rosswood from The Accidental Spy Series)

The Hope of Christmas Past

(Stand alone, but ties to Belmont from In His Eyes)

Novellas

The Heart of Home

The Hope of Christmas Past

www.StepheniaMcGee.com

Sign up for my newsletter to be the first to see new cover reveals and
be notified of release dates

New newsletter subscribers receive a free book!

Get yours here

bookhip.com/QCZVKZ

An Accidental Spy

THE ACCIDENTAL SPY
SERIES

Book One
Stephenia H. McGee

By The
Vine Press

Library Cataloging Data
McGee, Stephenia H. (Stephenia H. McGee) 1983 –
An Accidental Spy; The Accidental Spy Series Book One/ Stephenia H. McGee
368 p. 5.5 in. × 8.5 in. (13.97 cm × 21.59 cm)
By The Vine Press digital eBook edition | By The Vine Press Trade paperback edition | Mississippi: By The Vine Press, 2015
Summary: A woman finds a cryptic message and becomes involved in a plot to abduct Lincoln.
Identifiers: ePCN: 2020933672 Library of Congress | ISBN-13: 978-1-63564-046-5 (trade) | 978-1-63564-048-9 (ebk.)
1. Historical Christian 2. Clean romance 3. Civil War fiction 4. Action and Adventure 5. Courageous Heroine 6. Overcoming racism 7. Spies and espionage

For Jason,
Who never stops believing in me.

One

"No man has a good enough memory to be a
successful liar."
Abraham Lincoln

Rosswood Plantation
Jefferson County, Mississippi
February 4, 1865

Let the dead bury the dead. Annabelle Ross forced the spade
another few inches into the ground, then paused a
moment to wipe the sweat from her brow with a dirty sleeve.
Dead, indeed. Her arms were numb from digging, and her back
and legs were starting to cramp. A heart hardened against the
grisly task beat rapidly with exertion underneath what had once
been the gown of a privileged heiress. But that was before the
war, her father's death and…. Well, it didn't matter now anyway.

She hadn't had time for anything other than the soldiers
from both North and South who at one time or another had
filled her home to overflowing. Annabelle slammed the spade
into the earth, her fingers so numb from the cold she hardly
noticed the forming blisters. She gave these men the best she
could—a too-shallow grave and a few parting words. She
recorded every name, should their families ever come to look

for them. Until then, Annabelle had no choice but to share her land with the dead.

"Miss Belle, you done enough diggin' today."

Annabelle looked up from the hard ground and into a face that looked as tired as she felt. The waning light of another long day cast shadows on Peggy's dusky skin and made her look older than she should. Peggy lowered the rear legs of the makeshift cart to the ground, giving a soft grunt as she finally released the weight. Annabelle mustered a smile she hoped would soothe away some of the worry lines creasing Peggy's brow.

"I know. But I didn't think we could stand to leave him out another day."

Peggy pressed her lips together but said nothing. She was less fond of leaving dead men in the house than she was of Annabelle digging. Annabelle reached down and grabbed one of the worn boots and gave the body a tug. He felt twice as heavy as when they'd loaded him into the cart. "Help me get him in."

Peggy hesitated, and Annabelle wondered if this would be the time she refused, but, as usual, Peggy clamped her jaw tight and grabbed the other boot. They heaved and struggled until the body fell from the cart, scraped over the rough earth, and finally landed in the hole with an unceremonious thud just as the sun began to dip below the trees. Annabelle resisted the urge to place her dirty fingers under her nose in a futile effort to hold off the stench.

Peggy sighed. "It's a right shame we ain't got no preacher for them. You sure burying them here is a good idea?"

Annabelle pinched the bridge of her nose and let out a weary sigh. "Peggy, you've asked me that question a dozen times, and a dozen times I've given you the same answer."

"Still don't like it."

Annabelle nearly agreed, but she knew that would only give Peggy more footing to try to wear down her resolve. "Come on. It's getting dark. We need to get him covered. Lord willing, he will be the last soldier we lay to rest at Rosswood."

"Humph. You said that 'bout the last two."

Annabelle threw a scoop of dirt on the body and ignored her. Peggy grunted and grabbed the other shovel. By the time they patted down the mound and tossed on a few rocks in a scant attempt to keep the coyotes at bay, darkness had descended and blanketed Rosswood in a shroud of shadows.

"I got some water on the stove so we can get you a good bath tonight."

Annabelle looped her hand through Peggy's arm as they trudged back to the house. "No, I don't want you carrying all that water up the stairs again. It's too much trouble. I'll just wash from the basin."

They walked across dry ground that had once sprouted fields of cotton that had made Annabelle imagine what a thick covering of snow might have looked like where Momma had grown up in New York. She'd told Annabelle stories of snow that had fallen so heavy it had blanketed the ground like a quilt instead of huddling in icy patches as it did here, clinging to the shady places and crunching beneath her too-worn boots.

"Now you know your uncle might be here any day," Peggy said, interrupting her recollections of Momma. "Won't do for him to see you lookin' like a field hand and not a lady."

Annabelle drew in a long breath of air that smelled like soggy earth and the faint aroma of death from which she could never truly escape. "He's not my uncle," she mumbled. Peggy didn't respond.

It was bad enough she'd had to live under Grandfather's rule. She didn't welcome Andrew's. She clenched her hands at her side. "What does he expect to find here? Rosswood spent two years as a hospital and now as a makeshift haven for the wounded they left behind. Our people have long since run off, and war has stripped us all of what we once were. This place is a wretched waste. What will it matter if I look like a field hand? I work like one."

Peggy's fingers squeezed her own and she knew she'd let fatigue tinge her words with bitterness. Still, Peggy did not chide her because they both knew her words rang true.

"Forgive me, Peggy. You're right," Annabelle said, her shoulders slumping as they neared the house. "I should look presentable, even for him. Though I know Father would have preferred his own brother looking after Rosswood until I wed. Not Andrew."

Peggy nodded, her scarf-wrapped head bobbing in the darkness. "Ain't no doubt of that. But since he ain't responded to your letter, I don't see how you're gonna be able to count on him to come instead of Andrew."

If only Father hadn't died.

Annabelle huffed and turned the subject back to the original topic. "I still won't have you lugging all that water up the stairs. We'll move the tub into the kitchen. I can bathe by the hearth while you cook."

They stepped onto the back porch and Peggy lifted a lamp from the hook on the post, producing a match from her apron and birthing a tiny flame. Soon the flame filled the chimney with a warm glow, and a shiver that hadn't been caused by the chill ran down Annabelle's spine. She'd grown too afraid of the shadows. The flickering light danced across Peggy's face, illuminating worry lines that seemed to grow deeper with each passing day. Finally, Peggy nodded. "I guess I don't see no harm in it. Ain't like no one's gonna notice."

Grandfather had retired hours ago. He'd started staying in his chamber more and sleeping longer. Annabelle suspected he did it to hide how rapidly the sickness was getting worse. Or at least try to hide it until his son made it to Rosswood. And Grandfather would be the only one who would care if Annabelle bathed in the kitchen.

They turned from the dark house and again descended the steps, two of which had begun to sag. Only two soldiers remained within, and she'd already seen to their supper and bandages. Surely they would not need her again tonight. Guilt tugged at her anyway, and she paused.

Peggy turned. "What's wrong?"

"I better check on them once more. I've been out of the house for a good while. What if something happened again?"

Peggy's brows drew together. "You've done enough. You gonna run yourself into the grave."

"Do you think you can get the tub set by yourself?"

Peggy tilted her head. "Child, who you think toted that thing up and down them stairs all those years? I think I can get it into the kitchen."

You used to have help, Annabelle thought. But why bother saying it? "Thank you. I'll be along in a few moments." She turned to find another lamp, wondering if it would have any oil.

"I got a bad feeling about that one," Peggy said to her back.

"Won't be long before we're draggin' him through the yard, too."

Annabelle cringed. She knew little by way of nursing, only what she had observed when the house was used as a hospital, but she prided herself on having learned enough to care for the few who had been left behind. She refused to lose another one. She looked over her shoulder. "I only want to be sure Lieutenant Monroe's fever has not returned again. I won't be long."

Peggy dipped her chin and lifted her lamp. "Here. Take this 'un. I can get to the kitchen without it."

Annabelle hesitated, but realizing that arguing would only delay the comfort of warm water to her tired muscles, she consented and took the lamp. She unlatched the rear door and stepped into the house as quietly as she could, careful to avoid any planks she knew would protest her weight with a groan. She passed Grandfather's door and underneath the archway, turning to her left and into what had once been her father's library.

She turned down the flame until it barely glowed in the chimney and raised it to the open doorway. Two forms lay draped in thin blankets on the floor. A soft snore drifted from one of the forms, but neither moved. Relief spread through her. They both appeared to be resting comfortably. Neither thrashed about nor mumbled in his sleep, as each had often enough done when the fever raged. The officers hadn't thought these men would survive their wounds and had, thus, left five Confederate soldiers with her when they finally abandoned the hospital. Three died. Two remained. If she did not care for them, who would?

She stepped silently onto the rug and across to one of the pallets on the floor. The flickering light revealed the unshaven face of a man about the age her father would have been, had he not found his death in battle. The man's chest rose and fell evenly. Perhaps the fever had finally broken and he would no longer mumble strange, disconnected words in his sleep. She slipped in between the two pallets positioned so the men's feet pointed to the glowing embers. Annabelle prayed spring would soon arrive and give way to warmer nights, lessening the amount of logs she'd need to chop.

She lowered herself to her knees between the two forms, telling herself that having only one petticoat was a *good* thing, since it gave her easier movement. Annabelle peered into the face of Private Jack Hanson, who seemed nearly docile in his sleep. He'd lost his right arm at the shoulder and his right foot. She'd been there helping the nurses hold him down when the surgeon had sawed them off, listening to a string of words that would have infuriated her father, had he been alive to hear them spoken in her presence.

Annabelle lifted the light and checked the bandage around the stump on his arm, pleased to see it no longer seeped. She should check the one on his foot, but that would require removing his covering and—

A hand suddenly closed around her wrist, and she drew a sharp breath.

"Shhhhh," Edward Monroe hissed before the scream dislodged from her throat. He dropped his hand. "I didn't mean to frighten you."

She snatched her gaze from where it had rested at Jack's feet and whirled around to level it on Lieutenant Monroe's face. He offered a lopsided grin as his only apology for frightening her. She glared at him. "Are you mad? You could have made me drop the lamp," she whispered between clenched teeth.

He pulled himself to a sitting position and regarded her for too long. She was much too tired to indulge him in one of his long-winded conversations, so she thought to withdraw before her silence gave him the encouragement to continue.

"I know you took it from him."

Her heart lurched. *Impossible.* She narrowed her eyes, wondering if he could see the truth in them in the low light. "I don't know what you mean."

He regarded her with the same disappointed look her father might have given her over another poorly done page from the arithmetic primer all those years ago.

"It's of grave importance," he said in a strained whisper.

She settled back onto her heels and regarded him. "What is?"

He shook his head. "It was entrusted to us. I must leave here and get it to…." His voice trailed off, and she caught herself leaning forward in anticipation.

She rose and straightened her skirt. "If it were yours, then you would have it."

His eyes darkened. "You don't know what you're fooling with, girl."

Annabelle turned on her heel to leave, but he grabbed a fistful of her skirt. She looked down at him, just now noticing the sweat beading on his head. Perhaps fever hadn't fully left him, and she'd not been able to stop the festering in his leg after all. He drew a long breath and blew it out slowly, stirring the hair that hung damp across his forehead.

"Are you loyal to the cause?"

Annabelle's heart rate accelerated. She'd done everything to conceal her true feelings, hadn't she? "Of course I am. Why would you even ask such a thing?"

He frowned. "I've seen many a lady with a notion that she can conduct her own thinking, even when it goes against the men of her country."

Annabelle bristled. *Why, of all the....* She ground her teeth. She wouldn't learn anything if she snapped at him. "My father died resisting the Northern Aggression, *sir.* You would do well not to accuse me of disrespecting his memory." She looked down at his hand still holding fast to her dress. "Unhand me, Lieutenant Monroe."

He released her, slumping back onto his pallet. "It must get to him. I fear it's our only hope now."

"Must get to whom?"

His eyelids fell. "Not for you to know," he mumbled.

Annabelle leaned forward, but he had slipped into a fitful sleep, his eyes darting around behind their lids. She slipped out of the room and down the hall, not daring to breathe until she reached the safety of the rear porch. Once the door latched behind her, she let herself fall into the only remaining chair.

With trembling fingers, she slid her hand into her skirt pocket and touched the folded paper she'd removed from the jacket of the man she'd buried only a short time earlier. Thinking it would be a message to a loved one, she'd planned on trying to find where to send it when she found a spare moment to do so. Now, she feared what she held was something entirely different.

She pulled the slip of paper free and carefully exposed the strange message to the dying flame that could no longer hold the shadows at bay.

Two

"War is indeed cruel. But the South will hold out while
there is a man left."
John H. Surratt

The tree just two inches from Matthew's head suddenly
exploded. Bits of bark rained down on his hair and sent
him ducking for cover. He rolled across the soaked ground,
adding more mud to his already caked uniform, and crouched
behind the oak that had saved his skull. Blood pounded in his
ears, his racing heart thrumming to the familiar tune of battle.
Matthew leveled his rifle at the unseen enemy as the ragged
remainder of his company scrambled for cover, and disjointed
orders fell on men too disoriented after being roused from their
sleep to comprehend them.

"Blasted Yanks! They've found us again," George shouted
in Matthew's ear.

Matthew didn't glance back at his older brother. That Yank
Grierson had spent all winter raiding from Memphis to
Vicksburg, and it was no surprise he'd found their floundering
company here in Jefferson County. General Forrest had ordered
a few of his men farther south, but still the Yanks followed on

their heels.

A flash of blue darted through trees just touched with the clean light of early dawn, and Matthew followed it for only a few seconds before pulling the trigger. The rifle gave its familiar jolt and shoved his shoulder back. An instant later, the man fell to the ground. Once, such a thing had churned his gut. Now, he knew better than to think of the enemy as a man. He swung around to look at George through the lingering smoke. "Got one."

George grinned. "Who would have thought my carefree little brother would have become such a marksman?" He pulled his pistol up and fired across Matthew's shoulder, making Matthew's ears ring and muffling his brother's voice. "I just saved you a bullet in the back of the head. You can thank me later."

Matthew dropped the rifle's stock on the ground, pulled a cartridge from his satchel, ripped it open with his teeth, and dumped the black powder down the upturned barrel. "Then we're halfway to even, since I saved your hide twice in Tupelo." He dropped the Miniè ball down into the barrel. The smoke of a hundred guns drifted on the air, burning his lungs and giving the barely birthed morning an unnatural fog.

With practiced ease, Matthew dropped the ramrod down the barrel and had it back in place before George could respond to his prodding. He cocked the hammer back just in time to see a half-dozen men in blue charge through the woods and into the center of their camp. Where were the perimeter guards? A blast of lead volleyed toward them, and he heard George let out a cry of rage.

Matthew fired his rifle into the belly of a man with a bayonet just as the Yank had appeared to his right and thrust the shiny blade wildly at Matthew's face. He jumped to his feet and swung his head around to find George. Where had he gone?

Blasted man. Matthew had to keep George alive to give Father someone other than himself to pass Westerly on to. Lord knew Father would loathe leaving it to his youngest son, who'd done nothing to prepare for running 4,000 acres of cotton and tobacco. If any of it survived.

There!

Matthew slid down beside George, who grinned as if he didn't know anything about Matthew's struggle to keep his only remaining brother alive, and once more threw himself into the fray. The hum of bullets continued, hurtling fragments that made them shrink and cower in a way that ground against Matthew's nature. Having always been the largest man in any crowd, he was not accustomed to cowering before anyone. A bullet wound had since tempered his pride, and he now shrank away from whizzing bees of death.

He and George dove behind a prostrate tree about fifteen inches in diameter, finding scant security from the hail of iron as he drew long breaths. Despite the cold of early February, he had already begun to sweat in his wool uniform. Matthew cast a worried glance at George and saw his own fear reflected in his brother's eyes.

The balls beat a merciless rhythm into the outer surface of the felled log, thudding viciously as they sank in. A few flew off and rammed into a variety of other objects, thankfully none of which were their skin. Yet.

Matthew clenched his rifle. "Looks pretty bad this time, brother."

George nodded. "If I don't make it, don't forget your promise."

Matthew gripped his arm. "Don't say things like that. We'll get out of this the same as we have the rest of these scraps."

George grinned. "Yeah, sure we will."

Voices cried out as other soldiers dove to the Daniels brothers' scant sanctuary. Someone yelled between a string of curses that the fire was getting too heavy. Next to Matthew, a boy peeked his head just above the log, and before Matthew could pull the lad down, a bullet lodged in the center of his forehead. He fell limp in Matthew's arms, his blood spilling down his face and onto Matthew's uniform.

The familiar metallic smell was something he would never get used to. Matthew squeezed his eyes shut, but the image of the boy's bloody face remained.

He gently released the body to the ground and hoped that the boy had enjoyed a decent life somewhere before the inferno of war had added his soul to the ranks of youth too tender to be exposed to such horrors. Matthew let out a bellow of rage against another young life lost and turned his fury on the devils in blue who had robbed him of nearly everything he held dear.

Somewhere to the rear, an officer ordered the charge, and despite what was certain death, they responded to the shouts that demanded them forward. Matthew sprang to his feet, his war cry still on his lips, and allowed the surge of battle fever to spread like warm liquid through his veins.

He held on to it, needing it to push him to do what must be done. He would pray for the stains it left behind later. For now, he would need that fever to make him forget the peril thundering toward him. George at his side, they dashed forward, vigorously plying their weapons and stopping only to prime the pan and ram the load down. With practiced precision Matthew loaded, fired, and loaded again, stepping forward to dole out death as if he were the reaper. The Blues filled his vision, adding more to their numbers, and sent a feeling of dread snaking down his spine.

Behind him, someone raised the yell, and they pushed harder into the onslaught. Men grunted, and he knew many fell, but he no longer paused to look down. Matthew had long since learned there was nothing he could do to help them, and the time for mourning had to come after the battle, were he to live through it.

"Run them plumb-center!" George yelled as he unsheathed his salvaged cavalry sword and sent it slicing through blue fabric and flesh and bringing a man down.

They threw themselves behind whatever trees were near, darting in and out from their cover and moving ever forward. Time lost its meaning, and Matthew did not know how long his men held against the never-ceasing tide of blue uniforms.

"Watch out!" George screamed and slammed into Matthew, sending them both tumbling toward the sodden earth. They hit the ground, and the breath left Matthew's lungs.

They'd pushed the Yanks back and had now reached a clearing. But then the fleeing men stopped and began to sweep around. George cursed. No longer in the relative safety of trees, and finding that they would not live long in their current position, the brothers made a dash to a low hollow some twenty paces ahead rather than turn their backs to the Yanks forming up to meet them on open ground.

They dove into the hollow and narrowly escaped the volley

of bullets that passed over their heads. Breathing hard, Matthew gripped George's sleeve and prayed that the tiny hill would give him cover just long enough to break a hole through the oncoming line. He looked behind them to see the rest of their brothers in arms coming to a halt and delivering an answering volley. He and George were now caught in the crossfire.

George pulled on his sleeve. "Come on, we've got to retreat!"

No sooner had he said the words than the bugle blast sounded, signaling their company to fall back. Scrambling backward, they had no choice but to give their back to their enemy and run for the cover they had abandoned. Men shouted, volleys blasted, and Matthew wondered if they would survive the impossible journey. He leapt over fallen bodies, their blood painting the dead grass in strokes of crimson.

He'd often wondered how he'd stayed alive this long, given how they'd been on the run from Federals since their latest failure in Tupelo back in July. Matthew had begun to feel both relief and dread that the war would soon find its end. Now, as he heaved in a lungful of smoke-filled air heavy with the scents of the dying, he knew today they would likely find their deaths. George stumbled, and Matthew grabbed him, keeping him on his feet as they desperately ran for the trees.

Suddenly an eruption of pain seared through his calf, and Matthew's leg dropped out from under him. He crashed to the ground, his hands instinctively grasping at the spurting blood that covered his fingers. George dropped down next to him. "Go! Crawl on to the trees. I'll hold these Yanks off!"

Without waiting for a reply, George rose and plowed into the soldiers closing in on them. Matthew gave a grunt and hefted himself forward on one knee and his forearms, each movement bringing searing pain that threatened to blacken his vision. Forcing himself to stay focused, he turned, propped himself up, and began to level his rifle. He searched the fray for his brother, but George was nowhere to be seen. Panic gripped his chest. Matthew swung the rifle back and forth, not wanting to release his bullet until he could find his brother.

Matthew screamed, using the stock of the rifle to push himself to his feet. His knee buckled.

"George!" Matthew bellowed, forcing his leg to hold his weight.

A hand grasped his shoulder. "Got to make it out, Daniels! Come on, or you'll be dead!"

Matthew swung his gaze into the green eyes of David O'Malley, a man with whom he'd often shared stories of card games and beautiful women over a fire and army slop. He shook his head and wrenched his shoulder free. "George is still out there!"

His vision began to swim, and he cursed himself for his weakness. He would *not* surrender to the darkness tugging at him and leave his brother to his death! Matthew shook his head, trying to force the blackness from the edges of his eyes.

"No!" he screamed, leveling his rifle and firing it into a Yank not fifty paces away.

He swayed again, his single leg not obeying his command to hold his body upright. A hand once more gripped him, holding him up as his body sagged.

"You're losing too much blood, Daniels!"

Matthew tried to pull free but could not. The Yanks were nearly on them now. Where was George?

O'Malley screamed in his ear. "He surrendered!"

Matthew allowed himself to be tugged away and stumbled into the cover of the trees.

What did O'Malley say? It made no sense. The rain of bullets slowed, only a few pocking the trees.

The men in the field began to whoop. Matthew ground his teeth.

"Come on! We've lost. Your brother surrendered, and they already captured him! Be glad he's alive."

Matthew swayed. *Captured? No!* He had to save him, bring him back. Matthew pushed off a tree and took a step toward the clearing, but his leg buckled with a searing pain that dropped him to the ground and threatened to plunge him into darkness.

O'Malley's voice was near, though his face swam somewhere too far away. "They pulled him back through the line. There's no way you're going to make it to him, especially with the way that leg is bleeding."

Matthew ground his teeth. "I have to try!"

O'Malley looped his arm around Matthew and pulled him to his feet. "Too late. He's their prisoner now."

Matthew struggled forward, despair nearly robbing him of breath. The Union had long since quit the prisoner exchange, and there was little hope his brother would make it out of a prison camp alive. Prisoner was the same as dead. He dropped to his knees. Why move forward now?

O'Malley sank down next to him and put his face close to Matthew's ear. "I'll pull you out of here alive, big fellow. And if you're willing to help me, I'll let you in on a little secret that just might get your brother back."

Matthew's vision clouded. "Whatever it takes." Then the dreaded darkness robbed him of consciousness.

Three

"Watch and wait must be our motto for the present."
John H. Surratt

*A*nnabelle watched Peggy stir the pot on the stove and tried to remember what it'd been like to have sweet pastries and biscuits in the morning instead of stew, which they now ate at nearly every meal. Not that she would complain. At least they had food. Peggy had an uncanny way of bringing forth vegetation from the earth, no matter nature's resistance.

"What you thinking about so hard over there?" Peggy asked, dropping another slice of sweet potato into the pot from the end of her knife.

"Oh, nothing."

"Hmm. I figured you was worrying yourself silly over that letter that came in yesterday."

Annabelle had, in fact, been curious when Grandfather had snatched it from her fingers before she could open it. She shrugged. "Just a letter from Andrew. Nothing to be too worried about."

"Right odd he was wanting to try and read it hisself without asking you to do it. He knows his eyes ain't what they used to be."

Annabelle peeled the dry skin from an onion. "I suppose he was just excited."

"Hmm. I ain't seen that old man get excited 'bout nothing unless it suits his own purpose."

Annabelle laughed. "What purpose could he possibly have?"

Peggy lifted her shoulders and stirred her pot, disinclined to speak further.

"Besides," Annabelle said, "I have other things to worry about." Thinking now would be a good time to mention the strange scrap of paper, she pulled it from her pocket. "I found this on that soldier we buried yesterday."

Peggy took her time wiping her hands on her apron before turning around to look at the paper Annabelle held outstretched. "What you showing that to me for? You know I can't read."

Annabelle lifted a brow and gave the message a shake. "Well, I can't read it either. Here, look at it."

Peggy took the paper and held it close to her face, studying it. "Don't know what all these things mean, but they sure don't look like no words."

"Exactly. I think it's some kind of code." She lowered her voice, though there was no one around to overhear. "What if it's one of those spy notes?"

Peggy put her hand to her hip. "Now, don't you go letting that mind of yours run wild again. It probably ain't nothing."

"But, what else could it be?"

"Probably just somebody scribbling when he ain't got nothing else to do whilst he's holed up here."

"I don't give anyone paper and ink. I write all their letters for them."

"Maybe your grandfather gave it to him."

She gave Peggy an incredulous look.

Peggy waved her arms around. "All right, that probably ain't it. I just don't think it's nothing to worry over. You got enough to handle without worrying 'bout some scrap of paper."

"Perhaps. But, Lieutenant Monroe said...." She let her voice trail off.

Peggy crossed her arms over her chest. "You been talking to that man again? I told you he ain't quite right. I don't like him."

"He's just been run down with the fever."

Peggy placed her hands on Annabelle's shoulders and leaned close. "You leave that poor man be, and don't go listening to any of that fool stuff out of his mouth."

Annabelle sighed. There would be no point arguing. "Very well. But I do think it's strange."

"Men do plenty strange things. Why fret over it?"

"I suppose you're right." She brushed her skirts and crossed to the cupboard to fetch Grandfather's bowl. "I better hurry and get him breakfast before he gets sore again."

Peggy nodded and ladled two hefty scoops into the bowl. Annabelle glanced in the pot. Already half gone. She could make do with yesterday's bread. Peggy had lost too much weight lately because she'd tried to give Annabelle the best portions.

She pulled on her shawl, held the warm bowl in both hands, and set out into the piercing wind. She found Grandfather at his usual spot at the dining table, sitting in the one chair the Federals had allowed them to keep. They'd agreed not to burn Rosswood since Annabelle had allowed them to run a hospital here, but they'd still relieved the house of most of their belongings and nearly all of the furniture. After they left, she'd let the Confederates use it as a hospital as well. She still wasn't certain they wouldn't have made off with her things as well, had there been anything of value left.

She stepped through the door, keeping her eyes lowered, and placed the bowl in front of Grandfather. She'd taken two steps backward when the increased rasp in his voice caught her off guard. He was getting much worse, and very quickly. His rapidly declining health seemed to make his moods even worse.

"Come, dear. Stay a moment, and we shall talk."

She kept herself from lifting an eyebrow. A term of endearment? He'd given up on the pretense of kindness when he'd taken over the plantation.

"Yes, sir."

She stepped back to the table, keeping her gaze focused on the smooth, polished wood her father had brought from Natchez. The familiar ache flared in her chest. If only he had survived, then perhaps things would not be as bleak.

"I have good news for you, girl."

Annabelle inclined her head. "Truly, Grandfather? What news?"

A smile spread slowly across his face, revealing a full set of yellowed teeth. "I have decided it is time you wed."

Her heart pounded. Heaven help her, but she'd begun to hope that Grandfather would pass on and she would be able to run Rosswood in peace until… Her thoughts tumbled to a halt and she frowned. Why would he be eager to find her a husband? It was her father's will to give Rosswood to her upon her marriage. Until then, it was under Grandfather's control. Why would he now be looking to give that up? He'd chomped at the bit to be plantation master since he'd first set foot on their soil.

"That's not the look of excitement I'd expect from a plain girl without options. I would think you'd be quite pleased I was able to secure you a suitable match."

Annabelle squared her shoulders. "Surely now is not the time for you to have to worry with wedding preparations."

He narrowed his eyes, and that cold stare that often made her shrink away threatened to do so now. But she could not cower. This was too important. She didn't need to be shackled to a man. Father had promised her she would be able to marry for love.

"You think I don't know what's going on in that vapid little head of yours? Foolish girl, I know what you're scheming."

She swallowed hard. "I'm not sure what you're implying."

"You're just waiting on me to die."

She gasped. "Why would you say such a thing? Have I not taken good care of you...?" She trailed off, realizing her mistake too late.

He slammed his fist on the table, rattling his breakfast and causing her to jump. "*You* have taken care of *me*? Who came to this place and saved you from the Yanks?"

She lowered her eyes. "You did, Grandfather."

A fit of coughing overcame him, and he leaned back in his chair, trying to catch his breath. Annabelle remained where she stood, knowing any attempt to console him would only end in another tongue-lashing. Three weeks now he'd been having these fits, and this one was by far the worst she'd seen.

When the fit finally subsided, she filled a glass from the pitcher of tepid water on the sideboard and set it in front of him without a word. When he drained it, he set the empty glass down with a thud. "I know you think this place belongs to you, but I tell you it does not. Women do *not* own property."

Annabelle wrung her hands. She had to speak up this time. "My father left a will. Rosswood was to go to me upon his death. According to his wishes, I'm the owner," she said softly.

"No," he hissed. "It's under my trust until you are wed, then it goes to your husband. *That* is what the will states. It doesn't belong to you."

"Well, actually, the court said it was under Uncle Michael's trust—"

He slammed his fist down again, and she jumped, her words dying on her tongue. "And since he's away with the army, it falls to the next living male relative. Which is me. Heavens, child, you're a dense one. We've been over this!"

Grandfather fell quiet. There would be no point arguing about this again. Father had said he couldn't leave it to her for fear the courts wouldn't allow it. But his intention had been clear. The plantation was hers. She could choose a husband, and they would run Rosswood together. That had even been the plan before the war. When Annabelle wed, she would be given Rosswood, and Father would take up residence in the town home in Natchez. He'd even lined up a couple of young men he'd thought would be both favorable to her and suited to help her run the plantation. But now he was gone, and she was left to the whims of any male relative who could cast his authority over her.

The nervous flutter in Annabelle's heart continued to grow until it blossomed into a seething anger. She finally risked a glance up at him—the one she called Grandfather, though they shared no blood.

He sat there studying her, stroking his thinning beard. "I left my home and came here so this place wouldn't be taken. I've held this land for you, made sure you were not soiled and your home burned. And still, all I get from you is a look of contempt?"

Annabelle distrusted the compassion lacing his words, despite how much she yearned for his favor. "I do thank you for that."

He nodded. "If I hadn't been here, you would've lost this land to the Yanks and likely your virtue as well. What would have become of you then?"

"I don't know."

"This is why women are unfit for anything other than child-rearing. Trust me, my dear. It's what makes a woman fulfilled. A lady isn't meant to deal with the business of plantations." His words were gentler than any she'd heard from him in nearly a year. Still, they made her bristle.

"If there's any business left to handle," Annabelle said under her breath, despite her determination not to antagonize him further. He heard her anyway. His eyes might be failing, but his hearing was still sharp. When would she remember to hold her tongue?

The muscles in his jaw worked, but he plastered a honeyed smile back on his face. "You'll need a suitable man to rebuild this plantation and restore it to what your father intended, and I fear I'll not be able to do that for you for much longer. You want your father's legacy to remain strong, don't you?"

She purposely kept her features smooth. "Yes."

A strange triumphant look filled his faded eyes. "I've decided you'll marry my son upon his return."

Annabelle blinked repeatedly. Surely she misheard him.

"You... want me to marry my *uncle*?" *Who is nearly twice my age and is as handsome as an old goat?*

Grandfather frowned. "Don't sound so disgusted. He's smart as a whip and will do well with his own plantation. Besides, he's only your uncle by marriage. It's not as if you share blood. Yes, you see, this is the best choice. I'll not have to fear leaving you on your own, should I not recover from this lung sickness."

Annabelle stared at him, her mouth too dry to speak. Andrew. Her stepmother's brother, whom she had met only once and immediately disliked. Grandfather intended to marry her off to his son in order to secure the cur a sizable plantation. Annabelle's father's second wife had come from a poor family, though Father hadn't cared when he'd married her. Sarah's father, however, had always had gold in his eyes. She chided herself. Why hadn't she seen this coming? Of *course* this would be why Andrew was coming.

She bristled. "You don't need to worry about me. I shall marry whom I choose, just as my mother did. *I* will find a good man to *help* me care for my Father's land, as were his intentions. There's no need for you to secure a marriage for me."

His hand found her cheek before she could react. The smack sent her head sideways and she instinctively reached up to cover the throbbing. She stared at him with wide eyes. How had he moved so fast?

Grandfather sank back down in his chair. "Why did you have to go and make me do that? You know I don't like striking you."

Annabelle could only stare at him. It had been months since the last time. She knew better than to provoke him.

"Why must you be so disrespectful? After all I've done for you." He shook his head. Another fit of coughing took hold, and Annabelle could not look on him with pity, nor did she fetch him another glass of water.

He wiped the moisture from his eyes and leveled his stare on her. Her defiance had not gone unnoticed. "Don't be a fool, child. You'll marry Andrew when he arrives later this week."

Annabelle gasped. "This week? How is that possible?"

"They've granted a short furlough while his regiment is near enough to Rosswood."

Annabelle swallowed the bile rising in her throat. "What regiment?"

"Why?" He frowned, suspicion lighting his eyes.

"A wife is to pray over her husband's safety, is she not? I would pray for his regiment."

He paused so long she thought he might not answer. Finally, he drummed his fingers on the table and then pointed at her. "He's in company K. That's all you need to know."

She nodded. "And my other uncle? Perhaps I should add him to my prayers as well."

Grandfather smirked, her attempt to beguile proven futile. "Michael's joined up with the Army of Northern Virginia. He'll be of no use to you."

She pressed her lips together. At least he'd given her something. Not that it really mattered. She'd sent two letters to Uncle Michael after Father's death, and neither had been answered. What good would sending a third do? Even if he got it, by the time he did, Andrew would already be here.

"You'll marry Andrew, and, Lord willing, he'll secure a babe within you by week's end." He smiled. "And I'll be able to die knowing I've secured the future of this plantation. Now be gone with you." He waved his hand at her and looked down at his bowl.

Annabelle dashed from the room and found her way back out to the kitchen despite the tears blurring her vision. She burst through the door with a heaving chest, causing Peggy to yelp and drop her spoon.

"Miss Belle! What happened?" She rushed over and wrapped Annabelle in a hug, squeezing her tight. Annabelle dissolved into tears while Peggy stroked her back, the familiar comfort bringing her only a small measure of peace. When Momma had died, Peggy had become the mother she'd needed. Father had thought a new wife would give Annabelle a proper raising, and though Sarah had tried to be her friend and was a good woman, all these years it had always been Peggy she'd clung to. The relationship was yet another thing Grandfather hated about her.

"Oh, Peggy. What am I going to do?" She sank down onto a scarred ladder-back chair and put her head in her hands.

Peggy patted her shoulder. "He chide you 'bout the food again? I'm gonna march right in there myself and tell him he ain't getting no honey and biscuits 'cause I ain't *got* none! He should be glad he gets something in that greedy belly at all."

Annabelle stared at her in disbelief.

Peggy huffed. "I will. You just watch me…." Her eyes widened. "Did he hit you?"

Annabelle said nothing.

Peggy spun on her heel and headed to the door.

"He's going to make me marry my uncle," Annabelle said, choking on the last word and freezing Peggy in her tracks. She turned slowly and regarded Annabelle incredulously.

"That there is incest, and ain't something to ask of no Christian."

"He's my uncle only by marriage, not blood."

Peggy crouched down beside her. "Oh, baby girl. I'm so sorry. I don't know what we can do, but don't you worry, we gonna think of something."

Annabelle put a hand to her heart and nodded. She would find a way. Whatever it took, she would not be used as a pawn in Grandfather's greed.

Four

The ground underneath him swayed and jostled, and Matthew wondered if he'd spent too long at a card table letting a serving girl talk him into too much whiskey. He groaned and tried to turn on his side, the throbbing in his head threatening to relieve his stomach of its contents. When would he ever learn to…? But no, he was at war. He'd not spent yesterday in a tavern but at battle.

His eyes flew open, and he found himself piled in the back of a wagon with a half-dozen other bleeding and moaning soldiers. The events of the skirmish formed in his memory, and he bolted upright, pushing an unconscious man off his arm. His fingers wedged through the press of bodies and found the pain radiating through his calf. Someone had cleaned and wrapped it, and from what he could tell, it didn't look to be seeping. There was hope enough in that.

Matthew twisted and hailed the buckboard driver. "Hey, Private!"

The gangly youth turned to look at him with a grin. "Mornin', Cap."

"Stop and let me off."

The private turned his focus ahead and spoke over his shoulder. "Can't do that. I've been ordered to haul the wounded to our next camp."

"We're moving again?"

The boy nodded. "We lost a lot of men back there. I was told there's another company camped in Jefferson County that's better off than we are. We're to join up with them. Word is they've got a doctor, too."

Matthew sighed and shifted, receiving a glare from the man who had to pull his foot free from Matthew's weight. "It's far too crowded in here. I need to get out."

The boy shook his head. "Sorry, sir. I have orders to get us there as quick as possible, and we don't got time to wait on lame men hobbling."

Matthew clenched his teeth and regarded the men marching behind them. He hated riding in a wagon while they trudged along on sore feet. Many had bandaged arms, heads, and other various parts that were not required for walking. He swept his gaze over their haggard faces and wondered if he would ever again be the same man who'd joined this foolish campaign with such gusto. War had not brought glory. It had only brought misery.

His attention landed on David O'Malley, who met him with a steady stare and then gave a slow nod. Matthew owed the man a debt of gratitude for pulling him to safety. Otherwise, he would probably be waking up a Yankee prisoner, if he woke up at all. David lifted his eyebrows, the unspoken question passing between them. The muscles in Matthew's jaw worked. He gave another nod. He'd not forgotten. Whatever O'Malley had planned, if it would get George back, Matthew would do what he must.

They traveled along uneven roads for the remainder of the day, the wagon jolting wounds and causing men to groan. He hated sitting among the injured, too pathetic to walk on his own two legs. When they finally came to a halt, Matthew was in such a sour mood that one look at his face sent everyone who thought to address him turning a different direction. They endured the tedious task of roll call and then continued to the medical tent where the rancid scent of old blood and unwashed bodies greeted them.

Matthew resisted the urge to push past a man with a broken leg, knowing his foul mood and impatience were not this poor fellow's fault. When the men at the rear of the wagon finally unloaded, Matthew lurched off the buckboard. When his feet hit the ground, pain shot through his calf, but he ignored it and began shuffling off in the direction opposite the medical tent.

"Captain Daniels!"

Matthew drew a long breath and let it out slowly through his nose. Private Jones, the boy who'd driven him like an invalid all day, jogged around to stand in front of him. "Pardon, sir, but all the wounded are to report to the surgeon."

Matthew glared down at him. "I don't require medical attention."

The youth didn't waver. "Sorry, sir. Them's the orders."

Matthew ground his teeth and turned on his good heel, trying his best to walk without a limp, though his traitorous leg disobeyed his every intention. He walked through the flap of the medical tent and waited his turn.

When the surgeon finally made it to him, he lifted Matthew's leg without greeting and inspected the wound. "Looks like it made a clean shot, no shrapnel or pellets that I can see. Should heal up nicely," the doctor said, pushing his spectacles up on his nose. "Stay off it as much as you can, and as long as the gangrene doesn't set in, you should be fine."

He rose from his squatted position and turned to another patient before Matthew could respond. Where would he go now? He looked around, but everyone seemed much too busy to take notice of him. He slipped out the front of the tent and nearly ran directly into Lieutenant Colonel Hood.

Hood looked up at him with surprise. "Where are you going, Captain? Aren't you listed among the wounded?"

"Yes, sir, but the doc said to just take it light on the leg for a while. It was a clean shot and shouldn't give me much trouble."

"Very good. We're in need of men on perimeter patrol. Good place for a man who needs to sit still for a while but can still be useful. Report to the rear of the encampment."

Matthew gave a crisp salute. "Yes, sir." At least he would remain on duty. He made his way slowly through the lines of tents, thankful that their ragtag company had found another of Forrest's regiments to join forces with. Most of the army had moved up into Tennessee or had gone east to Alabama to hold off the Feds, and few remained deep within Mississippi.

The more he walked, the more the leg began to protest. He'd made it almost to the post command when he heard his name called from off to his left.

"Over here, Daniels."

O'Malley hurried to his side and grasped his elbow. "There's a creek right down here. How about you and I go refill our canteens?"

Matthew followed him a short distance into the tree cover, refusing O'Malley's offer to shoulder part of Matthew's weight. O'Malley knelt beside a small, muddy stream and busied himself unscrewing his canteen. Matthew was unsure what he should do, since he was not carrying his canteen. Besides, he was afraid to put himself in a squatted position, lest he find himself stuck in it. But his leg was throbbing, and he knew water was not the only reason for this particular location. He put his back to a young pine and allowed himself to slide down to the earth with a soft grunt.

"Do you want to get your brother back?" O'Malley said over his shoulder.

Matthew picked some of the dried blood from around his nails. "You know they haven't been exchanging prisoners. Unless you plan on helping me break him out, I don't know what you think you're going to do about it."

"You are too narrow in your thinking, my friend."

Matthew's brows drew together. "What do you have in mind?"

"I have friends, connections. There's a group of us—a secret organization, if you will—that has plans. Big plans." He studied Matthew, as if deciding if he should continue. Matthew lifted his brows to encourage him along. O'Malley narrowed his lids. "Do you want to be a part of something big? Something that will change the tide of this war and put your name in history?"

"I only want my brother back."

"To get your brother back, you need leverage."

"And *you* have that kind of leverage?"

"We will."

"And why help me?"

"Frankly, because we could use someone like you. A man of your size can come in handy. I'm taking a big risk including you on this, Daniels. Don't let me down. You won't need to do much, and in exchange I will be sure your brother is among the first released."

Matthew eyed him cautiously. What could it hurt to hear him out? "I'm listening."

O'Malley glanced around and lowered his voice. "I know how to get your brother back," he whispered. "All we have to do is abduct their president."

Five

"She had better keep out of any of his wild schemes;
they are barely practical, and he who undertakes them
must perish."
John H. Surratt

Annabelle carried two bowls of collards and two slices of cornbread on a wooden platter into the library. Despite Grandfather's grumbling about her continuing to feed the abandoned soldiers, he hadn't yet kicked them out of the house.

She swished into the room, her patched skirt skimming floorboards that needed to be swept and stirring up little bits of dust. Both soldiers were awake and seemed to be in a fair mood. A deck of worn playing cards was strewn between them on the floor. Jack held several fanned out in his only hand, and Annabelle wondered how he could even play with such a disadvantage.

"I bet Miss Ross could even beat you," Monroe taunted as Annabelle stepped closer to their game.

Jack frowned. "Women don't play cards."

Monroe rolled his eyes. "Precisely."

Jack Hanson was a gentle man, though not quick-witted.

Annabelle smiled down at him. "Don't pay him any mind, Private Hanson."

"I told you to call me Jack, Miss Ross."

She inclined her head. "So you have. Now, here, I've brought you fellows some supper."

They sat cross-legged on the floor and accepted her paltry offerings with nods of gratitude. She sank down on her knees beside them and arranged her skirts slowly. She tried to assess the stump at the end of Jack's leg without him noticing, keeping her eyes low as if she were studying her dress. The bandage still seemed to be clean, despite how much he'd been moving about lately. That probably meant it was nearly scarred over. That was good, because she had little medical experience and even fewer fresh supplies. If it got bad, there would be nothing she could really do for him. Beyond feeding them, changing a few dressings, and keeping them as comfortable as she could, she wasn't really much of a nurse.

She glanced up to see that both men stared at her, curiosity crinkling Jack's brow and suspicion lighting Monroe's.

"So…." she said. "Do you think anyone will be returning to collect you and return you to your units anytime soon?"

Monroe shoveled in a spoonful of greens, chewed them slowly, and swallowed before speaking. "No, ma'am. I wouldn't reckon they would. I think it's more likely that we will have to return on our own."

"You plan on heading out?" Jack asked.

Monroe nodded. "My fever has broken, and it isn't right to continue to take advantage of Miss Ross's hospitality. It's my duty to return to the army as soon as I am able. I'll find the nearest battalion and present my papers there."

Jack shrugged. "I was hoping to go home."

Monroe looked at him as though he were soft in the head. He opened his mouth, but Annabelle interrupted before he could cause any damage. "I'm certain you would be granted an honorable medical discharge, Private Hanson. Wouldn't you agree, Lieutenant Monroe?"

Monroe caught her eye and then nodded. "Oh, yes, of course you would. No dishonor in medical discharge. You've done your duty well, soldier."

Private Hanson gave her a grin that quickly faltered. "Do you think you could send a letter to my ma for me? I don't reckon I'll make it back to the Delta on my own. Some of my kin are going to have to come get me."

She nearly reached out to pat his arm but thought better of it. "Of course I will. And you can stay as long as you need."

"Thank you, ma'am. I'll make it up to you somehow, I promise." He finished the last of his meal, scraping the juices from the bowl with the crumbling cornbread, and then hefted himself up onto his crutch. "If you will excuse me, I need to head out back."

Annabelle rose to her feet. "Here, let me help you."

He shook his head. "No, ma'am. I can do it. I don't need a lady to escort me to do such business." His face turned red.

Annabelle caught herself. Did he not know that she had assisted with changing men's soiled clothing when they were too weak to leave their beds? She opened her mouth to protest, but she could tell his wounded pride required she let him be. "Oh, of course. Forgive me."

He shot her a lopsided smile and hobbled toward the door. She watched him make his way out and then turned to see

Monroe studying her.

"I'll need that paper now, Miss Ross."

She lifted her chin slightly and squared her shoulders. "I'm prepared to trade you for it."

"What do I possibly have that you would require?"

"A uniform."

A look of surprise washed over his angular face, followed by confusion. "What would a woman want with my uniform?"

She scooted closer to him than was proper, her words coming out in a rushed whisper. "I need your help. I have to find my uncle. He's in the Northern Virginia army." Monroe frowned, and she knew a rejection formed on his pursing lips. She hurried on before he had a chance to stop her. "Please, it's imperative I reach my uncle immediately. I've sent two letters and have heard nothing. I know you soldiers must have a better, faster way to communicate than by the regular post. All I ask is that you find a way for me to contact my uncle. I will handle the rest on my own."

"The rest?"

"That's not of your concern."

"Why is it so important that you find him?"

Annabelle stared at him.

Monroe crossed his arms and settled his frame against the wall near the hearth, putting distance between them. "Then we don't have a deal."

Heat flared in her face. "I must speak to him on a personal matter."

"Why?"

Infuriating man! "Because I require his help!"

"And why can your grandfather not give you the aid you

desire?"

She forced her teeth to unclench. "My grandfather is requiring something of me I do not wish to do. I must appeal to the only other living male in my family who can help me."

Monroe leaned forward with what looked to be genuine concern. "What is your grandfather requiring of you?"

"He's forcing me to marry."

Monroe heaved a sigh and leaned back again. "That's no monumental disaster, Miss Ross. He is likely only trying to secure your future. It's not an uncommon thing for a woman to enter an arranged marriage."

"To her own uncle?" she snapped, immediately regretting the words that shot through her lips without consent.

Monroe's eyes widened and then quickly narrowed with his deepening frown. "I don't understand. You wish to run to your uncle to inform him your grandfather plans to attempt to place the two of you into incest?"

She let out an exasperated sigh, looking around to see if they remained alone. The sound of Jack's crutch thudding on the floor gave no evidence of his return, and Grandfather should be asleep. She lowered her voice anyway. "No. The uncle whose assistance I require is my true uncle, my father's brother. Andrew is not really my uncle, but my stepmother's brother. Though I call him Grandfather, his family is not related by blood."

Monroe studied her a moment. "And I'm assuming this Andrew would be your grandfather's heir."

She snorted. "If he had anything of his own to leave an heir. He's had his eye on Rosswood since he first arrived."

"I see."

Did he? A small droplet of hope began to form. She looked at him expectantly, afraid to push while he contemplated.

"Then I agree it's necessary you inform your blood relative that his family lands are in danger. I would imagine they are his by right, as your father had no sons."

Her mouth unhinged, but she quickly snapped it closed, having to form words through clenched teeth. "Rosswood belongs to me and to the man *I choose* to wed. My father's will states it's in trust to Uncle Michael until I wed, at which point it belongs to me and my husband. Grandfather has taken responsibility of the trust, since he was here and I could not get in contact with Uncle Michael after my father's death."

"I see your dilemma, Miss Ross. And I do think it's right that your uncle be made aware of the intentions against him. I will see if I can get a message out to him."

She heaved a sigh of relief. "Thank you. We can leave to-morrow."

He lifted his brows. "I thought you wanted me to send a messenger. What is this about leaving?"

She dropped her eyes. Should she feel so ashamed to admit that she was too cowardly to stay? It didn't matter. "I don't have time to hope a message reaches him. Andrew arrives this week, and Grandfather intends to see me wed and with child the moment he does."

"An event you do not wish to be present for."

"Precisely."

"I see," he said again, stroking the beard on his chin. "Then I have a proposition for you."

"Oh?"

"You will take the message you already possess and deliver

it to my friend for me. Once I know that it's safely in his hands, I will personally escort you to my family lands, where you can wait with my mother and sisters for a response from your uncle. That way, you won't be here for the wedding you don't seem to think you can refuse to participate in."

It was bold, but it could provide a solution to a problem she hadn't found a way around. She'd thought about going to town and staying with her friend Molly, or perhaps asking Mr. Black for help. She didn't doubt they would be willing to aid her. But, she also knew that when Grandfather came for her, neither of her friends would be able to withstand his wrath or keep him from hauling her home. The people in town would likely agree with Grandfather that it would be better she wed and secure a family hold on the land. Why would any of them bat an eye at her desire to choose her own husband? Such a luxury was nothing but frivolity.

But how could she trust this man? He was little more than a stranger. How did she know there would be a safe place with his mother? What if he lied just to get her to do what he wanted?

She narrowed her eyes at him. "Why would you want me to deliver your message? I'm a woman."

"And that, for once, may actually be an advantage and not a hindrance."

"I don't understand."

"Who will expect a woman to deliver it?" he said softly.

The embers in the fire gave off a small glow, the room descending into evening's shadows. Annabelle felt an unexpected thrill scurry up her spine. She leaned closer to the lieutenant, close enough she could smell that she needed to wash his uniform again, and whispered, "You wish it delivered in secret?"

Monroe stared at her as if she were dense, and she quickly tried to right herself before he decided she wasn't up to the task.

She waved a hand. "Of course, you *would* want a coded spy note delivered covertly."

He said nothing, and Annabelle sat back to consider. What were her options? If she took this opportunity to deliver the message and get into a military camp, perhaps she could persuade an officer to send an army messenger with word to her uncle. They might even be so pleased she'd delivered them their spy information that they would be willing to help her in return. At least it would give her another option if Monroe did not hold to his end of the deal.

Annabelle pulled her lower lip through her teeth and stoked the embers in the hearth. Was she really considering dallying in something this dangerous? Something that might help the South and perhaps prolong the war? All because she didn't want to be wed to a man she didn't like? The answer was glaringly obvious. Yes. Heaven help her.

She turned back to Monroe. Could she trust him? Probably not. He studied her with a steady gaze, likely wondering if she was worth the trouble. Why not deliver it himself? The question nagged her, but she pushed it away. She'd heard of women spies running important information. They took a big risk, but they were valued. Maybe, if the camp was close enough to Rosswood, the Confederates would be so grateful for her information they might even send a few soldiers back with her for protection while she waited on word from Uncle Michael. It was a thin and foolish hope, but it was something. Somehow, she feared that even if she refused to wed Andrew, he would force her into consummation whether she'd spoken vows or not.

The lieutenant seemed honorable enough, but he was still physically weak, and she didn't think Andrew would allow either of the two soldiers to stay once he arrived. They wouldn't be able to help her.

She chewed on her lip. Monroe seemed content to let her contemplate. Well, it seemed finding the army was her best hope. Even if they wouldn't send soldiers back with her, at least then she might have two different messengers sent out to find Uncle Michael.

Decision made, she dipped her chin. She would not go with Monroe to his family's land, but he didn't need to know that now. Let him think she wanted his offer. She just needed him to escort her to the camp, since it would be too dangerous on her own. Once she got to the Confederates, she would leave him to his plans and follow her own.

"Very well," she said, her voice disrupting the silence and sounding more resolved than she expected. "I will play spy for you. I shall find a place to store the message where men wouldn't think to look, should we be stopped and searched."

His eyes dropped down her figure, and his eyebrows began to climb. She crossed her arms over her chest and tried to sound confident despite the heat burning in her ears. "Not there, Lieutenant Monroe. I'll roll it up in my hair."

"Oh." He dropped his eyes.

The rear door slammed, and they both looked toward the door. The steady thumping of Jack's crutch reverberated down the hall.

"I will rouse you early. We'll be gone by first light," she

whispered.

He gave a solemn nod. "And then, perhaps we shall see what sort of tenacity the lady of Rosswood keeps hidden under those shy eyes and that deceptively humble manner."

She let a smile tug one side of her mouth into a curve. "So you shall."

Six

"It would serve our turn quite as well to capture the despot, and keep him for a while in Libby Prison. I reckon the South would then gain the day."

John H. Surratt

*M*atthew stared at David O'Malley as if he'd suddenly sprouted a second head. "Their president? As in *Lincoln?*

"Keep your voice down, man. Do you want to be heard?" O'Malley snapped, glancing around their place by the creek.

Matthew lowered his voice. "I don't know what kind of operation you think you have going, but—"

O'Malley held up his hand and interrupted, "There's more going on here than you realize. We have fingers in everyone's pie."

He spoke the words softly but with such conviction that it gave Matthew pause. "What do you propose to do?"

"We have a solid plan, don't worry."

Matthew's ire rose, and he curled his cold fingers into a fist. "And what *is* the plan?"

"I'm not at liberty to involve you in that just now."

Matthew clenched his jaw. The man was an idiot if he

thought that Matthew would just follow along blindly. "You don't know, do you?"

O'Malley swept a hand through his hair. "Look, there are certain precautions that have to be made. We don't all know every bit of the arrangement. What if we were found out? Then everything could be ruined by one fellow with no gate on his mouth."

The man had a point, but it was too outlandish to consider—nothing but the wild dreams of men desperate to see an end to this misery. "This is harebrained." Matthew pushed himself onto his knees and struggled to his feet, pulling against rough pine bark that scraped his palms. "I can't let my brother's life depend on some half-formed plot to abduct one of the most closely watched men in the Union."

O'Malley stepped closer and clenched Matthew's arm. "We have a man who can get near him. He's even been invited to the White House on several occasions." Matthew frowned, but O'Malley hurried on before he could speak. "The target likes him. Trust me, he can get close. We know all of the president's moves."

"Let's say by some chance you actually pull this off. Then what? Do you really think you will get what you want?"

O'Malley released Matthew's arm and stepped back. "I do. I think the North is so bewitched by him they'll do whatever they must to get him back. Think of it. It could turn the tide of this war."

Matthew let his head drop back and looked up at towering pines filled with twittering birds that had no idea about the dangers the men below them discussed. What would it be like to be that free? Never to have to fight wars or see your family destroyed? He sighed. "I only want my brother back."

"And if you could get him back and return to your way of life in peace?"

Matthew let his gaze return from the peaceful treetops to the anxious—and perhaps hopeful?—look on O'Malley's face and ran a hand through hair that felt thick with grime. "I suppose that would be ideal."

O'Malley nodded fervently, excitement lighting his eyes. "So, you see reason."

"Well, I—"

"Hey there! You two!"

O'Malley whipped around as the owner of the voice stepped closer. "Hello, there!"

Matthew didn't recognize the soldier plodding through the underbrush; he had to be a member of the company they'd joined camp with. His bushy brows lowered over deep-set eyes as he regarded Matthew and O'Malley. "What are you two doing out here?"

O'Malley lifted his canteen. "Just getting a full jug after that long march. No worries, I've finished filling up and was just helping my friend here to his feet. He took a shot to the leg." He tilted his head in Matthew's direction.

The soldier slid his gaze to Matthew and studied him as if he would find the secret to life in Matthew's features. Finally he shrugged. "Well, now that you're finished, I'd be glad to help you get your lame friend here back to the medical tent."

Matthew stiffened. "I've been to the surgeon. He released me." The man looked skeptical, so Matthew hurried on. "Lieutenant Colonel Hood placed me on perimeter duty. Said it was a good place for me to go gentle on the leg and remain on duty."

Surprise and something akin to respect lit the soldier's features. "Admirable. Most men would have relished the opportunity to lie on their backs and shirk their load. Come, I will see you set up. My cousin's on perimeter." He grinned. "Might do him good to spend a little time with the likes of you." He whirled around on his heel in crisp military fashion.

David cast Matthew a loaded look. Despite his misgivings, Matthew feared a shot in the dark might be better than no shot at all, so he gave a single nod. O'Malley seemed satisfied with the halfhearted gesture and sauntered up to the retreating soldier, attempting to befriend him with a joke about two Yanks in a bawdy house.

Matthew ground his teeth against the pain in his leg and followed them, wondering about how each had insisted on helping him and yet neither did. Not that he wanted or needed assistance.

By the time O'Malley scurried off with a final wink and Matthew was properly introduced and settled on the rear perimeter, sweat had begun sliding off his forehead and into his eyes, despite the lingering chill in the air. He wasn't entirely sure of the date, but hopefully winter had given its last fanfare with that spattering of snow they'd seen a few days back. Maybe, if he was lucky, they would start to see spring soon.

"Here you go, sir," a young private said, offering him a place on a large tree stump. Matthew nearly refused. A good soldier did not lounge on duty. But even his pride could not outweigh the pain in his leg or the exhaustion that was creeping up on him. He nodded in thanks, lowered himself onto the makeshift stool, and let out a long breath. The young private gave a sloppy salute and mumbled something about returning in a few moments with instructions before he scurried off. Matthew watched him go, shaking his head.

A nauseated feeling sloshed in his gut like from the days when he'd guzzled too much red-eye in the taverns. But it'd been three years now since he'd even taken a swig. Probably not since that night he and his cousin Charles had helped a Yank out of an inn full of hot-blooded Southern boys who were still full of war fever.

If he ever made it out of this death march, he would have to make a visit to Ironwood. He heard Charles was expecting his first child. He stretched his leg out in front of him and gently massaged the sore tissue, his wandering thoughts returning to the outlandish plot he'd been presented. Could there be any hope in O'Malley's foolish plan?

"Hey, there."

Matthew turned to look into the face of the soldier who had escorted him from the woods and to his new post before leaving him with the sloppy private who'd offered him this stump. How long ago had that been? He was too tired to tell. Not long enough for the rest to do him any good, he knew that much. He stifled a groan that threatened to escape his throat as he forced himself up and his leg to hold his weight. "Hello, Captain Holt."

"It has come to my attention you have never been on perimeter patrol before."

Matthew nodded.

"Very well. I'll instruct you on the proper sentry duty."

What was there to instruct? If you saw an enemy approach, you raised the alarm. Even a child had enough wits to know as much. The muscles in his jaw worked, but he said nothing.

"If any Yanks approach, you are to give up a yell and then engage, unless they are carrying a white flag."

We are not to ask them to dance? Well, I'll be.... Matthew stopped the thought and forced himself to keep the odd mix of annoyance and amusement from showing on his face.

"And if it is a fellow brother in gray, you ask for his name, rank, and unit, and if he has a properly signed pass by an official."

"Understood."

"If he does not possess paperwork, he is to give the proper words of passage."

Matthew tilted his head. "I don't know the proper words."

Holt looked incredulous. "That's precisely why I'm here. It's time to deliver the new codes. We change them routinely. Now that we have new soldiers among us, I've been instructed to give a new countersign."

Feeling foolish, Matthew chose only to nod rather than to release another string of dense words.

Holt handed Matthew a small slip of paper. "This has what you need to know. If anyone, anyone at all, approaches, they must give the proper countersign. It doesn't matter who they claim to be or what tale they spin. If they don't give the proper sign, they are to be detained."

"Understood."

Holt narrowed his eyes. "Be sure that you do. It's imperative. We've had all manner of innocent-looking folk approach, spewing all types of lies. It's better for you to detain someone on suitable business than to let a spy pass."

Matthew had heard rumors of spies with secret messages and encrypted letters but had been too busy shooting Yanks and staying alive to pay it much mind. "I will see that it's done."

Holt seemed satisfied and stalked away to deliver the message to the next sentinel on the line. Matthew settled back on his seat and unfolded the paper.

It read simply:

Countersign, February 6, 1865

"Rome"

Official: M. Hood

Seven

"Another year begun, and still we struggle on with no
hope beyond despair..."
John H. Surratt

earest Peggy,

*I'm terribly sorry to leave you a note this way, but I know
if I told you what I was doing you would find a way to stop me.*

Annabelle lifted her pen, shocked at her own foolishness.
What was she doing? In her stress, she'd thought a letter would
be easier than saying goodbye. She had to be half out of her
wits, writing a message to a woman who couldn't read! She
crumpled the wasted paper in her hand and tossed it into the
embers of the near-dead fire in the kitchen hearth. The wad
caught, and a small flame flared, devouring her excuse to avoid
confrontation in a matter of seconds.

Peggy had retired to her room in the basement hours ago.
Annabelle wouldn't have much longer before she was supposed
to rouse Lieutenant Monroe and slip out into the moonlight.
She suspected if they left in the next hour, they could reach
town at dawn. It would be at least another hour or two after that
before anyone noticed their absence.

Annabelle paced the floor. What was she to do? If she did not let Peggy know her intentions, Peggy would assume Lieutenant Monroe had somehow abducted her. However, if she told Peggy her plans, she feared Peggy would either break her fragile resolve to complete this mission or Grandfather would find a way to rip the truth from Peggy's lips. She could not allow Grandfather to know what she intended, at least not until the messengers were on their way.

After the fourth trip around the kitchen, Annabelle determined fretting would do no good. She shouldered the pack in which she had guiltily stored two loaves of yesterday's bread, a handful of nuts, an onion, and three carrots. What would Peggy make for breakfast now? She shook her head and slipped out the door, pulling it closed as softly as possible.

She paused at the back door, changed her mind, and trudged around the side of the house to the slave quarter doors underneath. Thankful Peggy never barred the door, Annabelle entered the small but homey space as quiet as a dormouse.

There were no embers burning in the hearth, and Annabelle sent up a small prayer for an early spring. She tightened her paletot around her shoulders and stepped across the brick floor to the small bed against the wall. She could barely make out Peggy's form beneath the pile of coverings—a mix of thin blankets, tattered curtains that had once graced the parlor, and other random scraps of cloth Peggy had apparently hoarded.

Annabelle placed a hand on the softly rising heap. As soon as she began to lean closer, Peggy let out a yelp and bolted upright, the crown of her head smacking into Annabelle's nose. Annabelle stumbled back, her eyes filling with water.

"Hush!" she hissed before Peggy could scream again. She

placed her hand to the tender bridge of her nose, feeling for damage. There seemed to be none, although the sting released moisture from both her eyes and nostrils. She fought the urge to sniffle.

"Miss Belle! What you doing down here? Something wrong?" Peggy tossed off the coverings and swung her feet out of the bed.

Annabelle held up a hand to stay her, but she wasn't sure Peggy could see her in the meager light. "Don't get up, Peggy. You'll catch a chill in here. Haven't I told you to light a fire at night?"

Peggy remained where she was, the shape of her flimsy white nightdress the only part of her Annabelle could see. "Don't need no fire. I keeps plenty warm without it."

Now was not the time to argue. "Please, get back under the warmth," Annabelle whispered.

This was foolishness. She should not have come here. She glanced at the pack that had dropped to the floor. She just needed to distract Peggy with a proper explanation of her presence, return the supplies to the kitchen, and get herself into bed. There had to be another way to thwart the wedding. She could not leave Peggy alone here with Grandfather. She would likely freeze, or starve, or worse—what if Grandfather tried to sell her and then—

Peggy interrupted her galloping thoughts. "Child, what you doing down here in the middle of the night?"

"Nothing. I'm sorry. Go back to bed." She spun to retreat, but Peggy's cold fingers clamped down on her arm.

"What you doing?"

"I'm… I couldn't sleep."

"Hmm. No wonder. Seeing as how you're dressed for goin' out."

How could Peggy see her so well in the dark when she could barely separate the forms from the shadows in the room? "Well, I couldn't go about in my nightdress, now could I?"

No response.

"It doesn't matter. I'm going back to bed. I'm sorry I roused you."

Peggy did not release her grip. "You're dressed and carrying a bag. I ain't no half-wit. Where you think you going?"

Annabelle's shoulders slumped. "I was going to leave. Try to get word to Uncle Michael and inform him of my predicament."

"Yeah..." Peggy mused. "I reckon he'd be the one that could solve this here mess."

"Yes."

Peggy was quiet for a moment before she spoke again. "What's this really about? We can go to town and send a post in the morning. Why you wanting to go by you self before it's even first light?"

"You're right, I wasn't thinking. I was being foolish. We'll go to town after breakfast. Goodnight." She turned on her heel, but Peggy's quiet words stopped her.

"Miss Belle, I ain't never known you to act without first thinking on something right long and hard. I don't for one heartbeat believe you was just going to sneak out of the house without knowing what you was planning on doing. Now, what're you not tellin'?"

Annabelle sighed. "Very well. Lieutenant Monroe agreed to send my message by one of the army carriers to Uncle Michael if I delivered a secret letter for him in exchange. We were going to head to town before first light so Grandfather couldn't stop us."

"That all?"

Annabelle swallowed hard, now glad for the dim light. "Yes."

"Ain't that bad of a plan, I reckon. Seems a good way to reach your uncle. But, I don't like that part about you giving some letter. Why can't he do that his self? Don't seem right."

"I know." The strain in her voice settled on her own ears, and she felt Peggy's grip tighten. Soon she was circled in the embrace that had comforted away many a childhood fear. But this was not something that could be chased away with affection. "I don't know what I should do, Peggy," she said, stepping back. "I have never trusted *Uncle....*" Her voice dripped with disgust. No, she would call him that no longer. She straightened her spine. "I've never cared for Andrew. On the occasion we met, he seemed too slick with his words, too predatory in his gaze. I fear he possesses the black heart of Grandfather, and will not even attempt to keep it suppressed."

"Then you know what you gotta do. We can't let that man force his way in here and take advantage of you. You go on to town and find some help."

Annabelle paused. She hadn't expected Peggy to agree to a plot so rife with danger. She wasn't quite sure Peggy understood all her plan entailed. It wouldn't be a simple trip to town and back. What if finding the camp where she needed to take the letter took several days? What would happen to Peggy while she was away? "Come with me."

Peggy patted her arm. "No, child. Can't do that."

"Why not?"

"I need to stay here. Keep your grandfather's nose down the

wrong trail. It be better if I can keep him fooled long enough for you to get gone and get home without him knowing what you went to do."

She hadn't thought of that. A plan began to form in her mind. "That could work. You could tell him my feminine inclinations set in, and I'm excited to plan a wedding. Tell him I couldn't sleep—I was so undone with the flutters that I hurried to town before morning light so as to spend the day immersed in wedding details."

"That should work well enough. He won't like you going alone with that soldier, though."

"Tell him Monroe was ready to leave and offered to escort me to town. Grandfather will probably be glad to see him gone. He might rant a little, but what will he be able to do about it?"

But what to do if she were gone for more than a day? She couldn't tell Peggy she might spend the night alone with a man. She would never allow it. Hating herself for the lie forming on her lips, she took a deep breath.

"I think once I get the message out, I might stay with Molly a few days. If you think you'll be fine without me, I really could use the time with her."

"Of course, child! I been saying you work too much. You take a few days with your lady friend and talk about dresses and things like a girl your age is supposed to do." Peggy nodded with approval, and Annabelle's heart sank. But it couldn't be helped. She would simply have to ask for forgiveness later.

"Then just tell Grandfather I plan on staying with Molly a night or two so she can fit me for a dress." She thought a moment. Grandfather wouldn't be pleased with her not being around. "Also tell him while I'm in town I'll arrange for someone to come get poor old Jack and take him back to his family. He'll be glad I got the rest of the soldiers out of the house, so maybe he won't be too angry at me for wanting to stay with Molly for a bit."

"Well, all that seems fine enough, except for that part about a lady ain't to be riding with no gentleman unescorted."

Sometimes it seemed Peggy forgot the changes that war had rendered. Good thing she hadn't mentioned going with him to the army camp. "I understand your concerns for my reputation, but I'm afraid there's little that can be done about it. If I ever meet a gentleman I choose to wed, and he casts me away for riding to town with another man, then he isn't the man for me anyway."

"I just don't want folks in town to start saying you're a public woman." Annabelle gasped, but Peggy kept on talking. "And besides that, what's to say he ain't going to try to take your virtue whilst you're away from home?"

Annabelle placed her hand at the base of her throat. She'd never heard Peggy speak so crudely before. "Peggy! What a thing to say."

"Humph. Got to be said. You ain't slow, girl, and you ain't sheltered no more, much as your papa wanted you to be. War's done stole that from you. I won't see no soldier steal anything else."

A cold chill raced down her spine. "I suppose I have no choice but to trust him. He seems to be a man bound by duty and honor, despite his strangeness. I'll just have to be on guard and pray he holds to morals."

Peggy crossed the room without a word. She found a lamp, lit it, and flipped open a trunk. Annabelle watched her rummage through the contents until she finally found an object and held it out in Annabelle's direction.

Annabelle gasped. "Where did you get that?"

"It was my papa's. You need it now."

Annabelle reached out and took the small weapon. It looked like a dagger of some sort, but not like any of Father's. The handle conformed to her hand, carved from wood and worn smooth. She pulled the blade free from a simple leather sheath. The short metal blade seemed as if it had come from another knife and had been fitted into the homemade handle.

Annabelle's brow creased. Slaves were not supposed to have weapons. "Where did he get this?"

"He made it. Carved it with his own hands, he did. He took an old, broken scythe blade and worked it with a sharpening stone until he got it into that shape there. Momma made that leather sleeve for it."

The pride in Peggy's voice kept Annabelle from mentioning that if he had been found crafting weapons, he likely would have paid a steep price for it. What did that matter now? It was a family treasure to Peggy. Annabelle held the weapon back out to her. "I cannot take it from you."

"Yes, you can. You got to have some protection, in case you need it. I know you gonna take good care of it and bring it back to me."

Annabelle wrapped Peggy in a brief hug. "Thank you." She studied the odd weapon. "Where shall I conceal it?"

It took a bit of time, but they came up with some strings and a way to tie it around her waist and secure it between her skirt and petticoat, leaving only the tip of the handle sticking through the top and lying flat against her blouse. Even that could be fully hidden so long as she kept her medici belt over the top. She could then reach under the belt and pull the knife free if she needed it.

A stray thought wandered into her mind. At nearly twenty, she was past the age to be in a blouse, but she'd not had the time or material to fashion a proper bodice, so it would just have to do. Besides, she already looked young for her age.

Peggy looked at her with approval. "There. Ain't no one gonna suspect you're carrying that."

"No. I don't suppose they would." She smoothed her skirts. "Thank you. I do feel more secure."

Peggy held Annabelle's face in her hands and offered a sad smile. "There now, you see? Old Peggy be watching out for you no matter where you go."

Tears burned in the back of Annabelle's eyes, but she refused to let them fall. All she could do was nod.

"Now," Peggy said, "you best be gettin' on. I suspect it'll be light soon."

After a brief hug, Annabelle emerged into the deep darkness and hurried around the house to the rear porch. Her heart hammered as she slipped inside and past Grandfather's door. She found the lieutenant already waiting for her, dressed in his ragged uniform, which still bore resistant stains from his wounds.

"I thought I was to rouse you," she whispered.

He stepped close and leaned near her ear, his hot breath scurrying across her skin. "I'd begun to think you'd changed your mind."

"Against my own plan? Don't be absurd. Now, come, let's be gone."

He strode through the door and onto the rear porch, showing more strength than she thought him capable of. Surely he was now on his way to a full recovery. So long as he remained true to his honor, he might very well prove a decent escort for her mission.

She scooped up the pack she'd left on the stairs and made her way past the garden with Monroe on her heels. In the stable, she found old Homer strapped to the buckboard and standing exactly where she'd left him earlier that evening. She smiled and ran her fingers over his muzzle.

"Here, allow me," Monroe said, sweeping the pack from her arm and putting it behind the driving seat. He offered his hand, and she stepped up into the wagon, settled on the hard bench, and tried to remember what it was like to ride in a plush carriage.

Monroe slowly climbed in on the opposite side and sat a respectable distance from her. She reached for the reins, but his fingers closed over hers. "A lady should not drive."

Annabelle stiffened. Just because Father had allowed her to drive the surrey a few times when it had been just the two of them didn't mean it was proper to take the reins now. Thankfully, Monroe couldn't see her blush in the dark. "I've driven before." She pulled her hand away from his.

He frowned, his features only vaguely visible with the scant light coming through the open doors. Dawn would be coming soon. "It's not proper for a woman to drive a man."

She withheld her protest. "Very well. You're correct." She waved her hand. "Let's get moving."

He palmed the reins and with a gentle snap encouraged Homer forward. The old gelding, who'd probably dozed off, startled, and the buckboard lurched forward. Annabelle held tight to the side rail and found herself praying that she'd not just made a detrimental error.

As the wagon rolled down the drive, the unease in her chest loosened, and a tentative sense of determination dawned. She would not be a rug for men to tread upon. She would not sit idly by while men determined her future.

Her fingers slid down the hidden dagger, its solid form bolstering her confidence. For once, she would be the one in control.

Eight

"So far, I believe he is right, and agree with him that, if a
blow is to be struck, it should be an effective one, and
one that will make a lasting mark."
John H. Surratt

*D*awn broke over the horizon, and Annabelle glanced at
Monroe in the dusky light. What would people in
town think of her riding in alone with a soldier? She hadn't been
off Rosswood lands in nearly two years. Grandfather made any
necessary trips to town, and even those had become scarce.
Now that she thought on it, those two letters he'd said he'd
taken to town to send to Uncle Michael had probably never
gone to the post.

She clenched her jaw. How many people would even recognize her? She'd been to Lorman very few times, most of her
interactions having been with families of neighboring plantations or visiting family friends during the months they'd spent at
their home in Natchez. Only her friend Molly and Mr. Black, the
general store owner, would probably know her. Who would
think the girl in the patched skirt and stained blouse was the lady
of Rosswood?

She sighed. Perhaps it was better they didn't recognize her.

"Have you given thought to how we shall present ourselves to others?"

Monroe cut a sidelong glance at her. "What?"

"I'm an unmarried woman riding with a soldier."

His face remained blank.

"Without an escort."

"I assumed such things didn't matter to you." He clicked the reins to get Homer to quicken the pace. The poor beast could hardly maintain more than a trudge. The prominent ribs visible under his shaggy coat were evidence the winter had been no kinder to the horse than the rest of Rosswood.

"Beg your pardon?" Annabelle snapped.

He tilted his head to one side, his careless attitude grinding against her already battered emotions. Annabelle tried to stifle her annoyance. Taking a calming breath, she tried again. "Could you kindly explain to me, Lieutenant Monroe, what would cause you to determine I have no regard for my reputation?"

He kept staring straight ahead, as if he needed the utmost concentration to stay on the deserted road. He shivered as the cool wind buffeted his face and made his hair dance across his brow. The longer his answer took in coming, the more she felt the heat rising in her face.

"Well," he finally said, "you served as a nurse for, I believe, quite some time."

"That is true, mostly. I was more of an aide than a true nurse, but I did what I could." What did that have to do with their current topic of conversation?

"From my experience, a war nurse is exposed to all manner of things that would disrupt her...uh, *delicate sensibilities*." He ran a sleeve across his brow.

She considered his words. "Yes, I suppose. But those men needed my care. Without it, many would have died."

"Most did anyway."

The words cut, exposing a wound that guilt seared on her soul. She looked away, furiously blinking back tears she would not allow the liberty to spill.

After several moments, he sighed.

"My words were unkind. You're correct. Many were probably saved. I've just seen too many men—good men—find their deaths in this war. Too many died simply from poor conditions and lack of proper care."

Annabelle gave a curt nod and said no more. How could she explain how much of her had drained out with the death of each man she could not save? He would never know the toll it had taken on her. To men like him, her sacrifice was meaningless. They would forever see a woman as a weak vessel. Never capable enough to truly matter. Her toil meant little, her sacrifices were pitiable, and her tears—as Grandfather had pointed out—were the outward manifestation of a woman's innate inability to control even herself, let alone the world around her. Why did she continue to give of herself when it did so little good?

Oh, Momma, forgive me. It grows ever harder to keep my promise.

The lieutenant cleared his throat, and she could feel his eyes on her. Annabelle refused to look at him and kept her gaze on the lonely roadway surrounded by shaggy pines. The heat climbed up her neck and into her face, but she ignored that as well.

"Miss Ross?"

She forced a syrupy tone. "Yes, Lieutenant?"

"I meant no offense."

"Very well."

He sighed. "As to your original question, I assumed you wouldn't be concerned with what people thought of our companionship, because any woman who could withstand the horrors of assisting with amputations, see men in their worst conditions, and even bury them herself...." His voice trailed off.

He knew about that? She cut her eyes to his stiff profile in the gathering light. He darted his gaze to hers, but she looked away again.

"Miss Ross, any woman who can do all those things is too strong to worry with petty propriety."

She felt a flutter of pride and could not resist the smile that curved her lips. "Thank you, Lieutenant. However, I do think it might be prudent to come up with some other arrangement so that—"

Her words were cut short by a sudden gun blast. Homer stopped and threw up his head, jerking the buckboard to a halt. Monroe lurched to his feet, swaying slightly before he steadied himself. His hand settled on the scabbard at his side, and Annabelle's fingers lay over the comforting presence of her own secret weapon.

"Look what we got here!"

The voice preceded a man who stepped through the tree cover and then positioned himself in the center of the road with his gun pointed straight at Homer. "This here road requires a toll, if you was wantin' to pass through."

"I'll pay no toll to pass on a public road," Monroe said in a near growl. "I suggest you remove yourself."

Annabelle's heart fluttered. They had nothing to give, save

their own clothing and a few meager supplies they couldn't do without. She narrowed her eyes at the scoundrel. His thin frame, tattered clothes, and the hint of fear that tightened his features betrayed his attempt to look threatening.

The man raised his gun higher and aimed it at the lieutenant's chest. "Now look here, deserter, I ain't got no problem shooting you right where you stand and taking what I need."

Annabelle lurched to her feet. "Please, good sir. Do not harm my father. He was wounded in battle and is just now recovered." Monroe shot her a sharp look, but she hurried on before he could stop her. "All he wants is to return to service so he can put an end to those Yanks."

The man lowered his weapon slightly, and Annabelle took it as a good sign. She hurried on. "We don't have much, just a little bread and some nuts, but we would gladly share it with you. You seem like a fine Southern gentleman, guarding this route from those horrible Feds." She smiled sweetly at him, ignoring the trepidation rolling in her stomach. "That is what you're doing, correct?"

He dropped the muzzle to the ground, confusion etching his brow. She slipped her hand through the crook of Monroe's arm and felt him tense. She gave him an almost imperceptible squeeze, worrying at the heat seeping through his jacket.

The man on the road ran a hand over his scraggly beard and then straightened his shoulders. He frowned up at Monroe. "That true? You returning to duty?"

"I am. I'm traveling to catch a coach that will deliver me to my regiment, though I first had to see my..." He narrowed his eyes at Annabelle. "My daughter safely to my brother for safekeeping. After the Yanks burned our home, she has no one left to look after her."

Annabelle drew her lower lip between her teeth and looked to the side.

"Aw, look, I didn't mean to scare you folks." The man scratched his head. "But, see, I got three girls of my own at home what's looking to me to feed them. It's right sorry what I'm doing here, but I ain't been able to get any game in four days. I heard the wagon coming and, well...." He shrugged.

Annabelle pulled her arm from Monroe and scrambled down the side of the wagon. She pulled a loaf of bread from her pack and walked slowly to the man, who now seemed more pitiful than threatening.

"Miss Ross!" Monroe hissed as she passed by him.

She turned and gave him a smile, her eyes warning him against using her name. "Don't worry, Papa," she said loud enough for the stranger to hear. "This man acted only out of care for his children. Surely we do not begrudge him that?"

Monroe scowled at her but said nothing more. She stepped up to the man and held out the loaf. "I'm sorry, but this is all I can offer you."

The man shook his head and reached for the bread. "Thank you, miss. You're right kind offering to share with me. Especially after I threatened you."

"The war has taken from us all. What little we have must be freely given, so that all may make it through."

His eyes reddened. "You're too kind, miss." He scurried away with his treasure, disappearing back into the wood line.

Annabelle turned and beamed up at Monroe, but received only a harsh glare. "Let's go."

He looked a little too pale, his muscles too tense. Now

would not be the time to celebrate her success at averting a fight. She hurried and returned to the wagon, studying his face as she climbed in. As soon as her bottom hit the plank seat, Monroe snapped the reins and startled Homer into a brisk trot. Annabelle righted herself after the sudden jolt and looked at Monroe. Sweat lined his brow despite the chill in the air.

"You don't look well."

"Perhaps that's because you chose to act a fool."

Annabelle gaped at him. "A fool? For the mere price of a loaf of bread, which he seemed in need of anyway, I avoided a conflict. I count that a victory."

"Deceitful," he murmured.

"Perhaps a little. But that's precisely the type of thing I've been trying to talk to you about."

He scowled. "Leave it to a woman to jump to deception to get her way."

She bit back the retort on her tongue. Let him think what he would. She'd been the one to protect them, and from the look of Monroe's face, it was a good thing she did. He was in no condition to fight. "Perhaps you should stop for a moment and let me look at your wound."

Monroe shook his head. "No. I want to get farther away from here."

"But, I don't think—"

"I said no," he snapped.

Fine. She set her teeth and focused on the road. The sun climbed higher in the cold sky, its rays giving barely enough warmth to battle the chill. As they continued on, the sway of the wagon and the twittering birds almost allowed her to imagine this was simply a pleasant ride to town. If she closed her eyes, perhaps she could remember what it had felt like to ride with Father on the padded seats of a real carriage.

Suddenly Monroe's weight swayed against her, and her eyes popped open. "Oh, my! Lieutenant, are you well?"

He shook himself as if struggling to stay awake. "I'm fine."

"I don't believe you are." She reached for the reins. "I fear your fever has returned."

He ignored her. She snatched the reins from his hands, and he gave little protest. She tapped Homer but could not bring him to produce more than a slow trot. They continued at the jarring pace until she saw a break in the trees.

She pulled a single rein to guide the horse off the road and onto an open field. There had once been a fence here, but it had broken in several places, leaving rotting logs scattered across the dry grass. The wagon lurched over them, and Annabelle backed the vehicle behind a screen of two towering magnolias. Their branches hung all the way to the ground and provided cover. As soon as the wagon came to a halt, Homer dropped his head to the dead grass and began to graze.

Monroe didn't look well at all.

"Let me see your wound. You're burning with fever."

He shook his head. "Doesn't matter. We must deliver the message."

"We cannot deliver anything, or hope to travel, with you in this condition. We should turn around and return to Rosswood."

"No. You take the horse. Leave me here in the wagon to rest for a while. See if you can find the nearest Confederate encampment, and we'll simply deliver my message there." He held up a hand to stop her next words. "They'll also have a messenger you can send with a missive to your uncle."

"But—"

"Just go." He groaned. "I need the rest. Surely you're capable of riding into town on your own."

Annabelle clenched her teeth. "Fine," she snapped. *Let him sleep off this sour mood.* She could check his wound when she returned.

She unhitched Homer, and Monroe climbed over the bench to lie down in the rear of the buckboard. She shook her head but let him be. Now, how to get on the horse unassisted? She led Homer over to the crumbling fence, found a fairly stable place, and hoisted herself up on a cross piece. It gave a little but held her weight. Thankfully, the old gelding seemed to sense what she intended and swung his body around next to her.

She gave his bare back a pat. "Thank you, old friend," she whispered. With a bit of a struggle, she managed to balance herself on Homer's back, both legs hanging off to one side. Too bad she didn't have a riding habit to cover her feet. She might be bareback, but she certainly couldn't ride into town astride with her ankles exposed to the world. She'd just have to maintain her balance without the aid of her lady's saddle. "I suppose this will just have to do. Come on, boy, let's go."

Homer moved forward, and they returned to the road at a slow walk. She turned to look back at the wagon but could barely make out the shape behind the towering magnolias. How far was she from Lorman? From what she could remember, she was probably more than halfway there. But she couldn't estimate how long it might take with Homer at a leisurely walk.

At least Monroe should be able to rest without anyone happening upon him. She hated to leave him alone, but perhaps she would be able to get some bandages from town.

Annabelle rode for what she judged to be three quarters of an hour without incident and began to pass the outlying farms. Within another half hour, she crossed into the quiet town of Lorman. She drew Homer up in front of the general store and slid down the horse's side, her skirts raising nearly to her knees before her feet touched the earth. Humiliated, she quickly smoothed the fraying wool down and looked around, but no one seemed to have noticed. She tied Homer to the hitching post and patted his neck before turning to the store.

People hurried along the walk, their gazes fixed on the ground before them, too frightened, or at the very least too preoccupied with their own affairs to offer their neighbors even a cursory greeting. A sense of unease settled in her stomach.

She stepped into the store and suddenly realized the reason for the worried looks and shuffling feet. Two Union soldiers stood at the counter, talking to the shop owner. So, Lorman would soon be occupied as well. As far as she could tell, it would likely be a good thing. The Union troops could bring much-needed supplies. Perhaps she could learn something valuable from these two.

"I've asked you twice, and will not again," one of the men in blue said, his face red.

Annabelle slipped behind a shelf containing a few sacks of flour and other limited supplies and turned her ear in their direction. Perhaps if she stood unseen, they would not curtail their talk of important matters as men often did whenever a lady approached. Thankfully, it seemed they made no effort to keep their conversation private.

She feigned interest in the exorbitantly priced items in front of her.

"And I've answered you twice as well, sir," the shopkeeper said.

"You mean you haven't seen the first Rebel gray come in here?" the soldier said, his tone thick with annoyance.

Annabelle frowned and rubbed her hands together to return some warmth to her fingers. The shop owner, a kindly middle-aged man she'd spoken to on several occasions earlier in her life, answered in a clipped tone. "As I already told you, *no.*"

The soldier tapped his foot on the wooden floor. "We have word some of General Forrest's men broke off and are camped near this town."

Annabelle peeked around the edge of the shelves. The two soldiers glowered at Mr. Black, but he didn't appear concerned. "Well," he drawled, "seems like you fellows already have more information than I do. But if I see any boys in gray come by here, I'll be sure to tell them you are looking for them."

The red-faced soldier slammed his fist down on the counter, but the other man grabbed his arm. "Let's go. We won't get any more out of him."

The air grew thick with tension.

Finally, the man turned on his heel and stalked out the door. The other soldier, a handsome youth with dark hair, gave Mr. Black a shake of his head and then followed his companion. As soon as the door slammed behind him, Mr. Black's shoulders slumped.

Annabelle hurried from her hiding place and up to the counter. "My goodness. I worried they would make trouble for you."

Mr. Black's close-set eyes widened. "Miss Ross? Is that

you?"

She smiled. "I didn't think you'd recognize me. It's been several years since we've spoken."

"You look the very image of your mother." Before Annabelle could respond to the compliment, he frowned at her. "A summer bonnet? In this weather?"

She blinked at him, incredulous. Were there not more important matters than her style of head covering? She lifted her shoulders and gave an apologetic smile. "It's the only one I have left."

He gave her a look of pity.

She leaned close, her voice a small whisper. "Mr. Black, I fear I'm in need of some assistance."

He glanced around the store, but they seemed to be alone. "Yanks giving you trouble at Rosswood?"

"No." She puckered her lips. "At least not yet." She gestured toward the door. "But I heard what they said. Is there really a Confederate camp nearby?"

He frowned. "Camp is no place for a lady." He looked more closely at her, and his mouth turned down. "Is all going well out there? Since I heard your father passed...." He let the words trail off.

She straightened herself and held up her hand, trying to look more like a confident lady than a scared girl trembling in her slippers. "I'm afraid I can't give you any details. However, it's imperative I get a message to my father's brother, which can most quickly be done with an army message runner." She hesitated. But who else could she ask? "I also need help with arranging transportation."

He crossed his arms over his dusty full-length apron. "I

don't think it would be wise for you to—"

She leaned forward, stopping him mid-sentence, and lowered her voice. "Do you know I'm still caring for wounded at Rosswood?"

He shook his head. "I thought they'd moved on from there."

"Most have. In one way or another." She waved her hand. "Anyway, I have one soldier who wants to join back up with the army as soon as possible, and one other who has lost an arm and a foot. He needs to be sent back to the Delta. I just thought you might know someone who can help. I can no longer care for them." She took a long breath and let some of her desperation show in her eyes.

An expression she couldn't quite grasp crossed over Mr. Black's face. "You poor child. You should have never—" He shook his head, cutting his own words short. "There was a Confederate officer in here yesterday. I don't know where they are exactly, but I believe they've bivouacked somewhere just north of town. Maybe they'll send your message and take the men. If not, I'll see if I can find someone who's willing to take the man north with them, should they be traveling. Enough folks come in here. Surely I can find someone."

Annabelle offered him a tired smile. "Thank you, Mr. Black. I'm most grateful." She turned to leave.

"Wait."

She paused, and he shifted his weight. "Have you…come to harm?"

Annabelle angled her face to hide skin still tinged yellow from the fading bruise caused by Grandfather's hand.

"If there's anything I can do, just name it."

The concern in his tone reminded her of Father and twisted her heart. She had to trust someone, and her options were few.

"If you could find a way to get a message or telegraph to Lieutenant Michael Ross with the Army of Northern Virginia, I would be most appreciative."

"Messages past the line have been difficult, but not impossible. What shall I tell him?"

Annabelle thought a moment. She could likely trust Mr. Black, but if word got out no one had a firm hold on the plantation...well, she'd heard of property being stolen out from underneath widows and families without male protection. She didn't need anyone challenging Grandfather in his state. Better to deal with this marriage problem on her own than risk losing it all to a stranger.

"Tell him my father's wishes concerning Rosswood are in danger. He must come quickly. I fear he doesn't even know Father is dead."

Mr. Black nodded. "If you require more, please, let me know."

"Thank you. I must go now." She hurried out the door and unwrapped Homer's reins. Where would she find a mounting block?

"Might I help you?"

She looked up into the smiling face of the younger of the Union soldiers who'd been in the store. "Oh, I, um...."

"I don't mean you any harm." He held up his hands, palms out. "Just because I wear the wrong color doesn't make me an indecent man." He gave her a disarming grin.

She couldn't help the nervous laugh that bubbled up. "Yes, yes. Forgive me. I could use some assistance." She looked up at the horse's bare back and could not fathom a proper excuse for it. Thankfully, he didn't appear to be inclined to ask for one, as his stare had not yet left her face.

He smiled and stepped closer. He couldn't be more than a few years older than she. Then his brows pulled together. "Where's your saddle, miss?"

Drat. He'd noticed after all. She smiled, trying to appear as though a woman riding without proper tack was a usual occurrence. "I don't have one."

He appeared as if he expected further information, but she had none to give. They looked at each other for another moment. Then he simply laced his fingers together, and she stepped up on them. With a quick bounce, he hefted her up, and she clamped onto Homer's mane to stabilize herself. Thankfully, she didn't topple from the other side. She looked down at the face of the young man, who seemed kind and appeared to have the bright spirits of one not too long burdened with the horrors of battle.

Once again, words tumbled from her mouth without proper restraint. "How long have you been in this war?"

He shrugged. "Long enough."

He seemed no more inclined to explanation or exposition than she, which was likely for the best. She twisted the long reins into her ungloved palms and nudged Homer back a step. "Well, sir, I thank you for your assistance."

His lips curved slightly, and he nodded, his mouth opening to say more, but she pulled on the reins and turned Homer around. "My father is waiting on me."

The lie had slipped easily from her lips, and she wondered why she'd used it. Pretending Monroe was her father had been necessary before, but why would she choose to do it now? The sad truth settled on her. It had felt good to say—to pretend, if only for a moment—that Father really was nearby, waiting on her to come show him her newest hair ribbons.

Unexpected tears gathered in her eyes, and she blinked them away. Now was not the time for sentiment. She urged Homer along the lonely road and tried not to think too much on her situation. She'd made it within sight of the magnolias when she remembered the bandages she'd wanted to get for Monroe.

Annabelle found Monroe sleeping just as she'd left him, his face slick with sweat. She tried twice to rouse him, but he merely groaned and turned his head. Not sure what else to do, she began unbuttoning his uniform. Underneath the shirt, the bandage appeared clean and dry. She frowned. Why had the fever returned?

She tugged at the wrapping, doing the best she could to free the bindings without causing him pain. When she finally succeeded in removing them, what she saw made her heart sink. Amid the white pus, blackened flesh had begun to rot, putting forth a pungent odor. She placed a hand over her nose. The smell was worse than the sight, and she was suddenly glad she'd not eaten today.

Annabelle sat back on her heels. She'd seen enough wounds go bad to know there was little she could do for him now.

She put her head in her hands and began to pray.

Nine

"I would like to trust him, but dare not."
John H. Surratt

*M*atthew watched the sun dip down to the top of the trees and dreaded the thought of losing what little warmth it provided. He inspected the wrap around his leg. He didn't trust the doctors here. Or anyone who claimed to be one. It seemed too many had done little more than read a surgeon's manual and then taken up a bone saw.

He'd once seen them remove pus from one man's wound and transfer it to another man's wound. They said the ooze indicated a lesion was properly healing, but Matthew couldn't fathom that something that smelled rotten could be anything good. The man who'd received the pus had seemed to be recovering, only to plummet after they'd smeared him with the foul substance. Both of the men ended up dead, and Matthew hadn't trusted a doctor since.

He'd survived one gunshot—well perhaps it was more of a graze—by using his father's principles for horse care. When one of the mares suffered bites or other marks from the stallion, Matthew's father insisted the stable boys kept it washed and packed with poultice. Matthew had not paid attention to the ingredients of the poultice and doubted he could have scavenged them anyway, but the principle of often washing his injury had proven its merit. Where others had suffered fever and the dreaded gangrene, his wound had scarred over cleanly. He hoped the hole in his leg would do the same.

Matthew pulled the dressing free and inspected his ragged flesh. If the bullet hadn't passed all the way through, he would likely now be sitting in the medical tent without a leg. He tilted his canteen and let the cool water fill the bloody hole, clenching his teeth against the pain.

"Why you doing that, Captain?" said a voice behind him.

Matthew turned to see Private Gregory Holt, cousin to the deadpan Captain Holt who had provided him with the proper countersign two nights past. He gave a grunt. "I'm keeping it clean."

Holt knelt beside him and scratched his scruffy beard. "I don't know how clean that water is, seeing as how half of my company died from distemper after drinking from a stream a couple of months ago."

Matthew grinned up at him, a little of his good humor returning. "Good thing I wasn't drinking it then, huh?"

Holt frowned. "You ain't been drinking any water?"

Matthew grew serious again. "You know, Private, if a man pays attention, he can discover certain things that just might let him survive this level of Hades."

Holt's eyes rounded. "Like what?"

"You seem clever enough. You noticed that drinking right from a stream made men sick, didn't you?"

"Yeah. Ain't that hard to figure out."

"Ever notice a man losing his gut after drinking tea? Or coffee?"

Holt scratched his head. "I don't reckon I've noticed that, no."

Matthew shrugged. "Me either. So I've tried keeping to coffee and tea."

"How would you manage that? Y'all must have been rationed a lot more coffee than we were."

"No, I've just had to stretch it."

Holt looked at him with a blank expression, so he continued. "I noticed that even just a tiny bit seems to do the trick. So, I take a pot of water and boil it with just one tea leaf at a time, or a few coffee beans, if I have them. Then I put it in my canteen. Makes that pond water taste a mite better, and it seems to keep away the trots."

Holt rocked back on his heels. "Huh. I wonder why that is."

Matthew rinsed his bandage cloth and wrapped it back around his calf, ignoring the chill. "I don't know. But I've been doing it for three years now, and I've not heaved up any of my meals."

"Well, who woulda thought of that?"

Matthew winked. "Me."

Holt slapped him on the back. "Sure enough. You got any other ideas?"

"Just keeping wounds clean like my father always did the cuts on his horses."

Holt still looked skeptical, but he nodded. "Anyway, I came down your way to make sure you were all right to stay on shift."

"I'm not getting a relief?"

Holt shook his head. "Not anytime soon. We're thin on

men. The general says we don't have enough for regular on and off now that we lost fourteen to fever, so each man who's healthy enough stays out until about half-night, then gets his rest until dawn. The other shift will run from half-night until about midday."

Matthew stretched his shoulders and tried not to think of how nice it would be to lie down for a few hours. "Very well."

Holt slapped him on the shoulder again and sat next to him. "I'm supposed to sit here with you, seeing as you've never been on the line through the night before."

Glad for the company, Matthew smiled. "That sounds mighty nice."

"I'll go round us up some firewood and see if we can get a bit of warmth." He scurried off toward the woods, and Matthew's shoulders relaxed. He'd feared a long, cold night and was grateful for a man willing to build a fire.

A sound came from the edge of the woods opposite where Holt had disappeared, and Matthew's head snapped around in that direction. He raised his weapon and scanned the area, but seeing nothing, finally lowered it. Probably just a critter.

Annabelle shook Monroe again. He groaned, and his head lolled to one side, but he would not open his eyes. She placed a hand to his slick brow and cringed at the heat pouring from him. She'd need to cool him. She climbed down from the wagon and determined she would have to search out a source of water.

Oh, Lord, help me find it quickly.

She chose a direction and walked deeper into the field. She had to lift her skirts often to avoid the droppings littering the ground, so there must have been cattle somewhere nearby, and they would need a place to water. She just hoped not to find a bull anywhere near it.

Not long into her journey, Annabelle spied a glimmer that caught the rays of the quickly descending sun, and she hurried in that direction. It turned out to be a small pond, little more than a mud hole, but it would do. She knelt, ripped a section from the hem of her petticoat, and dipped it into the cold water.

By the time she reached the lieutenant again, his eyes were open. "Oh! You're awake!" She climbed into the wagon and sat beside him, pressing the dripping cloth to his head. She prayed she might break the fever without replacing it with pneumonia.

He looked at her with glassy eyes. "You must take it."

She bathed his head. "Hush now. Let's get this fever down first."

He reached up and clasped her wrist in his clammy fingers. "I'll not finish this journey. I thought I could ignore it long enough…." He heaved a ragged breath. "You *must* deliver the message."

Annabelle shook her head. "We can go over those things later. We'll get you back to Rosswood and then travel again when you're well."

"Annabelle. *Please.*"

The use of her first name stayed her hand. She'd seen enough death now to recognize its signs, and it appeared Lieutenant Monroe sensed the end would soon be upon him.

She let out a long breath and left the cloth lying on his brow. "What would you have me do?"

"Deliver the message now. Don't try to take me back to Rosswood. We've lost too much time already."

Annabelle drew her bottom lip between her teeth. "There's a Confederate regiment just north of here."

He brightened. "Do you know which one?"

She shook her head. "I'm sorry."

He drew a breath that seemed to rattle within his chest. "We have no choice. I'm convinced that Jonathan was right. It must be done. I can only hope one of our own is within."

Jonathan? Ah, yes. Lieutenant Smith. The man who'd first possessed the cryptic message. Annabelle's brow furrowed. "What do you mean? Are not all with the Confederate Army *one of us?*"

"It's not for you to worry with. You need only to...." he drew in a deep breath and his body lurched with a series of coughs. It took several moments for him to recover and finally draw his sleeve across his chapped lips. His features hardened in the way a man's often did when he loathed the thought of showing the slightest weakness. "You need only to do as I instruct. All will be well from there."

"And what of me? How shall I know where to find a messenger to send for my uncle?"

"Simply ask a ranking officer."

Annabelle clenched her teeth and said no more. What choice did she have?

"Go to the line and give them the countersign *Richmond.* That will get you past the sentry. From there, ask to speak with an officer from Crestview, Virginia. Deliver the message to him. *Only* to him." He stared hard at her, as if he feared she could not comprehend such a simple command.

Annabelle narrowed her eyes. "How do you know there will be a man from that town in this regiment? We don't even know which one it is."

"If no... officer comes forward from that town, that one alone, then... destroy the message and be, be done with it." He began to pant, and Annabelle worried his lungs were filling with fluid.

She wrung her hands. "But, I don't think—"

Monroe's eyes rolled back in his head. She grasped his hand. His fingernails had begun to darken. "Lieutenant! Stay with me."

He gasped and focused on her. "I don't have long." He pulled in another rattling breath.

Had she been too preoccupied with her own concerns to notice how near death he had truly been? "We've broken this fever before. We'll do so again."

The words were false hope, and his expression told her he knew the same. Even if the fever broke now, the infection had already taken over his body. Despite such logic, her heart rebelled against watching yet another man die, knowing she had not been able to save him.

He shook his head. "My heart beats far too quickly."

Tears gathered in her eyes and trailed down her cheeks. "Shall I pray for you?"

He scowled. "For...what purpose? I have... not life enough left for God to want my service now." The labored words were delivered with disgust and a tinge of regret.

"He took the thief on the cross, when that man was hanging to die and had nothing to give," she said softly.

Monroe turned his head away from her. "It's too late," he gasped. "All that matters is that you deliver the message."

Annabelle prayed anyway.

His body stiffened and lurched upward, his lungs gasping for breath they could not gather. Tears slid down Annabelle's cheeks. Would she ever grow accustomed to the hideous pain that accompanied man's final moments? "Please, before your heart gives out," she pleaded, "turn it over to the Lord, and find peace in the end rather than torment."

He opened his mouth as if to say something, but then fell backward, his eyes staring into nothing. She reached out gently to lower his lids. Annabelle sat back on her heels and drew her knees against her.

Never had she felt so alone.

The cold wind tugged at her hair, drawing her up from her sorrow and reminding her she had neither the time nor ability to allow herself the comfort of tears. She must mourn later. Here was another soldier who deserved a proper burial she could not provide, and this time she didn't even have a spade.

Her gaze wandered to the broken fence, and soon her feet followed. The rough wood left little scratches on her palms as she tugged, rolled, and hefted the pieces of the boards into a pile behind the wagon. She wiped a hand across her cheeks and studied the pyre in front of her as the final rays of sun dipped low, casting shadows across the dancing grass.

She pulled a match from the pack and rolled it between her fingers. What else was she to do? It would be crueler to leave him here for the birds and animals to nibble, finding his eyes and… she shivered. It must be done.

Using her bare fingers and a relativity flat stone, she scraped away the dry grass for a couple of feet in a perimeter around the pyre. Hopefully, the fire would remain contained and would not leap her moat to find the dry grass beyond.

Annabelle climbed into the wagon and placed her hands underneath the still-warm body of the lieutenant. "Forgive me," she said, and gave a mighty shove. The body rolled. In a few moments, the soldier she'd hoped would provide her protection fell from the wagon bed and onto the woodpile at an awkward angle.

She stepped down and set to work arranging him properly, then covered his body with handfuls of dried leaves. As the darkness thickened, she struck the match and held it high, whispering a prayer that his soul had found its rest.

Annabelle lowered the flickering flame, and in a moment the leaves began to catch and crumble. She watched until his clothing took hold, then placed her hand over her mouth and turned away. She climbed into the driver's bench and took up the reins, urging Homer forward.

As the flames glowed brighter, Annabelle turned her back on the shadows and rode deeper into the night.

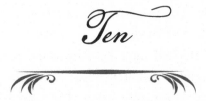

Ten

"They have no faith in Peace Conferences; neither
have I."
John H. Surratt

"*Y*ou hear that?" Holt asked, dropping the stick with which
he'd been poking the dying flames.

Matthew straightened. He'd heard rustling but had dismissed it. Perhaps he should not have. He reached for his rifle.
"I did."

Holt drew his weapon and pointed it to the dark woods
beyond their small circle of light. Matthew used the stock of the
rifle to aid him in getting to his feet, thankful the movement was
becoming steadily less painful.

A sound again came from the woods, and Matthew caught a
flash of color moving through the trees. He followed it for only
a second before it merged with the shadows and made him
wonder if he had merely imagined it.

"Halt! We see you, man. Come forth, or be shot!" Holt
shouted.

Silence. Matthew scanned the trees but could not distinguish
movement anywhere near where he had seen the snip of color,

but someone had to be there. Should they send up an alarm?

Suddenly, a distinctly feminine voice came from the darkness. "Please! Don't shoot me!"

Matthew and Holt exchanged a glance. Matthew returned his attention to the sound. "Come forth!" he commanded.

A small shadow emerged from the trees and stood cloaked in darkness. The figure was slight of frame and did not appear to hold a weapon. Matthew lowered the muzzle of his rifle but kept it at the ready. "Approach, ma'am," he said, "and give reason for your presence."

Holt steadied his stance and trained his gun on the woman as she neared. When she reached the flickering light of their wavering campfire, Matthew could now distinguish the slender form of a girl half hidden underneath a frayed paletot not nearly warm enough for this cold.

"Who are you?" Holt asked, suspicion thick in his tone.

"Please. I mean no harm. Could you lower your weapon?" the girl said with a slight tremor in her voice.

"Not until you give reason for your presence."

She sighed. "I've come to find an officer."

Matthew studied her. She appeared to be a young woman of perhaps seventeen years, her face streaked with dirt and her dress ragged. The waif probably came seeking supplies or a place as a camp woman. Many had come offering various forms of service. Matthew had been wise to stay clear of them all.

Holt laughed. "I bet you have. Aiming high, huh? Well, you seem pretty enough under all that dirt to fetch a fair wage."

The girl gasped.

Matthew placed a staying hand on the private's shoulder, his height once again giving him an advantage. The young man straightened and said no more.

Matthew looked the girl over. "Why don't you just state your business, miss?"

She lifted her chin, and his gaze wandered briefly down the smooth curve of her neck before returning to her eyes. He couldn't be sure in the dim light, but her eyes appeared to glitter as she fixed her steady stare on him, ignoring Holt entirely. "I'm here to deliver a message to an officer from Virginia."

He raised a brow. "Just any officer from Virginia?"

She hesitated. "He hails from the town of...." she thought a moment. "Crestview."

Holt snorted. "No one passes this point without the proper call sign. Too many spies about."

Matthew cast his gaze to the heavens. This waif? A spy?

She cast a disgusted look at the private and then once again dismissed him, speaking only to Matthew. "Oh. Yes. The sign. Let's see...." She fiddled with her dress. "Oh, yes. I remember now." She straightened and studied him, as if wondering if he were the proper one to deliver it to.

"Well?" he prompted.

"The countersign is Richmond."

Holt threw up his gun and aimed it at her. "Captain! Restrain that woman!"

Confusion rolled through Matthew. It was not the proper counter, but shouldn't they just send her away? The signs changed often enough that one might not have ample time to travel with any given pass before finding it had expired. And why would the private be so unnerved as to presume to give his superior orders? Matthew glared at Holt. "Explain yourself, Private."

The man looked at him with wide eyes, his gaze bouncing back to the frightened girl. "She's given the sign of Richmond," he said, as if restating the obvious were proper explanation of his behavior.

"Indeed, Private. And thus should be turned away."

Holt scowled. "I ain't got the time to explain. Captain, you must keep your rifle trained on this spy to keep her from escaping while I restrain her."

The girl gasped. "Spy? I'm no spy." She took two steps backward, and Private Holt lurched forward.

"Halt!"

She stopped, fear evident on her features in the flickering firelight. Holt grabbed her arm and pulled it around behind her back, and she let forth a small yelp that stirred Matthew's ire. "Private, must you restrain her so? I don't believe this tiny girl would cause any harm."

Holt tugged on her, and she followed him to Matthew's side. "Sorry, Captain, but I have my orders from higher than you. This woman is to be restrained and delivered."

She stared up at Matthew, searching his face. "But, I am *not* a spy."

"Perhaps not." He stared down at her. Her loveliness was evident even underneath the grime. Such beauty only made her more dangerous. He frowned, dismissing the attraction that would only lead him into trouble. "But then, I've seen many a woman who was not what she appeared. Private Holt is correct. You must be taken in. You may explain yourself there."

She blinked rapidly at him. "But the lieutenant gave me the countersign. He's been in my care since he was wounded and was on his way to rejoin the army."

Holt snorted. "A likely story. And where is this man now?"

She swallowed hard, fear lighting her eyes. "He's dead."

Matthew nodded. "You'll report to Lieutenant Colonel Hood."

"No, sir," Holt interrupted. "I'll go to one of this regiment's officers and see that—"

Matthew held up a hand to silence him. "It would seem that I'm not apprised of all that needs to be known on the line, Private. Perhaps it's best that I take her and you maintain your position here, seeing as you have carried on your duty so well. I shall have to tell your cousin of your aptitude."

The private stood a little taller. "Yes, sir." He hesitated. "But you *must* take her in." He looked at Matthew as if he expected rebuttal. When he received none, he continued. "We're supposed to bring in anyone who gives that sign as a spy, seeing as how the last man who used it carried off some...." He glanced at the girl. "Sensitive information."

Matthew nodded. "Understood." He reached out and cupped the girl's elbow. She made no effort to evade him and stood silently beside him while Holt handed him a torch. How was he to carry the light and his rifle and still maintain the girl? She would not attempt to flee, would she? He looked down at the top of her head. She must have sensed his stare, for she turned her chin up and steadied a crisp blue gaze on him. He offered a tight smile.

"You won't go running away on me, miss, now will you?"

She opened her mouth to reply, but Private Holt interrupted before she gained the opportunity to speak. "Captain, protocol says you are to maintain contact with the prisoner's person at all times."

She paled. "Prisoner?"

Matthew glared at Holt. "Private, as I do not possess three hands, I suppose only two will have to do."

Holt blinked.

"I don't believe I'll need my weapon, so I'll leave it here with you, thereby allowing myself to maintain restraint on this young woman while also retaining the ability to provide us with light without attempting to secure the torch in my mouth."

Holt's face reddened, and he gave a single nod as Matthew handed his weapon over. He looked down at the girl again, who stared up at him with rounded eyes. "Come, miss, and we'll see this sorted out. Do you have proper papers?"

She shook her head. "I'm afraid not. Only the message I was asked to give to an officer from Crestview."

He guided her around the fire. "I'll return shortly, Private Holt," Matthew said over his shoulder.

"Yes, sir."

They walked into the edge of the main camp and past several tents of sleeping men without the girl showing any inclination to run from him. It was a good thing, too. He was doing well enough concealing his limp, but he doubted he would be able to run after her if she proved quick.

She did not speak until they had nearly reached the officer's quarters at the center of the camp. "Sir?"

"Yes?"

"I'm confused. I'm not a spy. I'm only delivering a message for a friend." She lifted her shoulders. "And, well, perhaps hoping to find a messenger heading to the Northern Virginia."

Matthew stopped, bringing her to a stumbling halt. "Why do you want to do that?"

She scrunched her nose. "That is of a personal manner."

"That so?" Matthew bristled. Holt was likely right. She was up to some form of deception. And here he was, nearly swayed by another beautiful face masking a devious soul. He grunted. "Well, it's none of my concern. You can take it up with the lieutenant colonel." He continued on, pulling her along.

"But, I...." she stumbled beside him, but he did not stop, forcing her shorter legs to keep up with his stride.

"Here we are, miss." He raised a hand to the man on guard outside Lieutenant Colonel Hood's tent. "I do hope you have an honorable reason for coming into this camp," he said low enough for only her to hear.

He heard her sharp intake of breath but ignored it, instead raising his voice to the guard as he came to a stop in front of the tent. "You'll need to rouse the lieutenant colonel, Sergeant. This woman has come to the line without the proper countersign."

No need to mention what Holt had said about her being a spy. He didn't want to put ideas into anyone's head if they didn't have cause to be there. He glanced at the girl. Even if they might very well be true, he would allow the lieutenant colonel to come to his own conclusions.

The sergeant nodded and within a few moments returned with the lieutenant colonel, who looked as if he hadn't been sleeping anyway.

"What's going on, Captain Daniels?" Hood asked, his gaze traveling over the pair.

Matthew urged the girl forward. "This young woman has given the wrong counter. We figured it best to bring her to you."

Hood narrowed his eyes in the flickering torchlight. "You

thought her enough of a threat not to simply turn her away? You've likely disturbed my rest only to bring me a camp wench who's wandered away from some man's tent."

"I'm no harlot!" the girl snapped, ripping her elbow from Matthew's grasp.

The lieutenant colonel raised his bushy brows. "Then what business do you have here?"

She drew herself to her full height, little that it was. "I'm here to deliver a message."

Hood extended his hand. "Ah. A message of such urgency it needed to come in the middle of the night. This I must see." He wiggled his fingers. "Hand it over."

She shook her head. "I must give it to an officer from Crestview, Virginia. Do you hail from there?"

The amused look on Hood's face vanished, and his features tightened. "That will be all, Captain Daniels," he said, his eyes not leaving the girl.

Matthew frowned. "Yes, sir, but I—"

"I'll handle this from here. Return to your post."

The muscles in Matthew's jaw clenched, but he stepped away from the girl without another word. The lieutenant colonel took her arm. "Come, my dear, and we'll discuss this further." He guided her forward, and she cast a worried look in Matthew's direction before she disappeared inside the tent behind Lieutenant Colonel Hood. The flap fell closed, and the sergeant resumed his position in front of it.

Having no other choice, Matthew turned and limped away. The farther he walked from the tent, the deeper the unease settled in his gut. What fate might he have delivered that poor girl into?

Eleven

"Now we shall soon see the end of all, or the beginning
of worse."
John H. Surratt

Annabelle allowed the officer to escort her inside the
tent, where a wave of warm air greeted her and chased
a shiver from her frame.

"Come, my dear. It seems you've caught a chill. Please, sit
here while I stoke the fire." He guided her to a ladder-back chair
positioned in front of a small personal desk. She lowered herself
into the chair and glanced around her surroundings, unnerved at
being confined in such a small space with a strange man.

Annabelle rubbed her arms, glad at least to be out of the
biting wind for a few moments, even if it was by entering the
jaws of an unknown foe. The lieutenant colonel had managed to
cram a single-man bed, a washbasin, a table covered in all
manner of papers, a trunk, and the writing desk into the small
space. Even the ground underneath her feet was covered with
an array of various rugs that overlapped one another. The most
striking and most luxurious item in the tent was the small wood
stove in front of which the lieutenant colonel stood, holding the

door and prodding within. Her eyes followed the pipe up to the top of the tent where it protruded through the canvas ceiling. He even had a teakettle warming over the fire. Oh, how wonderful a hot drink would be on this frigid night.

As if reading her thoughts, the lieutenant colonel lifted the kettle and turned to her. "Would you care for a cup of tea?"

"Please."

He set to work and in short order presented her with a tin cup filled with the steaming liquid. "I apologize that I don't have something better to offer, but I'm afraid proper china is simply impractical out here."

"No apology needed. Thank you for the drink." She lifted the cup to her lips and let the aroma wash over her and the steam tickle her face.

He took a seat on top of the trunk near the foot of his bed, directly across from her. She looked at him from under her lashes and took her time sipping the tea in order to avoid speaking and give herself a little time to think. Never had she been alone with a man in the intimacy of his private quarters, and she certainly did not wish to be so now. However, it seemed she had little choice, and if she was going to free herself from this predicament, she would need to choose her words wisely.

The lieutenant colonel studied her, his dark brows turned down slightly in concentration. What did he think of her? As if suddenly remembering something, he slapped his knee and caused her to startle. "We haven't had proper introductions!" He rose to his feet and gave a small bow. "I'm Lieutenant Colonel James B. Hood, originally of the 31st Arkansas."

She inclined her head. "Miss Smith." Intuition told her using her real name would not be wise, so she simply spoke the first one that flowed from her lips.

He lifted a brow, but when she gave nothing further, he returned to his seat. "So, Miss Smith, you have come to deliver a message to a man from Crestview. Who told you to seek someone from that town?"

She lowered the cup and decided that in this, she would give the truth, so much as she knew it. "I was asked by Lieutenant Monroe of the Mississippi 35th."

"He wasn't able to deliver it himself?"

She wrapped both hands around the cup and enjoyed the sensation of warmth on her fingers. "He was wounded and has been under my care. When we believed he was getting well, he wished to return to the army." She paused, trying to judge the officer's reaction, but picked up on little more than intense curiosity.

"I see. You're a nurse?"

"In a manner of speaking. I was an aide until everyone in the hospital moved on. Then I did my best to nurse the few left to my care."

He stroked the short beard on his chin. "We could use another nurse."

"But, I'm—"

He waved his hand. "Forgive me, merely observance. Please, continue."

She shifted in her seat and glanced at the entry. There would be no way to leave this place except with the blessing of the man across from her. If she had any hope of asking him to locate her uncle, she would have to find a way for him to realize she was harmless. She offered the officer a sweet smile. "Where was I?"

He returned the gesture with a tolerant smile of his own, not unlike the one she had often seen from Grandfather when he believed her too dull to comprehend his words. "You were saying how you were a nurse."

"Oh. Yes. Lieutenant Monroe seemed to be recovering, and he wished to return to duty. He intended to locate the Northern Virginia and join up with them." Another partial truth.

"And why didn't he?"

"He died."

Silence fell on the tent, and Annabelle lifted the cup to her lips to take another sip and an opportunity to avoid the man's steady gaze. When she looked up, she found him still staring at her. She sighed. "I'd hoped he was doing well enough to travel. I didn't realize his wound had begun to fester, and the fever returned even stronger. There was nothing I could do for him."

Hood nodded. "I see."

Did he? She shifted again. "I was only returning a favor for him. If it's any trouble, I'll simply take it along with me as I continue my journey." Better to find another way to send her message than to be detained here.

"Oh, no. That will not be necessary."

Panic fluttered through her, but she fought to suppress it and tilted her head. "Then the officer I seek is here?"

"It so happens that *I* am a man from Crestview."

She kept her features even. "How convenient for me."

"I've never heard of a Lieutenant Monroe, so you must forgive my suspicions. We've had problems with spies, and as you can imagine, this war has caused even the best men to become leery."

Perhaps he did have a reasonable point. A small measure of relief loosened the constriction in her chest. "Then I'm glad I'll be able to help the lieutenant with his final request."

Interest lit Hood's face, and she suddenly regretted her words. Should she have given away how important the message had been to Monroe?

"Yes, yes. That's good, indeed."

She drew a long breath and threw out her request while he seemed to be in a pleasant disposition. "I was also wondering if I might be able to send a message out with one of your men, if any are going to the Northern Virginia?"

Hood leaned back in his chair. "I'm afraid I cannot help you with that, Miss Smith, as I presently do not know exactly where they are. We have no official correspondence between us at this time."

She leaned forward, feeling the first flutter of hope since she'd lit the match and laid Monroe to rest. "But do you know where their *general* location is? Perhaps that will help me."

"Why?"

She sat back in the chair, resisting the hopelessness that had begun to creep in. Clasping the cup, which had now grown cold in her fingers, Annabelle kept her eyes down, lest they give away emotions she did not wish to reveal. "I'm seeking my uncle."

"And why is that?"

She stiffened, her eyes snapping to his face. "That is of a personal matter, and I don't see how it pertains to our current conversation."

He stared at her, his expression sending the message that if she did not speak further, then he would in no way aid her. Her shoulders slumped. "He doesn't know my father died, and he's now my only remaining male relative."

The officer stroked his chin. "And who was your father?"

Panic stirred anew in her chest, and she lowered her gaze. "He was a captain, and he died in battle. I'm afraid I don't know too many of the details. Why do you ask?"

"You speak as a well-born lady and not at all like the waif you currently appear to be."

Her hand involuntarily rose to her face. "I'm not a waif. Nor a camp follower, and *certainly* not a harlot." Her voice rose in irritation.

"So, you are high-born, then."

She studied him. Seeing no harm in giving her status, and hoping perhaps it might aid her, she nodded. "I suppose. My father was a small plantation owner." Better not to give away any details on Rosswood, lest he deduce she had given him a fake name. He couldn't know all of the plantations in Mississippi, could he?

"Well, Miss Smith, as you are obviously not a threat to us, you are welcome to rest here tonight, and then you can be on your way on the morrow. As soon as you deliver what you have come to do, of course."

Relief flooded through her. "Oh! Of course." She reached into her pocket, pulled out the piece of paper, and handed it to the lieutenant colonel. She watched him closely as he unfolded it.

Surprise flickered across his face but was quickly concealed. "Thank you, Miss Smith. This is most helpful."

"You can read it?"

"Of course. We often do things in this manner to keep enemy eyes from reading our correspondence. Even when it's nothing more than news of home, as this is here."

"News of home?"

"Just letting us know our dear town is safe from Union raids and is faring well."

Annabelle frowned. Why would Monroe act with such urgency for something so mundane?

"But, you see, something still baffles me," Hood said.

"What?"

"There's not a family by the name of Monroe in our town. I wonder, then, why he would have such a salutation."

Annabelle lifted her shoulders, nervous words tumbling from her lips. "Oh, well, that's simple enough. I actually found the letter on another soldier, who died a few days before Lieutenant Monroe. But Lieutenant Monroe must have been close to the man, because he was rather insistent the message be delivered on his behalf. Perhaps this other man is someone you know."

Hood's eyes lit with interest, though his face remained passive. "That would make sense. What was this man's name?"

Annabelle made one up. "Joseph Franklin."

"Yes! The Franklins live not too far from town." He stroked his beard.

Fear clawed in her stomach. What game did this man play? She needed to get out of here.

She forced a smile. "Wonderful." Annabelle bounded to her feet a little too quickly. She had to catch the chair before it toppled over. "Since that's been resolved, I think I'll be on my way now."

Hood rose to his feet and stepped in front of her, his face darkening. "Oh, no, Miss Smith. I'm afraid that's not possible."

She lifted her brows. "But you said I could go on my way once the message was handed over."

"So I did." He clamped his hand down on her arm. "But that was before you proved yourself to be a spy."

Twelve

"The only hope the South ever had of late will certainly now fail her. The Knights are powerless either to aid or lead."

John H. Surratt

"Daniels!"

Matthew groaned and rolled over. Was someone calling his name, or was he dreaming again? Most every night brought with it the distorted memories of losing his brother, in the twisted forms of nightmares that caused his heart to gallop and his palms to sweat.

"Daniels! Wake up, man!"

Full consciousness crashed on him like a bucket of fresh well water, and he jerked upright. His tent was still cloaked in darkness. How long had he been asleep? "Who's there?" he growled.

"It's David O'Malley."

Matthew tossed his blanket off and opened the small flap near the end of his feet to find O'Malley crouched outside. "What are you doing out here?"

"Let me in."

There was scarcely room for Matthew inside, much less

another man. He pulled back the flap and drew his legs underneath him as much as he could, allowing a small amount of room for O'Malley to enter and crouch at the foot of his bedding mat. Sitting hunched like this reminded Matthew of the days in his boyhood when he would build forts out in the woods and duck inside, pretending he was a great warrior defending his lands.

Lands this war might render to shreds. The thought sent a pang through his chest, and his jaw clenched. He had to force it to unlock so he could push forth discontented words from their confines. "What's the meaning of this, O'Malley? Why in heaven's name are you coming to my tent in the dead of night?"

"You brought her in, didn't you?"

"The waif? How would you know...?" he let his voice trail off. Just how many things did O'Malley really have his fingers in?

"I told you. It's our duty to know things. That girl might be one of us."

Matthew snorted. "Impossible."

"And why is that?" O'Malley asked, his hunkered form nearly indistinguishable from the shadows.

Matthew hated not being able to read a man's face when they were speaking. One gathered more information from what played across a man's features than from anything that spouted from his mouth. Not being able to see in the dark made Matthew feel at a distinct disadvantage.

"That girl looks like she wandered in from some field," he said, waving away O'Malley's paranoid concerns. "It's not likely she's some conspirator in a plot to abduct—"

"Hush, man!" O'Malley interrupted. "Do you want to get us

killed?"

Matthew ran a hand through his long hair. "I'm afraid you're going to have to explain yourself."

O'Malley drew close enough that Matthew once again noticed the often forgotten scent of unwashed bodies. "We have to be careful. It's going to require some stealth to get her out."

"*What?*"

"They're keeping her prisoner. We need to get her out before sunrise, when they will start questioning her. We need to talk to her first."

"You want me to help you break out a *prisoner?*" The man was completely mad.

"Hurry. We don't have much time." O'Malley turned and began to lift the tent flap, but Matthew caught his arm.

"Wait. Don't you have others in your... *organization...* who would be better accomplices?"

O'Malley sighed. "Look, Daniels, I put my neck on the line for you. It took a good bit of convincing to get the others to accept my nomination for you. I'm going through a lot of trouble to give you the opportunity to see your brother freed. You said you were with me. Are you retracting your word?"

"Daniels men do not go back on their word," Matthew snapped.

"Good," O'Malley said as he lifted the tent flap and crawled through. "Then come on. We don't have much time."

Pushing down his misgivings, Matthew followed O'Malley into the night. They stalked through the camp like a pair of criminals on silent feet. Matthew inwardly groaned. He should have grabbed his boots. This had better not take long. How ridiculous was it to be slinking about in only his woolen socks?

They neared the rear of Lieutenant Colonel Hood's tent, where light still flickered and shadows moved within, and Matthew had no further opportunity to contemplate the measure of wits residing in O'Malley's skull. Why were they here? Weren't they supposed to be talking to the girl?

O'Malley gestured for them to drop to their bellies and crawl to the base of the tent, where they pressed their ears as near to the bottom of the canvas as they could.

"I tell you, we have one of them," said a voice Matthew didn't recognize.

"Perhaps," said the distinct voice of Lieutenant Colonel Hood.

Something rattled within. "I'm telling you," the other man replied. "I've been tracking this for months. There's some sort of group within the ranks that's plotting something. Something that could be detrimental."

Matthew's heart began to hammer, and he forced his breathing to remain even.

"Come now. You're being paranoid."

"Didn't I tell you about their password just two nights ago? What further proof do you need than one of them giving it just this very night?"

The lieutenant colonel was silent for several moments, and Matthew began to wonder if the men had left the tent or had heard the eavesdroppers outside. He tried to keep himself perfectly still. He glanced at O'Malley. The man seemed unaffected, keeping his eyes closed and his ear to the tent.

Something crawled from the frigid ground and into the leg of his breeches. As the ant began to bite, Matthew slowly moved his opposite foot and tried to scrape the vile insect free.

O'Malley placed a staying hand on his arm. Matthew gritted his teeth and was just about to suggest they move when Hood finally spoke again.

"I must agree. The evidence is quite compelling. And they did discover some type of homemade dagger hidden upon her person."

"So you see what must be done. Good wits, man, playing along with the ruse and getting the message."

"It seems that if she is a spy, she's not a very good one. I had to do little more than say I was from the location she mentioned to get her to hand it over."

A small whoosh of air escaped from the man beside him, and Matthew threw his gaze in that direction. O'Malley's hand clamped down tighter on his arm.

"Where is it, then? This message. I must see it."

"There's not much to see. It appears to be in code. Little more than a series of odd pictures," Hood said with a sigh.

O'Malley tugged on him and backed up. Matthew followed, regaining his feet and slipping through the shadows unseen. They found some manner of distance from the lieutenant colonel's tent before O'Malley spoke. "This isn't good. They have more information than I thought. They might even have what we've been waiting on. We're going to have to enact the dispersion plan."

"The what?"

"I have to warn the others so they can get out. If we're scattered, they're less likely to piece together any more information," he said, beginning to pace. "If I could just get that message," O'Malley mumbled under his breath.

Matthew was about to object to the wisdom of such a plan,

but O'Malley reached up and gripped his shoulders, speaking quickly. "I need you to get the girl. They have her in a tent just outside the medical station. You'll need to take her and head south. I'll meet you on the outskirts of the town of Lorman. There's a house there with a red barn. The owners sympathize with our cause and will pretend not to know you're there. I'll find you in the loft. Now, go."

Matthew caught his arm before he could leave. "You're talking about deserting! Never mind aiding a prisoner in escape. We could hang for this."

"If you don't, she'll be executed. This is her only chance." He pulled free and disappeared into the night. Matthew watched him go until he could no longer distinguish his form. He had never heard of a woman being executed. He stood there thinking, his feet beginning to grow numb from the cold seeping in through his socks. Then he snapped his teeth against the curse forming on his tongue and crept through the still camp toward the medical tent.

As O'Malley had said, in the rear sat a single tent away from the others, hidden from view of the encampment. Matthew drew closer, wondering why they would not have placed a guard on duty. Something wasn't right with this entire situation, but he didn't have time to dwell on it. He eased open the tent flap. The silver light of the moon gave just enough illumination to reveal the girl.

"Miss?"

The girl retreated further into the recesses of her small confinement. "Who's there?"

"Captain Daniels. I've come to take—" A bugle blast cut through the silence of the night, and it would soon bring slumbering men from their pallets with weapons in hand. "Miss! We have to go!"

"I won't go anywhere with you," she hissed. "I'm not a spy, and I'll not be treated as such."

Matthew crawled into the tent. "Listen to me, girl. I don't know what sort of business you're involved with, but if you don't come with me right now, you won't live to see the sun set tomorrow."

She hesitated, stoking the fire that burned in Matthew's gut and pushed nervous energy through his veins. When she finally spoke, her voice was purposeful. "I'm bound. I don't see how I can run even if I chose to."

The bugle sounded again, and shouts mingled with the blast. It wouldn't be long before someone came around and found him here. His fate was already sealed. He grabbed the girl by the ankles, ignored her screech, and hefted her over his left shoulder.

She pounded her small hands on his back, her shifting weight making his balance more difficult with each step he took toward the woods.

"Unhand me this instant!"

Other than her initial cry of alarm, she hadn't screamed for help. If nothing else, Matthew would take that as a sign of consent and keep moving, regardless of how awkward it felt.

"I cannot do that, miss. Right now either we run or we die, and since you are incapable of the former, I will strive to keep us from the latter."

She moaned but did not protest further, her body growing stiff against him. Despite the fire burning in his leg, he pushed on through the darkness, weaving through low-hanging limbs and pushing vines out of the way. Twice he stumbled and feared he would drop the girl, but he maintained his grip and plunged deeper into the cover of trees. When the sounds of the camp began to fade into the distance, he risked setting her down on the damp earth.

"I'm sorry for carrying you so, but it was necessary."

"So you say," she said, lifting her chin. "I think it may well have been an excuse to place your hands upon my legs."

Heat flooded his face. What would give her such a ridiculous idea? "If I didn't hold you, you would have found yourself sprawled on the ground."

She looked up at him, the curve of her jaw appealing even in the dim light. "I suppose that's true." She eyed him, and he once again felt the disadvantage of inadequate light. "I wouldn't wish to fall from so great a height," she said with a small sigh that bespoke of resignation. "It would be like tumbling from the saddle."

He stifled a chuckle that threatened to escape despite the dire nature of their situation. "Good. Then we are agreed. Let me see if I can undo the ropes so you might travel on foot and save us both the indignity of me having to carry you."

"And to give your injury a lighter load to bear," she said softly.

"What injury?" He'd thought he'd done well concealing his affliction.

"I'm not a fool. Besides, I've spent a great deal of time tending wounded men. I know the signs of injury. From the way you favored your right side, I would say you have an injury to your lower leg."

His brows pulled together. Perhaps he hadn't concealed the

weakness as much as he'd thought. "How very observant of you. Now, the ropes, miss. Give me your legs."

She pulled her feet underneath her long skirts. "I think not. I'll not have another strange man putting his hands on my ankles."

Matthew sighed. "We don't have time for you to waste trying to untie them. If you could do that, you would have done so by now."

She drew in a sharp breath, and he knew that even though he could not make out her features in the dark, she wondered how he'd been able to guess what she'd been doing. Not that it was such a difficult thing to discern. Who wouldn't attempt to untie the feet when some idiot had left the hands unbound?

"And since I have a knife with which to cut them," he continued, "I suppose you'll just have to allow me access."

"I'll do no such thing. You can hand me the knife, and I will free myself."

Stubborn girl. He held up the blade. "And how do I know you won't try to stab me with it once you are free?"

"And how do *I* know you won't try to take liberties with me while we are alone out here in the darkness?"

Matthew chuckled. "I suppose we will just have to trust one another."

"Indeed. So, hand it over." She thrust out her hand, and he placed the pocket knife in her small palm.

To his surprise, she flicked open the blade with practiced ease, sawed through the ropes in short order, and returned the closed knife back to him. He'd have to remember that not all women were the pampered ladies he'd known in his days at the plantation. There were plenty of working women who thought nothing of such things.

She rose and stood close to him, her head reaching only to his chest. Without looking up she said, "We'd better get moving before they start searching for me." She started out through the woods, not giving Matthew the opportunity to lead.

He fell into step behind her, but after having to push back several limbs that she simply ducked under, he moved around her and assumed the position of clearing the way.

After they had walked until his leg screamed and the sky began to lighten with the first rays of a new day, he finally stopped and lowered himself onto a fallen log, amazed they had not been overtaken. The girl remained standing, not looking as if the walk had tired her in any way.

"Where are we going?"

He massaged his aching calf and kept his eyes turned down. "Lorman."

She stiffened. "And then?"

He cut his eyes up at her, for the first time able to make out the distinct features of her face. What he saw stirred something within him that he quickly dampened. She was strikingly beautiful, despite the streaks of dirt marring an otherwise perfect complexion. She watched him with piercing blue eyes that suddenly lit with concern as her hand flew up to smooth the flaxen hair that had escaped from its pins.

He cleared his throat. "Then we wait for the others."

She gave a small nod and turned away, her stride confident.

"I think we can tarry for a few moments."

"Oh, of course." She hesitated. "Forgive me. You must need to rest."

Annoyance flared within him. He wasn't an invalid in need

of special tending. But regardless of his wounded pride, the leg would need to rest. It was beginning to seep, and he couldn't afford to have it open back up.

"I don't believe we have been introduced," he said, turning the conversation away from his injury.

A mischievous light entered her eyes. "No, we have not."

"I'm Captain Matthew Daniels."

She inclined her head. "Miss Smith."

"Pleased to meet you, Miss Smith."

"And I you," she said, though the words were thick with sarcasm.

Matthew stretched his leg out in front of him, listening to the early morning twittering of birds and trying to dampen his frustration at his missing boots. He glanced at the girl, who stood quietly watching the woods.

"How old are you?" he asked, pulling her attention back to him.

She frowned, confusion settling in her eyes. "Nearly twenty."

He tilted his head. "There's no reason to be dishonest with me. I've no interest in your profession."

She gaped at him. "How dare you! Why do people keep assuming I'm a harlot?"

"I mean no disrespect, miss. But, women don't generally come to the camp in the middle of the night unless they are seeking…. certain companionship."

She crossed her arms over her chest. "I am *not* a harlot! Or a spy. I was merely helping a soldier who'd been under my care. Before he passed on, he asked me to deliver a message for him. I tried to honor his final request before continuing on my mission to locate my uncle. I didn't know that such a simple thing as delivering a message would land me in this predicament."

He studied her a moment, with her flushed face and flashing eyes. There was no way to know if she was telling the truth or not, so he tried coming at the solution from a different angle. "So, you really are nearly twenty?"

She glared at him. "I was born on the fifth of March, in the year eighteen hundred and forty-five."

He lifted his shoulders in an if-you-say-so shrug. "You look like a girl of no more than seventeen, and that's being generous."

"So I have been told," she spat. Then as if remembering herself, she straightened and smoothed out her tattered skirts. "However, I don't see how my lack of development has anything to do with our situation."

Lack of development? Before he could ponder the odd statement further, she said, "And just how old are you, Captain Daniels?"

"I'm twenty-five."

"Well, since that's settled, and you are properly rested, I suggest we be on our way."

He stared at her for a moment, then shook his head and returned to his feet.

She glanced down at his socks. "I'm sorry to be so rude, but I simply cannot stand it any longer. Why are you without boots?"

"I didn't have the time."

She looked incredulous but simply walked away. Matthew once again had to position himself in the lead, this time earning a small snort from the woman behind him. He pushed into the woods, feeling her eyes staring into his back.

It took them only perhaps two hours more to clear the woods and locate the farmland that marked the proximity of the town they sought. Matthew kept to the edge of the trees, the girl on his heels, and skirted around the field. By the time the sun hit its zenith, he located the barn O'Malley had mentioned, just out from a large white farmhouse. There didn't seem to be anyone about, so he looked back at Miss Smith. She gave a small nod.

Matthew walked up to the rear door of the barn, his eyes darting around for danger. Seeing not the first sign of life— beast nor man—he grabbed the rusted handle and pulled the large door open.

The place appeared unused, with cobwebs hanging from the rafters and the musty scent of lingering animal waste permeating the stale air. He stepped inside and quickly checked the four stalls, but it didn't seem any horses had been housed in here for some time. Good thing, because despite O'Malley's assurances the owners would look the other way, Matthew felt more comfortable knowing they might not know he and Miss Smith were here at all.

Near the rear of the barn stood a ladder to the upper loft. If they didn't leave any footprints in the soft red dirt, they might remain there unnoticed for as long as needed. Matthew glanced down at his soggy socks and thought about the best way to cover their tracks down the center aisle. But first he must get the girl safely above. Then he could worry about the trail.

He turned to offer Miss Smith assistance with the climb but found only the open door held ajar on rusty hinges. Alarm bubbled in his chest as he hurried the short distance back to the door and stuck his head outside, hoping she'd merely decided to wait for his assurance that it was safe to enter.

Curse that woman!

He should have known better. True to her kind, she'd fooled him into trusting her. *Blast!* Where could she have gone? Matthew poked his head around the barn, but found only swaying grass.

The girl was gone.

Thirteen

"Such attempts, if they fail, will only make the Yankees
strike the blow harder; for, it must be acknowledged,
they have the power, and if the South can obtain no
outside assistance, she must fall."

John H. Surratt

Annabelle hiked her skirts to her knees and dashed through the underbrush with little heed to the brambles that further ruined her dress. She felt a ridiculous pang for the loss of her change of clothes in her small traveling trunk, which was still in the abandoned wagon she had left on the outskirts of the army camp.

Such a foolish thing to mourn, but she had little enough clothing as it was. Worse, she'd been stripped of Peggy's weapon when they had searched and bound her before tossing her in that tent. Now she would never be able to return the priceless family treasure. Hot tears burned in her eyes, but she blinked them away. Now was not the time to worry with things she could not change. The present moment presented far more pressing troubles, such as keeping her footing and praying she could outmaneuver the giant who would not be long in noticing her absence.

She ducked under a low branch and drew in a deep breath of cold air, which burned her lungs in a way something so frigid should not. Annabelle almost felt remorse for leaving the man behind, but not regret. Though he had likely saved her from being tried as a spy, he just as likely had landed her in an even greater predicament. Captain Daniels seemed kind, and she'd studied the eyes of enough men to recognize one with honest intentions. Whatever was happening, Captain Daniels truly seemed to believe he was helping her. But what she really needed was freedom. She could not risk asking for his aid as she had with the lieutenant colonel.

She glanced up at the sky, but the canopy of limbs obscured the location of the sun. Not that it mattered. She'd passed by this place before. If she remembered correctly, if she continued forward she would eventually end up back in Lorman. Perhaps if she could reach it, she could find someone to help her untangle this mess and get a ride back home. Lungs burning, Annabelle ducked behind a large pine and drew labored breaths. She needed to rest, or her heart might explode.

Something rustled in the distance. She held her breath, despite the protest from her chest, and strained to hear. Twigs snapped, leaves crunched, and without a doubt Captain Daniels was in pursuit. *Drat!* How had he gained so quickly? Certainly he could not have tracked her path so easily. She'd dashed through the yard, past the house and across the road before ducking into the trees again. As cautious as he'd been of the house, she'd expected him to try to locate her retreat back the way they'd come.

She had not the time to contemplate his actions. Annabelle sprang through the woods and into a sprint in much the same manner she expected a doe might when she'd spotted the hunter. An odd sense of exhilaration warred with her fatigue, and she nearly delighted in the wind that tugged on her tumbled hair, her bonnet having been lost at some point she could not even think to remember. Perhaps if she had paused to find it and make herself more presentable before approaching the camp, she would not currently be sprinting through the woods.

Annabelle leapt over a large, exposed root, her feet landing nimbly on the soft earth, and ducked under a tangle of vines in nearly one motion.

She would escape him now. A man as large as he could not possibly contend with the agility she did not know she possessed. She was like the deer, light and quick and….

Her foot caught on something and sent both Annabelle and her thoughts of freedom crashing to the unforgiving ground below. She scrambled to her hands and knees and struggled to regain the breath that had been forced from her lungs. Pain shot up her left leg, and when she pulled herself to her feet, her ankle buckled. Annabelle clenched her teeth. How foolish! Like a deer, indeed. Now she would be found for certain.

She struggled forward, her ankle not harmed enough to refuse her weight, but certainly tender and unable to be forced into another run. What was she to do now? With little time to think as the sounds of her pursuer drew closer, Annabelle pushed through the woods to her left, careful to stomp harder into the ground as much as her pain would allow and snap small limbs. With any luck, she would make a decent trail for a man in a rush to follow.

When she'd gone as far as she dared, pressing her foot lighter each time, she carefully stepped backward into as many of her footprints as she could find until she reached the upturned root that had fouled her plans. Dropping to her knees, she pushed around the leaves as best she could in an attempt to cover her fall, and then she headed in the opposite direction, balancing on roots and stepping lightly on damp leaves or moss.

A rustling sound indicated her pursuer neared. If she were to find a hiding place, now would have to be the time. Up ahead, a massive tree had fallen and long been forgotten, its innards having been foraged by all manner of crawling insects. The huge and somewhat hollow trunk would serve her purpose. Annabelle shivered and tried not to think too much on the rash action she was about to take.

She dropped to the ground and peered inside the log. Perhaps she could simply crouch behind it. Maybe he wouldn't even come this way at all.

Heavy footsteps pounded nearer, and without further time to dissuade herself, Annabelle wiggled inside the tight confines of the log. The rough, damp inner bark scraped any exposed skin it could find and caught on her hair. She pulled herself as deep into the recess as she could manage, pulling up on her skirts and hoping the toes of her shoes did not protrude past the end of her cramped refuge. But she could not draw her legs in any further nor make herself any smaller, so it would simply have to do. Who would think to duck down and look for her here anyway?

The pounding footsteps drew closer and suddenly stopped. She waited, listening. After what seemed much too long, she finally heard another twig snap a little farther away. He was following her false trail! Soon he would be gone, and she could get herself out of this deplorable sanctuary. Just as she'd begun to feel relief flutter about in her chest, his voice cut through the still air.

"Miss Smith!"

She drew a sharp intake of musty air. Had he found her?

"Miss Smith!"

She clenched her jaw. If he was hoping she would answer his call, he was mistaken.

"You must stop this foolishness. I know you couldn't have gone far."

How would he know such a thing? She wouldn't move and give herself away. How much time passed outside of her thudding heart, she could not know. It felt as though half the day was already lost to this standoff. Finally, she heard him move again. Annabelle tried to swallow against her dry throat. The footsteps came closer.

She squeezed her eyes tight and held her breath.

Matthew clenched his fists in frustration. He didn't have time for this foolishness. Conflicting desires warred in his chest. Perhaps he should just leave the girl. She was likely a spy, and he didn't want to be entangled in the likes of that.

He studied the ground. Someone had raked the leaves in an odd heap in a manner that bespoke of human hands. What reason would she have for stopping to dig in the ground? Up until this point, she'd been easy to follow. He'd caught a glimpse of bright fabric ducking into the woods across the road from the farmhouse, and from there she had left an easily discernible trail.

Her laughable lack of stealth would have made her easy to pursue even without the line of broken branches and trampled brush. He doubted a frightened horse could have made more noise tearing through the forest than this strange girl. What was her reason for running anyway? As one of O'Malley's band of short-sighted conspirators, she should have been ready to meet up with the rest of them. He frowned. Something just didn't fit.

A short distance from the leaf scraping, he noticed a footprint. He narrowed his eyes. Why was this one deeper than the others? Had she lifted some sort of weight? Regardless, the small print was unmistakably hers, and he followed it off on the tangent to the left of the relatively straight path she had thus far forged.

The weighted prints continued for a short distance and then stopped suddenly. Matthew turned and studied the steps behind him until he found one that confirmed his suspicion. She'd messed up on this one and placed her heel too wide, leaving a print that gave away her backtracking.

Intrigued, he squatted down and admired her attempt to deceive him. Why go to such lengths? He stepped carefully around the prints and returned to the raked leaves. In a moment, he spotted what his eyes had been trained by years of tracking game to find. A depression on the ground indicated where she had likely slipped off a fallen branch and left him a clue he was certain she did not expect him to find. He stepped over to it, then looked ahead in a straight line from the indention.

Not six paces away, a rotted log lay on the ground. At the end of it, a slip of pink fabric fluttered in the breeze. He stroked his chin, then shook his head.

"Miss Smith!"

She didn't respond. Didn't she know she'd been found? A smirk tugged at his lips. Perhaps not.

"Miss Smith!"

No response. He crossed his arms and watched the log. "You must stop this foolishness. I know you could not have gone far."

He took three steps closer, but still she refused to abandon her ruse. Matthew frowned, his amusement melting away. What manner of deception was this woman weaving? He thought a moment, then turned and stomped away. She was not the only one who could play such games. If O'Malley had a traitor in his midst, then they could all be in danger. This girl knew his name and rank, and she could easily spin a tale that he had kidnapped her and deserted his unit.

He noisily retreated down the false path she'd created and then, despite his protesting calf muscle, shimmied up a large oak and settled down to wait.

Fourteen

"We are to perish, and none will help us! The cause is
deserted by God and man."
John H. Surratt

Annabelle waited for as long as she could stand the
thought of remaining in the log. Convinced he'd
followed her false trail, she finally slipped free of the dank bark
and slowly rose to her feet. She brushed at her skirt and flipped
her loose hair over her head, shaking it to dispose of any
unwelcome creatures that might have found it inviting.

If only she hadn't lost *all* of her pins. It would be bad
enough to go into town with a tattered dress and a missing
bonnet, but loose hair hanging down her back was unacceptable.
She pulled her fingers through the tangled mess and quickly
bound the length into a plait. Now, if only she had something
with which to secure it. Her gaze fell on the ragged hem of her
skirt, and with a sigh she reached down and tugged a portion of
her petticoat free with a heart-sinking rip. She twisted the strip
of fabric around the end of the braid and knotted it, then tugged
free another piece a little longer than the first. Winding the braid
into a tight coil at the nape of her neck, she was able to secure it

with the fabric tied into a bow.

She shook out as much dirt as she could from her skirt, hoping that she looked presentable enough that her story of a runaway horse would be believed. It seemed a decent excuse for her missing bonnet and dirty dress, though she briefly wondered at how quickly such lies now came to her. When had she become desperate enough to begin fabricating tales before she even needed them?

Likely around the time she had been thrown into a hidden tent with her feet bound. Annabelle pressed her lips into a thin line. If she were going to get herself out of this situation, she would have to rely on quick wits and pray forgiveness for her deceptions later. She had very little time left until she would have to return and face Grandfather. If he knew she had been out all night with a man... she shivered and pushed the thought away.

Ignoring the pain that shot up her leg every time she took a step on her sore ankle, Annabelle turned and headed in the direction of the road. She would not run through the woods any longer. Deciding her best option would be to find someone traveling into town who might be willing to assist a lone woman who'd fallen from her horse, she drew a calming breath and pushed forward until she eventually saw a break in the trees.

Heaving a sigh of relief, Annabelle paused at the edge of the road but saw no one in either direction. She'd just have to walk. At least it was easier than the forest.

Annabelle trudged down the road, hugging her paletot against her until the sun had risen high enough in the sky to chase away some of the chill. With each step her thoughts grew ever more resolute. This errand was foolish and had only gotten her into a mound of trouble. When she'd had an escort, a wagon, and a horse, the idea had seemed less ridiculous.

Even if she *had* gotten the army runner to deliver a message to Uncle Michael, did she really expect him to abandon his unit and ride to Rosswood to confront Grandfather? Resolution stirred in her.

Annabelle straightened her spine and felt her determination grow with each passing step. She would no longer let Grandfather intimidate her. Each day he was less the fearsome presence he had once been and increasingly became nothing more than a frail old man with a sharp tongue. No, it was Andrew she truly needed to worry about. What lengths might he pursue to secure Rosswood?

Annabelle was so lost in her thoughts that she didn't hear the hoofbeats approaching until they were nearly upon her.

Matthew had followed her since she'd finally crawled out of the fallen log, slinking through the shadows on silent feet that still did not possess shoes. Curse O'Malley for making him leave them behind! He had not dashed across the ground with uncovered soles since he was a young boy.

Despite the discomfort of the hard, wet ground and toes that had begun to ache from the chill, he'd trailed her all the way out of the woods. She'd paused at the edge of the road, drawing her wrap around herself, looking very small and somewhat helpless. For several moments, he'd stood there and allowed himself the luxury of admiring her—up until he'd shifted his weight, and a twig snapped underfoot, cutting the silence like a blasting cannon.

Miss Smith had whipped around, a stray strand of blonde hair dancing across her face, her blue eyes narrowed in his direction. Matthew had been certain she'd see him crouching behind a pine barely large enough to conceal his frame, but after staring in his direction for a few moments, she'd hurried on toward the road, limping slightly.

When had she been injured? She'd certainly been moving slower than the mad dash she'd made prior to her ruse, but he'd not noticed the limp. Regardless, it would have been better if he had abandoned his curiosity about the girl and returned right then to the barn to wait on O'Malley. If this girl was a traitor to the group, O'Malley could deal with it himself.

Leaving the girl to her deceptions, he turned to go, but the sound of an approaching rider gave him pause.

Matthew bristled as he watched the young man approach. *Yankee.* Private, by the looks of him. What was this boy doing by himself in enemy territory?

Matthew clenched his teeth. If he needed to know whether the girl was in danger or if she truly was a Union spy, then this would surely tell him the truth. He slipped from behind the pine and crept closer.

Startled, Annabelle spun around to find a Union soldier not twenty paces behind her. She stopped and shielded her eyes from the sun and waited for him to approach.

"Well, hello again, miss."

She blinked against the bright light and squinted up at the young man she'd seen in Mr. Black's store. The one who'd helped her up onto Homer's back. Poor old Homer. Guilt panged her, but there was nothing she could do but hope the old boy had found his way home.

She smiled up at the young soldier, genuinely relieved to see a friendly face. "Hello again." She gestured to her dress before he could ask. "It appears I once again find myself in need of your assistance."

He easily swung down from his gray horse. "Well, now, I'm afraid I cannot help you."

Annabelle blinked at him in confusion, too tired to do more than stare.

"You see, miss," he said, stuffing his hands into his pockets, "I make it a policy only to aid young women who are polite enough to give me their name."

Annabelle pulled her wrap tighter as a cold burst of wind ruffled her hair. The mischief in his eyes caused a nervous laugh to bubble out of her throat. "You must forgive my lack of manners." She inclined her head. "I'm Anna Smith."

Not even the slightest hesitation at giving her false name this time.

He frowned. "And what are you doing alone on the road, Miss Smith?"

She dropped her eyes. Would he believe her story? "My horse spooked and threw me."

He was quiet a moment. "Ah. So then it would seem that riding without a saddle may *not* have been the best idea?"

Annabelle cut her gaze to his face, a sharp retort forming on her tongue. But the glimmer in his deep brown eyes shooed it away. "How observant of you, Mister...?"

"Private Joshua Grierson."

Grierson. Why did she recognize that name? Something tugged at her memory, but she let it flitter away like a lazy butterfly. "It's a pleasure to officially meet you, Private Grierson."

He bent forward slightly at the waist. "The pleasure is mine." He straightened and ran his hands down the front of his crisp uniform. "Since that's settled, Miss Smith, shall I ride out and locate your mount?"

She shook her head. "Oh, no, I'm sure he will return home on his own." That part was true enough. If he had gotten away from the camp, Homer likely would have found his way home by now. That meant Grandfather probably knew she was missing, and Peggy was likely sick with worry. What a predicament. "Perhaps you can just give me a ride back to town instead?"

"Perhaps. Why are you traveling without an escort? Roads can be dangerous for a woman alone."

Annabelle pushed down her frustration. A legitimate, if inconvenient, question. "It's only me and my father now, and he's... not feeling well. I left him at home and was going to return to Mr. Black's to see if he might have something to soothe Father's stomach."

The young man nodded, seeming to accept the lie that felt sour in Annabelle's mouth.

"I'm returning to town now. I'll take you to the store and then escort you home. A young woman shouldn't be out alone, especially when we're at war."

"Thank you." No sense pointing out that technically he was her enemy, and therefore not considered a proper escort.

He offered his laced fingers to boost her into the saddle, keeping his eyes down as she arranged her skirts. As soon as she was settled, he swung up behind her. Private Grierson wrapped his arms around her to secure the reins, and heat rose in her face. Though she was turned to the side so that her legs were properly covered, she was practically sitting in the young man's lap!

Annabelle stiffened and tried to create as much distance between his chest and her back as she could, but as soon as the horse took a step forward, she found the task impossible. The saddle was simply too small to keep her distance. She squirmed. "I think it would be better if I walked."

She looked at him out of the corner of her eye, afraid if she turned her face, her nose would brush his. He chuckled, and she couldn't help feeling he was enjoying her embarrassment.

"Perhaps you're right." He placed the reins in one hand and swung down from the saddle. "Though I would not require you to walk. That would be rather impolite, don't you think? You hold onto the pommel, and I'll lead him into town."

Relief surged, and she gave him a grateful nod. She'd feared her ankle would not stand the long walk into town. "Thank you. I simply feel it would be improper to ride in such a manner with a stranger."

He grinned and began to lead the horse, looking back over his shoulder. "Well now, we're not truly strangers. We've met twice. I should think that would make us acquaintances at least."

His jovial manner made her feel more at ease, and she let herself smile. "Indeed."

The horse's feet plodded across the ground, creating a steady rhythm. Twice the private attempted to coax her into conversation, but Annabelle found it hard to concentrate on his words. The best she could manage were brief remarks she feared were rude, but her mind was too busy figuring out how to explain her appearance to Grandfather.

"Miss Smith?"

"Hmm?"

"When I return you to your home, might I ask your father if I may come call on you sometime?"

Her full attention turned to the back of the private's head, his dark hair partially covered by his blue cap. Surely, she'd heard him wrong. "Excuse me? What did you say?"

He turned slightly to look over his shoulder at her again. "I asked if I might call on you."

"You cannot be serious."

He lifted his shoulders, laughter dancing in his eyes. No, he most certainly could not be serious. He was merely toying with her. But then, the merriment left his features and he turned to face her, bringing the horse to a stop. He stared up at her with sincerity, fiddling with the reins in his hands. "Well, why not?"

Her brows gathered. Was this young man short on wits? Handsome though he might be—and at any other time a plain girl such as herself would have been flattered—she could not believe he would even consider such a thing. "Have you forgotten we are at *war*?"

"It will soon be over."

Annabelle huffed. "So I've been told for the past four years."

He cocked his head. "The Union occupies most of the

South, and Lee is on the run."

Despite the fact she wished to see this war over and had always secretly agreed with keeping the country intact, his flippant attitude that the South soon would meet its end poked at a sore place she wasn't entirely aware she possessed. "Is that so? And why should I believe *you*? You are merely a private with the enemy."

She'd expected the words to sting, but the look that flittered across his face made her feel a pang of regret. She had no reason to be cruel. Heaving a sigh, she let her shoulders drop from the defensive tension that had pulled them up. "I'm sorry. That was rude of me."

He turned and pulled the horse along, continuing their slow, plodding pace. She stared at the back of his head, trying to reconcile her tangled emotions with her beliefs. Annabelle had begun to figure out what manner of apology she should come up with when he finally spoke again.

"I know we're on two sides of a conflict that, I believe, should have never been started. And, yes, I do know I'm nothing but a low-ranking man who has too recently joined the fray to truly understand the horrors of war that others have thus far endured."

Something in the way he said it poked at her heart. Was this a man who had been told of his inadequacy time and again, just as she had?

"However," he continued in his solemn tone, "I'm also a man who looks to the future and hopes for the best. I apologize for offending you, Miss Smith. I do hope you will forgive me." He kept his gaze forward.

The sincerity of his words nipped at her. How callous she

had become. She drew a long breath, the cold air pulling into her lungs and giving her another chill. "No, it's I who should apologize. You're correct. It's only... well, after caring for so many of the wounded and losing my...." She stopped. She'd nearly forgotten herself and mentioned Father's death. Oh, keeping these lies straight was difficult!

He looked at her over his shoulder, and she offered him an apologetic smile. "Losing my brother in the battle of Corinth, I've grown more cynical than I ever thought I would be." Though based on a lie, the truth of the underlying emotions and self-revelation settled heavily on her heart.

"I understand, miss. I was too presumptuous."

Annabelle stared at the road ahead, drawing ever closer to a problem she had not yet figured out how to face. "Secretly, I *do* hope to see this war ended and the country whole again. I wish only to be left at peace with what is mine." The words slipped out before she could regain them, and she pressed her lips into a line.

Private Grierson turned his profile to her, a small smile tugging against the corner of his mouth. Heat rose in her cheeks. When he began to laugh, she feared her face would turn the color of her mother's finest roses.

"Don't worry, Miss Smith. I'll keep your patriotic secret to myself."

"Patriotic, or treasonous?"

"I suppose that depends on one's perspective."

Undeniably. What exactly was her perspective? It seemed the Confederacy had already labeled her a spy, and that was treason on its own. As they reached the edge of town, she decided that this young man had been nothing but kind and, despite herself, she found him quite pleasant. "Private Grierson?"

"Yes?"

"When this war is over, if you ever find yourself back here in Lorman, would you be so kind as to pay me a visit? I find I rather enjoy your company."

"I would be honored."

Guilt tugged at her as he tied the horse to the hitching post outside the general store. She slid from the horse without waiting for his assistance and immediately regretted it as pain shot up her leg. She tried to hide her grimace as she mounted the steps to Mr. Black's store, her ankle screaming in protest.

Fear wound through her. How could she get out of this with Private Grierson at her side? Mr. Black knew her father was dead. Could she simply ask for stomach medicines and be on her way? She had to at least make it to Molly's, therefore avoiding one more lie she would need to tell.

She pulled open the door and strode inside, Grierson on her heels.

"Miss Ross!"

She faced the surprised store owner and tried to offer a confident smile. "Hello, Mr. Black."

He frowned, his gaze traveling over her disheveled state and then coming to rest on the soldier behind her. His eyes lit with fury, and Annabelle hastened to explain before he could come to any conclusions on his own. "This young man was kind enough to assist me when I got thrown from my horse. If it weren't for him, I would have had to walk all the way here, and I do believe I've injured my ankle."

Mr. Black didn't look convinced. He came closer, wiping his

hands on his apron. "Does your grandfather know you're here?"

She drew a quick breath. "Um, well, he knows I came to town and was going to spend a few days with Molly."

Mr. Black's frown deepened, though Annabelle would not have thought it possible. "You sure don't look like you've been with the dressmaker."

Annabelle straightened herself. Why should she need to explain her whereabouts to the shopkeeper? "I'm in need of a new dress, as you can surely tell. Even more so, I'm afraid, now that this one's nearly useless."

Private Grierson spoke up from behind her. "Didn't you need some medicine for your father's stomach?"

Annabelle cringed. Just as Momma had always said. *If ever we spin tales of falsehood, they will soon unravel around us, leaving nothing but a heap of tangled mess.* "Well, you see...I...."

The front door burst open, slamming against the wall as three Confederate soldiers strode in. As soon as Mr. Black and Private Grierson turned, Annabelle slipped behind a row of shelves and hurried toward the back of the store, where she prayed there would be a rear entrance Mr. Black used for receiving supplies. Escape was soon becoming her first response.

"We're looking for a pair of spies." The voice carried through the store, clear even as she continued to retreat. "Have you seen a deserter and his female companion? The man is exceptionally tall, with long pale hair."

Annabelle's heart tripped over itself, and she hobbled faster. There would be no safety for her here. How would she ever return home now? She had to figure out a way to smooth things over. If he heard she was accused of being a spy, Grandfather would turn her over and take claim of Rosswood. And then even if she survived to return home, there would be nothing to return to.

Think! How could she undo this mess?

Despite her command, her mind could focus on nothing more than getting away and ignoring the throbbing in her ankle. She pulled open a back door, revealing a sparse storage room. Blessedly, another door stood at the rear.

She dashed outside and down a short flight of stairs, the bright sunshine causing her to blink. As she rounded the corner of the building, she ran full into something solid, and strong hands suddenly grasped her shoulders.

She nearly screamed, but the sound cut off in her throat as soon as she looked into the concerned face of Private Grierson.

"Come on," he whispered.

She followed him through a back alley and past several buildings until her ankle began to give way, and she started to stumble. "Please. I can go no farther."

Private Grierson looked down at her. "It's only a little way now. Should I carry you?"

She shrank back. Why had she been so quick to trust him? "Where are you taking me?"

Uncertainty played across his eyes. Then, as if deciding, he gave a curt nod. "To an inn. Then I'm getting you a doctor."

"Why?"

"Because you're injured."

"But...."

He held up a hand. "I'm aware you're in some sort of trouble. And no doubt you weren't going to get medicine for your father. But, regardless of what your intentions are, I'm going to offer you my protection and assistance." She opened her mouth to thank him, but he didn't give her the chance. "At least until you have the opportunity to explain yourself."

He deserved the truth. Perhaps the Union Army might even assist her, once they understood her story. At this point she feared she wouldn't find help within the Confederate ranks. Annabelle gave a small nod.

The soldier swept her up into his arms, and she let herself be carried away.

Fifteen

"Every failure which may attend our operations now,
will add all the more to the final day of reckoning, when
the Western wood-chopper will have to pay up for all
the shortcomings."
John H. Surratt

As Matthew watched from the trees, the audacious
Yankee boy placed Miss Smith on his horse and
wasted no time in pulling her close. Though Matthew tried to
dismiss the irrational irritation that flared in his chest, it would
not be denied. Thankfully, Miss Smith appeared to have enough
decency to request that the boy dismount.

Perhaps she'd been truthful about not being a camp follower. Otherwise she wouldn't have turned such a deep shade of
pink. Her actions spoke of a young woman who was untried in
the ways of men.

Matthew found that to be a comforting thought. So, despite
the call of logic to return to his meeting place, he convinced
himself he was responsible for Miss Smith's well-being and that
O'Malley deserved a little more information on the girl's
intentions. He would simply see that she made it to town safely
and was not taken advantage of by the Yank. He kept to the

woods, far enough behind so as not to be noticed, until they reached town and came to a stop in front of the general store, where Miss Smith quickly dashed inside.

There. He could return now with a clean conscience that he'd done all he could. He turned to leave just as three soldiers stepped onto the general store's porch.

Matthew dipped his chin, hiding his face as best as he could. He recognized these men from his own unit. If they'd come into town, it didn't bode well for him.

Matthew ground his teeth. His uniform hung on him like the banner of a deserter, flagging him as a coward who'd abandoned his men and turned his back on his country. He slipped behind the general store, dropping to his knees and kneeling behind a heap of discarded crates. Even the scent of refuse reminded him he'd not eaten since before he delivered Miss Smith to Lieutenant Colonel Hood. In league with his thoughts, his stomach let out a low grumble.

He eyed the door on the rear of the large brick building. Should he sneak inside and see if the soldiers said anything about him, David O'Malley, or the escape of a female prisoner? He needed more information.

Before he could move, the door flew open and slammed against the wall. Miss Smith dashed outside, tattered skirts flapping around her legs. They must be after her. Before he could call out and offer his aid, the Yankee boy appeared and grabbed her hand. They hurried away.

Matthew let out a low rumble, something his brother George had likened to the deep growl one of the hounds made when another dog tried to steal its bone.

He'd been a fool. Her rendezvous with the Yank only

strengthened her position as a spy. She might not be a harlot, but she certainly consorted with the enemy.

A movement to his rear drew Matthew's attention out of his rapidly heating thoughts, but as he started to swing around, something slammed into his skull. Pain ripped through the back of his head and pulsed through his eyeballs, darkening his vision. Dizziness caused him to sway, and he slumped to the ground.

"I'm sorry, friend," a man's voice said above him.

Then everything went black.

Annabelle swayed in Private Grierson's arms, her exhaustion battling with her fear. The comfort of being off her feet almost made her forget the circumstances that had landed her here. Almost, but not quite.

The air warmed considerably, and Annabelle wondered if the winter had begun to break. An early spring would be a miracle she could use right about now. Private Grierson carried her up to the front steps of the inn as if they were simply two travelers weary from their journey.

Or a groom bringing his bride away on their post-wedding jaunt. The second thought jarred Annabelle back to her senses, and she squirmed in his arms. "I can walk now."

Private Grierson set her on her feet and lifted his brows. "I'll have that explanation now."

May as well get this over with. "My father is dead." His face remained passive, and it felt good to speak the truth again. "I live with my grandfather, who's determined to marry me off to a man I despise. On the way to try to get a message out to my uncle—my father's brother, and only remaining male relative—to aid me, I was accused of being a harlot and then a spy."

He stared at her, understandably dubious.

"When you found me, I'd just escaped the man who took me from the Confederate camp holding me as a spy."

Annabelle stared up at him, her heart fluttering in her chest. He remained silent. Should she have disclosed so much?

The muscles in his jaw worked, and emotions scurried across his face, but finally Private Grierson gave a curt nod. "Thank you for your honesty."

Her shoulders relaxed.

"First, you require a doctor. After that, we'll see what else I can do."

He'd help her? Why? "Thank you."

He leaned forward, speaking quietly. "Keep your head down. Let me do the talking."

She followed him into the inn, limping on her sore leg. After a few hushed words, the private handed the man behind the desk a handful of bills. A moment later, he carried her up a flight of stairs and to a room at the end of the upper hall. Private Grierson set her down on the small bed, which groaned slightly under her weight.

"Well," he said, "It will have to do."

She hardly noticed the sparse room. "Private Grierson?"

"Call me Joshua."

She didn't return the familiarity. "I hope you'll forgive the forthrightness, but to my knowledge, privates don't usually have such freedoms."

He studied her a moment. "No, I suppose they don't." Then he opened the door. "I'll return with the doctor."

Alone, she surveyed the small room. It contained only the rickety bed, a single chair without a cushion, and a worn rug on the floor. The wood slat walls held no adornments, and no curtain hung on the single window opposite her bed.

As she sat quietly, fatigue swept over her, reminding her of the limits to which she'd pushed herself. Perhaps she could lie back for a few moments and allow her tired muscles a little rest. Her lids soon grew heavy, and before she could stop herself, she drifted off to sleep.

A knock at the door startled her, and she bolted upright. How long had she slept? Sunlight still flooded the room, so it couldn't have been too long.

The knock came again. "Yes?"

"I'm Doctor Hall. I was asked to come to this room?"

"Oh, yes, Doctor, please do come in."

Annabelle swung her feet over the side of the bed and ran a hand over the front of her dress in a vain attempt to smooth the wrinkled fabric.

The door opened, revealing an aged man with a medical bag. He stepped into the room, his black shoes thudding on the floor. "Are you Miss Smith?"

"Yes."

The doctor carried himself like a man who'd discovered weariness could seep all the way down into one's soul. He stepped forward and bent to one knee, dropping his large black bag next to him.

He extended his hand. "Foot, please, ma'am."

Annabelle complied and lifted her leg, unable to contain a

wince as he took hold of her ankle.

The doctor bent close and examined the tender flesh. "Some swelling, but little bruising. When did the injury occur?"

"Earlier this morning."

He didn't ask how it had happened, and she didn't offer any more information. Instead, she shifted the topic to slaking her curiosity. "You're not the local doctor."

"No." He bent her foot up toward her leg. "Does this hurt?"

"Not so much. Then who are you?"

"Doctor Hall."

"As you said. But, where did you come—"

He turned her foot inward, and she cried out in pain, losing the end of her question.

"As I suspected," he said, ignoring her outburst and continuing to rotate her foot. Annabelle clenched the quilt underneath her and bit down on her lower lip. "You strained one of your ligaments. If you stay off it for a few days, you should be just fine. You can walk when necessary, but otherwise keep it elevated as much as possible until the pain subsides."

Annabelle nodded, but she didn't have time to follow his orders. "What do I owe you for the service?"

"Nothing." He scooped up his bag. "Good day to you."

He put on his hat and ducked out the door before she could say anything more. Had the private covered the fee? Annabelle lay back on the bed and propped her foot up on the footboard, using the pillow as a cushion. She needed to think.

But only a couple of moments after the doctor departed, another knock sounded.

"Yes?"

"Supper, miss."

Annabelle frowned and sat up. "Come in."

The door opened, and a young girl, probably no more than twelve years of age, popped inside carrying a tray topped with a heaping plate of meat and vegetables and a glass of milk.

The girl looked around the sparse room, and then with a small shrug handed the tray to Annabelle. "Here. Hold this a second."

Leaving the tray in Annabelle's hands, the girl grabbed the room's only chair and dragged it across the floor and up to where Annabelle sat on the bed. "Now, then," she said. "We can put the tray on there, and that should work well enough, seeing as how we ain't got a table." The girl grinned, looking pleased with herself.

Annabelle couldn't help but smile. "Thank you." She placed the tray on the low chair in front of her. The tantalizing scent stirred her hunger.

"You're welcome. I've never brought food up before. Most people just eat down in the main room with everyone else." She shrugged. "Poppa said you had a hurt foot, so you were just going to eat up here."

"How did your poppa know that?"

"The soldier told him when he paid for the room and your meals. Poppa made him pay more than double, since he's a Yank. Didn't seem to bother him none." The girl eyed her suspiciously. "He your beau?"

Annabelle shook her head.

The girl looked curious but said nothing more about it. "All right. Enjoy your supper." She turned and went out of the room, pulling the door shut behind her. Left alone, Annabelle shoveled ham, peas, and okra into her mouth much too quickly to be ladylike. It'd been months since she'd had so much food.

The sunlight faded as she finished the meal. Stomach full, her weariness returned. Annabelle pushed the chair away from the bed and pulled the covers over her. For the moment, she was safe.

The rest of her problems would just have to wait until to-morrow.

Sixteen

"Every plan has failed. Now, perhaps, we may hope for
the success of our movement, for it is only by that that
the South can save herself."
John H. Surratt

*M*atthew's head pounded furiously. He groaned and
rolled to his side in hopes of relieving a small measure
of the pressure in the back of his skull. As he did, his stomach
lurched and bile burned at the back of his throat. Drawing a
long breath, he willed down the nausea that threatened to make
him retch and forced his eyes open. With a few blinks, his vision
cleared enough to reveal a small, sparse room with lamplight
dancing across the unplastered walls.

Alarm swelled, and Matthew pushed himself up on one
elbow on the quilt spread across the floor underneath him.

"Easy now," said a man's voice from across the room. "You
don't want to move too much. You took a good blow there."

Matthew trained his attention on the man as he stepped
closer. How had he missed the presence of another in the room
with him? He'd always been more aware of his situation. War
had a way of teaching a man always to keep an eye out for his
enemy. A wonder he was still alive, given his foolishness. The

stranger offered him a mug of tepid water, which Matthew gratefully downed while studying the fellow from one eye.

Middle-aged, portly, and dressed in a shopkeeper's apron. Probably not a threat. Not seeming bothered by Matthew's silent scrutiny, the man took the empty cup from him and crossed the room to place it on a low table near a sitting bench.

"Sorry for making you lie on the floor," he said, his back still turned, "but I don't own a stick of furniture that would fit a man like you."

Matthew gingerly pulled himself into a sitting position, hoping his stomach would stop tossing about like a ship on a windswept ocean. He stretched his legs out and adjusted himself so that his back rested against the wall behind him. As he settled, the pounding retreated somewhat.

"Who are you?" Matthew finally asked the stranger, once he'd determined that the water would remain settled in his stomach.

The shopkeeper sat on a low bench near the hearth glowing with embers that barely chased the chill from the room. Twisting his hands in front of him, the man ignored his question. "I didn't mean to hit you so hard, you know." Apologetic concern etched the planes of his face. "You're just such a big fellow and, well...." He shrugged.

Matthew rested his head against the wall but kept his focus on the man in front of him. Another miscalculation. This shopkeeper was more dangerous than he appeared. "Why did you strike me?"

"There wasn't time to explain."

So he knocked him unconscious? "You're not making sense."

The man rose and paced. Keeping his eyes on him proved difficult, so Matthew let his lids droop. If the shopkeeper wanted to kill him, he would have done so already. It would be no more indignity than he'd already suffered in the course of this wretched day.

"I'm Edward Black. I own the general store."

Worry constricted his chest, but Matthew kept his face impassive, leaving his eyes closed and speaking with an even tone. "What cause did you have to pummel me, Mr. Black?"

Mr. Black ceased his pacing and came to a stop. "I fear Miss Ross has landed herself in a dangerous situation, and I have a feeling *you* know something about it."

Matthew cracked his eyes and had to tilt his head to look at the man's face, a position he was not accustomed to, nor did he appreciate. He pressed his lips into a thin line and waited for the man to continue, not trusting his words to remain civil.

Mr. Black sighed. "You were lurking at the back of my shop. But I only meant to stun you. Didn't think I'd knock you out cold, I swear." He scratched at the scruff growing on his chin. "Took three of us to get you up the stairs after those Yankees left."

Matthew clenched his teeth, which renewed the throbbing in his head. Three more men had seen him. How long before someone handed him over as a deserter? Why had he ever agreed to any of O'Malley's schemes? He wished he was still sitting on the line with his unit where he belonged, and not here on the floor, being scrutinized by some shopkeeper.

After four years of fighting bloody battles, he'd been taken down by a portly man in a blasted *apron*. Matthew tried to keep his frustration at bay, but it manifested itself in the clenching of his fists.

"You're poorly mistaken, sir," Matthew said, the venom in his voice thinly veiled. "I don't know any woman by the name of Ross."

"Don't try to deceive me, young man. I know you're the deserter they're hunting. Can't be too many men in this world who fit your description."

His size had always seemed an asset. Now it appeared to be a disadvantage. He would stand out wherever he went. "I am *not* a deserter," Matthew snapped.

The man lifted his hands and took a step back. "I don't right care what you are and what you aren't, mister. That's your business. What concerns me is Miss Ross."

"And, as I have told you, I don't know her." The man began pacing again, and Matthew closed his eyes. "Do you suppose I could trouble you for something to eat?" Curse his pride at having to beg for food. Either he ate, or this confounding roiling in his stomach would reduce him to an even more pathetic state than he currently embodied.

The man stopped his heavy footsteps. "Of course. And then, you can tell me about the girl they said escaped with you."

Matthew didn't open his eyes as the footsteps retreated and the door closed. How had he come to this? Disabled, captured, and held prisoner by a merchant nearly twice his age. His brother would tease him for the rest of his days for such a thing. If he ever saw George again.

A few moments later the footfalls returned, and Matthew opened his eyes to find the shopkeeper offering an outstretched plate. His stomach growled as soon as the scent hit his nostrils. Matthew grunted his thanks. He shoved a hunk of cornbread between his lips without taking his eyes off Mr. Black. He quickly finished off the pile of peas, carrots, and slice of cold pork, but the meal seemed to do little more than further awaken his hunger. But at least it settled his stomach.

As soon as he placed his fork on the empty plate, Mr. Black took the dish and set it aside. "Now," he said eagerly, "tell me of the girl who escaped the camp."

Matthew narrowed his eyes, the throb in his skull receding to a near-tolerable level. "What do you know of it?"

The man sighed, resting on his haunches in front of Matthew and thankfully situating himself at eye level. "Some soldiers came in saying a woman spy escaped with a large man from the encampment north of town. Miss Ross happened in my store just as they came in, looking a frightful mess. As soon as she saw them, she disappeared."

Matthew nodded, thoughts churning.

Mr. Black studied him for a moment. "Now, from what they say, they don't know what's going on with the officer." He lifted an eyebrow suggestively. "Could be he's trying to capture the spy. Or, could be he's a deserter in league with her."

Matthew could easily return. Say he chased after her. Lost her. He could forget O'Malley's schemes and that feisty little woman, and return to life as he'd known it for the past four years—bad water, long marches, sweat, and the companionship of men who'd shed blood together and survived to share glorious tales of battle with their sons.

Those men had become dear friends. They'd been with Matthew as he'd transitioned from a wayward youth to a man hardened by war, and they deserved his loyalty more than a pretty young spy, no matter how confounding and oddly enticing she might be. But, what of George? Who would seek his freedom if Matthew returned to the army and claimed to have chased but lost the girl?

The Yanks had long since stopped the prisoner exchange, and from what he'd heard tell, most men didn't survive the harsh conditions in the prison camps. If infection and gut rot didn't send them into ground, then starvation was a slow predator that would gnaw a man to his bones.

Matthew set his jaw. He had to get George out. They'd not been close in his youth, with George always being the serious and responsible type and Matthew finding a bit too much pleasure in cards, red-eye, and infuriating the fathers of nearly every pretty face in the county. But war had changed much of that. He was no longer the hot-blooded youth who had rushed to join the glory of battle, and through those hopeless times, he and George had learned much about one another. And now, George was all he had left. Regardless if this scheme got him imprisoned or hanged, he would see George freed and set over Westerly where he belonged.

The shopkeeper cleared his throat, and Matthew realized he'd gone too long without answering. "Again," Matthew said, "I don't know a Miss Ross."

Mr. Black opened his mouth as though to refute him.

"However," Matthew said, stalling the man's interruption, "I do know Miss Smith, who appeared at the encampment wishing to deliver a message. As she did not have the proper call sign, she was escorted to the lieutenant colonel's tent to discuss it with him. That's all I can tell you."

The man lifted a brow. "Smith, huh? And did this *Miss Smith* have golden hair and bright blue eyes?"

"You know her?"

"I know a Miss *Ross*, who lives just out from town, where her family owns a large plantation. Rosswood did well farming and brick making before the war. It's mostly empty now—having been used as a hospital, and the slaves all running off—and now both of her parents are gone."

Rosswood. He remembered the name, though he'd not realized he'd come this close to it. He had travelled there before, some years ago. What had it been? A ball? No. A wedding. A realization hit him, but he pushed it aside and focused on the shopkeeper.

Matthew shook his head. "They may have physical similarities, but Miss Ross cannot be the Miss Smith I encountered. Miss Smith is a working-class girl of no more than sixteen or seventeen years, despite her insistence she's nearly twenty."

Black scratched at his chin again. "Such a strange coincidence, though, since Smith *was* her mother's name." He studied Matthew intently, eyes saying something more that Matthew couldn't place. "How can you be certain it's not the same girl?" He ran a hand over his head, signs of guilt creasing the corners of his eyes. "I should have stopped her when she came in here telling me she desperately needed to get a message out to her uncle. Ross's second wife's father—I don't think he does right by her. I don't know much about it, but people talk." He shook his head.

Matthew remained quiet. Mr. Black spilled his beans without any prompting.

"Something's wrong. I sent the telegram she requested and found someone to take that soldier home, but I should've tried to do more."

Mr. Black stood and crossed the room to a trunk in the corner. He pulled out a worn blanket that was more wadded than folded. "You're welcome to get your rest here tonight. I owe you that much for smashing your head." He tossed the blanket, which Matthew caught with one hand.

"Thank you." He offered a friendly smile. "Both for the hospitality and not turning me over to the Yankees."

Mr. Black regarded him another moment, then offered a tense smile. "Goodnight to you then." He shut the door and left Matthew in deepening shadows.

Matthew pulled the blanket over him and plucked through his memories. Ah. He remembered now why they'd gone to Rosswood. His family had come for a wedding, then ridden on to Natchez that summer. Elliot Ross had married for a second time, a woman from lowly background but with a lovely face. He'd danced with the Tucker girl at that wedding and had set a fire to Marilia, the brunette he'd been courting at the time. She'd made quite a scene. Her father had physically removed her from the lawn. Matthew had feared the man would try to run him through, but he'd seemed glad enough for his daughter to be finished with Matthew. He'd never called on her again.

Matthew pushed away his regrets over his wayward youth and tried to recall the Ross family. There *had* been a girl. A shy thing who stayed near her father as he and the new bride mingled with their guests. Easy to dismiss. But he did remember big, blue eyes.

Miss *Smith* couldn't possibly be Miss Ross, the girl his father had once considered a good match for him. Could she?

The Ross family was known for the quality of bricks they produced. Father considered the alignment with Rosswood a perfect match, as lumber and brickyards were the new conquest Father sought.

Those days seemed so far away now. Plans forgotten in the fever pitch of war.

Elliot Ross had agreed to Matthew's suit, stipulating Matthew would wait until her sixteenth year and debut into society before they began to court. But war came first and the courtship had been forgotten.

Matthew tried to remember the face of the young girl so he might compare it to the face of Miss Smith, but could not recall it with any clarity. Could she truly be the same waif who'd wandered to the line? It seemed unlikely. The stiff Mr. Ross would have insisted his daughter be an impeccably proper lady. Miss Smith was anything but. The mystery surrounding this woman grew ever thicker.

Matthew breathed evenly but did not lie back on the mat. He would not sleep here tonight, despite how much his body cried out for rest. As soon as the shopkeeper slept, Matthew would make his escape.

Seventeen

"Lincoln had better be wise or he will have to pay
the penalty."
John H. Surratt

David O'Malley studied the footprints in the red dirt of
the barn floor. No mistake—these belonged to
Matthew Daniels. He stood and scratched his head. Where
could they have gone?

"Ain't nobody up here," Harry called down from the loft.

David had hoped to find the girl up there cowering. But,
since he didn't see any female prints in the soft ground, he
hadn't actually expected to find anyone.

"I *knew* he'd turn on us," Benson said. He spit a stream of
amber tobacco liquid. "I done told you he was too much of a
risk."

David frowned but didn't respond. Why had Daniels left?
Perhaps he had a good explanation. David had seen the
desperation in Matthew's eyes when he'd lost his brother, and
desperate men were a fearsome force. Just needed to focus
Daniels in the right direction. "We stay here for the night."

Harry dropped down from the final rung of the creaking

ladder. "What for? I told you ain't nobody here."

"I can see that. We're going to wait."

Benson spat again. "Gettin' dark anyway."

Harry shrugged. "I reckon."

David stepped outside into the gathering dusk and studied the farmhouse on the hill. The soft glow of lamplight flickered in the window and brought a sudden pang of memory. He'd once had a home like that—a warm haven from the world.

The thin curtain suddenly swept back, revealing a man holding a rifle. David held up his hand and opened and closed his right fist three times. The man in the window did the same, then dropped the curtain. They'd be safe here tonight.

David turned away from the inviting scene and the memories it provoked. The barn suited him. He wouldn't let himself long for the comforts of the life he'd lost until he saw this thing completed. He'd honor them by remembering his penance.

Benson, the smell of tobacco surrounding him like a swarm of flies, stepped close. Once, the scent of tobacco had been sweet, calling up the thoughts of relaxing in front of a fire with a pipe at the end of a hard day of labor. Now, it only churned his stomach. He scowled. "Speak, man, if you have something to say. Don't just stand there."

Unfazed, Benson made a sucking sound as he cleaned bits of tobacco from his teeth, then spat again. The muscles in David's jaw worked, but he refused to repeat himself.

"We're not just staying here to bed down for the night, are we? You're waiting on him."

"I am."

Benson leaned back against the side of the barn and began picking at his teeth with an overgrown fingernail.

"We need him," David said, though he didn't have to explain himself to this lout.

Benson watched him for a moment. "Well, you keep saying that, see, and we are startin' to wonder why you put such a priority on a man who hasn't even been with us for a week. How do we know he's not out there now, betraying us?"

"He's not."

"How do you know?" Benson pressed, his eyes narrowing.

David drew a deep breath and admired a group of clouds turned pink and orange with the final rays of the sun. Such beautiful colors. People rarely bothered to enjoy them. "Benson, have you ever noticed the way the sky erupts with color when the sun sets?"

The man grunted. "Yeah. What of it?"

David closed his eyes. With Liza gone, who would be left to appreciate such things? He turned his focus back on the scrawny man in front of him. "Nothing."

Benson pushed off the wall and stepped in front of David, so close David could see the flakes of brown tobacco in the crevices of his yellowed teeth. David took a step back, though not from intimidation. No, he simply preferred to look into the taller man's eyes without craning his neck.

"Now look here," Benson said. "Just because you're the closest to Booth doesn't make you the leader here."

Didn't it? What did they know about the plan other than the crumbs David had shared with them? He kept a smirk from twisting his mouth and merely waited for Benson to continue.

"We want to know what's going on with this Daniels fellow."

"Yeah," Harry said, stepping outside to join them. "We've

got a right to know."

David let out a long sigh, demonstrating his disappointment with their lack of trust in his leadership. "The plan's for Daniels to meet us here. Maybe he just went into the woods to catch a rabbit or something. He'll be back."

The two men exchanged a loaded glance, and a spike of uneasiness coursed through David's veins. If he'd learned anything from this cursed war, it was how to sense danger. If he didn't offer up another morsel, these two were liable to cause him more trouble than they were worth.

What would it hurt to treat them to a little play of logic? "Have either of you ever seen him?" David asked, crossing his arms.

"Daniels?" Benson asked. "Of course we have. We're in the same regiment."

David shook his head. "No, you lout. The man whose name we do not speak."

Harry perked up. "I saw a sketch of him once, in the paper. He's got a funny beard and a real angular-like face, like he's half-starved or somethin'." He scrunched his nose, making him resemble a wrinkled rat. "Seems a man like him could afford to eat more."

David lifted his brows but ignored the imbecile. Benson pulled on the scraggly hairs protruding from his chin, a motion he did whenever faced with something that caused the rusted cogs in his brain to turn.

"We've never seen him, O'Malley, but I don't see what that's got to do with Daniels."

Disappointed the train didn't leave the station, David explained. "Oh, it has everything to do with him. You see, our quarry is an unnaturally tall man. Whether you've ever seen him or not, everyone knows he stands more than a head above most men."

The two fools nodded eagerly, as if remembering where they'd stashed a sweet.

"That's right," Harry said, his head bobbing. "He sure does."

They stood there dumbly, neither possessing the ability to come to any logical conclusions on his own. Like hounds without snouts, he'd have to lead them down the trail. Smothering his frustration, David spoke slowly so as to allow them to keep pace. "So, how do you suppose to capture a man of such size?"

Benson harrumphed. "He's skinny as a rail. His height won't make no difference."

Harry glanced at Benson. "Don't know about that. You're thinner than a sickly girl, and yet you still beat me at a strong arm contest every time."

Benson puffed out his chest, stepping into Harry's space. "What did you call me, you cur?"

David thrust his arms in between them and shoved, sending both men stumbling backward. They regained their balance and stared at him.

"Enough. He's managed to snag the truth of it, Benson." The man clenched his teeth, and David hurried on before he ended up in a senseless display of swinging fists for delivering a perceived slight. "You can't tell me most men don't underestimate your strength. I'd guess that's exactly why you challenge them to a contest, am I right?"

Benson's shoulders relaxed, and he deflated somewhat but

kept his eyes trained on David.

"As I thought. They take one look at you, figure they'll beat you right easy, and end up losing their coins."

Benson frowned. "Well, yeah. How'd you know that?"

Because not everyone is as thick-skulled as you. "I thought the same myself, my friend, until I watched you push over two separate men, each with arms twice as thick as your own." An exaggeration, but it would play to the fool's pride.

Sure enough, Benson puffed out his chest, and David half expected him to start strutting like a pup with a fresh bone in its jowls.

"I see it now," Harry said, understanding dawning in his dull eyes. "You can't take the chance that a man that size won't be stronger than we think. You need someone at least as big as him to be the one to snatch him, so it'll be quick like."

David smiled. "See? There you have it. Well done."

Harry grinned, obviously pleased with himself. Benson remained silent, his bushy brows settled low. Disappointed he hadn't made the conclusion first, or still befuddled altogether? "And have either of you ever seen a man as tall or as stout as Daniels?"

They both shook their heads.

"Then you see why I chose him."

Benson tugged at the scruff on his pointed chin again. "But that don't mean nothing if he's run off and is sharing our secrets."

David looked back to the sky, but the light had faded, the beauty of the sunset having been trampled by the two clods in his company. He let out a sigh at the loss and continued the cyclical conversation. "Daniels wants his brother back, and he'll do anything to get him. That's motivation enough."

"How you gonna do it, O'Malley?" Harry asked. "Can you really find Daniels's brother in all them camps?" His voice actually sounded hopeful, though David couldn't fathom why.

"I can try, though the man will probably be long dead by then."

The silence confirmed their confusion, but he grew tired of dragging them along, so he dismissed them and stepped inside the barn. He only needed Daniels to *believe* he'd get his brother back. Once they had their leverage, Daniels would have to be dealt with. A shame, really. Daniels seemed the type who would be fiercely loyal, if he chose.

David hauled himself up to the loft and settled down into the moldy hay. Below, the boys complained about having nothing more than hardtack and jerky and rambled about imagined feasts. David ignored them. What was food but a necessary product to keep the body moving? If he needed to, he could go several days before he had to find a meal to keep his mind clear. He didn't need to eat tonight.

He turned his thoughts back to Daniels, letting the concern he'd kept hidden from the cretins take hold. What if Daniels really didn't return? He needed that girl to discover the message the army had stolen.

Daniels wouldn't disclose their plans; he knew too little. Despite what he'd said, a good blow to the head would subdue any man, regardless of how tall and lanky. David didn't think they actually needed Daniels as much as he'd let on. At least, not solely because of his size. But Booth had insisted on muscle for the job, and David was determined he'd be the one to deliver it. Maybe then he might actually get as close to Booth as he'd claimed. He'd found the perfect prize.

David rolled to his side. He could convince Daniels to do the grab. David could have been just as famous of an actor as Booth himself if he'd joined the troupe. But he didn't regret his choice to care for Liza instead. No, he could never regret that. Besides, his skills served them better here. Who else could so easily slip on the countenance of any man he chose?

David let his lids droop. Too bad they couldn't keep Daniels for the duration of it. He would make a good guard. But there was too much hesitancy in Daniels's eyes to make him a full member. Such a shame.

The two dullards gave up on their foolish conversation and settled on the other side of the loft. Good. At least he wouldn't be overwhelmed with their stench.

"You sure he's gonna come back?" Harry said, disturbing the silence a few moments later.

"I'm quite certain, Harry. Go to sleep."

"How can you be so sure?"

David groaned, his mask slipping further the more the fatigue pulled at him. "My dear friend, it's as I've already told you. Daniels is a desperate man, and desperate men will do anything to get what they want."

"If you say so," Harry said, then blessedly fell silent.

David did not doubt. Desperation was the demon ever on his own shoulder, and he knew well what it could oblige a man to do. If Daniels's heart was a mere portion as hollow as David's own, David would have no trouble convincing Daniels to succumb to the sweet revenge that desperation always promised.

Eighteen

"They all seem ready to do anything to secure success."
John H. Surratt

When the only sounds Matthew could distinguish were the chipper calls of crickets and his own tempered breathing, he abandoned the mat and picked his way across the room in the darkness. The doorknob turned easily in his hand, and he let out a sigh of relief. He'd almost expected to find it locked.

He opened the door only wide enough to slip through, grimacing as the hinges squeaked. Matthew stood with one foot in the hallway and listened. Silence. He felt his way along the hall and to a set of narrow stairs that likely led to the mercantile. The stairs didn't betray his descent, and he soon found himself in a small room behind the counter.

Matthew crept through the shop, trying to find what he sought by the paltry moonlight coming through the two large front windows. Finally, on a low shelf in the far corner, a row of boots took shape in the gloom. He usually had his shoes specially made. None of these would fit, but better he escape in too-tight boots than socked feet.

The largest pair would have to do. He pulled one onto his

foot and stood. It pinched his bent and cramped toes, but he'd manage. The leather would eventually stretch. He quickly pulled on the other boot and laced it up.

Matthew had never stolen a single thing in his life. Not even a sweet from the kitchen when the cook wasn't looking. The starving army hadn't been paid in months. His only possessions were government-issued. Except his knife, which he refused to trade. He'd have to remember to send payment through the post at his first opportunity.

Slipping through the storage room, Matthew found the door at the rear that would lead him into the alley where he'd been felled by the portly Mr. Black. He lifted the thick bar securing the door and propped it against the wall, then stepped out into the cold night air. The new boots would most likely leave blisters on his heels, but he ignored the discomfort and stepped into the alley.

Now, which way had the girl gone? It'd be harder to track her through town than the woods. Especially in the dark. He stood where he had seen her with the Yank, thinking. Had the meeting been planned or accidental?

Matthew walked carefully down a long narrow alley, trying not to overturn any garbage heaps or disturb any cats lurking in the shadows. At the end of the alley, he stepped onto a main street lined with darkened shops. Now what?

They were likely deep in a Union camp by now. Up ahead, warm light spilled onto the street, carrying with it the sounds of laughter and the merriment of people who had apparently forgotten they were at war.

Matthew ducked his head and hurried under the sign that marked the place as an inn, though it sounded more like a tavern. No one seemed to notice him.

He trudged through the moonlit town and to the road that would lead back to the barn. Indecision clawed at him, and his anger grew with every passing step. Curse this war, the North, and the Yanks who'd taken George. Though he might long to return to his unit, he'd likely spend weeks in detainment for leaving, regardless of the reason. Unless he brought the girl back, they'd string him up by the thumbs for defecting during the night. Might even accuse him of conspiracy.

Fatigue begged him to bed down in the barn for the night. He could decide in the morning if he wanted to risk trusting O'Malley or take his chances with the army.

When the barn came into view, Matthew left the road and stomped through mid-calf grass. Good thing he had boots in case he came across any cow patties. He entered the dank building, glad to be out of the cold wind. Safely closed inside, he eased forward in the complete darkness, feeling ahead with his outstretched hands. After making his slow shuffle down the aisle, he eventually brushed his fingers against the rough ladder on the rear wall.

He'd just put his foot on the first rung when a voice startled him, and he leapt backward, his hand instinctively going for the knife at his side.

"Who's there?" the voice said from above.

Matthew strained his eyes in the darkness but couldn't make out the man above. He lifted his blade.

"Answer me, or I'll shoot!"

Matthew fell into a fighting stance, his blade at the ready.

"Harry! Get out of my way."

Matthew lowered his blade. O'Malley. He hadn't expected

him so soon.

"Daniels, that you?"

"You expecting someone else?"

"Excellent. I *knew* you would return."

Matthew frowned. Something in O'Malley's tone set his intuition on edge, but he couldn't quite place why. "Who else is here?"

"Just me, Harry here, and Benson who's sleeping like a dead horse."

Matthew waited. The other man grumbled something about lost sleep and then fell silent.

"Well, come on up."

Matthew scaled the ladder and crouched on the platform, his senses wary of danger. He waited for an ambush, but nothing moved. At least, as far as he could tell. He couldn't even see the knife he held out in front of him.

"Over here, Daniels. There's a big enough pile of hay for you near the corner."

Matthew kept at the ready but followed O'Malley's voice. When his searching hand came in contact with a heap of musty straw without incident, he pocketed the knife and sat.

"Where's the girl?" O'Malley asked, his voice only an arm's length or so to Matthew's right and low enough so as not to be heard by the others.

"Gone. Maybe even in the middle of a Union camp by now," Matthew said in a harsh whisper, the annoyance in his voice surprising even him.

O'Malley remained quiet for a long moment, and Matthew began to think he'd come to the same conclusion. The girl was either never a part of the group or she'd betrayed it.

"We'll have to get her back," O'Malley finally said.

"Why?"

O'Malley shuffled closer, lowering his voice even further, so much so that Matthew had to strain to hear. "I need to know the contents of that missive."

"Don't you already?"

"Not exactly."

There it was again, that subtle shift in tone that fueled Matthew's unease. Suddenly O'Malley's hand patted his shoulder. Matthew stiffened. How could the man even see to find him in this inky darkness?

"Easy now, friend. You're more nervous than a mouse in a room full of starving cats." O'Malley leaned close, his breath on Matthew's ear. "We were waiting on that delivery for weeks. It came from our contact up north with instructions on when to put the plan into action. Without it, we can't make our move."

"As I see it, the plan's forfeited. Return to the army with me in the morning. I'll figure something out."

The fingers on his shoulder tightened. "Return?"

Matthew shrugged free. "I'm not a deserter. I'll tell them I chased after the escaped girl, then lost her. A few nights strung up won't kill me."

"And you think they'll believe that?" O'Malley hissed.

"I'll take my chances."

O'Malley controlled his breathing with long, deliberate inhalations. After the fourth one, he finally said, "That wouldn't be wise. Who will help your brother?" Matthew clenched his jaw. O'Malley took his silence as a chance to continue. "Go north with me and use our sources to find out which camp your brother's in. Then you can decide what to do."

Matthew considered it. If he found where they held George, he'd find a way to get him out on his own. Somehow. "I'll go, but I'm not making any promises."

"Oh, but you already did."

Matthew let out a low rumble and sensed O'Malley scooting a little farther away.

"I'm only reminding you of your word."

Matthew leaned back against the stack of hay. "Let's get some sleep."

"Of course, my friend. You certainly deserve it. Only one more thing, and then I'll let you be."

"What?"

"Do you know anything about this girl?" he asked, once again scooting closer and dropping his voice. "I'm beginning to fear she's not who we thought and therefore may be in grave danger." The concern in his voice seemed genuine enough that Matthew agreed.

"Either she unknowingly got caught up in this, or she's a northern spy."

"Daniels," O'Malley said urgently, "we *need* to know where she is."

He was probably right. "She went with a Yank. I don't know where he took her."

"Do you know anything else about her? Anything that might help us?"

"Perhaps...." he hesitated. "But you'll have to let me handle it."

"Of course, of course."

"I may know where she's going. Assuming she's not a spy."

"Excellent. Where?"

Matthew rolled to his side, putting his back to O'Malley. "It's a very unlikely scenario, one I don't even believe myself." Matthew's lids grew heavy, his body unable to refuse sleep much longer. "I'll make you a deal of my own. I'll go and see if there's any truth to my suspicion. If there isn't, we'll assume she's a traitor or a spy and go north without her."

O'Malley was quiet for a moment. "And if you *do* find her?"

"Then you agreed to let me handle it."

"Indeed, I did. And I'll not go back on my word. A man is nothing without his word."

Matthew bristled at the prod at his honor. "Good night, O'Malley," he said through clenched teeth.

Rustling indicated O'Malley settled into the hay. "Sleep well, my friend. We have quite a journey ahead."

Despite the worry that desperately clamored for his attention, Matthew closed his eyes and told himself it would all be clearer in the morning.

Nineteen

"How disheartened the Southern papers read. 'Sherman is riding rough-shod over the whole South, carrying destruction everywhere.'"

John H. Surratt

*P*rivate *Grierson,*

Annabelle paused with the pen hovering across the rough paper the young serving girl had delivered after breakfast. The ink dropped, marring the page.

I'm sorry to leave you this way, but it's of utmost importance I return home. All the things I told you yesterday are true, and I do hope you'll believe me. I will be ever grateful for your aid after I was thrown from my horse.

Despite the girl's promise Annabelle could leave a sealed letter for the young man who'd paid for her lodging, she knew well enough that nothing would be delivered to a Yankee soldier unread. Even if the Union now controlled Lorman. She'd have to be very careful with how she worded her letter.

I do hope that aiding the enemy will not go poorly for you and will be seen only as an honorable act of helping a lady in need, despite her status as a Southerner.

May as well try to staunch any rumors. She held the pen over the page, contemplating how she should sign it. Another drop of ink fell and splattered on the page. She sighed. Years ago, her governess would have made her begin again for such sloppiness.

Making up her mind, she quickly scrawled the remainder of the short message.

I thank you again for your assistance.

Sincerely,
Anna

She folded the paper and poured a dollop of candle wax across the fold. It would have to do. She stood, relieved to find her ankle felt much better this morning. It held her weight without the discomfort immobilizing her. She'd rest it again once she returned to Rosswood.

After securing her hair as best she could, Annabelle tried to straighten her tattered dress, then descended the steps. No one noticed her walk out the front door and into the cool, clear morning. Who would ever think such a dirty girl was actually the lady of Rosswood? With her uncovered head, they probably thought her a lady for hire anyway. Better no one recognize her, even if the implications gnawed at her sensibilities.

Turning to her left, she walked as quickly as she dared down the street, made a left and then two rights, and came to the front of the dressmaker's shop just as the throbbing in her ankle began to demand she stop.

The bells on the door tinkled as Annabelle stepped inside,

thankful no other people examined the few bolts of cloth remaining on the shelves.

Molly appeared from behind a curtain on the rear wall, her pale cheeks flushed. "Annabelle! Oh, my heavens! How nice to see... oh, dear." Molly stopped and placed a hand over her mouth.

Annabelle grimaced. "I know. I look a fright."

"What happened?"

Molly remained her closest friend, even though they hadn't seen each other in a long time. Father had allowed the friendship when she was a child, letting the girls play while he and Molly's father talked of business or whatever else men spoke of. Back then, Molly's father had been a successful merchant, and Molly was near enough Annabelle's station that staying nights at Rosswood had been proper.

War brought the death of both of Molly's parents and, like Annabelle, Molly had found out that survival required great changes. Though their circumstances had kept them apart, just looking upon her friend's concerned face now brought a surge of relief.

Annabelle admired the store. "You've done very well to care for yourself. It isn't easy for a woman to have her own business."

Molly's generous lips stretched into a tight smile. "Thank you. Now, what happened to you?"

How like Molly to not let her steer the conversation away from her disheveled state. "I was thrown from my horse, and I'm in need of a new dress. Or a skirt and blouse, at least." Sometimes Molly made skirts from the leftover fabric when she finished a lady's dress and sold them to the poorer women. But, since the line between the privileged and the poor became thinner every day, Molly might not have even remnant patch skirts on hand.

Molly lifted her dark brows. "*Homer* threw you?"

Heat surged into Annabelle's face. Caught. She grabbed Molly's wrist and pulled her back behind the curtain that separated the storefront from the sewing space. "Come on. I'll tell you what happened."

Molly followed her into the sewing room littered with fabric remnants and spooled threads. A nearly finished dress lay across a wide table in the center of the room. Annabelle studied her friend's troubled expression for a moment, then decided it would do her good to spill her heart.

"Grandfather wants to force me to marry Andrew."

Molly gasped. "Your uncle?"

"Only by marriage." She grimaced. "It's legal."

"Oh, dear. Your father always said you could choose."

Annabelle straightened. "I won't do it. I tried to find my father's brother, but...that's been difficult." She'd keep the army and spy part to herself. Though unlikely, if anyone were to ask, she didn't want to cause Molly any trouble. "Anyway, Grandfather thinks I've been with you to be fitted for a wedding dress."

Molly snorted. "As if I'd be able to make a proper wedding gown these days."

"Well, I doubt he's thought of that."

"So, what happens when you don't have a dress?"

"I'm going to tell him you started all my measurements, but I changed my mind and decided not to marry."

Molly looked Annabelle over. "And how shall we explain your current condition?"

Annabelle sighed. "I'd hoped you'd help me avoid that particular explanation."

"It just so happens I might." She pointed to the mound of patterned blue fabric lying across the table. "Mrs. Jones ordered it but came in just yesterday to say she couldn't pay for it." Her voice nearly cracked on the final word, and Annabelle's heart constricted.

"Oh, Molly. I'm sorry." Annabelle knew how many hours Molly put into her dresses, and she needed what little money her work brought to fill her stomach. Molly's father had left the buildings to her, but the remaining money that he'd been able to pass down upon his death had run out last year.

Molly waved her hand. "It's nothing. I understand." She blinked, likely to ward off unwanted tears. "None of us has much anymore. But I planned to finish it anyway, hoping that maybe one of the Union officers might have a wife with him, and she might be in need of a dress about this size." Doubt thickened her voice. "Regardless, with a little bit of adjusting, it should fit you nicely."

"I couldn't." How could she take something that could fetch Molly a good price? "I just need a patch skirt and homespun blouse."

"It's all I've got, and I won't allow you to go home like that." She glanced at the dress, her forced chipper tone crumbling into a grumble. "Besides, what *was* she thinking to want such a thing made in times like these? I should have known better."

Annabelle assessed the sorry state of her appearance. It would be easier to tell Grandfather why Molly had given her a new dress than to explain her current one. What choice did she have?

"I'll pay you back."

Molly smiled. "I know you will. Soon Rosswood will be thriving again, and you'll come to me for twenty new gowns!"

She giggled, and Annabelle joined her, both of them knowing the fantasy would never come to pass but not wanting to ruin the moment by admitting it.

In just two short hours, Molly stepped back and let Annabelle look in the mirror. "There. It's obvious it wasn't made for you, but it still fits you decently well."

Annabelle turned to admire the delicately patterned fabric that made her eyes appear an even brighter blue. It might not look like a perfect fit to Molly, but Annabelle would have never been able to tell the dress wasn't always meant for her. Tears welled in her eyes, and she tried to blink them away.

"Come now, it's only a dress."

Annabelle pulled her friend into a hug. "No, it's more than that."

Molly squeezed her and then stepped back. "I'm sorry it's an evening cut, but I think we're going to be blessed with an early spring, so perhaps you won't freeze for too long with the wide neckline."

The dress fell across the edges of her shoulders and dipped down in the front to expose all of her collar bone. How scandalous would it be to go about with so much showing during the day? Well, she could wear her paletot or a shawl for a while; it would be fine. At least it had long, creamy sleeves that brushed the backs of her hands.

The skirt at the bottom was a little less full than any of her previous gowns had been, and she wore only a layered petticoat underneath instead of a hoop skirt, which neither of them had. Hoops would be ridiculous in this situation, anyway. Who needed to worry with silly fashion standards when they were nigh on starving?

No sillier than a girl in a ball gown with her shoulders showing on a winter day.

Annabelle dismissed the thought and pressed the fabric down with her fingers, which she refused to let tremble. The blue fabric split in the middle, revealing an underskirt with delicate white lace that matched the trim on the bodice.

Annabelle stared at herself in the looking glass. In a proper bodice, she looked more a woman and less like a child. *Let's see if Captain Daniels thinks me a girl now!* The unwelcome thought startled her. Why should she care what he thought? She'd never see him again.

"Ah. One more thing," Molly said, clapping her hands together and pulling Annabelle from her musings. She slipped behind the curtain, and Annabelle could hear her rummaging around in the store. She returned a few moments later. "Now, with this band and a little of the lace, we can make a nice head covering to match."

Annabelle's lips turned up. "A bonnet will do fine. I don't need a complete ensemble. You've done plenty already."

Molly frowned. "Hold on." She snatched up a piece of the blue trimming from the dress, completely ignoring Annabelle. "No, no. It's easy to make." She held it out and then pulled it back. "Oh! But we must do something with that hair."

Annabelle lifted her brows but said no more. Molly unwound Annabelle's braid and let a mass of spiraled hair tumble down her back.

"Oh, yes. These curls are much better," Molly said, gathering them up and securing them to Annabelle's head with several pins before placing the headband on top and pinning it down.

Annabelle had to admit the style did look rather fetching. If she were ever to have an evening out, she might even be the finest dressed lady in the room.

Annabelle grabbed Molly for another hug. "I'm indebted to you."

"Nonsense. I'm sorry I didn't have a proper day dress for you. I do hate to cause you such embarrassment."

Annabelle laughed. "As opposed to the embarrassment of walking about in a tattered skirt with my head uncovered and my hair a mess?"

"Well, yes, there is that."

Annabelle sobered. "Thank you, Molly."

She smiled. "Anything for my oldest friend."

Annabelle stepped out into the late-morning sun and felt like a new woman. With a proper dress, she could hold her shoulders back and no longer have to hide herself in shame.

Now all that remained was to hire a hackney and secure a ride home. With purpose in her step and a determined posture, Annabelle steeled herself for what lay ahead.

Twenty

"This shall be terribly avenged by-and-by."
John H. Surratt

*M*atthew swiped his hand across his brow. The mid-afternoon sun shone down on him and chased away the thoughts of a cold night spent in the hay loft. Mississippi's fickle springs could never decide if they wanted to appear in early February or late March. The weather could send a man into a sweat one day and then bring a frost the next. He almost shed his jacket, but decided against it.

The men had let him sleep almost to the sun's zenith, then after a quick noon meal of hardtack and jerky, he'd set off. He'd half expected O'Malley to change his mind. The fact that he hadn't left Matthew both worried and baffled. He'd tried to keep vigilant in discovering which one of them trailed him, but the fellow must be good. Matthew hadn't seen any of them on his heels the entire way. But one had to be there somewhere.

He stopped at the beginning of a long drive, the remnants of once plentiful fields lining either side like dead sentries. He remembered it well now. His cousin Charles had introduced Elliot Ross and Matthew's father.

The dried-up acres stretched before him, revealing neither man nor beast. What exactly did he think he would accomplish here? Likely, he would do nothing more than prove himself a fool. Better a fool who knew the truth than a fool outmaneuvered by a tiny woman with a sharp tongue. If he found her here, he *would* confront her and get to the bottom of this mess she'd caused.

To the far side of the drive, Matthew noticed a section of ground dotted with mounds of rocks. Many of the older-looking ones, where the stones appeared more settled, had crudely built crosses at the head of the rock mounds. Graves? By the looks of it, there could be nearly two dozen of them. Why would so many be buried here?

As he neared the house, the answer greeted him by way of a flag tied to the upper balcony. Made from what appeared to be a bed sheet or quilt, the yellow banner had been painted with a large white H.

Hospital.

A tingle snaked down his spine. He hated hospitals. However, that would explain a few things about Miss Smith.

The house stood quiet, its porch unoccupied by healing soldiers. They'd likely moved on. Seeing no one around the yard, slave or free, he continued closer.

He remembered stepping down from their carriage on the circle drive and passing through the wrought-iron gate to a small garden area at the front of the house. It had been vibrant. Now the dead, thorny branches of a no-longer-tended rose garden surrounded a small dried-up fountain. He passed the cracked fountain and neared the front porch.

Shouts split the calm air, setting him on edge.

Matthew tensed, studying the house. Despite the date, the unusually warm day had lured the occupants into opening all the lower windows on the front of the house. Odd, really. Who would want the breeze dispersing the stored heat when fires were still needed at night?

"I will not be disobeyed again!" A male voice bellowed from the room to the left of the front door. Matthew frowned.

"Grandfather, please! Just listen to me."

That voice. It *was* her! Matthew clenched his teeth and stepped quietly onto the front porch despite too-tight boots that nearly made his feet numb.

"This matter has already been settled!" The man she'd identified as her grandfather had a raspy voice, and his last word nearly disappeared into a fit of ragged coughs.

When the fit subsided, the grandfather spoke again. "Andrew has received his leave and will be here at any time to secure this arrangement."

Matthew pressed his back against the house and eased closer to the window, which, strangely, had no curtains. If he could angle himself just right, perhaps he could see inside.

"I will *not* marry my uncle, Grandfather. You cannot force me."

Matthew halted. Her *uncle*?

"You will marry him, or you'll be put out on your own. There is a choice for you, since you always demand to have one. Let's hope you aren't quite as simple as you are plain."

Anger churned in Matthew's gut. How dare this man speak to a woman, let alone his own kin, in such a manner?

The silence stretched on, and Matthew began to think they'd left the room. He started to step away from his position when she spoke again, this time without a waver in her voice.

"I choose not to wed, and I will not leave. This is my home, left to me by my father, and you cannot—"

Her words were suddenly cut off by a resounding *crack*, followed by a small whimper. Matthew's blood boiled, and without pausing to consider his actions, he pounded a heavy fist on the front door.

A harsh whisper came from the open window, but Matthew couldn't decipher any words. Then the coughing came all the way to the door. It cracked open slowly, revealing a spindly man with graying hair and a hawkish face.

Matthew shoved down as much emotion as he could, but his voice strained. "Good day, sir. I'm here to see Miss Ross in regards to the arrangement her father set forth with my brother."

The plan formed quickly. A ruse near enough the truth to pass as believable. He hoped.

"Excuse me?" The man narrowed his eyes. "We aren't expecting visitors, and my granddaughter has no arrangements. Good day."

The man started to close the door, but Matthew caught the edge and held tight, refusing to let the elder man push it closed.

"Forgive me for not sending prior notice, but as we are at war, such things have become difficult. I've been granted a short leave while we're near, and I insist I speak to Miss Ross before returning to my unit." Matthew forced a grin, but instead of coming across as pleasant, it must have betrayed a deeper feeling, because the man's face grew pale. "Allow me to introduce myself. I'm Matthew Daniels, son of Winston Daniels of Westerly. Perhaps you remember my family?"

The man narrowed his eyes. "I can't say that I do."

Liar. His eyes told otherwise. Matthew lifted his brows. "You're certain?"

The man stared at him, jaw clenched.

Matthew cocked his head, still holding firm to the door. He pushed until he felt the old man strain, then said, "Perhaps you should let me in, so that we may come to terms on my brother's betrothal."

The man's eyes widened. He tugged harder on the door but could not pry it from Matthew's grasp. When a gleam of sweat appeared on the man's forehead, he began coughing and lost his grip. He barely stumbled out of the way as Matthew pushed past him. Now, where was that girl?

She stepped out of the room on the left in a swish of blue fabric. Matthew paused, his eyes traveling up the fine dress to her exposed smooth shoulders and long neck. This could not be the waif who'd come to the line. Here stood a lady. Not some camp follower or...anything else. She narrowed her eyes at him, and as she did he no longer had any doubt. Lady or not, this was the same little woman who had time and again caused him undue trouble.

The side of her face burned an angry red and a drop of blood welled from her swelling lower lip. The fire in Matthew's veins stoked again. Despite what predicaments she'd caused him, he had to get her out of here.

The old man bent behind him, succumbing to a fit of coughs. Sick or not, he was no suitable guardian. Matthew locked eyes with Miss Ross and mouthed *trust me*.

She did nothing more than glare at him. Would she play along? How could he help a stubborn woman who would refuse his every aid? He turned his back to her and faced the man recovering from his fit. He dabbed his lips with a handkerchief, but not before Matthew noticed the blood staining it.

"I apologize for my intrusion," Matthew said, straightening to his full height. "But my leave is short. I've been granted permission to fetch my brother's betrothed and see her safely to Westerly. As previously arranged by my father and hers, she is to consider a wedding with the Daniels family upon reaching her twentieth year, which I do believe is not far off." That last bit seemed like a good addition, as she'd already revealed her coming birthday.

Miss Ross let out a small gasp.

The man grabbed Matthew's arm. Matthew looked down at the gnarled fingers, letting a little of his fury escape from his eyes. The man immediately withdrew.

"That arrangement was forfeited before the war!"

Matthew smirked. "Ah, so you do remember my family."

Another sound came from Miss Ross, though he couldn't quite pin the emotion behind it. Surprise, perhaps? Regardless, he had what he needed. The man did remember his family, and he obviously knew something of the arrangement. That would have to be enough.

"Oh, the arrangement was not forfeited, not at all," Matthew continued, his voice calm and cold. "The arrangement still stands. And now that my father is gone and my brother has become the master of Westerly, he wishes to honor Father's arrangement before seeking any other options for the lady of Westerly."

He gave a small nod to Miss Ross, who looked rather pale but thankfully said nothing.

"There's no need. She's already betrothed to another."

"I am not!" Miss Ross said with more venom than he expected, and a small smile tugged at his lips. She glared at Matthew. "I'm betrothed to *no man* and will *not* marry."

Matthew inwardly groaned. Couldn't she see he was trying to *help* her? She stared at him, and behind the bravado and erect posture, he sensed her fear, her anxiety. He forced a smile.

"As I was about to say, our fathers agreed for you to come to Westerly and decide for yourself if you wished to bind your family to mine, which, I do believe, they thought would be mutually beneficial and provide you with some protection." He let the final words fall a little heavier and hoped she picked up on his implication.

Her delicate brows pulled slightly together, and she hesitated, then gave a small nod. "Oh, yes, I do remember it now, though it was so long ago. I had all but forgotten my father mentioning it."

Matthew grinned as the older man began to sputter.

"I'll have no such thing!"

He stepped closer to Miss Ross, who immediately shied away. Matthew moved to stop him. The man halted, shooting Matthew a heated glance that did not hide his fear.

He looked past Matthew to Miss Ross. "You will stay here," the man said, his raspy voice growing low and his hands forming into fists, "or you will forfeit any claim you think to have on this land."

Miss Ross opened her mouth, but Matthew cut her off. "That seems unlikely to me, sir," he drawled, "As I know her father intended for this plantation to become hers upon her marriage."

This he knew for certain, as it was precisely why Father had wanted to push for the marriage. Elliot Ross had planned to turn over the plantation to his daughter while he and his wife took up residence in their Natchez home. The immediate bestowment of such an asset had made Father determined to see Matthew wed. Matthew had balked at the time but looking at her now....

He forced his thoughts, and his eyes, away from her and addressed the man. "Since her inheritance of this land is instrumental in the discussion for the betrothal, I don't see how you can think she would forfeit any claims to it."

The man snarled at him. "Women do not own lands."

Matthew smirked. "Regardless, as she is already betrothed, and upon marriage her husband will gain control, I find it hard to believe the court would see you trying to eject her from her own land as anything other than illegal."

The man gaped at him. Suddenly, a small hand slipped onto Matthew's arm, giving him a slight squeeze. She narrowed her eyes slightly, as if trying to figure out exactly what to do with Matthew's offer. Finally, looking resigned, she turned to her grandfather.

"You know this to be true. My father did have a suitor in mind for me, and I remember him talking about the family being a match for us."

She glanced at Matthew, confusion flickering in her frosty eyes before she looked back at the other man. "Since you're so eager for me to be wed in order to secure my future, I'm sure you're pleased that we've been blessed with this fortuitous rediscovery of my forgotten betrothal to an affluent family. Certainly, my marriage to someone who can help restore the lands would be the preferable choice?"

The man's face darkened, and Matthew silently cheered Miss Ross on. How could this be the same harried girl he'd followed through the woods? The woman on his arm was smart, confident, and the picture of a proper lady.

"I'll not have you leave with this stranger."

Miss Ross lifted a delicate brow. "He's not a stranger. As I recall, we met at Father's wedding."

Matthew's eyes bulged, and he had to scramble to cover his surprise. She remembered? How much did she know? If she'd recognized him before, why pretend otherwise? She continued speaking, cutting off both his own words and the stuttering ones beginning to spew from the older man.

"I'll take Peggy with me for a chaperone, and will travel to Westerly with Captain Daniels to see this matter settled. Then I shall return."

"I forbid it!"

She lowered her eyes, and her grip on Matthew's arm tightened, but bless her, her words were strong and steady. "I don't see how you can stop me."

Pride and a strange sense of protectiveness welled in Matthew, and he patted her hand gently, hoping it bespoke of his approval. He would see her removed from here. And, if he could help it, he'd see her safely returned to claim her right to the plantation. What if his lie were to be made true? She certainly needed a husband, and George was widowed.

The thought caused a stirring anxiety that unnerved him, so he pushed it aside. "It's settled. Miss Ross, why don't you ready your belongings, and we'll be on our way."

She slipped free without a word, and Matthew ignored the sense of loss as she removed her hand. Then he turned his attention to the cur seething in front of him.

Twenty-One

"The best laid scheme seemed blocked on every side."
John H. Surratt

*A*nnabelle rushed out of the house and down the rear steps, her heart pounding in her chest. She pushed through the kitchen door, slamming it against the wall. Peggy let out a sharp yelp.

"Child! What in the heavens are you doin'?" Peggy looked at her with wide eyes. One hand pressed against her chest while the other clutched a rolling pin.

Annabelle closed the door against the cool air and enjoyed the smell of bread and biscuits enveloping the warm kitchen for only a second before hurrying around the table.

"We need to start packing our things. Hurry now."

Annabelle rummaged for a basket or sack to start stuffing supplies into, but Peggy's flour-covered fingers grasped her wrist. "Now, look here, child. You just swept in here this very morning with your fancy dress and shaky story, and now you want to run off again?" She placed her hands on her hips. "You ain't making no sense. You said you'd stay here and refuse to marry Andrew. You know if you run off, they's gonna take this place from you."

Annabelle stilled and regarded the worry in Peggy's deep brown eyes. "Well, it seems I've just been presented with a different solution."

Peggy huffed. "And what's that?"

"An old arrangement I'd completely forgotten."

"Talk sense," Peggy said with an exasperated sigh.

Annabelle dropped onto the kitchen bench, clenching her hands together in her lap. They didn't have time for this, but Peggy wouldn't budge until she had her answer.

As if to confirm her inner assessment, Peggy lifted her brows and gave Annabelle that familiar "best be out with it, or we'll be here all day" look.

Some pair they made. What would she do without Peggy? She'd decided to stay with Annabelle when all the others had fled. And as soon as it was in her power to do so, Annabelle had made sure Peggy was legally free, and no longer property of Rosswood. Not that she'd ever thought of Peggy as anything other than her dearest friend.

"Not long after he married Sarah," Annabelle said, turning her attention back to the current conversation, "Father mentioned introducing me to a wealthy family's youngest son—when I was ready to court, of course. It was to be the next summer, after my sixteenth birthday."

Peggy frowned.

Annabelle waved her hand. "Nothing became of it. I'd actually forgotten all about it and didn't even remember the family's name."

Peggy's brow furrowed deeper, but still she waited for Annabelle to continue. Annabelle gestured back toward the house.

"One of those sons just showed up at our door, claiming to want to take me to meet his brother and secure the arrangement."

That got the reaction Annabelle expected. Peggy threw up her hands, then pointed a finger at her. "How you know he's telling the truth?"

Annabelle shrugged "Well, he—"

"Lawd, girl!" Peggy interrupted. "How you know this stranger ain't some fortune-seeker looking to snag this land and you with it?"

She couldn't tell Peggy about having already met Captain Daniels, lest that be the thread that began to unravel her chain of secrets. She pulled her lower lip through her teeth. "Well, he did give the right name. Once he began talking about it, I remembered." She crossed her arms. "I don't know why I didn't put it together sooner," she grumbled.

"Sooner than what?" Peggy asked, narrowing her eyes.

Drat. She waved her hand. "Nothing."

Annabelle clenched her teeth. Why *hadn't* she remembered? True, it had been long ago, and at the time she'd dismissed the discussion. Never mind that she hadn't yet been interested in courting, even though many of the local girls could talk of nothing else. Regardless, she *should* have remembered him.

He'd been the big lout who'd started a ruckus at the wedding. Who could have forgotten such a scandal? But all she remembered of the fool was that he had been an exceedingly tall man with short, blond hair and a flapping jaw. All of his other features were vague in her memory, but she had no doubt he and the officer in her house were indeed the same man. Had he known all along? Heat flooded her cheeks. Why would he have accused her of being a harlot if he'd known her true identity?

"What's wrong?" Peggy said, her knowing tone breaking into Annabelle's seething thoughts. "You look mighty riled up."

Annabelle cut her eyes to Peggy, squeezing her arms across the decorated bodice of her dress.

"Yes, ma'am," Peggy drawled. "I do think it'd be best if you started telling me the truth now."

How did she know? Annabelle sighed. "Fine." She gave a condensed version of her journey. She'd already told Peggy about Lieutenant Monroe's death and asking Mr. Black to send her telegram—a part she'd hidden from Grandfather—and then had skipped to where she'd visited Molly and received a new dress before returning home. Now, she had to fill in all the undesirable sections of the tale that would certainly put Peggy into a tizzy.

Peggy peppered in "Oh, Lawd!" and "Mercy!" at several points in Annabelle's hurried outpouring. She thought Peggy might fall over when she reached the part about being accused of being a harlot, then a spy.

"Then Captain Daniels set me free from the camp," Annabelle summed up. That part was true enough. She dropped her gaze. "And then I ran back to Lorman, to Molly's. You know the rest. I didn't recognize him at the time, though I was foolish not to."

She glanced up to find Peggy studying her thoughtfully.

"But it *is* him." She rubbed the back of her neck. "I suppose he must have recognized me, and that's why he decided to free me. But I don't know why he didn't immediately tell me."

Annabelle picked at her fingernails. Why come now? If he really planned on going through with their fathers' arrangement, then why would he have come only after seeing her at the army line? And, for heaven's sake, why wouldn't he have said *something?*

Peggy stared at her. Annabelle thought it best not to show too much of her ire, lest Peggy try to undo the fragile resolve forming in her mind. Annabelle lifted her brows and gave a small shrug. "I don't really know why he chose now to bring this up."

"Ha!" Peggy wagged her finger. "Well, I know. It's because he's wanting to grab himself a pretty wife who's got a standing plantation. How do you even know his family still has all their lands? What if it's been burned down, and he's just come here to take yours?"

She hadn't thought of that. "I suppose it's a risk worth taking. I think he's trying to help me. Let me meet this brother he told Grandfather I'm betrothed to, and—"

Peggy threw up her hands. "Betrothed! You *ain't* betrothed. Meeting and courting ain't the same as betrothed! Your daddy said he wasn't going to arrange your marriage."

Annabelle smirked. "You know that, and I know that, but Grandfather doesn't."

Peggy huffed. "I reckon."

"Besides, let the Daniels man think what he wants. I'll play along with it until we meet this brother of his. As I see it, this gives a solution to a couple of problems."

Peggy turned back to her dough, forming it into a loaf and placing it in the oven.

"First, it gets me safely…." Peggy snorted at that, but Annabelle ignored her and continued, "It gets me safely away from here when Andrew comes. Despite what I said about them not being able to force me to marry him, I'm afraid Andrew could, and likely would, force me into consummating a marriage, whether I had spoken my own vows or not."

Peggy closed the oven and turned to her, pain evident on her face. She came to sit near Annabelle and wrapped one arm around her shoulders. "I want to say that wouldn't happen— and it right pains me to know you're aware enough of such things to have thought of that on your own—but you're right. I got that same fear."

Annabelle drew a long breath. "It makes sense not to be here. Second, what if I go up there, and they have a good family, and he's a decent man?"

"Who skipped the war?"

Annabelle frowned. "There are some men who couldn't go, for various reasons."

Peggy lifted her eyebrows.

Annabelle waved away her concern. "Anyway, what if he's a decent man with a strong family that can restore Rosswood? I have to take that chance."

"And marry a man you don't love?"

Annabelle offered a sad smile. "Love is a luxury I no longer have. It was a nice dream once, but now what I really need is security. Lots of women marry men they can respect and who provide for them, even if there isn't love. Right now, safety and survival are simply more important."

Peggy took Annabelle's face between her hands. "When did you become a strong woman and not the sweet little girl at my skirts?"

Tears welled in Annabelle's eyes, and she let them fall. Peggy quickly dabbed them away and then cleaned the flour she'd deposited on Annabelle's cheeks. "Now, now. You're right. We're gonna have to go." She huffed. "It's a better chance than staying here and waiting on that nasty old Andrew anyways."

Annabelle rose, drawing a steadying breath. "Then gather your things, and pack as much food for us as you can." She turned and headed to the house without looking back, lest she lose her nerve.

When she opened the back door, she found Grandfather with his back pressed against the hallway wall and the imposing figure of Captain Daniels towering over him. She'd never seen fear etched across Grandfather's face before.

The two men turned to her as she crossed the threshold, and Captain Daniels stepped back, tugging on his jacket. "Are you ready to go, Miss Ross?"

She flicked her gaze between him and Grandfather, who had not moved from his position against the wall. "Not quite. I have my maid readying supplies, but I still need to gather some personal things." What little remained of her clothing after losing her trunk. She pushed away the guilt at knowing Homer had never returned home.

"Now, wait here, you can't take all the food...." Grandfather's voice trailed off under the heaviness of Captain Daniels's scowl. He turned his head opposite and began coughing again. Pity stirred her.

"Come with us to town and stay at the inn. You'll be cared for there."

Grandfather's face turned an ugly red, and the vein in his forehead bulged. He dabbed his lips with his handkerchief and glared at her. "I'll not have you ousting me from this house, girl. Andrew will be here soon enough."

The threat in his words hung heavy in the air. Annabelle straightened. "Have it your way. Andrew can take you with him when he leaves."

Grandfather snorted but said no more. Annabelle hurried to the staircase, casting a worried look at Captain Daniels before grabbing the banister. He gave her a tight smile and nodded for her to continue. Warily, she ascended the steps, but she heard no further words from either man.

She found a carpetbag in Father's room and then returned to her own chamber to gather one pair of boots to replace her soft slippers, a night dress, and her spare chemise. Then she removed the gown, carefully trying to fit it in the bag without causing the fabric to wrinkle overmuch. She couldn't risk ruining the only good dress she had. She would simply have to travel in her work skirt with a frayed hem and a stained blouse. She sighed. At least she had a proper, clean gown to meet Captain Daniels's brother in when they arrived.

After tossing in her comb, hand mirror, and three hair pins, she secured the bag and surveyed her room. Almost forgetting her most prized possession, Annabelle unlocked the top drawer of her bureau and pulled the little black bag free. She pressed it to her chest for just an instant before she tucked it securely into the carpetbag's inner pocket.

Setting her jaw against the emotions that threatened to overtake her, Annabelle put on her paletot and descended the stairs. Both men stood below, staring at her.

"That is all you will bring, Miss Ross?" Captain Daniels asked, narrowing his lids.

She shoved down her ire. "As it's all I possess, I'm afraid so."

Sadness bloomed in Captain Daniels's eyes for only an instant, then disappeared. He lifted a shoulder. "For the best anyway, I'm sure. Taking a trunk may prove difficult."

She dipped her chin. "If you'll excuse me, I'll fetch Peggy."

He stepped away from the stairs and motioned for her to continue without the questions she'd feared he would ask. Grandfather seated himself in the ragged hall chair and stared at the wood floor.

For the first time in a long while, Annabelle remembered what her home had once looked like: polished furniture, colorful rugs, and paintings on the walls. Now all that remained in the main hall was a poorly repaired ladder-back chair and a small side table she'd found tossed in a back corner of the stable, one that some Union soldier had missed in his plunder. Would Rosswood ever be the same? Would her sacrifice save the home her father had loved so dearly?

Annabelle opened the small door set underneath the staircase that led to the basement. Pulling it closed behind her, she stepped down into the noticeably colder rooms under the house.

She shivered. It would be good to have Peggy out of here. She'd wanted to move her into one of the empty rooms upstairs long ago, but Grandfather had refused to have a *slave* staying in the house. When he was gone, she would see Peggy in a room with a proper window.

As expected, she found Peggy in her sleeping chamber, stuffing the tattered bedclothes into a burlap sack. She turned when Annabelle stepped into the small room, its low ceiling only a few inches above her head. Before the war, Peggy had lived here with three other unmarried house women who'd shared the two sleeping chambers and the common room.

Peggy hefted the sack on her shoulder. "I think I got everything."

Annabelle regarded her for a moment. "Do you think this is the right thing to do?"

Peggy's features softened. "Honestly, I don't know. But I reckon it's better to take a chance on something good than it is to wait for the bad you know is coming."

Annabelle nodded and picked up the basket on the floor, sifting through the contents. "Did you leave enough for Grandfather?"

Peggy snorted. "Shoulda taken everything and left that old crow with nothing."

"Did you?"

Peggy plucked the basket from Annabelle's hands. "No. I left him two loaves of bread and a pot of collards."

"Thank you." Annabelle lifted Peggy's sack, but it was soon pulled from her fingers.

"Nope. You let me carry that." She smirked. "Ain't right for the lady to carry more than the slave."

Annabelle laughed. "Those terms no longer apply to either of us."

Peggy glided past her. "You think traveling through Mississippi as two poor women would be smart?"

Annabelle rolled her eyes and lifted her carpetbag, following Peggy up the stairs. She didn't give an answer, because she knew Peggy didn't expect one.

Peggy opened the door and stepped out, eyeing Captain Daniels. She stepped over to the wall opposite Grandfather and lowered her eyes. Grandfather stalked to his room, slamming the door behind him. Annabelle cringed at the sound but straightened her shoulders. Captain Daniels took her elbow and guided her to the door. Peggy fell in behind them, and they made their way out of the only home Annabelle had ever known.

As they stepped out into the clear sunshine, Annabelle breathed a prayer that she wasn't making a huge mistake. Then she squared her shoulders and took the lead.

Twenty-Two

"But the opportunity will yet come. Well, better late
than never."
John H. Surratt

February 15, 1865

Annabelle clenched her teeth to keep them from
clattering. The biting wind tugged at her hair, and she
stuffed freed wisps back underneath her bonnet. Why had
winter returned and chased away the warmer weather that had
promised an early spring just yesterday?

It had been clear and beautiful when Captain Daniels had
led them back to the very barn from which Annabelle had first
escaped. There they met up with a trio of men with suspicious
eyes and dirty Confederate uniforms. After spending a long time
in discussion with these men, Captain Daniels had asked that
they spend the evening in the barn while the one he called
O'Malley retrieved an additional horse for Peggy. Annabelle had
wondered why these strange men already had horses ready for
her and Captain Daniels, but she didn't ask. She was simply
thankful not to have to walk all the way to Westerly on an ankle
still not completely healed.

Annabelle rubbed her eyes. Neither she nor Peggy had slept well. How could they? They'd made their beds in a moldy hay loft with no way past the men sleeping at the bottom of the ladder. She'd dozed fitfully, always afraid that one of them would creep up in the middle of the night. But they'd snored peacefully, and none had seemed interested in bothering the women. They weren't overly friendly, but neither were they intimidating. She was beginning to feel slightly more at ease, though she would be a fool to let down her guard.

Annabelle slowly stroked the red coat of the gelding tied just outside the large barn doors. She'd chosen this one to be her mount because his gentle eyes reminded her of poor old Homer. Annabelle's fingers smoothed the horse's mane, but her thoughts were set on the men making travel preparations. She covertly watched the tense man who seemed to consider himself the leader of the group. He smiled too much and his friendly manner appeared forced.

If they thought she was fool enough to believe this entire crew was simply aiding her to Westerly Plantation while they took their furlough, then they were duller than they thought her. She hadn't yet figured out exactly what they were hiding, but she suspected it had something to do with the message that had started this entire problem. O'Malley had asked her about it and didn't seem pleased that she knew nothing about its meaning.

Why hadn't she just left the thing in that soldier's pocket? Then it would be buried with him, and none of this would have happened. Whatever had been written there, it seemed to be at the center of some secret they all guarded very closely. How Captain Daniels fit into the plot, she couldn't yet be sure. He seemed to be straddling a line between being caught up in this and being in on the entire thing.

She watched the men speak to one another in low tones, sometimes cutting their eyes in her direction. She regarded them flatly, which made them uncomfortable. Good. They might as well be as uncomfortable with her as she was with them.

A group of spies, Peggy had called them. Annabelle tended to believe her.

Captain Daniels stepped into her line of sight, hefting a saddle across his shoulder. "I'm sorry about not being able to find you a lady's saddle, Miss Ross."

She patted the horse's thick neck. "Thank you for your concern, but I'll manage."

Annabelle stroked the horse's mane and tried to keep an aloof composure. She had to work doubly hard to present herself as a lady. Perhaps if she ignored their embarrassing first meeting and subsequent flight through the woods, then maybe he would as well. Neither of them had spoken of their time together prior to his showing up at Rosswood. She planned to keep it that way.

Captain Daniels finished readying the horse and secured her bag behind the saddle without another word, then left to continue with other preparations. She watched his wide shoulders retreat, and her brows pulled together. The horse stomped, cold breath billowing from his nostrils.

"Easy, boy," Annabelle soothed. Her words carried on the fine mist like a puff of smoke. Oh, how she wished for spring.

Peggy made a wide berth around the horse's hindquarters and stepped up to Annabelle, eyeing the creature the entire time. "You sure they can't get a wagon?"

"No. I already asked." She twisted the black mane through

her fingers. How had a group of soldiers on furlough been able to find, and afford, six well-tended horses? She didn't doubt they would've been able to get a wagon if they'd been so inclined. Mr. O'Malley's insistence they didn't need one didn't sit well with her, but she wasn't about to voice that to Peggy.

Peggy snorted. "I told you, I ain't riding one of those things."

"I don't see where you have a choice. You can't just walk along behind us."

The horse bobbed its head, and Peggy jerked back. "I still don't like it," she grumbled.

"I'm quite aware." Annabelle smirked.

Peggy ignored her jab and tugged up the hem of Annabelle's skirt. "You got the trousers on?" she whispered.

Heat rose in her cheeks. She didn't have a proper riding habit or even a lady's saddle. The men seemed to think nothing of the indignity of making her ride astride the horse. Thankfully, they hadn't questioned Peggy's request for extra pairs of men's pants to be added to the list of supplies.

What would Father think to know his daughter wore trousers under her petticoat?

She nodded. At least her legs would be covered when her skirts hiked up. Wearing pants felt the lesser of the two humiliations.

"All right then," Peggy said. "I just hope what we're going to ain't worse than what we're leaving."

Annabelle gave Peggy's hand a small squeeze. "As do I."

Mr. O'Malley's voice rose above the quiet conversations and sounds of jostling tack. "The time has come, friends. We ride for Washington!"

Washington?

Before she could open her mouth to protest, Captain Daniels appeared at her side. "We'll have to go farther than expected." He shifted his weight from one foot to the other, clearly agitated.

Worry wormed through her gut.

Captain Daniels cleared his throat. "It, uh, seems my brother is no longer at home. We'll have to meet him in Washington."

Peggy snorted, not buying this sudden change of plans any more than Annabelle.

She narrowed her eyes. "Our arrangement was for me to travel to Westerly. Not Washington. You cannot think such a journey prudent."

He looked decidedly uncomfortable. "I'll see that you arrive safely."

Annabelle glared at him. "You can see me safely to your family home."

His shoulders tensed. "I'm afraid I cannot."

"Why?" she pressed. "Does it no longer stand? Is this entire thing just a scheme to get me away from my home so you can take Rosswood from me?" She regretted the bitter words as soon as they leapt from her tongue but could not call them back.

Confusion creased his brow for only a moment before it melted into anger. "Miss Ross." His low voice sent a shiver through her not associated with the chill. Around them, the others had mounted their horses and stood quietly by. He leaned closer, his long hair curtaining the side of his face. "I assure you, my family lands are completely intact, and I sought only to give you a measure of escape from your circumstances. I have never intended to take anything from you."

She could only stare at his glassy eyes.

"However, if you no longer wish to meet my brother, you're free to return to your grandfather at any time."

Annabelle took a small step back. She couldn't reconcile the boisterous youth from her memory with the serious man before her.

Despite the uncertainties, Captain Daniels offered her a chance to save Rosswood. Would it be worth the risk?

She dropped her gaze. "Forgive me. I think my fear of traveling so far into the unknown has gotten the better of my self-control."

She could nearly feel the tension release from his frame. He placed a hand on her elbow. When she looked into his face, his eyes were soft. "No need for forgiveness. Your concern is valid. I didn't expect for you to need to travel so far, and I assure you, if I could avoid it, I would."

His words seeped sincerity, so she offered him a small smile. Behind her, Peggy grumbled something that they both ignored.

Captain Daniels helped her get her foot into the stirrup, and she swung her leg over the side of the horse. She noted the surprise, followed by amusement, spark in his eyes when he saw the trousers sticking out from under the ruffles of her petticoat, but he made no mention of it.

He looked up at her, a small smile tugging at the corners of his lips. "Just think, at least someday you'll be able to tell your children you attended the second inauguration of the sixteenth president of the United States."

With that, he turned on his heel, leaving her staring after him, baffled. In a moment, he had Peggy sitting on top of a brown mare and looking more harried than Annabelle had ever seen her. Annabelle placed a gloved hand to her mouth to cover her smile, but Peggy wasn't fooled. She rolled her eyes and sat straighter in the saddle, her hiked skirts showing a pair of dirty boots and tall, woolen socks.

Mr. O'Malley called for them to move out, and in a few moments Annabelle found herself trailing a group of soldiers, who were more likely spies, into a cold morning and down the road that would lead her ever farther from home.

Matthew tried to ignore the guilt clawing at his stomach. O'Malley insisted that the girl knew too much and had to remain with them until the plan was safely carried out. They'd talked long into the night, and try as he had, Matthew could think of no safer place for her than at his side. Finally, he'd given in and come up with the only lie he could think of—that George waited for them in Washington. Clearly, she suspected his deceit, yet she still came with him. Her trust knifed through his gut.

He told himself he meant only to protect her, and that the arrangement would indeed be beneficial to George, but the truth of it continued to surface. He liked her near. Despite the fortifications she'd now thrown up against him, he'd seen the capable woman with quick wits and quiet determination underneath. He'd glimpsed the fiery lady she now tried to smother under a mantle of forced refinement. Why did she think the cold, stuffy person she tried to imitate was more appealing than the spirited woman who'd made him give chase?

Matthew glanced over his shoulder and caught her eye briefly, but she quickly turned her face from him. He looked forward. The answer was simple enough. She didn't wish him to find her appealing at all. The horses stepped onto the main road, and O'Malley called for them to get up into a quick canter. If they were to make it to Washington in time, they would have to push the horses hard and change them often. O'Malley had assured him that funds for the venture were secure, and they would not have to worry with travel.

Apparently, O'Malley had gotten word from someone named John Surratt, who said something about having secured the necessary aid. The more O'Malley revealed, the less it seemed like a wild scheme and more an active secret mission.

O'Malley had mentioned contacts in Canada and connections within the Confederate government who were not only privy to the idea, but supported his plan if the opportunity arose. How much went on within his unit under his nose?

How had the men riding in front of him become involved in something so monumental it could change the course of history? For that matter, how had he?

Would this plan truly shift the tide of the war? Gain the South's independence and see them returned to Westerly with George safely at its head?

Gritting his teeth against the biting wind, Matthew lowered his head and urged his horse faster. If that little woman could hold on just a little longer, perhaps she'd soon find herself in the company of heroes.

A rifle shot cut through the air and in an instant, Benson toppled from his saddle and hit the ground. Matthew pulled up hard on his horse's bit. The animal reared and nearly threw him from the saddle. When the creature returned to the ground, Matthew jerked on the reins to spin the horse around. Another crack came from his right, and O'Malley screamed at them to run. Matthew found Miss Ross barreling toward him, hunkered low and riding evenly in the saddle. Behind her, the Negro maid screamed and dropped the reins. The strips of leather trailed behind the spooked horse.

Matthew spun his mount around just as Miss Ross reached him and the two horses galloped in stride, the maid screaming behind them. Miss Ross threw anxious glances behind her.

"Captain Daniels!" she screeched.

Another gunshot split the air. A squad of five Confederates gained on them.

Curse it. They wouldn't be able to lose them on this road.

"Take to the woods!" he shouted at Miss Ross. She gave him a quick nod, and as they topped a hill, Matthew saw a break in the tree line.

He swerved the horse to his left, and Miss Ross peeled off along with him. He glanced behind. The slave woman held onto the saddle. She bent forward over the horse's neck and began to slide off one side.

"You have to help her!"

The woman's terror catapulted Matthew into action. He kicked his heels into his horse and spun it back toward the road, a plan half formed in his mind. "You catch her! I'll distract them." He didn't wait to see what she would do. Matthew whipped the reins around behind him, slapping the horse's hindquarters and urging it faster back in the direction they had just come.

Please, God. Don't let them have a loaded shot.

Matthew unleashed the rebel yell he'd never used against his own and plowed straight into the onslaught. One of the men lunged for him and nearly succeeded in unhorsing him, but by some miracle Matthew was able to shift his weight and wrench the man's hand free. The soldier fell to the ground with a grunt.

Matthew didn't recognize any of the soldiers. They weren't from his company. Regardless, the looks of determination on their faces meant they would bring him in. Dead or alive.

In a matter of seconds, he broke through to the other side and galloped headlong back toward Lorman, hoping the soldiers would pursue him and allow the women to get away.

In a fervor of shouts, two of the remaining four pursuers managed to get their sweating horses to spin around and give chase. Matthew glanced over his shoulder just as one of them pulled a pistol and leveled it in his direction.

Grinding his teeth and lowering himself as much as he could, he yanked hard on the reins and jerked the horse left just as a bullet whizzed by his head.

Twenty-Three

"I have arranged all our plans, and secured the
desired assistance."
John H. Surratt

Annabelle gripped the heaving horse with her thighs,
suddenly grateful for a man's saddle. She squeezed
harder, and the horse surged forward, coming alongside Peggy's
mount. The two horses bobbed awkwardly, their bodies swaying
dangerously close as Annabelle reached out and tried to grab the
horse's fallen rein.

Peggy screamed, too frightened to even form her terror into
words.

Annabelle strained across the gap, the ground beneath passing by at an alarming rate. Despite the frigid air biting at her
face, sweat popped up across her brow. If only she could reach
just a little farther.

Her fingers brushed the side of the horse's neck. The
dropped rein dangled precariously from the horse's bit and
down its chest, flapping between its front legs. If it were to step
on one, the sudden lurch would send Peggy flying. She urged
her own horse faster, and he finally gained a stride on the other,

bringing Annabelle closer to the other horse's bridle. Finally, her fingers were able to grab the rein close to the bit. She clenched it tightly and quickly pulled the length of it up from the ground.

Annabelle dared a glance behind her. Two men were still in pursuit, but neither aimed weapons at them. She lost sight of the other men in the captain's group. How long would the horses be able to keep up such reckless speed?

Peggy finally quit screaming and leaned all the way forward in the saddle with both of her arms wrapped around the horse's neck. Thankfully, she kept both feet in the stirrups.

"Peggy!"

She didn't answer. Her eyes squeezed tight, and her lips moved silently.

"Peggy!" Annabelle screamed.

Peggy's eyes snapped open in terror.

"Reach with your right hand and grab that other rein!"

The horses galloped wildly down the road, sending up clouds of dirt behind them. Annabelle wouldn't be able to control Peggy's horse with only one rein. She'd have to have both, and to reach the second she needed Peggy's cooperation.

Peggy shook her head and tried to bury her face in the black mane that whipped through the air and slapped across her cheeks.

"Peggy! You have to get it. If the horse steps on it, you're going to fall!"

Peggy snatched her head up and stared at Annabelle in shock.

"Grab it. *Now!*"

Peggy struggled forward and, after a couple of attempts, managed to grasp the rein and pull it to her. Knowing that

Peggy would not steer the horse on her own, Annabelle reached out and took it, gathering both of the horse's reins in one hand and urging her own mount to gallop faster with the other.

Both horses frothed with sweat, but her mount managed to gain even more of a lead on Peggy's until she was in front of the other horse and leading it with the outstretched reins. She glanced back over her shoulder. Peggy hung on for her life. Behind them, the two men were still in pursuit, though the distance between them grew. She breathed a prayer of thanks for a fast horse and leaned lower in the saddle.

Up ahead, she finally caught sight of the other men. David O'Malley caught her eye and frantically waved for her to follow them. As if she could do anything else!

Her heart beat furiously. How would they escape the pursuers who would see her tried as a spy? If they'd had any doubt before, her escape from their camp and current company had plastered her with guilt.

Suddenly O'Malley and the other man, Harry, veered right and plunged into a small clearing off the road. Annabelle urged her horse to catch them, the one behind slipping back until she only grasped the end of the leads.

Please, horse, keep up!

If the horse pulled free, she doubted she would be able to regain it. They thundered across the meadow and into the woods beyond. Annabelle was forced to lay low against the horse and trust him to follow the others of his kind ahead of him, lest she be swept from the saddle by a low-hanging limb.

How long they wove through the woods she couldn't be certain. Time lost all meaning as the horse leapt, stumbled, and darted through the trees. Finally, they came upon a shallow creek and steered the horses into it.

Thankful for the open air above her head, Annabelle sat straighter and turned to look over her shoulder. Peggy was still atop her horse, thank the Lord. And she didn't see the soldiers!

After a time, they pulled the horses from the creek when the footing became rockier and the water deeper.

They took to the woods again, limbs tugging at her arms and hair and....Oh, dear. She'd lost another bonnet. Her hair streamed out behind her. What would Captain Daniels think—

Her crazed thoughts jerked to a halt. Where *was* he?

She hadn't seen him since he'd plunged toward the soldiers and given her the chance to pull away. Her stomach tightened.

Please, don't let him have been captured or...worse.

She ducked her head low and let tears of frustration chill her face further. Her horse stumbled, his sides heaving. Despite her squeezing, he slowed to a walk and could not be convinced to move any faster.

Ahead, Mr. O'Malley drew up his horse and waited for them to approach.

"I think we may have lost them."

Annabelle glanced behind them, then nodded.

"Where's Daniels?"

Her lips trembled. "I don't know. He ran into them so Peggy and I could get away."

Mr. O'Malley's face darkened. "He ran *toward* the soldiers?"

"Yes. He was distracting them so that—"

"What exactly did you *see* him do?"

She narrowed her eyes. "I saw him give an awful yell and run straight for them, causing them to scatter and giving me the chance to get away."

"And after they scattered?"

"I don't know. I was galloping in the other direction," she snapped.

His nostrils flared. "Five to start. Two that pursued us. That leaves three. Wonder what happened to them?"

Annabelle glared at him. "I would guess they followed Captain Daniels."

"Or, he joined them."

Annabelle blinked. "What? Why would he do that?"

"Why, indeed?" Mr. O'Malley studied her for a moment.

Despite her discomfort, she refused to wilt under his scrutiny and held his gaze. Finally, he seemed to make up his mind on something and gestured ahead. "We're off course. Best we keep to the woods until dark. Then we'll camp."

Annabelle balked. "Out here?"

"No, at the inn just ahead." Sarcasm no gentleman would use on a lady dripped from his words.

She stared at him flatly.

The muscles in his jaw worked, and then he plastered a false smile across his lips. "Forgive me. As I'm sure you're aware, we're off course and in the middle of the woods. As there are no local bedding establishments or any homes to offer hospitality in this vicinity, it seems to me the best course of action is for us to continue on today for as long as the horses will carry us. Then find a place to hide for the night."

Annabelle swallowed a lump in her throat. Peggy peeled herself off the horse's neck and sat taller in the saddle. She stared at Mr. O'Malley with thinly veiled hostility.

How safe would they be, alone in the woods with these two men? Harry seemed harmless enough, but Mr. O'Malley... she suppressed a shudder. And, what had happened to Benson?

Mr. O'Malley didn't wait for her reply. He spun his horse around, determined the position of the sun, and then headed north.

Annabelle watched him go for several paces. He didn't glance back at her. Then, seeing no other options, Annabelle sighed and urged her exhausted horse forward.

Matthew slapped the horse again and ducked another branch. He'd led the two remaining soldiers back down the road until he'd reached the barn he'd hoped never to see again, then looped around, dove into the woods, and doubled back toward the women.

He'd still not managed to shake his pursuers.

The poor beast beneath him wouldn't be able to hold out much longer. He needed a good place to throw them off his trail.

He hated to lose the horse, but he couldn't outrun them. Up ahead, an ancient oak spread her branches wide, taking up the majority of the ground's resources and choking out the other life. It just might be his salvation. He quickly wrapped the reins around the pommel of the saddle and tied them tight. Then he slapped the horse's hindquarters and lifted himself in the stirrups.

The horse lowered his head and plowed toward the low limbs of the tree. Matthew swung one foot free of the stirrup and with all his might lurched himself from the saddle.

He hit the branch with his midsection, his air leaving his lungs with a grunt. Matthew clawed to hang on, then swung his leg up and wrapped it around the limb, pulling himself to his feet and scurrying up to a large fork in the trunk. From this vantage, he could see his horse barreling ahead, free of the weight of its rider. With any luck, the animal would stay far enough ahead of the soldiers that they wouldn't notice the empty saddle.

Seconds later, the two soldiers galloped into the clearing, shouting to one another. They passed under him without pause, and Matthew let out a sigh of relief.

He held still until he could no longer hear anything more than twittering birds and the occasional squirrel. He shimmied down the tree. His boots hit the damp earth, and the jolt sent pain through his right side. He prodded beneath his jacket with gentle fingers.

His ribs probably weren't broken, but they hurt something fierce. At least his leg held up. He had a long walk ahead of him.

Good thing he knew the entire planned route to Washington. O'Malley had mapped out several safe places to stay along the way, and if Matthew kept moving he could eventually intercept the others. He stepped through tall grass the wind sent dancing in multiple directions. The sun had climbed well into the sky during the chase and had now begun its descent back toward the horizon. He turned north and worked his way through the woods with the skills he'd learned as a hunter. It was a little slower going, but Matthew did his best not to leave a trail, just in case the soldiers discovered his deception and doubled back.

He trudged on in silence, his ears straining to pick up on the sound of approaching hoofbeats. As the sun began to sink lower, Matthew inched his way through the underbrush, finally coming to the road. He paused and watched for a moment, but not a soul appeared to travel it. Still, Matthew didn't dare leave his cover.

He needed to find Miss Ross, and soon. He didn't suspect O'Malley to be the type to take advantage of women, but she'd be frightened after her flight of escape. If she *had* escaped.

He pushed the thought aside. He had to believe she'd made it to freedom. To dwell on the alternative would only stoke his anger.

Matthew continued forward, thinking only of the relief that seeing her safe would bring. Step by step he pushed on, until the night fell thick and the moon shone upon the weary man below.

Twenty-Four

"Booth wants his life, but I shall oppose anything like murder."

John H. Surratt

"Are you mad, woman?"

Annabelle crossed her arms and glared at the spindly man in front of her. Peggy dropped her armload of firewood on the ground at Annabelle's feet.

"I'm not asking for your assistance. I'm perfectly capable on my own."

She was tired, hungry, and above all else chilled to the bone. She was in no mood to be treated as a helpless female. She'd have her fire whether they wanted it or not. It was bad enough she'd have to sleep on the ground. She wouldn't die of pneumonia.

"And what happens when the soldiers still hunting us see that smoke?" Harry said, twisting his face into a scowl.

Annabelle drew her lips into a line. He had a point.

"If we use the dry wood, it won't smoke as much as that green," Peggy inserted. Harry looked at her as if seeing her for the first time.

"'Sides," she continued, "if we get a fire going, I can make y'all some supper."

Harry put a hand on the back of his neck. "A hot meal would be kind of nice."

Annabelle took that as consent and knelt to arrange the firewood. Harry sighed and tromped away. Annabelle expected Mr. O'Malley to protest her efforts, but he sat on a log staring up at the sky, lost in thought. Content to leave him distracted, Annabelle focused on her task.

She and Peggy scraped the grass and dried leaves away from a small circle of earth and stacked a handful of pine straw at the center. Then they built a teepee of smaller sticks.

Most women of Annabelle's social class probably had no idea how to start a fire. In her younger days, the slaves kept their hearths warm and cooked meals. A lady never handled such mundane tasks. Now, her calloused fingers were familiar with building fires as well as gathering and chopping wood. She no longer possessed the soft, useless hands of a pampered young lady.

Peggy produced a match, and in a few moments she breathed a flickering flame to life. Annabelle removed her gloves and stretched her fingers toward the paltry but welcome warmth. Flames soon devoured the smaller sticks and Peggy added stouter limbs until the fire crackled pleasantly and offered a small ring of light to chase away the gathering shadows.

Harry brought a pot of water, and soon they filled it with chunks of dried meat, carrots, onions, and potatoes. Peggy even had a little flour to thicken it. They'd not had this much food on hand at Rosswood all winter. How had this band of spies afforded so much?

Annabelle tended the fire while Peggy stirred the stew, the delicious aroma reminding her stomach that she hadn't eaten since early this morning.

"You got that ready yet, cook?"

Peggy didn't look up at Mr. O'Malley but continued to stir. "No, sir. Not yet. Needs a little more time."

He walked over and looked down. "I say it's done. Serve it up."

Annabelle caught the almost imperceptible shake of Peggy's head and snapped her mouth closed against a snippy retort about to spring free. Peggy was right. Best not to stir them up or a little disrespect could be the least they'd have to endure.

Night settled on the camp, and the deepening chill formed ice crystals in her bones. Annabelle gathered tin bowls with shaking fingers, then held them out for Peggy to fill. She served them to the men with a smile though neither of them thanked her.

Crickets sang their welcome to the night as Annabelle settled on an old curtain from Peggy's pack. She tucked the edges of her skirt around her ankles in an effort to hold in warmth and motioned for Peggy to sit near. The older woman hesitated for only a moment, then sat cross-legged next to her.

Annabelle sipped her soup. "You were right. It needed to thicken a little longer. The meat's still chewy, and the flour tastes a little too raw."

"Um hum, but you can't tell them that."

Both men hunched over their bowls, shoulders tense. Perhaps their sour demeanor came from mourning their lost companion. When they finished, the men handed their scraped bowls to Peggy. She quietly set aside the rest of her meal and rose to rinse them with a little water from the canteens. Annabelle knew better than to offer assistance in front of the others. Peggy wouldn't allow it, and she needed these men to see her as a lady. Still, she felt guilty.

When the camp settled down for the night, Annabelle scooted as close to the flickering warmth as possible. Exhaustion tugged at her, but she couldn't succumb to sleep. She'd keep the fire going and pray it provided the captain a guiding light.

Matthew kept to the woods until it was too dark to see, then ventured out onto the road, confident he would hear anyone approach before they picked him out of the darkness.

What had happened to the others? He didn't even know what direction they might have gone in order to evade the soldiers. His only hope would be to follow this road and try to beat them to the next stop, where they had planned to change out the horses. O'Malley might have a different place to hole up for the night, but he likely would still have to make it to the correct stables.

Whoever backed David O'Malley had deep pockets. Matthew set his teeth against the cold and continued his trudge northeastward. Some time later, he topped a small hill, and something caught his eye. He'd almost missed it. He wasn't even sure what had drawn his eyes that direction, but as he squinted in the moonlight, he grew certain: white smoke. It had to come from someone's campfire. Matthew stared at it for a moment.

Reconnaissance would be worth the risk.

Matthew slowly made his way through the underbrush, placing his feet as well as he could in the darkness. The deeper he went, the less the moonlight revealed. He crunched leaves, tripped on roots, and smacked himself with branches. It would be a wonder if he wasn't shot.

He stepped up to a big pine, muscles coiled for danger. When nothing stirred, he peered around the trunk. A small fire flickered in the clearing, surrounded by three sleeping forms and one vigilant watchman.

Make that watch*woman*.

Relief flooded his veins and he had to stifle a chuckle. No mistaking the beautiful face staring with wide eyes in his direction. His bumbling had likely frightened her from sleep, but he couldn't help but withhold his presence for an instant longer to watch the firelight dance across her smooth features.

He stepped away from the tree, holding up his hands. "Miss Ross? It's Matthew."

Her shoulders slumped, and she gestured him closer. He made his way to her, doing his best to avoid at least some of the leaves that rustled and cracked beneath his boots. Matthew knelt beside her pallet, trying not to notice her mussed hair and flushed cheeks.

"I feared you were dead!"

A small smile played on his lips. "You worried about me?"

She glared at him. "Of course." Then she hastily added, "As I would anyone. I'm afraid poor Benson was killed."

Matthew nodded solemnly, the hint of humor dissipating as the weight of their situation settled. "I feel responsible." He'd not meant to say it, but as her hand rested on his arm, he was almost glad he had.

"They were after all of us. We share responsibility."

Matthew regarded her quietly. Such a woman would do George good. A man needed a wife who would help lessen the weight of his burdens. The sudden thought surprised him. Matthew had determined women were more dangerous to handle than an unbroken colt. He'd never once thought of one as a calming presence.

She patted his arm and glanced at the others. "Should I wake them?"

His thoughts jerked back to the present. "No. Let them sleep." Fools. If he'd been the enemy they'd both be dead. "You should return to your rest as well."

"I've not yet slept."

His leg beginning to ache, Matthew lowered himself from his haunches and sat just off her pallet. When she didn't protest, he asked, "Why not? Surely you must be tired after such a day."

She picked at a frayed edge on the blanket spread over her lap. "I believe it's the nature of the day that's rendered me unable to keep my eyes closed long enough for sleep to take me."

"Then let's talk of something else."

A small smile bent the corners of her mouth. "That would be pleasant, if you truly don't mind."

"I would find it distracting as well."

She thought a moment, and then something sparked in her eyes. *Uh-oh.* He should have thought before—

"Did you know me when we first met?"

Too late. "I did not."

She narrowed her eyes, suspicion flickering as brightly as the reflected firelight.

Two could play this game. "Did you know me?"

She blinked. "No."

"Then why do you find it unbelievable I didn't recognize a woman whom I had only seen once when she was but a shy young girl at her father's coattails?"

He'd meant to lighten her mood, but as pain flooded her eyes he regretted his levity.

She nodded. "Of course." She waved her hand as if to shoo unwanted emotions. When she looked back at him, her eyes were cool and distant. "At what point did you remember my name?"

Matthew's hand involuntarily returned to the base of his skull, where the shopkeeper had bested him. "Something reminded me," he mumbled. At her silence, he continued. "When I thought about where I remembered you from, it all came back to me. Your father's wedding, my own father's plans."

Miss Ross wrapped her arms around herself.

"Are you cold, Miss Ross?"

She dropped her arms and sat a little straighter. He waited. She turned the conversation, yet again keeping him off balance. "If you are to be my brother, perhaps you should start calling me Annabelle."

Brother. Why did that word feel like a punch to the gut? "And you may call me Matthew." He barked a laugh. "Besides, *Captain* Daniels no longer applies." The bitterness in his tone surprised him, but her smile washed some of it away.

Matthew unlaced his boots and pulled his feet free, rubbing one to coax circulation. "So," he said, stretching his legs out in front of him and toward the fire's warmth, "at what point did you remember me?"

She wrinkled her nose. "When you showed up at my house and told Grandfather I was betrothed. Which was an exaggeration, by the way."

"A gamble." He shrugged. "I'm thankful you went along with it."

She gave a small laugh. "Marriage to a man I don't know isn't exactly appealing. Tell me something of your younger brother."

"How do you know he's younger?"

She lifted a shoulder. "Father said I would court the youngest Daniels son."

His throat constricted. What would she do if she discovered Matthew was the youngest son? He clenched his teeth and forced any hopes aside. He must consider his brother before any foolish notions about women. Besides, George would inherit Westerly. And George would be able to give her a life she deserved. Not him.

"George is a good man, Miss Ross."

"Annabelle."

He stared into the flames. "He's kind, decent, and will be able to provide for you. And you'll make a good lady for Westerly."

She remained quiet for several moments. When she finally spoke, her tone held concern. "Do you think he'd come to Rosswood instead?"

Did she fear Westerly wouldn't provide adequate comforts? "Westerly is the larger holding. I'm sure you'll want your main residence there."

Her shoulders slumped. "I wish to remain at my family home."

The quiet words settled on him. If George had Westerly, could she perhaps settle for a brother who would come to her plantation? He cut the thought short. *Foolish.*

"I'm sure that's a discussion better left for my brother." Matthew cleared his throat. "I cannot assume to speak for him." A little voice nagged that in setting up a wife without George's permission, he'd already overspoken for his brother. He just hoped George would see reason, and Annabelle would never be the wiser.

"Of course."

They sat quietly for a while, until the flames began to wane. Then Matthew stacked a few larger pieces of wood on the fire and brushed his hands on his pants. "I fear morning will soon be upon us. Perhaps we should find our rest."

"Yes, of course."

He found a spare place on the ground not far from her feet and lay on his back, his hands laced behind his head.

"Matthew?"

The way his name slid from her lips stirred something in him. "Yes?"

"Thank you for talking to me. I feel safer now that you're here."

His chest warmed. "I'm most glad. Rest assured you're protected."

"Thank you." Her soft voice brushed over him, stirring places best left forgotten. "Goodnight, Matthew."

"Goodnight."

After a few moments, her breathing fell even, and he relaxed. Still, Matthew could not sleep. He spent the remainder of the night staring at the stars and trying to remember that the woman slowly stealing his heart belonged to his brother.

Twenty-Five

"We have planned out the roads to be taken, if we only
succeed in capturing Lincoln."
John H. Surratt

Mount Crawford
Augusta County, Virginia
February 28, 1865

Annabelle didn't ever want to ride a horse again. This
was the fourth—or was it fifth?—horse she'd ridden
throughout this seemingly never-ending trip. Long days of hard
riding had been followed by short nights of insufficient rest at
various inns, homes, and camps along the way. She was tired,
cold, and more than a little irritable.

A cold drizzle had been falling on them for most of the
morning, and the long woolen mantle Mr. O'Malley had given
her was nearly soaked through. Annabelle pulled her hood down
lower over her face, glad that she had been outfitted with
something warm—something that actually covered her legs,
even though she still rode astride.

The men had even traded out their uniforms for plain attire,
which had likely helped them avoid further confrontation along
the way. Finding properly fitting, ready-made clothes had

proven to be somewhat of a feat for Matthew. Fortunately for him, there'd been a curvy seamstress in Tennessee who was more than willing to stay up deep into the night with him and let out seams. She'd even convinced a cobbler to stay open late and fashion Matthew a proper set of shoes.

Annabelle tried not to remember the way the seamstress had been able to walk with a sway in her hips. Some women seemed to know exactly what to do with their womanly wiles. Annabelle didn't think she even *had* any feminine wiles, much less the ability to wield them. Not that she should be thinking such things.

Why had she ever agreed to such a trip? Riding hard, always with an eye out for danger, might have seemed like some grand adventure the girl in her would have longed for, but the reality was anything but exciting. It was exhausting. Why hadn't she insisted harder that she stay behind and wait for George Daniels to come to her?

She still didn't know much about him. Or his brother, for that matter. Since that first night in the woods, she'd had only mundane conversations with Matthew, who for some reason seemed set on keeping her questions at bay. What did he have to hide?

Maybe she was being too harsh. He was likely just too tired at the end of the day to endure her questions. Even an army man had to be getting weary of the jostling rides and spine-jarring hooves. Who would have thought she would come to despise a horse?

At least they let the animals walk for a change as they neared a village. But the cluster of homes could hardly even be called that. Annabelle didn't see the first shop, let alone an inn. But surely they wouldn't be coming here if they weren't planning on staying?

Annabelle was so focused on the thought of climbing off this loathsome beast that she did not immediately understand why Matthew held up a hand and called for them to stop.

Hundreds of Confederate soldiers, several of whom gathered to study their approach, were positioned at the bottom of the hill. The rest guarded a covered bridge spanning the river snaking along the edge of the town. Her throat constricted. Would they be recognized? Restrained?

Annabelle looked at Peggy. Though she'd grown more accustomed to the saddle, the older woman never seemed comfortable there. At the moment, she looked as nervous as Annabelle felt. Since that first day, they had managed to avoid most other trouble, a grand feat indeed for a group of spies traveling through a war-torn country. How foolish of her to begin to think they would make it the entire way without being chased again.

Matthew had said the trip through the Shenandoah Valley would be the most dangerous by far. How he managed to keep apprised of the armies' movements was a small mystery she hadn't quite solved, but she shouldn't have dismissed his warning so easily.

They paused there on the hill for only a few seconds. Then, without waiting for discussion, Mr. O'Malley nudged his horse forward and headed straight for the town, ignoring the Confederate band altogether. Matthew hunched lower in his saddle and followed. Annabelle and Peggy followed suit, though Annabelle kept her eyes averted from the group of soldiers and her hood hanging low across her face.

They walked the horses to one of the homes near the edge of the village, uncomfortably close to the river and the Confederate camp. Shifting her attention away from the soldiers, Annabelle studied the quaint home. Anything warm and dry was a palace.

Matthew slid from his horse, took the reins from the women, and secured the horses to a hitching post just inside the small fenced yard.

A couple of chickens squawked and scurried away as Matthew lifted his arms to assist Annabelle down from the saddle. She swung her leg over the side, and he grasped her waist and gently lowered her to the ground. His hands lingered, and she looked up into his face. The worry in his eyes and the nearness of him made her chest tighten.

"Annabelle, I think there's something I should...." He shook his head.

"Should what?" She frowned, studying the tight lines of his face beneath the weeks of scruff covering his jaw.

"I should tell you that—"

"Daniels!"

Mr. O'Malley's voice cut through Matthew's words and the tension hanging around them, and Matthew's hands dropped from her.

"Now's not the time." Without waiting for her reply, Matthew turned and strode toward Mr. O'Malley. The stiffness in his shoulders indicated he'd wanted to tell her something important.

"Humph. Sometimes being an old Colored woman is just worse than other times."

Annabelle tore her gaze from Matthew's retreating form.

"These old bones sure woulda appreciated some handsome boy helping *me* down from that beast."

Annabelle frowned. "What?"

Peggy lifted her brows, the humor in her features turning to something akin to smugness. "You seem a might taken with that big fellow."

Heat flooded Annabelle's face. "I'm no such thing!"

Peggy stared at her, her expression disbelieving.

"Besides," Annabelle said, lowering her voice, "he's not the brother I'm to court. It wouldn't be proper."

Would it? She wasn't actually bound by a betrothal.

"Quit your mulling, and let's get in that house. My toes are freezing."

Annabelle snapped out of her thoughts and pulled her mantle closer. Her stiff legs reluctantly carried her up a set of wooden steps and onto a small porch just as Mr. O'Malley's knock was answered by a portly woman in a faded yellow dress and a white apron.

"Hello there! I was afraid y'all might not ever make it."

Mr. O'Malley tipped his hat. "Forgive the delay, Sallie."

"Nonsense. Come on in out of this chill."

The woman smiled at the men as they passed her, but gave Annabelle and Peggy a curious look as they stepped up to the door.

"I didn't know there'd be a lady and her slave traveling with you, David." Her eyes didn't leave Annabelle.

Annabelle straightened her shoulders and answered for herself. "I'm merely a traveling companion on my way to the same destination, though for a different purpose."

The woman crossed her arms. "That so? What kind of

purpose?"

"A personal one," Annabelle said, lifting her chin.

Matthew appeared and cupped her elbow. "Come this way, Annabelle."

Annabelle inclined her head to the curious woman and followed Matthew into a small sitting room. The wooden floors were covered with brightly colored woven rugs topped with simple furnishings. No paintings adorned the walls, but a fire roared in the hearth, filling the room with warmth. Annabelle lowered her hood, and no sooner had it hit her back than Matthew's hands were there to help her remove the mantle.

Sallie bustled around the room, collecting their damp coats and outerwear and hanging them on pegs on either side of the mantel to dry. Annabelle sat in a straight-backed chair near the fire and watched the others. Peggy took a place near her, standing against the plank wall.

Annabelle's eyes followed Mr. O'Malley across the room. He pulled Sallie aside, whispered something in her ear, and pressed something into her hand. The woman nodded, and then the two of them slipped from the room. Annabelle narrowed her eyes. What were they up to?

Matthew paced in front of the fire. She turned to watch him, wondering what kind of secrets he kept and just how deeply he was involved in the plot that the others were clearly trying to hide.

"Sure am glad to be off that horse," Harry said, pulling her attention his way. He rarely talked directly to her.

She gave a small nod.

He looked at her intently. "What do you expect to do once we reach Washington? You haven't yet said where we're going to leave you."

"Leave me?"

Matthew stepped up beside her. "She'll remain with me."

Harry scratched his chin. "I don't see how that's going to work."

Matthew stepped closer to Harry. "She stays with me until I can safely hand her off to my brother."

Annabelle bristled. Hand her off?

Before the tension could grow thicker in the room, Mr. O'Malley and Sallie returned with trays of food. The smell filled the small room, and everyone's eyes turned in their direction.

"Come on to the table," Sallie said as she swayed through the room. "I made a feast worthy of the heroes gracing my home."

Heroes? Annabelle glanced at Peggy, who gave a small shrug. Annabelle rose from her seat and began to follow the others before realizing Peggy remained against the wall.

"Excuse me, Sallie?"

"Yes?" the woman's voice said through the other doorway, which Annabelle assumed separated the dining area from the living space.

"Where shall my maid eat? She's in need of a good meal as well."

Peggy glared at her, but she ignored it.

Sallie slid around Matthew, who took up most of the doorway, and looked between Peggy and Annabelle.

"I'm not accustomed to having slaves inside the house."

Annabelle maintained her best ladylike calm but refused to budge.

The woman scratched at the small white cap on her head.

"She can eat out in the kitchen, so long as she doesn't steal anything."

Annabelle suppressed her annoyance. "I assure you, Peggy is quite reliable."

Sallie didn't look convinced but gestured for Peggy to follow her. "Come on. You can help me bring in the rest of the cornbread and the pie, and then you can have some of what's left on the stove."

Peggy cast a sour look at Annabelle but followed the woman without a word. Annabelle clenched her teeth and spun around to find Matthew watching her.

"What kind of relationship do you have with that slave?" The look of honest curiosity on his face stifled the retort that popped onto her tongue.

She leveled her gaze on him, trying to project the proper image of a refined lady. Despite her effort, emotion still filled her voice. "Peggy has been with me since I was born. When my mother died, she comforted a grieving child. From then on, she raised me as a mother would and has been the nearest to one I've had since."

Understanding dawned in his eyes rather than disgust, and her heart immediately leapt toward him. "I, too, was mostly reared by a mammy," he said. Then softer, he added, "Thank you for sharing that with me." Curiously, he winked at her.

Had she given away something too personal? Nervousness fluttered in her stomach. She offered him a tentative smile, which he returned with enthusiasm. Curious again. Why was he acting so strangely? Matthew gestured for her to enter the dining room. She kept her eyes downcast as she stepped past him and chose a seat.

Matthew sat next to her, and in a moment Sallie and Peggy delivered the remaining meal. Sallie seated herself at the head of the table, and Peggy disappeared without a word. They passed the food around, and Annabelle served herself smaller portions than she truly wanted, making little piles of peas, okra, and greens on the chipped plate. Interesting, how a lone woman had such an abundance of food.

No sooner had they begun to eat than shouts arose from outside. Mr. O'Malley leapt from his seat and dashed out the door. Matthew glanced at Annabelle only briefly before following him out. Harry and Sallie scurried to the windows in a flurry of tossed napkins and rustling fabric. The appetite that had snapped like a starved wolf withered as Annabelle swallowed down the fear rising in her throat. Deciding it would be better to look over Sallie's shoulder than to get too close to Harry, Annabelle chose the window farthest from her chair and strained to see outside.

Men in gray rushed about; several carried torches. Annabelle clutched the fabric at her throat. "What are they doing? Are they going to burn the town?"

Sallie swung around to face her, her eyes incredulous. "Why would our own burn our homes?"

Annabelle just stared at her.

Sallie turned back with a huff, and Annabelle watched the streams of men flow past the window. Seconds behind them, men in blue crowded her vision. Sallie squealed and jumped back from the window, knocking into Annabelle and making her lose her footing. She stumbled out of the woman's way as she hastily pulled the curtains closed.

How did Sallie still have curtains? The thought distracted

her as Sallie pulled her back into the sitting room. Stunned, she allowed Harry to push on her shoulders and lower her into a chair.

Matthew and Mr. O'Malley burst through the front door just as she plopped down in the chair hard enough to jar her teeth. Matthew strode across the room and knelt in front of a small couch, pulling a rusted rifle out from beneath it. Annabelle gawked as he positioned himself near the front door. How had he known where to find a weapon?

Witless woman, her mind mocked. *The enemy waits outside the door. Do you think to escape them again?*

Mr. O'Malley cursed, snapping her attention to him. "That *Custer* is here." He said the name as if it were another foul word she wasn't supposed to hear. He stalked the room like a caged lion. "Rosser's trying to hold the river, keep those Yanks from joining up with Sheridan."

Fear flooded her veins. *Peggy!* Annabelle lurched from her seat. "I'm getting Peggy!"

In her shock, she'd forgotten Peggy ate in the kitchen. Guilt accompanied her fear, and she strode for the door.

"You're going outside to fetch a slave when there's Yanks storming through here?" Sallie's brown eyes bulged. "She's probably already run off, soon as she saw blue!"

Annabelle ignored her and dashed through the door at the rear of the house. A walkway led to the kitchen just to the right of a miniature garden. Annabelle hurried across the path and flung open the kitchen door. Peggy stood near an open window at the rear wall, watching soldiers file past.

"Peggy!" Annabelle cried. "Come on!"

Peggy startled and shuffled across the room, grabbing a

hunk of cornbread and shoving it into her mouth before following Annabelle out the door.

The drizzle had stopped, but the cold wind hit Annabelle hard in the face. She blinked away the sting of moisture that sprang into her eyes, only to find a man in blue standing in her path.

He sneered at her. "Hey there, little Rebel."

Without thinking, Annabelle spun on her heel, grabbed Peggy by the wrist, and darted behind the kitchen.

"Hey!"

They didn't stop. Without protest, Peggy ran with her around the back of the kitchen and across the grass as Annabelle tried to angle out to the other side of the yard. She scurried around the house and stopped short so quickly that Peggy ran into her with a grunt.

"Child! What you doin'?"

Annabelle tugged Peggy's wrist and gestured ahead. The Confederates had lit the covered bridge on fire and were struggling to keep it going as waves of men in blue slammed into them. Gunfire erupted and peppered the air with blasts of smoke.

On the road just in front of her, a man in blue fired a shot at the back of a man in gray only a few feet in front of him. The man's body lurched, and blood sprang from the wound as he fell, his face in the dirt. His body still twitched as the Union man stepped over him and continued forward.

Annabelle's mouth went dry.

"Let's get back into the house!" Peggy's pleading voice tore through Annabelle's shock.

Annabelle pressed her back against the wall but could not

tear her eyes away from the carnage. "We might need to get the horses instead."

The horses pawed at the ground in agitation, one of them dancing about and tossing his head. The Union soldiers ignored the animals and hurried forward to engage the vastly outnumbered Confederates. Annabelle's heart hammered in her chest, the pounding blood in her ears mixing with the shouts of the men and the blasts of gunfire.

"Miss Belle!"

Peggy's shout awoke Annabelle from her stupor. She spun on her heel, wringing her hands. "What should we do?"

"Get you back inside the house!"

Peggy tugged on her, and they ducked their heads, hoping not to be noticed as they ran up the front steps. Annabelle lifted her hand to pound on the door, but it opened before she had the chance. A gun barrel flew up only inches from her face. The scream that wanted to claw free remained lodged in her throat.

"Annabelle!" Matthew barked, lowering the gun and grabbing her shoulder, wrenching her inside. "What were you thinking?"

She swallowed hard, trying to regain her stammering voice. "What...what's happening?"

He pushed her behind him, slamming the door. After several seconds without her being followed, Matthew turned and pressed his back against the door, ignoring her question. His gaze roamed over her frame. "Are you hurt?"

She shook her head.

"That was foolish," he spat. "Why didn't you come back in from the kitchen, where Harry was giving you cover?"

Her nostrils flared. "I had to escape a Union soldier in the yard!"

The muscles in his jaw worked. "Are you sure you wouldn't rather run off with him instead?"

Surprise melted her indignation. "What?"

His face hardened. "Seems like you're pretty comfortable in a Yank's arms."

He thrust himself off the door and pushed past her before she could respond. What was he talking about? Suddenly Private Grierson's face filled her memory. Had Matthew seen her with him? She clenched her fists. Had he been spying on her?

She stalked after him, forgetting the terror thundering outside. Peggy grabbed her wrist, but she ripped it free. How dare he! Was he already back to making her the harlot?

"I say we ride," Matthew said as she stepped into the living space off the front hall.

Mr. O'Malley nodded. "Agreed. We need to get moving before the battle heats up."

Sallie put her hand on Mr. O'Malley's arm. "Get your horses. I'll get what I can in some sacks for you. Take the back way out of town, and avoid the river. They're more interested in getting across than they will be in you."

"Let's hope," Mr. O'Malley said, catching Matthew's eye. "Can you keep it under control?"

Matthew glanced at Annabelle, his expression hard to read. He gave a curt nod. "Let's go."

Annabelle opened her mouth to free the fire building inside, but a sudden blast rattled the walls, and she forgot her anger. If they survived this, she would deliver her ire later.

Annabelle bolted after Sallie to the dining table, and she and Peggy dumped bread and bits of cheese into a flour sack. The men had already swooped up their packs by the front door.

They hurried down the front steps to the lawn, where the men waited with the horses. Without a word, Matthew thrust both Annabelle and Peggy onto their saddles and swiftly mounted his own horse in a matter of seconds. The Union soldiers had cleared the road in front of the house and concentrated on extinguishing the fire and overtaking the Confederates on this side.

Matthew led the band of horses around the west side of the house, through a gate just beyond the chicken coop, and out into an open field. Annabelle looked over her shoulder. Several of the Union soldiers had crossed the river and engaged the small band of Confederates on the other side. Smoke rose into the air, black and ominous. The wet weather had not helped the men in gray. The bridge fire sputtered out, and more Union men rushed across.

Annabelle mumbled what felt like a hopeless prayer for lost life, then turned and kicked her horse into a gallop. The sounds and smells of the battle faded behind her with each of the horse's thundering strides, but she could not purge the horror of it from her heart as they raced away. As the five of them flew across the hills of the valley, the cold wind buffeted her face and tried to dry the tears streaming down Annabelle's cheeks.

Twenty-Six

"[He is] too closely surrounded by his friends. No chance before the inauguration."
John H. Surratt

*F*or likely the tenth time, Matthew checked over his shoulder at Annabelle. This time, as each before, she met his eyes with a flat stare. He stifled a groan and turned back in the saddle.

The winded horses could not be coaxed to run any farther. He was glad for it. They had pushed the poor creatures hard, putting distance between themselves and the skirmish. Matthew drew in a long breath of crisp air that smelled of damp soil. Above, the sky shone a pristine blue, unmarred by a single cloud. The day had warmed considerably, offering a slight reprieve from the cold.

His horse plodded along, the steady rhythm in stark contrast to Matthew's chaotic thoughts. His attention darted from wondering about his brother's condition to his status as either deserter or conspirator, then to the disappointment of spending another cold night outdoors when he had been anticipating the comfort of a roof and four walls. Despite the multiple topics he attempted to set his mind to, it stubbornly returned to the woman riding behind him.

Twice already he'd berated himself for his harsh words against her, words that had bubbled up from anger caused by his fear and fueled by jealousy he hadn't realized still simmered. It seemed any ground they'd gained in their friendship fizzled under his heated accusations.

He resisted the urge to look at her again and stiffened his shoulders. Better she didn't feel overly friendly toward him anyway. More than once, something had sparked in her eyes that had caused heat in his chest. To his shame, not only had he relished it, but he'd encouraged it. He must remember Annabelle would someday be his *sister*.

O'Malley slowed his horse and fell into step with Matthew, drawing him out of his mental flogging.

After a few paces, O'Malley spoke in that smooth tone he used when he wanted everyone to comply with his wishes. "We still have nearly a hundred miles before we get to the meeting house in Washington. Since we've lost the luxury of our last allied residence before we get there, I say we ride on as long as we can before we have to rest the horses."

"Agreed."

Matthew watched the man from the corner of his eye. O'Malley rode with stiff shoulders, a rigid posture, and his hat pulled low over his rumpled brow. He hardly looked the part of a confident conspirator.

"Are you sure this thing will work?" Matthew whispered just above the crunch of leaves and dried grass under the horses' hooves.

Matthew caught a flash of worry in O'Malley's eyes an instant before the smolder of frustration returned. "I grow weary of your doubts, Daniels."

"Doubts are founded in such a situation as this."

"And yet, you have more doubts than are necessary, or even understandable. I'm starting to think you seek to shirk your duty."

Matthew scraped a hand over his face. "I grow tired of your jabs to my honor. I'm set on seeing this through, if only for the puny hope I might see my brother freed. Don't begrudge sound logic that says your plan is nearly impossible to accomplish."

O'Malley eyed him for a moment, then took a long breath. "Haven't you noticed the help we've received along the way?"

A suspicious amount. "I have."

"And have you also not noticed the funds I've used to secure clothing, supplies, and horses?"

Why did he feel like a child being reprimanded? His knees involuntarily tightened, and his horse bobbed its head, trying to give its rider a faster gait. Matthew released the tension, and the poor beast relaxed, falling back into a slow walk next to O'Malley's mount. "I'm not dull. I can see you're well funded."

O'Malley jutted his chin, a smirk playing on the corners of his mouth. "So, you're bright enough to notice someone with means has given their support, but you haven't pieced together who'd have such a long arm, have you?"

There were plenty of Southerners with hefty assets, but how should O'Malley expect him to know which…? His thoughts tumbled to a halt, and he swung his gaze to O'Malley's lifted brows.

"Ah. So you've figured it out."

"Davis." Matthew whispered.

"Now, of course, I cannot confirm any suspicions you may have involving our government. However, our president has appointed two men to head the secret service, a rather well-funded operation that is safely set up in a remote location. But surely you know that already?"

Matthew's gut tightened. "Canada."

Pride flooded O'Malley's features, and Matthew immediately regretted letting his thoughts escape.

"See there?" O'Malley nearly cooed. "You're endowed with both height and wit. Surely you understand now that your doubts are wholly unfounded."

Are they? Matthew gave a curt nod. Perhaps the plan was feasible. Why then did he still feel so uneasy?

"Since that is settled, let's speak on it no more?" O'Malley's words slithered across more as a command than a request.

Matthew drew his lips into a thin line.

"The inauguration draws near," O'Malley said after a few moments. "We'd hoped to move before now, but with the complications caused by our misplaced correspondence, we lost too much time."

Matthew dropped his gaze from the hawk gliding overhead to O'Malley's creased face. "When did you originally intend to do it?"

O'Malley pulled the collar of his jacket closer as a cold gust of wind buffeted them. "Before he was set upon by a bunch of goons that never let him out of sight."

Matthew lifted his brows.

"I suppose it's better this way." O'Malley rolled his shoulders back. "He'll be firmly in his position, which makes his capture all the more potent."

"When will it happen?"

"The opportunity will soon arise."

How long did they intend to stalk in the shadows hoping to catch Lincoln alone? "And what of Miss Ross?"

O'Malley still let out a huff. "She will accompany us to the boarding house in Washington, where she'll remain until this is safely seen through. Then you may do with her as you please." O'Malley dipped his chin, clicked to his horse, and trotted ahead to rejoin Harry, leaving Matthew to stare at his back.

Matthew slowed his horse further, increasing the distance between him and the other men, expecting Annabelle to catch up. He should talk to her about George and figure out an explanation about why they might need to stay in Washington. Maybe he could get her mind off it with some outings.

She still had not reached him, so he smothered his pride and turned in the saddle to look at her. Annabelle and her maid rode silently about two horse lengths behind him. Just as his gaze settled on her, she nudged the reins to draw up her horse and maintain distance. Matthew tightened his calves on the saddle fenders, and the horse increased his pace until Matthew rode at the midpoint between the trouble in front of him and the trouble at his rear.

They rode until the sun set and the horses were near collapsing. O'Malley finally stopped in a hollow in the shadow of a small mountain range. Matthew slipped from his horse and started over to Miss Ross to offer his customary assistance with her dismount. Rather than waiting for him, she slung her leg over the saddle with a flurry of fabric. She landed with one foot on the ground, but the other remained stuck in the stirrup. Before he could reach her, she yanked her boot free but lost her balance. She landed square on her backside.

Peggy yelped and scrambled down from her horse, but Matthew reached Annabelle first.

"Let me help you." He extended his hand but did not want to touch her without her permission.

She glared up at him with flashing eyes above cheeks tinged pink—whether from embarrassment or fury, he couldn't be certain, but the color gave her creamy skin a fetching glow. Since she didn't tell him to leave, he reached down and placed his hands under her arms, easily lifting her and placing her on her feet. She gave a small gasp and tilted her chin to look up at him.

Her eyes sparked like blue diamonds in the waning light. How long would she stand here, letting his hands rest upon the curve of her waist?

Peggy made an awful show of clearing her throat, and Annabelle's eyes widened just before she took a large step backward and out of his hands. Matthew lowered his arms but kept his focus on her face. She dipped her chin and turned from him without a word.

Matthew spun and returned to his horse. He loosened the girth strap and unhooked his pack, letting the weight of it drop to the ground. After he found a place to leave his pack, he unsaddled his and the women's horses and secured them to a length of rope tied between two young trees.

O'Malley and Harry both handed over their reins with a nod and went to ready the campsite. After two weeks, they'd fallen into a routine. His job didn't bother him. Horses were more peaceful than people.

Running his hands down their forelegs, Matthew felt for

heat in the cannon bones. Sure enough, he found it in the right foreleg of Peggy's mount. Poor creatures. Hopefully they wouldn't be lame in the morning. Hardly bothering to graze, the animals tested the length of their overhead tethers and lay down.

Night settled quickly, and soon Matthew could hardly see more than a few feet in front of him. He should help the women with the fire. He scooped up a few shed limbs and gathered as many boughs as he could for the frigid night ahead. Three winters he'd spent huddled in army camps, and still he hated the cold. The body never quite grew accustomed to hard ground and no walls. If he was dreading it, he could only imagine how a lady would despise it.

But Annabelle had yet to complain.

She coaxed a small flame into a roaring fire and positioned her bed roll. Harry complained that the cornbread he'd stored had disintegrated into crumbs as though the women could do anything about it.

Ignoring him, Matthew dragged his saddle next to the fire. Using it as a makeshift seat would curl the leather, but he couldn't bring himself to care. The women busied themselves spreading out blankets. From the looks of it, Peggy had no intentions of making a meal tonight. The men would have to fend for themselves.

The irony of it struck him, and he chuckled. If Matthew hadn't insisted on bringing the women along, they would have been gnawing on hardtack the entire time. He stretched his legs and massaged the wounded muscle. It didn't ache nearly as much now.

After Harry finally quit grumbling over the food, he made his way around the circle of subdued conspirators and offered them each two slices of hardened bread, a hunk of cheese, and a strip of dried meat.

Despite his ravenous hunger, Matthew forced himself to chew his food slowly and savor what little flavor could be found. Yesterday he'd had to tighten his belt another notch. That made the third time he'd tightened it since he'd left the army. At this rate, by the time he was supposed to grab Lincoln he'd be nothing more than a walking skeleton.

As a blanket of darkness settled on the camp, the night creatures began their lullaby, and weariness settled heavily upon him. But he could not rest just yet. He had something he first had to address, lest it continue to gnaw at him. He waited as the others finished their treks away from camp for private business before settling down for the night. When everyone stilled on their pallets, Matthew rose and skirted the fire.

"Miss Ross?"

She looked up from where she'd settled on her blankets, her rumpled dress evidence of her inability to change her clothing in the presence of several men. It would be good to get her to the boarding house.

"Yes?"

"Might I speak with you?" he whispered.

She smoothed away a stray lock of hair that had slipped free of her tight braid. "In the morning would be more appropriate."

He immediately thought back to that first night when they'd talked under the starlight while the others slept. Another pang of regret pierced him, but he inclined his head. "I only wished to apologize for my rash words. I'll not bother you further."

Her lips parted, but no words left them, so he turned and walked around the small campfire to where the other men had already buried themselves beneath jackets and blankets.

Matthew reclined against his saddle and positioned his socked feet toward the fire, leaving his rifle resting in his lap. One of the two men beside him snored softly.

Something touched his arm. He jerked suddenly, his hands instinctively gripping his weapon.

"Captain Daniels! It's me."

His grip relaxed, and he squinted at the form crouching beside him. Had he so soon drifted to sleep? He sat up straighter. "What's wrong?"

Annabelle remained silent a few heartbeats too long, and he leaned nearer, trying to read her features but finding the paltry starlight inadequate. The firelight danced behind her, creating a halo around her head but leaving her face shadowed.

"You said you wished to talk," she finally said.

He drew himself into a full sitting position and crossed his legs underneath him. Taking his cue, she settled down and arranged her skirts around her ankles.

"I did." Matthew rubbed at the back of his neck. "I apologize for my harsh words."

"Which ones exactly?"

An owl hooted somewhere nearby, startling a few birds from their roost. He watched one flap by overhead before returning his attention to Annabelle. "All of them."

"Thank you." She sat quietly, and Matthew gave her time to gather her thoughts. When her words came, they didn't hold as much venom as he'd feared. "Why did you think I'd leave with some random Union soldier? Haven't I said I'd go with you and meet your brother?"

Matthew chose his words carefully. "That day at the barn,

when you first ran off. Why did you do it?"

"I was afraid. I didn't know you, or what your intentions were, and I wanted to go home."

Matthew set his weapon to his side and shifted his weight so he could face her more directly. "I understand. But under the circumstances, I was inclined to believe you might be a spy."

"Like you?" she said softly.

His muscles tensed, and he rolled his shoulders back in an effort to release them. "I'm not a spy. I am, as I assume you are, just someone who seems to be caught up in something bigger than myself."

"I see."

Did she? "I was simply trying to help you when I freed you from my army's camp, so you can see my confusion as to why you would rather run than ask for my assistance."

She regarded him with stoic features. What wouldn't he give to know what thoughts churned behind those arresting blue eyes?

"In answer to your original question, when you ran, I followed you. Which I assume you know, since you attempted to elude me by making a false trail and hiding in a log."

She gasped. "You knew?"

"Of course."

She gave a small nod. "You saw me with the private who gave me a ride back into town."

Matthew rose and tossed two more limbs onto the fire. The embers flared and tiny flecks of light danced in the air. When he sat back down, he could feel Annabelle staring at him. He chose a spot slightly off from where he'd been before. As he'd hoped, she shifted to face him better, and her face was now half-turned to the fire. At least he could make out her profile in the light.

"I suppose I can appreciate your suspicion." Her soft words sent a flood of relief that surprised him. "However," she continued with a little more steel in her tone, "I would have you know that I did not previously know him. Well, not really. I'd seen him earlier in passing, and he'd assisted me in mounting my horse."

Matthew gave a small nod.

They sat in silence for what Matthew counted to be ten breaths before she huffed. "Just so there's no more suspicions between us, I should clear up these misconceptions you keep flinging around."

He kept his features even so that she wouldn't see the self-satisfied smirk that attempted to bloom on his lips. He was trying for patience, not manipulation, but he doubted she'd see it that way.

"When the Union private happened upon me on the road, he offered to take me back to town. He sent a doctor to see to my twisted ankle, and I have not seen him since. I have no connections with anyone in the Union Army."

Her words sounded both defensive and slightly desperate. Did she want so much for him to trust her?

"I believe you."

"You do?" The surprise in her voice panged him.

"At the time, I still thought you were Miss Smith." He let the implications hang in the air. If she wasn't a spy, why give a false name?

"Oh. I'm sorry about that."

She gave no further explanation, and he didn't ask, despite his curiosity. She'd likely done it to protect herself, even if it made no sense to him. "Your reasons are your own."

"I…." she sighed. "Thank you." She shifted. "There's something I'd like to know."

He stiffened. If she noticed, she didn't let on.

"You're *sure* you didn't recognize me when we first met?"

He gave a soft chuckle. "No. I figured it out much later."

"When exactly?"

Memories of the shopkeeper sparked humiliation. He couldn't tell her he'd been unmanned by a portly fellow in an apron. "I spoke with a shopkeeper who asked me if I knew anything about a Miss Ross. From his description, I realized she and you were the same. I remembered having once been to Rosswood, and after that, everything about my father's plans."

"Mr. Black? What did you tell him?"

Why did fear lace her hurried words? "That I didn't know Miss Ross. And the girl the Confederate soldiers were searching for was Miss Smith, which technically, I suppose, was true."

Her shoulders slumped. "Oh."

Matthew tossed a stick into the flames. "I'm glad I decided to come find you."

"Why did you?"

He kept O'Malley's suspicions to himself. "Curiosity. Imagine my surprise to find that the lady of Rosswood was the same waif who'd run from me in the woods."

She huffed, and he couldn't contain his chuckle. One of the others stirred, and they fell silent.

Finally, she whispered, "I never really thanked you for that."

"I'm glad I did."

She shivered. From the cold, or something else? "The very reason I tried to get to the camp at all was to get a message to my uncle about my grandfather's plans to wed me to..." She hesitated and picked at her fingers. "To someone I don't wish to marry. I don't think any of my previous letters actually made it to him. Taking Lieutenant Monroe's note was only secondary, a means by which to gain entrance. Which, as you know, turned out poorly."

She seemed relieved to have shared the tale. Had it burdened her? He should steer the conversation away from secret messages and the questions they might stir. Besides, something had bothered him ever since he'd overheard the odd conversation at Rosswood. He'd been unable to figure out a way to ask her about it without giving himself away.

"Your grandfather...." Matthew scratched his chin. "He... seems to be a man without honor."

She let out a bitter laugh. "So you saw." She picked at her fingernails. When she looked up, he couldn't read the expression in her eyes. "He's also not truly my grandfather, but merely a step relation."

"The male relative overseeing your plantation until you're married."

"Yes."

"And this man he chose for you?"

She let out a long breath. "Andrew. His son."

Things clicked into place. "It makes sense. He has to marry you to someone in his family if he wants to maintain any legal claims on the land."

"Exactly." She spat the word through clenched teeth.

They sat in silence for a while, and Matthew left her to her thoughts. No wonder she'd agreed to come with him. As her male relative, blood or not, her grandfather should have been seeking to care for her, not to further his own gain. Anger boiled in Matthew's stomach.

"How much older are you than your brother?" she asked, jerking him from his thoughts.

Matthew's brow furrowed. "There's three years difference between us."

"Hmm."

"Why?"

"When we first met, you told me you were twenty-five."

"I am."

"Then he would be twenty-two, correct?"

Matthew bit the inside of his lip. An answer this time would not be an evasion, but an outright lie. He forced a laugh. "Twenty-five less three does make twenty-two."

She stared at him in the dying firelight and he forced himself not to shift under her gaze. "Why the sudden interest in age?"

"Just more information, that's all."

Why didn't he believe her?

He jumped to his feet a little too quickly and gathered some more wood. He tossed it on the fire. "We should rest."

Without a word, she rose and shuffled off into the darkness. He heard her settle down on her pallet, though he could barely make out her form in the firelight. He gritted his teeth and returned to his place, propping himself up on his saddle and turning his cold feet to the fire that he doubted would survive until dawn.

In a couple more days they would be in Washington, and he would be forced to tell her the truth. What would happen then? How much would she hate him? Guilt poured through him like hot water, though it offered no relief from the coldness seeping up from the ground.

Stillness settled on the camp, broken only by lonely crickets. For a long time Matthew sat and listened to their song, trying to calm his thoughts. Though try as he might to do otherwise, his thoughts continually circulated to the beautiful blonde just on the other side of the camp. She might as well be miles away—a woman who, in another reality, could very well have been his wife.

Twenty-Seven

"My hopes and prospects rest solely on this attempt,
and should it fail, I am ruined for ever."
John H. Surratt

Surratt Boarding House
Washington, D.C.
March 3, 1865

Three days had passed since she'd spoken with Matthew by the firelight. Annabelle couldn't stop herself from playing the conversation over in her mind. How many times had she tried to analyze every word and gesture?

He'd been avoiding her since she'd asked about George. Was he hiding something, or had it merely been a reminder to them both that she grew too comfortable with the wrong brother?

True, they'd ridden hard and collapsed onto their makeshift beds each night, but not once had he tried to talk to her beyond polite and mundane words. She shouldn't miss the deeper conversations and shared feelings, should she? But she felt she had managed to gain and lose a friend all too quickly. Were they not past meaningless pleasantries and strictly necessary words?

Something pinched her arm, pulling her back to her current

surroundings and out of the thoughts swarming in her head. Peggy stood in the front parlor of a tidy boarding house in Washington as rigid as an iron sapling. She caught Annabelle's eye and gave a tiny shake of her head.

Oh, heavens. So much for paying attention! Not that anyone in their exhausted group had much to say while they waited on the landlady. The grandfather clock in the entry ticked quietly, counting the seconds.

They'd arrived at the narrow house a few moments ago and had quickly been ushered inside. A strange residence entirely too close to one's neighbors, in Annabelle's opinion. The house connected to another narrow home on one side and separated itself from yet another building on the other by only a small strip of land. The entire house looked like a book wedged into place onto a shelf already crammed full.

Yet, in a town filled to the brim with people, the inside of the boarding house was surprisingly empty. They would be the only guests tonight. Annabelle couldn't help but find that strange. Her gaze traveled over David O'Malley and Harry, then came to rest on Matthew, who shifted his weight from one foot to the other. He wouldn't look at her.

A tall woman brushed into the parlor in a sweep of fine black silks and the men rose to greet her. She wore a fine dress with a large bow and cameo about her neck, her white undersleeves crisp. She carried herself with the confidence of one accustomed to being in charge. She must be Mrs. Surratt, the landlady.

Suddenly, the woman's gaze snapped to meet Annabelle's. The expression framed between the woman's dangling earrings contained a strange mix of surprise and suspicion. As though she knew Annabelle didn't belong.

"Come, miss," the woman said, gesturing for Annabelle to leave the cushioned seat her tired body sank against. "I'll take you upstairs to your room. It's quite late, and surely you don't wish to be down here amongst the ramblings of menfolk."

Annabelle forced a submissive smile and pushed her weight onto sore legs. Without a word, Peggy fell into step behind her as she followed Mrs. Surratt. Annabelle gathered her skirts to keep them from brushing the walls squeezing on the staircase. At the second landing, a single door led to the third floor. Mrs. Surratt held it open, and Annabelle and Peggy passed through into a small upper room. Built into the roof, the low slope of the ceiling dipped close to the two small beds flanking either side of the chamber.

Mrs. Surratt clasped her hands and hovered in the doorway. "Captain Daniels insists you accompany him tomorrow to the inauguration. I trust you have something more proper to wear?"

The clipped words raked across Annabelle's nerves. Where she went and what she wore were her own business.

She glanced at Peggy, who held up her father's carpetbag. "I do." Not that she needed to explain herself.

Mrs. Surratt turned to Peggy, as if noticing her for the first time. "You'll need a place for this slave, of course."

Annabelle waved a hand. "She stays with me."

The woman's face reddened. Was this not the North? Annabelle straightened herself to her full height and kept her gaze on the woman steady.

Finally, Mrs. Surratt retreated without another word. As soon as the door clicked, Annabelle's shoulders drooped.

Peggy made a clicking noise. "I don't like this one bit. We

ain't seen this man yet you're supposed to be courting, and I don't like the looks of what's going on here. Something's up."

Peggy should be upset by Mrs. Surratt's behavior. Annabelle's heart tightened. But Peggy didn't even notice because she'd been disrespected her entire life.

"I'm suspicious as well," she whispered, wary of listening ears on the other side of the door.

As if reading her thoughts, Peggy eyed the door and then sidled closer to Annabelle's side. "They're plannin' something. I just know it."

"I agree. But I don't know what it could be." She tugged on the laces at the back of her dress, and Peggy immediately took over, her experienced fingers flying through the task. Oh, how nice it would be to sleep tonight without being fully clothed! "I think they run a spy ring, but I don't see what we can do about it. It's probably best if we stay out of it."

Peggy pulled the blouse over Annabelle's head, and Annabelle stepped out of her petticoat and skirt. Stripping down to just her chemise and pantaloons, she padded over to the fire glowing merrily in the hearth. This small room at the top of the house felt warmer than those below, and Annabelle reveled in the comfort of being indoors in front of a fireplace. She turned her back to the flames and enjoyed the heat on her skin while Peggy turned down the thick quilt on Annabelle's bed. In addition to the two slender beds, a washbasin and stand and a small writing desk and chair completed the simple furnishings.

Peggy arranged Annabelle's skirt over the back of the chair, though Annabelle had to wonder if she worked more from habit than anything else. Wadding the skirt and tossing it in the corner couldn't produce any more wrinkles.

"Do you think I'll meet him tomorrow?"

"The new Mista Daniels?" Peggy crossed to her own bed and tugged back the quilt, then tightened the ropes. "I reckon." Peggy stripped down to her shift and came to join Annabelle over at the fire. "Least, I hope so." Whatever appearances they kept up in front of the others were easily dismissed when they were alone and exhausted. "You know I can't go with you tomorrow, right?"

Another injustice. "What will you do?"

Peggy snorted. "See if that woman's got a decent washtub so I can get some of the horse smell washed out of these clothes."

The corners of Annabelle's lips lifted. "That would be nice."

Peggy stretched and yawned. "Come on, girl. To bed with you. You'll have permanent dark circles under them eyes if you don't start getting proper rest."

Annabelle slipped under the blankets, the soft mattress a haven for her aching muscles. "Goodnight, Peggy."

The reply came as it had for as many years as Annabelle could remember. "Goodnight, sweet girl. Dream of beautiful things and a bright tomorrow."

The sun had barely slid into the room when Peggy shook Annabelle from her slumber. "Come on. I want to get you washed this morning."

Annabelle groaned and cracked one eye. "Can't it wait?"

Peggy crossed her arms. "You want to meet that man smelling like a stable?"

"Am I that bad?"

"Yep." Peggy laughed. "Get up."

Annabelle yawned and snuggled deeper into the covers. She had just enough time to register Peggy's snort before the blankets flew off of her.

"All right, all right. I'm up."

Peggy scurried out of the room, and Annabelle contemplated sneaking a few more moments of rest. Then she sighed and rose from the bed, choosing to warm herself by the fire instead. Peggy must have been up for a while. While Annabelle slept, Peggy had dressed, made her bed, and built up the fire.

She looked out the window and grimaced. Another wet day. When they'd finally made it here yesterday, it had been by plodding through inches of thick mud that had stuck to the horses' legs like paste. The thought of ruining her only nice dress in the muck made her wrinkle her nose.

Peggy burst through the door with a pitcher of water and poured it into the basin. "It ain't hot, but it's warm enough so it won't give you a chill."

Annabelle took the cloth Peggy offered. She scrubbed every last trace of horse and dirt from her skin. When she finished, Peggy tackled her locks.

"This hair needs a good washing, but that can't be helped. Captain Daniels is pacing downstairs, already waiting on you. Says he needs to talk to you before you go."

When Peggy finished twisting and pinning her hair and she'd smoothed the fine fabric of her blue gown, Annabelle turned in a small circle. "How do I look?"

Unexpected tears swelled in Peggy's eyes. "Like a lovely

young woman, grown too fast."

Annabelle smiled and grasped Peggy's hand. A sudden knock made them both jump. Peggy pulled away from Annabelle, straightened her face, and opened the door to find Matthew crowding the doorway. He glanced between them and twisted the hat in his hand.

"Annabelle, I need to speak to you."

Peggy frowned. "Gentlemen ain't allowed in a lady's room. She'll be down in a minute."

Annabelle smirked at Peggy's boldness. Perhaps the news that the Union president had signed all slaves into freedom gave her some confidence. Even if Mississippi would never accept such a thing, this was, after all, Washington.

Matthew didn't budge. He swung his gaze over to Annabelle, ignoring Peggy entirely. "I would like to speak with you privately. It's very important."

"Humph. Of course it is." Peggy put her hands on her hips.

Matthew finally addressed Peggy, confusion pulling his brows together. "It concerns my brother."

Annabelle's breath caught. Had she come all this way only to be rejected *before* she met the man? She gritted her teeth. How could he cast her away before he even laid eyes on her? What would make him change his mind? A nasty thought sunk its claws into her: what if he wasn't here at all? Worse, what if he didn't know his brother planned to force him into a marriage, just as Grandfather had planned to do to her?

Worry scurried over her like a hundred ants, and she quickly grasped Peggy's hand, pulling her past Matthew, who stumbled out of the way.

"Wait for me on the steps," she said to Peggy, her voice

low. "We'll leave the door open."

Peggy shook her head. "But you'll be out of sight."

"Only for a moment." She pleaded with her eyes.

"Fine, but only for a few minutes." Peggy glared at Matthew, then shot Annabelle a warning look before turning her back to them.

Annabelle left her on the stairs and stepped past a confused Matthew and back into the room, gesturing for him to join her.

"I have a confession to make," he blurted.

Panic gripped her chest, making her breaths harder to draw.

Matthew dropped his gaze. "I haven't been honest with you."

Her heart galloped. "And?"

"My brother isn't here."

She knew it! He'd abandoned her already. "And why not?" The words came out more scathing than she intended, and the look of pain that flashed in Matthew's eyes almost made her wish she could call them back.

"Because he is in prison."

"*What?*"

Her screech sent Peggy scrambling back into the room, her gaze darting between Annabelle and Matthew.

Matthew straightened. "Please, if you would allow me to explain."

"He was never going to be here, was he?" Annabelle clenched her fists at her sides, her chest heaving.

"No."

Heat flared in her chest and traveled into her face.

Peggy threw up her hands. "Oh, Lawd, what we gonna do?"

The muscles in Matthew's jaw worked as he set his earnest

gaze on Annabelle. "I meant only to protect you."

"By *lying* to me? Apparently, marriage to an unwilling criminal or to a cur twice my age are my only options. I should know what sort of miscreant you thought to throw me upon!"

Matthew's nostrils flared. "His only crime was to try to save his brother from certain death! He got himself captured by the enemy instead."

Anger left her in a sudden whoosh. "Oh." He glared at her, and she dropped her gaze. A prisoner of war. Not a criminal. "Forgive me. I didn't know."

His breaths exhaled long and deliberately, and it took several seconds before Annabelle dared to look up at him again. When she did, she noticed Peggy had left the room, and the man before her stood tense and erect, but not exactly angry.

She tilted her head and studied him. This would not be a man who let his anger blossom into strikes. Though she'd riled him, he didn't lift a finger. He appeared to have conquered his anger and now stared back at her intensely but calmly.

She licked her lips, trying to force moisture back into her mouth. "I'm sorry. My words came from anger and fear. I didn't mean them to wound."

He gave a single nod. "I'm the one who's gotten myself into this mess by not being honest with you from the beginning."

She shifted her weight. "Why didn't you tell me?"

"I feared you wouldn't come."

Annabelle thought on that a moment. Would she have? "Why bring me here rather than take me to your family's plantation as you first said?"

"I was not...able to make that happen, and I thought you would be safer with me."

Something in her heart stirred, but she pushed it aside. "You came to find me, to see if I was the same woman you met at the army camp, and discovered the predicament I was in, so you brought up my father's arrangement in order to remove me from Rosswood?"

He rubbed the back of his neck. "In a manner of speaking, yes."

Her chest tightened. "So, your brother is not aware of any of this, is he?"

Matthew drew a long breath and stepped closer to her, placing his hand on her shoulder and forcing her to tilt her head to look into his eyes.

"I'm afraid not."

Her lids dropped closed.

"But I assure you," he hurried on, "George will be most pleased with you and the arrangement."

Annabelle swallowed hard, then stepped out of his grip. "Very well." Matthew meant well. She tried not to let herself think on the possibility that George might never make it out. "Though I don't see how I can court a man in prison."

Matthew's features hardened. "He won't be there long."

Lord forgive her. How could she be so selfish? She was so concerned about using this man for security that she was angry he was unable to provide it. The poor man suffered in a war prison! He could die there or....Wait. What had Matthew said? She snapped her gaze from the rug to his face. "And why is that?"

He shrugged, clearly uncomfortable. "Prisoner exchange."

Annabelle crossed her arms. "Even I know they no longer exchange Confederate prisoners."

Matthew pulled his hat onto his head. "Don't worry. We have certain…leverage."

With that, he stalked out the door and left Annabelle staring behind him.

Twenty-Eight

"The city is full, and all the office-seekers are buzzing around him like so many bees. Can't yet be done."
John H. Surratt

President Lincoln's second inauguration
Washington, D.C.
March 4, 1865

An hour later, Matthew gripped Annabelle's elbow and led her down the boarding house steps, his other hand holding the umbrella over their heads. Breakfast had been rather tense, but she'd taken it fairly well, all things considered. He'd expected a slap across the face or, at the very least, for her to storm out and leave him in the wake of her wrath. Instead, she seemed to be a forgiving woman, one with enough patience to cover them both.

He tightened his grip on her arm and told himself it was only to be sure she didn't slip. She looked up at him with those big, blue eyes and a smile sprang onto his lips before he could catch it.

She pulled her lower lip through her teeth. "There's a parade?"

His grin widened. "Have you ever seen one?"

"No. What do you suppose a parade for President Lincoln will have?"

He shrugged as they turned onto the crowded sidewalk. "I guess we'll see. Come on, let's catch the others."

They hurried down the sidewalk after O'Malley, their progress slowed by the press of too many bodies heading in the same direction. Annabelle stiffened, apparently uncomfortable with people jostling her.

Taking her hand firmly in his own, he drew her behind him and used his body to open the crowd. He gained a few annoyed looks, but mostly a jovial spirit permeated the city and the majority of the crowd let him pass freely. Their anticipation and jubilance proved contagious.

After what felt like an endless trek through the mud, they reached Pennsylvania Avenue and found a place at the edge of the road next to Harry and O'Malley, the Capitol across from them. They would be able to both watch the parade and see the president without changing locations.

Annabelle held her blue skirts nearly high enough to be scandalous. She offered him an excited smile before slipping her hand free from his grasp and rising on her toes to look down the road. She looked stunning in a proper gown. He never wanted to see her reduced to rags again.

"We'll be able to see him from here!" O'Malley said, rare excitement peppering his words and commanding Matthew's attention.

"Lincoln? Of course we will." Matthew chuckled and pointed at the Capitol. "He's going to be there on that decorated platform, just under the new dome."

O'Malley's face soured. "Not *him*," he hissed. "Booth."

"Who?"

O'Malley tugged on Matthew's lapel, urging him to lean in closer. "The one I told you about. He's close to the lanky fiend! The western woodcutter loves the theatre. Fool has even invited Booth right into the White House." He jutted his chin toward the platform. "He's going to be up there."

Matthew followed his gaze to the rows of reserved spaces just beneath the platform. He frowned. How did they expect to snatch the man in the middle of such a crowd? And, if this Booth were to do it, how could O'Malley help him from here?

Matthew simply nodded and voiced none of his thoughts. A trumpet blared, and he turned his attention down the road, where a band played a loud and merry tune. The crowd erupted with cheers, men waving their hats and women fluttering handkerchiefs.

Annabelle remained still, her hands secured to her dress to hold it above the muck, but her eyes lit up at the sound. She cast Matthew a quick glance and smiled, her childlike glee sending a pang into his heart. How could he have deceived her? Unlike the other women he'd known, this one seemed as genuine as she was kind. Well, except for that whole *Miss Smith* thing.

The band marched down the street, its drummers banging furiously and banners waving gleefully despite the dreary cloud cover. At least it had stopped raining. Only a fine mist hung in the air, as though reluctant to miss such a moment. Matthew snapped the umbrella closed and lowered it to his side.

Behind the band came troops of Colored soldiers in grand regalia, their faces shining with triumph. The people waved to them just the same as they had the band. A sense of witnessing something monumental settled on him as he assessed the crowd.

Dark-skinned people brushed shoulders with white men and women, and no one seemed to notice it. Not a one seemed to care. No separation, no distinction. Something haunting washed over Matthew, and he felt as if he were standing in the very center of a turning point in history. He pushed the thought aside. The South would never see the races shoulder to shoulder.

O'Malley growled. Matthew shook himself and looked to the man who had so drastically altered his own personal course of history. "Look at them! Acting like they are citizens." He spat. "How dare they think they are better than us?"

Matthew grunted. *Better?* He studied the faces flowing past, actually taking the time to analyze those who were different from him. These weren't the faces of gloaters, but faces of joy. They carried themselves with triumph. The kind that came after a long, hard battle finally won.

He sounded like a Yank! His father's admonishment of his boyhood questions returned. Things were as they had to be. How would Westerly survive if Lincoln's thirteenth amendment was ratified? Their business and all his father and grandfather had built would be lost.

His gaze jumped to Annabelle again. She dropped her skirts and waved her handkerchief as joyously as any Northerner in the crowd. How would he provide for her if she disagreed with their way of life? He jerked his thoughts to a halt. That was for George to consider.

A carriage rolled down the street, and the cheers swelled to a near-deafening volume. O'Malley gripped his arm, lifting himself onto his toes to speak in Matthew's ear.

"He's not really in there, you know."

Matthew frowned. "What?"

"Only his wife. He's already inside. Been there all morning signing papers."

How would O'Malley know that? He cut his eyes to the platform at the Capitol. Maybe this Booth truly did have access to Lincoln. No sooner had he thought it than O'Malley pointed. "There!"

Matthew followed the length of O'Malley's arm but could not identify the man he indicated from the crowd of people flowing onto the reserved platform.

"Yes, yes," O'Malley mumbled, mostly to himself. "Of course. He came with Lucy. *That's* how he did it."

A roar of applause shook the air and spread through the people packed together for as far as Matthew could see. People flowed onto the street in the wake of the parade and pressed forward, trying to move closer to the Capitol. Only his height allowed Matthew to see over the swarm of cheering Yankees. If he had to guess, he would say over thirty thousand had come to witness the second inaugural address. Finally, the applause died away on the outer fringe of the throng, like how Matthew imagined a sweeping ocean wave might eventually crash and then dissipate.

Abraham Lincoln stepped up to the podium. Overhead, the cloud cover suddenly broke, and a stream of bright sunlight bathed the president in a splendid glow. People mumbled to one another, and a few pointed to the sky.

The president's clear voice rang out across the restless crowd, and in that surreal moment, Annabelle Ross gripped his hand like they belonged together.

"Fellow countrymen!"

The onlookers stilled, and awe washed across them. What manner of man could command such a presence? A strange feeling pulsed through him. An unnatural mixture of hope and resignation.

The most controversial man ever to lead the states, Lincoln had brought this war upon them. Matthew ignored O'Malley's murmurings.

O'Malley and his band railed against the Union president. Swarms of Southerners called him a tyrant. Had he ever truly considered his own thoughts about this tall, melancholy figure he was supposed to abduct? Lincoln didn't look the part of the evil warmonger Matthew had pictured.

Something about that unsettled him deeply.

"At this second appearing to take oath of the presidential office, there is less occasion for an extended address than there was at the first." The clear words washed across them and held Matthew's rapt attention. "Then a statement somewhat in detail of a course to be pursued seemed fitting and proper. Now, at the expiration of four years—during which public declarations have been constantly called forth on *every* point and phase of the great contest which still absorbs the attention and engrosses the energies of the nation—little that is new could be presented."

Matthew stilled. This man, who seemed in every way humble and unassuming, spoke with great power. Lincoln addressed the crowd with fervor about the pain of war, declared none had wanted it, and then pronounced them all guilty of letting the war come.

He blamed them all. Not just the South.

Then Lincoln spoke on the issue of slavery and, surprisingly, Matthew found his heart stirred by the passion that lit the president's words.

He glanced at Annabelle, whose eyes glistened, and then at several other rapt faces full of compassion. Had he missed something vital?

"Both read from the same Bible and pray to the same God, and each invokes His aid against the other."

Matthew swallowed hard, the truth of the words cold in his veins. Had they not asked the Almighty to aid them in slaying soldiers who were once their fellow countrymen? Had he not prayed that God would see the enemy bathed in blood and dead upon the earth? Guilt wrapped tight fingers around his chest, restricting his air.

"It may seem strange that *any* man should dare to ask a just God's assistance in wringing his bread from the sweat of other men's faces."

Matthew's heart quickened.

"But, let us judge not, lest we be judged."

O'Malley swore under his breath, but Matthew could barely hear him over the pounding of blood in his ears. What was this war to a God who loved all—slave as much as free? North as much as South?

"The prayers of both could not be answered. That of neither has been answered fully. The Almighty has His own purposes. 'Woe unto the world because of offenses; for it must needs be that offenses come, but woe to that man by whom the offense cometh.'"

The president spoke fervently, the light around him brightening the crowd and his stirring words intermittently interrupted with the spatter of applause. The anticipation swelled to bursting, and the president lifted his hand.

"With malice toward none. With charity for all. With firmness in the right as God gives us to see the right—let us strive on to finish the work we are in! To bind up the nation's wounds, to care for him who shall have borne the battle and for his widow and his orphan. To do all that may achieve and cherish a just and lasting peace among ourselves and with all nations!"

Cheers erupted around them. Annabelle waved her handkerchief fiercely, a small cry jumping from her lips. The people pushed forward in a vain effort to get closer to the man who'd delivered the most stirring speech Matthew had ever witnessed.

O'Malley caught his eye and gave a solemn nod. "Don't worry, my friend. Soon, he'll get what he deserves."

Matthew studied Lincoln's exalted face and tried to ignore the heavy weight that settled in his gut like a boulder.

Twenty-Nine

"Lincoln attends a review on the 7th. We have it all
arranged now, and nothing can fail."
John H. Surratt

Surratt Boarding House
Washington, D.C.
March 5, 1865

nnabelle lay awake in the darkness and waited for the
sun to warm the window of her attic room. Yesterday
had been a whirlwind of information and activity. She'd been so
caught up in all the emotions of the president's inauguration and
the flurry of activity that she'd been exhausted upon their return
and had gone to bed last night without even taking the evening
meal.

It would be a little while before Peggy awoke. She finally
had a few moments to mull over Captain Daniels and his
shocking confession. She rolled over onto her back and drew
the quilt up underneath her chin.

George Daniels was in prison. He had no idea Matthew
intended to match them together. Annabelle stifled a groan. And
the worst of it?

It should have been Matthew.

She'd figured it out, but had pushed the idea away. The truth remained. Father planned for her to court the youngest Daniels brother, the one five years her senior.

Five. Not three.

She played the conversations over in her mind. The first time she'd asked, Matthew seemed surprised she'd called George the younger brother, and then he'd grown strangely uncomfortable. The next time, though she prodded, he circumvented any direct answer about birth order with a vague quip about three years separating the brothers' births.

That led her to only one conclusion.

He knew. And he preferred to shift her onto his brother. She chewed her lip. She couldn't confront him and have his private rejection aired between them! Something in her ached, but she stomped out the ember of regret before it could burst into flame. She would *not* care for a man who didn't want her. Besides, the marriage served one purpose. Saving Rosswood. So long as George proved decent, it didn't matter.

Light streamed through the window, coating the small room in warm rose and amber. Peggy groaned and stretched. Annabelle could sleep through a sunrise, but Peggy never did.

"Morning, Miss Belle. You're up early."

"Must be because I went to bed with the sun."

Peggy got up and quickly dressed, finishing her morning ritual by winding a red scarf around her head. She tied on her apron and smoothed it down. Her eyes sought Annabelle's. "I'm right sorry."

The sorrow in Peggy's tone had Annabelle tossing off the warm quilt. "Whatever for?"

"I tried to see if I could get some chocolate to make you a

pie, but that lady's a—" Peggy stopped short and shook her head. "She won't get me none."

Annabelle swung her feet off the bed and cringed when her toes touched the cold floor. "I don't need a pie, Peggy."

Peggy put her hands on her hips. "I've made you that pie on your birthday every year since you was five."

In the chaos, she'd forgotten. Tears pricked her eyes. Peggy never did. Even in the throes of war and the disarray of the house being used as a hospital, Peggy had marked the day of Annabelle's birth each year with a chocolate pie. How she'd managed it remained a secret.

She crossed the room and wrapped her arms around Peggy's shoulders. "The fact that you keep track of the days means the most."

Peggy shook her head with a sad smile. Then she gathered Annabelle's freshly laundered garments and helped her dress. Peggy plaited her hair, twisted it into a simple roll at the nape of her neck, and secured it with pins.

With hopes of an early breakfast or perhaps some coffee, Annabelle descended the stairs. Hushed voices came from the front room. She paused midway down to the parlor and listened but could not make out the words.

What were they up to?

Annabelle inched silently down the stairs. A soft tinkling sound indicated someone stirred sugar into a cup. Annabelle pressed herself up against the wall in the foyer and edged as close to the doorway as she dared. The inviting scent of coffee drifted to her nostrils, and her stomach responded with a low growl.

Horrified, she pressed the palm of her hand into it and

willed it to silence.

"If we don't do something soon, it will be too late," David O'Malley said.

Annabelle chewed her lip.

"Yeah, but how are you gonna do it? We've been trying, but he's always surrounded."

Harry. Annabelle's brows gathered. Who were they talking about?

"It could have been over for good yesterday, you know."

"Yeah? And how's that? He was in the middle of thousands of people," Harry grumbled.

O'Malley sighed. Annabelle wished she could angle herself so she could see their faces, but that would be too risky.

"That he was. But I ask you, who stood above him? With a perfect angle?"

Harry was quiet a moment. "That actor fellow?"

"Precisely!"

"He wanted to try to snatch him there?"

Snatch him?

"He says he had the opportunity to kill him, if he'd wanted."

Annabelle's heart pounded. Murder! She'd suspected they were spies, and they were here in Washington to carry out some plan—why else would fervent Southerners go to such lengths to reach the Union Capital?—but murder?

"I don't like that fella, O'Malley. I don't think he's stable."

"Watch your tongue, man!" O'Malley snapped. "He has accomplished more for the cause than you have. Without him, we wouldn't have someone close enough to get the information we need."

"But, he's talking about murder," Harry insisted.

At least one of them has some sense!

"It won't come to that. All we have to do is carry out the plan."

Annabelle let out the whoosh of breath. Oh, heavens! These men planned something dangerous. She should find help and—

They stopped talking. Had they heard her? Her heart pounded furiously. She stepped a little farther from the door. Could she make it up the steps without being seen?

"It's all arranged now," Mr. O'Malley barked. "We won't fail. Come, man, we've gotten this far."

Relief weakened her knees and she pressed into the wall. She watched the staircase. What would she do if she were discovered listening in on some nefarious plan?

Her mind whirled. What had Lieutenant Monroe said? She must get the message to *one of them*. The plan had to be carried out.

No! Monroe had been a part of this scheme? And by delivering his message, she'd not only been labeled a Union spy but had helped with a plan for someone's murder?

Memories fell into place, stealing her breath. Matthew chasing her through the woods. Matthew hunting her down and coming to Rosswood. Matthew lying about her coming to Washington to meet his brother.

Her mouth went dry.

Whatever had been in that message, it had something to do with these men and their plot. Their questions regarding the soldiers she'd cared for. It all made sense now.

Had Matthew known about her true identity all along? Had they tracked her since she'd first intercepted their spy plans? No. Their *murder* plans?

She ground her thoughts to a halt. *Listen!*

"Word came this very morning with the dawn," O'Malley said. "He'll be going to the Soldiers' Home on the seventh without escort. We'll intercept him along the way. Then we take the route to Richmond."

It had to be someone important. An official, perhaps? An officer? She needed more information. She couldn't go to the authorities with vague accusations and risk discovery. Worse, what if they also accused her of being a spy?

Heavy footsteps sounded from the back of the house. Annabelle's heart thudded. *Come on! Who is it?*

"We are soon to make history, my friend!" O'Malley said.

"The South will sing our praises!" Harry replied, the laugh in his voice turning Annabelle's stomach.

The footsteps thudded closer. She would have to move before—

"And their president will find his due in Richmond," O'Malley growled.

Annabelle dashed to the stairs, leaping them two at a time. Halfway up, she whirled around and attempted to appear as though she just now made her way downstairs. No sooner had she made the turn than Matthew stepped into the narrow hall.

"Good morning, Miss Ross!" he said a little too loudly, his gaze cutting to the front room.

Scoundrel!

She forced a serene smile. "Good morning, Captain Daniels."

Matthew came to stand at the bottom of the stairs, and Annabelle stopped her descent two steps up. A good vantage, since she didn't have to tilt her head back to study his face.

Accusations and scathing demands for answers crowded her mouth, but she bit them back.

"Did you sleep well?"

She dipped her chin. "I'm adequately rested to return home."

Matthew shifted his weight. "Well, that wouldn't be wise, would it? Seeing as how the situation with your grandfather hasn't changed."

She clamped her hands together in front of her to keep them from shaking. They wouldn't let her go.

"Then we're traveling to your family's plantation?"

"Yes, of course."

Liar.

"We'll just be here a day or so more to rest after such a long trip."

"Why did we come here at all?" The question leapt from her lips before she could stop it.

Matthew rubbed the back of his neck. Annabelle forced her gaze to stay on him and not to wander to the other room. The men inside remained silent. Were they still in there?

"As I said, I wished to keep you safe."

"Yes, so you said. But what you did *not* say is why you came here to begin with, if your brother was never here."

Hush! You will give yourself away!

Annabelle ignored the inner voice vying for her attention.

He held her gaze, his golden brown eyes boring into hers. "I'm here to see if I can find out which prison holds George. And, once I find it, I'll do whatever I must to get him out."

Annabelle studied him. He seemed sincere. How could he lie so easily? Unless he thought that Lincoln would release his brother in exchange for freedom? Was he truly that foolish? That desperate?

Desperate men were dangerous. She took a step backward and nearly fell on her skirts. Matthew moved to grab her, but she hiked the skirt and snatched it out from under her feet. She took another step backward, avoiding the hand he held out.

Rejection skittered across his face for only a second before he smoothed it away.

"If you will excuse me, I think I'll return upstairs for a moment before we gather for breakfast."

"Of course." He inclined his head, all too eager to get her out of the way.

Annabelle climbed the steps with as much calm as she could muster. When she reached the top, she dashed to the upper door and slipped inside. As she leaned against the latched door, her pounding heart birthed rapid breaths in her lungs.

"Miss Belle! What's wrong?"

Annabelle's eyes flew open. Peggy dropped the undergarments she'd been folding.

"Captain Daniels." She forced her rapid breathing to calm. "I don't think he ever intended to see me matched to his brother."

Peggy grabbed her shoulders. "What do you mean?"

Annabelle blinked away the tears forming in her eyes. What to tell Peggy? The truth? If she did, would Peggy stop the plan already forming in her mind?

"Peggy, I think they are spies."

Peggy's dark brows drew low. "We've been thinking that since the start."

"Remember that message, the one I got off the dead soldier

we buried at home?"

"The one with the funny writing?"

"Yes. I think they lied and have kept me with them because of it."

Peggy paced, the tension in her stiff movements increasing Annabelle's worry. "But that makes no sense. What are the odds that Captain Daniels would be one of them *and* show up at Rosswood? The Daniels family *is* the one your daddy wanted to match you with. He didn't make that up."

Annabelle scowled. "I don't understand it either. But it doesn't matter. If George is a prisoner of war and Matthew is involved in a spy ring, we don't need to be here."

"You right about that. But where do we go?"

"Home, I suppose. Where else?"

"We're gonna travel all the way back to Mississippi whilst there's a war still going on?" Peggy threw up her hands. "It was bad enough getting up here with them men and they weapons. Ain't no way a Southern lady and an old slave woman is gonna make it back to Mississippi on our own."

What were they going to do? "We have to get out of here."

And try to stop them.

"Come on." Annabelle squared her tense shoulders. "Let's go out while they're at breakfast and find a stagecoach or something for safe passage."

"How you gonna pay for that?"

Annabelle drew a steadying breath, then crossed the room and grabbed the carpetbag. She reached inside the pocket sewed into the liner and drew out the small pouch she'd hidden inside.

"With this." She held up her mother's necklace, its pendant catching the morning light and bursting into sparkles.

"No! You ain't trading your momma's diamond for a coach."

Annabelle dropped the diamond into her palm and let the gold chain fold in upon itself. She gripped it tightly. "I think Momma would rather see me safe without this trinket than dead, still clutching it."

Peggy was silent for a moment. "Oh, Miss Belle. What happened to the life you was supposed to have?"

Annabelle gave a wry smile. "War."

Peggy's features grew resolute. "I say we go north, not south."

"Why?"

"They still fighting. It ain't safe."

Annabelle clasped the necklace around her throat. "Where would we go? No one will be willing to take us in." She stuffed the diamond under her bodice.

"Your momma had family in New York."

Annabelle grunted. "You know they won't help us."

"They might."

"I'm a *Southerner*."

"You're family. One in trouble, with half Yankee blood and a whole Yankee heart. Why would they turn you away?"

"Shhhh. Not so loud. If any of them hear you, we won't ever get away from here."

Peggy snapped her mouth shut.

Maybe Peggy had a point. Would her mother's family forget the bad memories between them? Or, would they still shun her because of her father, a man they had never liked for taking their only daughter far away? She'd only seen her grandmother twice in her early years.

Annabelle would have to worry with that later. "All right. Let's go."

She had a presidential abduction to thwart.

Thirty

"He goes out unattended, and we shall be enough…"
John H. Surratt

$\mathcal{A}$nnabelle stalked out the front door without anyone noticing. If she hurried, it might be a few more moments before anyone thought to summon her. And if they were lucky, she and Peggy would be too deep into the city for anyone to be able to find them. Behind her, Peggy lugged the carpetbag stuffed with everything they could fit. Peggy had insisted on bringing it with them, just in case.

The extra blankets the spies had given them had to be left behind, though Annabelle hated to discard something so valuable. She wore both her paletot and her mantle to shield her from this brutal northern winter. It would have to do.

Annabelle tried to avoid as much of the mud as she could, glad she had grabbed her boots from home. They might be a bit worn and were not nearly as comfortable as her slippers, but they kept her feet dry.

"You know where we're going?"

Annabelle startled at Peggy's voice behind her. She rarely ever spoke to Annabelle in public. Annabelle halted and took a step back, falling into stride with Peggy on the busy sidewalk.

Peggy looked at her incredulously. "What you doing?" she whispered.

"You're not a slave. You can walk with me so we can talk."

Peggy's eyes lit, but she shook her head. "Ain't proper."

"Says the woman who didn't see scores of Colored folks standing shoulder to shoulder with white people at the inauguration yesterday."

Peggy cut her eyes at Annabelle. "That true?"

"Why would I lie to you?"

The words chafed as soon as she spoke them. She hadn't really been lying to Peggy, had she? She'd only left out some things.

Lord, forgive me.

She needed to tell Peggy the truth. Annabelle leaned close to Peggy's ear. "They're going to abduct President Lincoln and take him to Richmond."

Peggy stumbled to a halt, causing several people behind them on the sidewalk to jump out of the way. They shot annoyed glances at Annabelle, but she ignored them. She grabbed Peggy's hand and pulled her into the covered doorway of a watch shop.

"What in the heavens?" Peggy wailed.

"Hush! Don't call attention."

Peggy put both hands on her head, dropping the carpetbag with a thud. "I knew they was doing something bad. But, lands, not this!"

Annabelle smiled and nodded to the strangers passing by with curious looks. "Contain yourself, Peggy," Annabelle said through her plastered-on smile.

Peggy straightened, snatched up the carpetbag, and stepped back out into the flow of pedestrians so quickly that Annabelle had to scramble to gain her side.

"We've got to tell someone," Peggy whispered, keeping her eyes forward.

"That's what I'm trying to do."

"Then we find some law officers."

Annabelle nodded to a gentleman who tilted his hat to her. "And tell them what? We're involved in a spy ring, but we're turning on them?"

Peggy glared at her. "*What* then?"

They stepped around a large mud puddle, and Annabelle glanced behind them to see if they were followed. As best she could tell, all the faces looked unfamiliar.

"All we need to do is make sure someone close to Lincoln knows about it," Annabelle said with more confidence than she felt. "Then they can handle it."

They stepped around another mud puddle and turned a corner, passing in front of Ford's Theatre. Advertisements for the play *Clark in de Boots* graced the side of the building with bold words and bright colors. Annabelle had no idea what such a title might foretell, but if she'd had a dollar to spare—and wasn't trying to thwart a presidential abduction—she would very much have liked to see a performance.

"You need to ask directions."

"What?"

Peggy looked incredulous.

"Oh, of course." Ninny. How could she be enjoying sights? A man's life was in danger. "Excuse me, sir?" Annabelle reached out and touched the arm of the nearest person. The older gentleman glanced down at her fingers, startled. Annabelle quickly dropped her hand. "Forgive me. Do you happen to know where I might secure a traveling coach?"

He narrowed his eyes, no doubt judging her accent. "Turn right at this corner," he said, gesturing to the end of the nicely square block they seemed so fond of in Washington. "Then go down four more street crossings, and take another right. Pumphrey's stable is on your left. If you reach the National Hotel, you went too far."

"Thank you."

The man tipped his hat and stepped around her.

"Oh! Wait!" He turned back. "Do you know where they keep records of the war prisons?"

Peggy gasped. The man blinked at her then stepped close, lowering his voice so near her ear that it tickled. Her heart pounded.

"As it turns out, I happen to be on the same side as you." The old man glanced around before he spoke again. "Who did you lose, my dear?"

Annabelle let her bottom lip quiver. "They took my...betrothed. I only wish to know where he went."

Sympathy filled the man's eyes. "A lady won't be able to sashay in there with her Southern charm and get that information from the Yanks."

Her heart sank. "Oh."

He wagged his brows. "But... who knows, maybe you could talk some young fellow into fetching it for you."

She ducked her head low. What would people think of them, huddled like this on the street? She took his arm and started down the sidewalk. He didn't protest but escorted her in the direction of the stables. Peggy grumbled something behind them, but followed.

"Would you be so kind as to tell me where I might go to find this office?" she asked, keeping her eyes on the people they passed. How did one tell who was loyal to what side?

"You'll have to go to the office of William Hoffman, Commissary General of Prisoners. It's not far." The man nodded to others on the sidewalk and steered her around a small puddle.

He kindly escorted her a few streets over. They came to a stop in front of a large brick building. The old man patted her hand. "Here we are, dear. I do hope you find what you need."

"Thank you, sir."

He pointed his finger, turning stern. "Don't expect too much out of them."

"Yes, sir. I won't."

He raised his cane to her and turned opposite, hurrying away and leaving Annabelle and Peggy staring after him.

"What in heaven's name were you thinking?" Peggy whispered.

"I think we should give it a try."

Peggy gave her a sour look. "You lost your senses?"

Annabelle dismissed the comment and assessed the formidable building. "You wait here. I'm going inside."

"Fool thing to do."

"Perhaps. But what could it hurt?" She didn't wait for Peggy to answer. Annabelle squared her shoulders and strode up the steps.

Inside, she found several empty desks and a solitary young man with a pair of spectacles perched on his nose. He studied a stack of papers before him.

She waited for a moment, but he didn't notice her. "Um, excuse me, sir?"

His head snapped up, and he scrambled to his feet, his crisp blue uniform tidy. "Yes? What can I do for you?"

Annabelle tried her best to come across the polished lady her father would have wanted. "I've come to speak to General Hoffman."

The fellow came around his desk, his polished boots clicking on the floor. "Do you have an appointment?"

She twisted her hands. "Well, no, but—"

"Then I'm afraid you can't see him." He made his way back around the desk and sat down.

She waited until he was seated and leveled his brown eyes on her. "Perhaps you could help me?"

"Oh, no, no. I don't think—"

Annabelle cut him off. "Please, I just need a simple thing. I suspect a fellow as smart as you knows where they keep all the records?"

He narrowed his eyes. "I do."

Annabelle let her shoulders droop. "I'm very sorry. I shouldn't be so presumptuous. It's just that, well, we don't know where he is, and…." She put her hand to her mouth and turned away.

"Miss?"

She looked back at him, dabbing at her eyes.

"Who are you looking for?"

Annabelle thought quickly. *Forgive me for another lie.* "My foolish brother. I can't believe he would join the Confederates. It made Momma nearly go mad to have one son on each side."

The man's eyes softened.

"He's been taken prisoner, and poor Momma... I just think if she knew where he was, then she would be more at ease, you know?"

The young Union soldier straightened his glasses, picked up a writing pen, and dipped it into a well of ink. "What's your brother's name?"

"George Daniels."

"Rank?"

Her heart fluttered. "I don't know."

He sat back in his chair. "What *do* you know, miss? I'll need more than a name."

She scoured her memory for every detail Matthew had mentioned. "He was in General Forrest's contingent. To our best knowledge, George served in a company located in Mississippi, somewhere around Jefferson County. That's where he was captured."

The Union man scribbled it down. "This might be enough."

"Oh!" She clasped her hands. "Thank you, sir!"

"Do not thank me yet, Miss Daniels."

A shiver ran down her spine.

"I'll see what I can find." He offered her a tight smile and pushed his spectacles to the bridge of his thin nose. "I understand your pain. My cousin joined the Confederacy as well. Tore my uncle up something bad."

"I appreciate the effort. Anything you can find would mean so much."

"It may take some time." He folded the paper and placed it on his tidy desk. "Where might I reach you?"

"I'm staying at the Surratt Boarding House."

"If I find anything, I'll send a message."

Elated, Annabelle offered him her best smile. "Thank you!"

He nodded and turned back to his work.

She scrambled out the door, beaming at Peggy. "I might be able to find George."

"Really?" Peggy cast her an incredulous glance.

"He's going to try."

Peggy gave her a knowing smile. "That's right good, Miss Belle. I hope he finds something."

Annabelle left the office of the Commissary General of Prisoners with more hope for a good outcome than she had for her next task. How was she going to stop an abduction?

They found the stables exactly where the man had indicated, only a few streets away from the Capitol itself. She paused out front.

How would she find someone to warn the president before she left? And how could she leave now, knowing she could find George? Maybe Matthew had been swept into this the same as she had. What if finding George stopped Matthew, and that stopped the abduction? And possibly a murder?

As if reading her thoughts, Peggy said, "Come on, Miss Belle. Let's see if that necklace will buy you a proper passage. Then we'll see if we can get a message to that man before they try and run off with him."

First, they would find a driver to take them to New York. And, well, coachmen would be familiar with everything in the city, so maybe one of them could direct her to where she might be able to contact someone at the White House. The task was too big, and she too small.

Lord, we sure could use Your help.

She squared her shoulders, stepped into the stable, and

looked around to find someone to help her.

"Miss? You need something?"

Annabelle smiled at a young man behind her. He tipped the hat stuffed down on a head full of curly, brown hair.

"Are you employed at this stable?"

"Me? Naw. But I come here often enough when we need horses. I might can help you find what you need."

"I'm looking to hire out a coach to take me to New York. I don't suppose you're a driver?"

He grinned. "I'm a driver, all right, but I don't think my employer would let me drive you to New York, though I sure would if I could."

He winked at her, and she dipped her chin. "Well, thank you anyway." She turned to keep looking, but something made her pause. She looked back at the young man. "Who do you drive for?"

He gave a small bow. "I'm Thomas Clark. Personal driver for President Lincoln."

Annabelle's heart skipped over itself. How could it be possible?

Peggy's eyes bulged. "It's an answer to prayer!"

Annabelle stared at her, and the young man looked confused. His face reddened. Annabelle stepped closer, hoping she could trust him. What choice did she have? "Do you truly know the president?" she whispered.

The fellow scratched at his chin. "Well, I don't rightly *know* him, but yeah, I'm his driver. Been so for two months now."

"Mr. Clark!" Annabelle clasped her hands together. "I'm in great need of your help!"

He tilted his head. "I already told you I can't take you to

New York." He scrunched his nose. "And please, don't ask me to introduce you to Mr. Lincoln. I can't do that. It's amazing how many folks ask."

Annabelle wagged her head. "I don't need you to introduce us. I only need to give him a message."

Mr. Clark's placating smile flashed straight teeth. "You can send it through the post."

"This is a matter of grave importance. It must be delivered immediately."

The humor left the man's face. "Look, miss, I don't know what kind of games you're playing, but I need to get on with my duties."

She grabbed his arm. "Please, just listen." She glanced around the stable and, seeing no one other than the three of them, hurried on. "I overheard a plot meant to harm the president. I'm looking to find someone who can stop it."

He raised his bushy brows. "Lady, you said you were looking to go to New York. Besides, if you have something important to report, there are plenty of law officers you can tell."

He pulled his arm free and began to walk off. Annabelle hurried along behind him. "I know he is going to attend a review on the seventh at the Soldiers' Home!"

Mr. Clark stopped and looked down at her, his brows pulling together. "How would you know that? It hasn't been announced."

"I told you. I know their plot. They're going to take him on his way there."

Mr. Clark scrubbed the scruff on his cheek and let out a low whistle. "Oh, man. Why are you telling me this?" He narrowed his eyes. "How'd you know I'd be here?"

She sighed. "I didn't know you'd be here, or even who you were. Please, believe me. I cannot go to a policeman. I'm in danger and need to get to New York without being detained."

He studied her a moment but didn't offer a protest.

"All I need you to do is take a different route. Please, Mr. Clark. You're the driver. Surely you can do that much? If I'm wrong, what would it hurt? But, if I'm not, you may very well save the president's life."

He swallowed hard, then gave a small nod. "I'll see what I can do."

Thirty-One

"The suddenness of the whole thing will prevent any attempt at rescue until it is too late. And once safely in Richmond, the independence of the South is certain, and my fortune made."

John H. Surratt

$\mathcal{M}$atthew diverted the matron's questions and asserted Annabelle was probably still just tired from the long journey and the excitement of the inauguration. All through breakfast, he kept her at bay. But O'Malley watched him too closely, his sharp eyes always returning to Matthew when he thought Matthew wasn't looking.

It came as no surprise, then, that when Matthew rose from the table and started for the front door, so did O'Malley.

"Where are you going? To locate your lost little flower?"

The muscles in his jaw tightened, but Matthew kept his face passive. "That would prove unnecessary. No, what I seek is a barber."

O'Malley cocked a brow. "I suspect you doubt she's actually here, same as I. Why then, I wonder, carry on such a charade at the table?"

Matthew stuffed his hand in his pocket. "Why rouse animosity toward her? She's not even aware of your schemes. If she went anywhere, it's likely only to take the opportunity to see Washington."

O'Malley didn't look convinced. "If she doesn't return soon, it's on you. I don't care what you do with her after this is finished, but until then, I want everyone close."

Matthew drew his lips into a line and stalked out the door. O'Malley was paranoid. What harm could Annabelle possibly do? She probably just needed a little time away from male company, or she wanted to see the city.

He offered himself any number of reasons as to why she would have slipped out without a word. None of them felt valid. The look on her face this morning when he'd found her on the stairs didn't bode well, but she wasn't his captive, and he wouldn't treat her as one. He shoved his hat low on his head and went in search of a hot shave and a haircut.

He'd almost refused the notes O'Malley had pressed into his hand last night. A stipend, O'Malley had said, in case Matthew needed anything to aid with the cause. A trip the barber to avoid looking like a vagabond would have to do. What else would he spend it on? O'Malley claimed Matthew would restrain the president, but since they planned on overtaking Lincoln's carriage and trapping him inside, he couldn't see what part he really played.

He wandered down the street, nodding at bundled-up pedestrians. An unexpected ache settled on him for unappreciated spring days spent at Westerly.

Two streets later, a silversmith's sign caught his eye, and he ducked into the store before giving it any real thought.

"Morning, sir! How may I be of service?" A young apprentice stepped out from behind a display counter, his thick apron smeared with soot.

Matthew felt foolish. "Uh, I...." He shrugged. "I'm not sure what I'm looking for."

"Trying to decide on a gift for a young lady, I assume?" said a voice behind him.

An older gentleman with a set of thick spectacles perched on his nose wiped his hands on an apron identical to the young apprentice's and then held one out to Matthew.

Matthew shook his hand. "I suppose you help many confused men?"

"Quite." The shopkeeper's eyes glimmered with humor. "I have a nice necklace any young woman would swoon over."

"I was thinking something...different."

The shopkeeper scratched his head, then waved a hand. "Come with me."

Matthew followed him through the shop and into the workroom beyond, where a smelting fire warmed the air considerably.

"Perhaps this?" The man lifted a small figure up for Matthew to inspect.

He took it and turned it over in his hand, guessing at the weight. It would take nearly all his notes...but, wouldn't it be worth her smile? "It might do."

They haggled on a price until Matthew still retained a few of his greenbacks to cover a shave. After paying the man, wrapping his gift in a handkerchief, and stuffing it in his pocket, Matthew pushed open the door and headed back into the cold.

He found a barber a few streets over and allowed himself the long-lost luxury of a good shave. He didn't even feel guilty about turning over the last of his funds. He'd become a deserter for O'Malley. A good shave hardly made them even.

When Matthew returned to the house, it had erupted in a flurry of activity. He closed the door behind him and watched quietly for a moment as O'Malley and his lackey wrapped several rifles in a blanket. O'Malley gestured to Harry. "Take these and send them on ahead. Mrs. Surratt has made arrangements for our man to store them at her home in Surrattsville. They will be there, should we need them."

Harry nodded to Matthew as he walked past him and toward the rear of the house. Matthew addressed O'Malley. "What's he doing?"

O'Malley regarded him like one did a dullard, then the practiced smile fell on his features once again. "I thought you also heard my instructions."

"I'm just wondering why you need a storage of weapons sent to another town when we're traveling to Richmond."

O'Malley waved his hand. "Merely a precaution. It's a shame you missed them. It would have been good for us."

"Missed who?"

"Mrs. Surratt's son, John, and Mr. Booth himself."

"That actor?"

"More importantly, the man who's given us the necessary information to carry out our plan. But no matter, you'll see both tomorrow, and by the time this is finished, you'll be well acquainted. Think on it, man! Two days from now, we will all be heroes!"

"Did he give you the information on my brother?"

O'Malley's brows drew together, dashing the pride from his features. "What?"

Matthew took a step closer, his height towering over the smaller man. O'Malley looked unconcerned. "Oh, of course. I did ask, as I told you I would. Booth is working on it. Takes time to find out these things, you know."

Was this the same man he'd shared a fire and hardtack with? One of the men who'd laughed with him over a deck of cards as they'd tried to pass the grueling winter days? It had been only a few weeks, but that life seemed ages ago. Much had changed. But then, had he ever really known this fervent man with something haunting in his eyes?

In that moment, Matthew knew that O'Malley would never divert his attention into finding George's location. His obsession focused on Lincoln.

"Why do you hate him so?" Matthew asked softly.

O'Malley feigned confusion. "What?"

"Something tells me more than patriotism drives you."

Sunlight drifted through the windows, creating dust motes and lighting O'Malley's flashing eyes. The room grew stifling underneath the palatable tension.

Suddenly, O'Malley's façade dropped.

"We all should *hate* him!" O'Malley bellowed, his face darkening. "Who sent soldiers into our lands to destroy our homes and our families? Who unleashed Sherman upon us to burn all that stood in his way?" O'Malley's eyes bulged in his reddened face.

Matthew took a step back. "What did you lose, David?"

"Everything," he growled. "When you go home to find your crops smoldering and your burned son lying in your dead wife's arms, *then* you can tell me if he is someone to hate."

O'Malley spun on his heel and left Matthew staring after

him. He'd known O'Malley had lost his family before he'd joined the Confederate Army. He'd also seen O'Malley engage the enemy with an intensity few men had shared. But he'd focused all of his loss and anger on a single man? He blamed Lincoln for it all?

What would he do if he were left alone with the president?

"Captain Daniels?" Annabelle stood in the doorway. Sunlight danced off her golden hair and across her lovely face.

He offered a tight smile. No matter what, he had to keep her away from O'Malley. "We missed you at breakfast."

Her eyes bore into his. "I'd like to speak with you, please."

"Of course." He gestured to the couch.

Annabelle twisted her hands in front of her and glanced around. "Somewhere else, perhaps?"

Matthew offered his arm. "A walk?"

She hesitated, then nodded. "But not too far."

He held open the door, and they descended the steps on the front of the house. She released his arm as soon as she stepped onto the raised sidewalk and strode forward. Matthew matched his stride to hers and clasped his hands behind his back.

"What are you not telling me?"

Her clipped words knifed through him. What could he say that would both gain her trust and still keep her from danger? They were nearly finished. He would see them to Richmond, be sure O'Malley kept his word about George, and then be finished with them all. She glanced at him, and the mistrust in her gaze flooded him with guilt.

"I'm not sure what you mean."

Her look of disappointment was worse than her suspicion. "I grow tired of these games."

His Adam's apple bobbed. "I know. But please believe me when I tell you I have only your best interest at heart."

She snorted. "I should be the one to decide that, not you."

Again she cut him with double-edged truths.

She looked up at him with eyes as blue as the sky, and he nearly stumbled into a man walking the opposite direction. The fellow raised his cane at Matthew and grumbled something before passing on the other side of Annabelle.

"I shouldn't have brought you here," Matthew said low. "I came to reach an informant who would be able to tell me where my brother is being held. I'm told they are working on it. Once I have the information I need, then I'll go find George. I sincerely hope you'll stick with me just a bit longer, Annabelle. I want to keep my word."

They made the block and approached the boarding house again. Annabelle said nothing more and ascended the steps without his aid. When she reached the landing, she searched his face so earnestly his insides twisted.

Please. I cannot give you knowledge that might see you arrested.

He took the steps two at a time and reached into his pocket. "Here. I have something for you."

She stared at the bundle in his outstretched hand. "What's this?"

"Just a little something for your birthday."

Her eyes widened, and he couldn't help the smile that spread onto his lips.

"You remembered?"

"Of course." He shrugged. "It's not much."

She gently took it from his hand and unwrapped the cloth, revealing a small silver horse about the size of her palm. He'd been right. The twinkle her smile brought into her eyes was worth all he'd spent.

"It's quite pretty."

"It's a token of your bravery during our long trip here. I hope that each time you look at this little horse, you'll remember how you made it through war and strife. How you survived many days upon horseback and too many nights outdoors." Her lips parted slightly, and heat stirred within him. "I hope you'll look at this trinket and, no matter what happens, you'll always remember that you're the strongest woman I've ever known. You'll remember that you're capable of anything."

Tears filled her eyes, and one spilled down her cheek. She quickly wiped it away with her glove. She drew a long breath and clutched the trinket to her chest. "Oh, Matthew."

The way she said his name filled him with longing, and he stepped closer. She looked up at him, her bright eyes blinking rapidly. She ran her tongue over her bottom lip, drawing his attention to her mouth.

Without giving it proper thought, he lowered his head a fraction. Suddenly she gasped and took a step back, hurt chasing away the light in her eyes. She shook her head.

"Goodbye, Matthew."

She dashed into the house and left him standing on the landing, feeling more lost than he ever had before.

Thirty-Two

"All is prepared. Tomorrow afternoon!"
John H. Surratt

Surratt Boarding House
Washington, D.C.
March 6, 1865

Annabelle paced the narrow center of the room, her nerves fluttering. The night grew deep, creeping toward morning, and still she'd not untangled her thoughts. Nothing made sense. But a decision had to be made.

"Miss Belle, you're gonna wear a hole in the rug."

"He remembered my birthday," she blurted.

Peggy's forehead crinkled, creating a deep line in between her brows. "That's what you're pacing about?"

"He lied to me."

"'Bout your birthday? Humph." Peggy rolled the blanket in her hand a little tighter and stuffed it into the carpetbag. "It won't close, but I don't think that matters."

Annabelle gaped at her. "Peggy! Are you listening to me?"

Matthew had lied to her, but she'd lied to him as well. Matthew wasn't a murderer. David O'Malley must have forced him into this by using George.

"'Course I am, child. But I don't see how your fretting needs to stop me from getting this here stuff together. That driver gonna be here first thing in the morning." She squeezed the bag against her chest as if she could force the contents to get smaller.

"I'm not going." She couldn't let them abduct the president.

Peggy dropped the bag. Annabelle put on what she hoped was her best you-won't-change-my-mind face.

Peggy lifted her brows. "That so?"

Annabelle lifted her chin a notch. "It is."

"Hmmm. You said we needed to get out of here as quick as we could."

She had. She'd even located a shady-looking man who had agreed to take her to her grandmother in New York. But she'd have to give him Mother's necklace. He'd said her Confederate currency was worthless, but that diamond would cover his troubles. She thought it would cover three trips, but he'd insisted the added danger upped the costs. She should have never showed it to him.

She clenched her teeth. "I can't run north." She dropped her voice. "They're going to abduct the *president*, Peggy. Possibly kill him. We have to do something."

"We already done something. It was a miracle we found his driver."

That couldn't be denied, and she was thankful for it. Still, anxiety sat heavily in her gut. "I have to see what happens. What if he didn't believe me? If nothing else, we need to follow them."

Peggy's eyes flew wide. "We ain't doing no such thing!"

Annabelle shushed her. "Lower your voice. They can't know

we're on to them."

Peggy groaned. "It's too dangerous."

"We won't let them see us." Annabelle gripped Peggy's shoulders. "We won't engage anyone, I promise."

Peggy looked dubious.

"We'll just watch. If we can't stop it, we'll at least be able to tell the law where to begin their search."

Peggy scowled.

"You know it's the right thing."

She pressed her lips into a thin line. "Why don't we just find the law now? Before they try and get him?"

Annabelle shook her head. "We've been over this. You know we can't take that risk."

Peggy gave a dramatic sigh. "Fine, but I don't see how you think we're going to make this work."

The corners of Annabelle's lips tugged up. "I have an idea."

March 7, 1865

Matthew pulled the brim of his hat low over his forehead. Annabelle had said goodbye. His breath billowed in the stables, mingling with the morning fog. Something about it didn't sit right. The pained look on her face had seared into him, and he couldn't shake it.

She'd stayed in her room all day yesterday as they'd finished their preparations, and Mrs. Surratt seemed perfectly content to have Annabelle's meals sent up to her. O'Malley said Matthew could return for her once they saw Lincoln to Richmond. But would she think he had abandoned her when he didn't return today? How would she ever trust him?

Curse it all.

Matthew slung the saddle onto his horse and patted the animal's neck. Anxiety crawled over him like a swarm of ants. In the stalls next to him, O'Malley, Harry, John Booth, and three of Booth's men readied their horses. Matthew had yet to see the greatness O'Malley boasted about Booth. An oiled dandy, if you asked Matthew.

"You ready?" O'Malley asked through the stall bars.

"Nearly." Matthew pulled the cinch tight and tied it off. He turned to O'Malley. "Following you."

O'Malley led his horse from the stall and down the aisle, and Matthew joined in behind him, with the others following silently. A young groom at the door bent his head over a saddle he was polishing and paid them no mind as they passed.

Once they mounted, Matthew expected to be told where they were going, but no one seemed inclined to discuss it. There was no choice but to follow. He tugged on the collar of his jacket and glanced at the heavy gray clouds hanging low in the sky.

They took their horses onto the muddy road, which never appeared to clear of the multitude that clung to Washington, not even at this hour. Matthew didn't think he could ever grow accustomed to living in such a crowded place.

Booth took the lead, and the group flowed through the unsuspecting people. Anticipation practically seeped from O'Malley. By the time they stopped at a small restaurant at the edge of town, Matthew felt as if his stomach would twist itself into a knot.

Inside, they gathered together without bothering to remove their coats and hats, let alone sit down at one of the empty tables. The establishment, likely lively and filled with hungry customers most days, sat shrouded in an unnatural silence that further unnerved him.

"Let's go over the plan once more," O'Malley said, his voice dripping with excited words that fell hollow on Matthew's ears.

Matthew expected Booth to deliver the final directives, but he and the Surratt fellow, the landlady's son, were hunched together in private discussion. Matthew swung his gaze back to the man he'd once thought a friend. O'Malley looked pleased, puffing out his chest as he addressed the men, calling them heroes.

Throughout this ordeal, O'Malley had taken credit for the plan. But within moments of meeting Booth, the truth had become painfully clear about which of the men was the mastermind. And who was the pup at his heels. The fact that Booth let O'Malley grandstand while he planned only confirmed it.

The muscles in Matthew's neck stiffened as he watched O'Malley's animated hands fly along with his words. How dull did he think they were? They'd gone over this part at the boarding house already.

"Daniels!" O'Malley suddenly thrust his finger at Matthew.

"What?"

"Did you hear what I just said?"

Matthew scowled. "Of course. Same as I did when you said all of this the first time."

O'Malley narrowed his eyes. For some reason, O'Malley had presented Matthew like a prize when he'd introduced him to John Booth. For what reason, Matthew couldn't fathom. But whatever it was, it made O'Malley keep a sharp eye on him as though he feared any move Matthew made could humiliate him.

Booth walked over to the group, his chest puffed and his brown eyes shining.

O'Malley raised a hand to him, immediately forgetting his glower. "Hear! Hear!" O'Malley's grin nearly split his face. "As we make ready, let's not forget the man who brought us the means to play this most dangerous of games. The man who has given of his own possessions to see that justice is done and the tyrant removed!"

Booth had funded them?

"I have only an army to give," Booth said, nodding to each of them. "My brains are worth twenty men, my money worth a hundred."

Matthew struggled to keep his face even. He'd thought *O'Malley* was stuffed with ego!

"And your information even more!" O'Malley exalted.

Booth offered him a sly smile. "I have free passes everywhere. My profession, my *name*, is my passport. My beloved, precious money—oh, never beloved until now!—is the means, one of the means, by which I serve the South."

The men nodded in agreement, and Matthew could feel their anticipation rising. Here stood a group of men who saw it as their duty to bring Lincoln to heel. Looking over their faces, seeing the glimmer in their eyes, Matthew wondered if it would end there.

Harry grinned. "Today, he shall be ours. The South will be avenged!"

Matthew tried to put moisture back into his mouth, but it felt filled with cotton.

Booth chuckled, and the mirth in it seemed out of place. "My love is for the South alone. I do not deem it a dishonor in attempting to make for her a prisoner of this man, to whom she owes so much misery."

The men raised a shout, and someone patted him on the shoulder, but Matthew couldn't share their elation. Dread wormed through his gut, a sense of unease so heavy its weight demanded he speak above the clamor. "When we have him, then what?"

Every eye turned to him, and silence dropped like a lead weight.

Though intuition told him they were words best left unspoken, the hatred boiling from these men made Matthew fear capture wouldn't be the end of their scheme. The leverage wouldn't stop at seeing Confederate soldiers released from prison. It wouldn't stop until they'd squeezed every drop of humanity from the object of their wrath.

Booth cocked his eyebrow, sharing a glance with a disgruntled O'Malley before addressing Matthew with the smooth voice of a man of practiced words. "This man's appearance, his pedigree, his coarse low jokes and anecdotes, his vulgar smiles, and his policy are a disgrace to the seat he holds."

Matthew tipped his chin. "Still, he is the elected president, brought to office by a people who will stop at nothing to see him returned to lead."

"Other brains rule the country," Booth growled.

Did they? Matthew couldn't rebuff the statement. What did he know of politics?

Booth stepped closer to Matthew, not intimidated as some men were to have to crane his neck back to meet Matthew's gaze. His eyes glimmered with passion.

"He is a Bonaparte in one great move—by overturning this

blind Republic and making himself a king."

What? Matthew's brows drew together.

"This man's reelection, I tell you, will be a reign! You'll see." He nodded vigorously, poking his finger into Matthew's chest. "You'll see that reelection means succession. His kin and friends are in every place of office already."

O'Malley pushed in between Booth and Matthew. "So, we see it ended today! The time has come!"

Booth whirled and stalked out the door. Matthew stared after him until O'Malley placed himself fully into Matthew's line of sight. They had not answered his question.

"Didn't I tell you? He's sat in the White House! He's dined with the tyrant. He knows, oh, he knows." O'Malley slapped Matthew on the shoulder. "Come, man! Today we become heroes."

Matthew followed him out and mounted his horse, telling himself the prisoners' release was his only concern. Once that was accomplished, he would have no more to do with their schemes.

Just as he swung into the saddle, a movement caught his eye. Someone darted around behind the restaurant before he could get a good look at him. Were they being followed?

Matthew set his jaw. He was likely just being paranoid. He'd be glad when this was over. He clicked the reins and urged the horse into a trot, drawing up alongside one of Booth's men, who didn't look at him.

In less than a quarter hour, they positioned themselves in the trees along the road to lie in wait. Time crawled by slowly, though Matthew couldn't tell if it was truly taking too long or if it only seemed so to him. He wiped his sweaty palms on his trousers. The horse stomped beneath him, sensing his rider's unease. Matthew patted the animal's neck.

Across the road, Booth sat straight in his saddle, satisfaction evident on his face. With his mustache and his long hair styled perfectly beneath his hat, the man looked every bit the pompous actor. How many had taken in his looks and quick smile and deemed him harmless? Certainly Lincoln.

Booth kept his gaze steady upon the road, as if the slightest flicker of attention away from it would cost him his quarry. Matthew couldn't help but wonder how a man famous in the theatre had become so deeply imbedded in the spy ring. How could he sit as a guest at the White House while plotting to steal away the president? How good of an actor was he? Could a person ever really know a man's true nature if he could wear any face he chose? How could anyone trust such a man?

A sound reached his ears, and his pulse quickened. Hoof-beats—faint still, but approaching.

Booth held up his hand, giving the signal for them to hold their positions. Matthew strained to see. Time slowed even further, though Matthew had not thought it possible, and his heart pounded with each step of the approaching hooves.

The soldier in him recounted his orders. He didn't particularly care for this plan. There was something cowardly about taking a man by stealth.

He swallowed his doubts and pushed his anxiety from his mind.

For George.

The carriage rounded the corner, and Booth gave the signal to move.

The women pulled their horses to a stop at the top of a small rise and remained hidden behind a grove of young pines. The horses had to wedge into the trees, and the rough needles tugged at Annabelle's trousers. They'd followed the men through town, waited behind a restaurant while the group seemed to be finalizing details, and then hurried out past where the conspirators waited in their current positions along this road.

After following and then skirting behind the group of men, Annabelle and Peggy found a place farther north on the road. Hopefully, if the president came this way, they would see him first. Annabelle tugged her man's cap lower on her head. The hair stuffed underneath it made it difficult to keep in place. But with the jacket pulled close and the cap low, no one would suspect her to be a woman, especially if she kept her distance. All those days astride a horse now came in handy.

Peggy, on the other hand, appeared just as uncomfortable as she had the first moment she'd been forced to ride. The worry on her face reflected the same fears churning Annabelle's stomach.

Please, let him have listened!

The wind stirred and tickled the back of Annabelle's neck, making her shiver. She prayed Mr. Clark had taken her seriously. Hopefully, they would wait here, watch this band of miscreants leave empty-handed, and then beat the men back to the house. The president would be safe and no one would be the wiser to her part in thwarting this scheme.

The hired driver meant to take her to New York hadn't shown this morning. Annabelle had wanted to send him away quietly. If he came to the boarding house now, she had no doubt Mrs. Surratt would tell the others. Would they let her out of their sight again? Worse, would they put the pieces together and guess what she'd done?

"Well, they ain't seen us yet," Peggy whispered.

Thankfully, the men had been so engrossed in their mission that they hadn't once looked back to see if they were followed.

The road remained quiet. The men's horses shifted in the cover of trees. It had to be past the time now. Mr. Clark must have—

Annabelle's heart dropped. The crunch of carriage wheels broke the silence, announcing her failure.

He hadn't believed her. Oh, heavens, why hadn't he listened? Conceited men. They never took a woman seriously!

Peggy groaned. "I'd hoped that fool boy would listen."

The black carriage approached at a leisurely speed. She narrowed her gaze. The young man at the reins seemed tense. He swung his head, eyes nervously darting back and forth across the road.

"Idiot," Annabelle spat.

"Miss Belle!"

Annabelle threw her an annoyed glance. This was hardly the time to be a lady.

"Look at him!" Peggy said, pointing. "He's on guard, sure 'nough."

Annabelle let out a breath. They didn't change plans, but at least they were prepared. She hoped it would be enough.

A cold breeze picked up and hit her in the face, and she had to smack the hat down on her head to keep it from blowing away. How did men keep their hats without pins?

Annabelle scrunched her brow, the truth of it digging in. "Just because he's keeping an eye out doesn't mean he's going to be able to do anything about it. There are seven of them!" And Matthew! How could he? At the end of this day, George wouldn't be the only Daniels brother in prison.

Suddenly, a shrill whistle cut through the air.

The men burst out onto the road.

Matthew spurred his horse forward and thundered out into the open. To his left, Booth let out a whoop and galloped forward as the other men exploded onto the road. Seeing them, the carriage driver slapped the reins onto the pair of matched grays, and the startled horses leapt forward.

The carriage jerked, and the driver's hat flew from his head. Did he think to outrun them?

The familiar call of battle swelled within him, taking over his thoughts. Matthew barreled ahead. A soldier with his orders. He no longer felt the cold or heard the voice inside compelling him to stop.

Every sound drowned beneath the horses' hooves pounding like war drums.

The carriage shot past him as he angled his horse. Something about the look on the driver's face as he lowered his head and pushed the horses forward plagued Matthew, but he didn't have the time to consider what it might mean.

He pulled on the reins, and the horse lunged to the side, coming up at the right rear wheel of the carriage and falling into sync. Another man—Matthew thought his name was Lewis—took position at the opposite wheel, and the others fell in around them.

The carriage suddenly lurched to the side, and Matthew's horse jerked to avoid collision. Ahead, the others regained their positions surrounding the carriage. It was a gallant attempt on the driver's part, but it would not gain him success. Even if Matthew had fallen, the other six wouldn't be thwarted. Giving up on disabling them, the driver gave a fervent shout, and the carriage team picked up speed.

Matthew leaned lower in the saddle and used his knees to keep his body in rhythm with the animal beneath him, using only one hand to grip the reins. The horse bobbed near the edge of the carriage, and Matthew reached out to brush his fingers along the crease of the door. He nearly had it!

A drawn curtain covered the small window, hiding the occupants. He kept an eye on it, lest the curtain sweep back and reveal a revolver. Matthew veered close to the carriage again, but couldn't grab hold.

Just ahead, one of Booth's men drew up to the front of the carriage and threw himself from the saddle. He crashed into the driver's seat and collided with the man urging the horses forward. The carriage jerked again, careening away from Matthew.

His fingers slipped, and he dipped precariously in the saddle. He threw his weight to the opposite side to right himself. The horse jerked to compensate, nearly sending Matthew to the ground. He tightened his grip, gained his seat, and got the animal settled underneath him.

The carriage shuddered and jerked. Matthew shot past the door, coming even with the front wheel before he could pull back on the reins and regain his position. In the split instant that he rode at the front, his mind catalogued the scene in a snap of memory: Booth directly across the team of grays from him with a look of intense determination upon his features; Lewis wresting the reins from a harried driver, his own features resolute; the horses throwing their heads in opposition to the battle against their bits.

Cold air bit him, and the carriage thrust forward again, cutting off his view. He heaved his weight to the left and threw the horse nearly into the side of the carriage.

There! His fingers grabbed onto cold metal, and he swung his leg across the saddle. A horse let out a high-pitched squeal, and the carriage swung again, nearly throwing Matthew from his precarious hold. He clawed the side of the carriage and pressed his body against it.

His horse bolted away from him, leaving Matthew clutching the side of the carriage with naught but his fingertips and the toes of his boots.

Just as he thought his cramping fingers would lose their hold, the carriage began to slow. After a moment, the horses came down to a trot, then a walk. The carriage steadied, and Matthew inched his way down to the side step.

With a grunt, Matthew grasped the handle and flung the door open.

Annabelle ignored Peggy's screech and dug her heels into the horse's sides. It lurched forward and she had to grip the pommel to keep her saddle. Regaining her balance, Annabelle leaned forward and moved in easy rhythm with the horse.

They flew down the hill, trailing the carriage and the men surrounding it. She would not lose them!

The carriage swung dangerously on the road. The rear wheel hit one of the horse's legs. The poor creature leapt sideways, nearly throwing its rider.

The carriage tilted, the wheel lifting off the ground. It hit the road again with a hard crash. The president had to be having an awful time of it inside.

Oh, just hold on.

Where were his men? Shouldn't there have been some kind of guard riding with him? Her eyes darted to the other side of the carriage.

Her heart lurched. *Matthew.* Why did he have to be a part of this? The true reason she refused to go to the law, or even to run to New York, slapped her in the face. She couldn't turn him in, despite what he did. She could understand desperation. Even sympathize with the distant hope a foolish plot would solve one's problems. She couldn't send him to prison for it.

Help us, Lord.

The carriage jerked again, and Matthew swayed in his saddle, leaning dangerously close to his horse's churning hooves. Wind buffeted her face, and the cold air stung her eyes. Tears welled and further clouded her vision, but Annabelle couldn't tell if they were a product of the stinging wind or blistering fear.

Suddenly, Matthew jumped onto the side of the carriage. His foot slipped, and Annabelle's heart plummeted. She opened her mouth to shout his name, but he regained his feet and pressed his body close.

Annabelle tugged on the reins and slowed the heaving horse. The carriage topped a hill, and just before it lurched down the other side and out of sight, Matthew threw open the door.

Empty!

Matthew swayed as the carriage came to a stop, and he plopped down on the plush seat. O'Malley leapt inside, and then spewed a string of curses.

Matthew sat there dumbfounded as O'Malley leapt from the carriage, yelling to the others. Booth shouted something Matthew couldn't decipher against the pounding blood in his ears, and then hoofbeats thundered away.

Someone knew.

Matthew leapt from the carriage. On the hill behind him, a man on horseback watched him. Before Matthew could pin down what looked familiar about him, he galloped away.

They'd been seen!

O'Malley paced, ranting about Lincoln.

Matthew assessed the others. One conspicuously missing.

Booth had abandoned them. As though that would save him. The driver had seen them all. Did Booth think the law wouldn't come after him?

"Where is he?" O'Malley bellowed.

"Mr. Graves? He isn't here." Every eye leveled on the driver. The man straightened his jacket, obviously trying to appear like wasn't afraid of the men surrounding him. He located his cap and shoved it down over a head full of curly brown hair.

Graves?

Just as Matthew approached the driver's bench, O'Malley roared and leapt onto the carriage. His fist landed solid on the young man's face, spraying blood. The driver's head rocked back.

O'Malley stood over him, heaving. "Graves?"

The driver touched his bloodied lip and glared at O'Malley. "You just tried to rob his carriage."

"We—" O'Malley snapped his mouth shut with a growl. He scrambled from the driver's seat and leapt onto his horse. The others snapped into action, their horses' hooves churning up dirt.

Matthew hesitated, eyes lingering on the driver. "You knew."

Something flashed in the man's eyes so fast Matthew nearly missed it. He pressed his lips together.

Anger and relief battled within him, a strange stalemate rendering him motionless.

"Look. I don't know you," the driver said. "But whatever you're involved in, fellow, it would be best if you got out."

The haunting words slithered through him, mingling with the persistent inner voice warning him away. Matthew glanced at the churning dust of the men leaving him behind. "How? How did you know?"

The driver's brows drew together with determination. He would say nothing more.

Matthew dug his heels into his horse and hit a canter in a

single breath. As he left the carriage behind, one thought pulsed in his head and sent chills down his spine.

They were known.

Thirty-Three

"Ruined! My prospects blighted! The whole thing
has failed!"
John H. Surratt

*A*nnabelle galloped away from the approaching men
and toward a terrified Peggy. Peggy awkwardly spun
her horse and urged it forward just before Annabelle nearly
plowed into her. Annabelle overtook her easily and threw a look
over her shoulder that told Peggy she had better forget her fear
and get that horse to do more than trot. Thankfully, the
pounding hooves behind her soon attested to Peggy's acquies-
cence.

The plot had been thwarted! She breathed a quick prayer of
thanks heavenward that the driver had believed her. But if
President Lincoln wasn't in the carriage, where had he gone?
Why did the driver even come down the road at all?

They galloped to the edge of Washington. Annabelle drew
up the reins, and Peggy came up beside her.

Annabelle jerked her head to the side. "Let's turn this way.
Keep your head down. If we look normal, maybe no one will
notice us."

They slowed the horses to a walk. Peggy grumbled something under her breath but followed Annabelle's instructions.

Annabelle's heart thudded. Did they know? She had to get back to the house.

She kept her head low, trying not to look at the people on the street. After what felt like hours of taking an indirect course and thankfully not getting lost, Annabelle and Peggy finally came to a stop just down the road from the stable. Annabelle dropped down from the horse, proud of herself for learning to do so without a man's assistance.

She handed the reins over to Peggy, who clenched her teeth as she led the horses away. A female slave returning the horses to the groom was a lot less odd that a woman dressed as a man doing it. Annabelle ducked into the shadow of a brick building, just inside a narrow alleyway that separated this structure from the next.

Even the biting wind and the ominous clouds could not dampen her spirits now. They'd saved the president! She smiled to herself. If they hurried, they could sneak back to the outhouse and get changed before anyone wondered—

A calloused hand clamped over her mouth.

Annabelle tried to scream, but the sound lodged in her throat. She kicked at her assailant and clawed at the thick arm wrapped around her waist. The brute pulled her deeper into the shadows.

"Cease," the man growled in her ear. Then he groaned. "I should have known."

Annabelle stilled at the sound of the familiar voice, her chest rising and falling rapidly.

He thrust her away from his chest. "You had better explain

yourself!"

Annabelle whirled around to face Matthew, heat coursing through her body like flashing lightning. "How dare you!"

His eyes glinted and he grabbed hold of her wrist as he stalked deeper into the alley.

"What are you doing?"

"I'm not letting you run from me again," he said, his voice low.

Annabelle stumbled along behind him. What did he mean to do? He tugged her deeper into the small space between the two brick buildings and then flung her around to face him.

She winced, and he instantly dropped her wrist. She rubbed at it, staring hard at him. His gaze dropped and regret flittered across his face, but he offered no apology. Annabelle thrust her arms behind her and away from his probing gaze. She looked at the ground to hide the traitorous tears that flooded her eyes.

She refused to blink and instead stared at his feet until her eyes dried. Then her gaze traveled up Matthew from his feet, set shoulder width apart, to his wide chest and arms held behind his back. When she reached his face, she found his features hard. Even so, her heart lurched just as it had when he'd given her the silver horse on the steps. Why did that seem like ages ago?

Clean shaven, he looked much younger than he had during their long ride. And she had the strangest impulse to release the long hair tied behind his head and see what it would feel like between her fingers.

Enough! Annabelle stiffened. She must not allow the softness she felt for him make her forget his lies.

"What did you do?" His clipped words jolted her back to reality. The man who'd plotted to steal away the president and had dragged her through his lies glared down at her with anything but tenderness.

She crossed her arms. Even in the heavy overcoat, she felt exposed in trousers that hugged her legs too closely. She suddenly missed the protective curtain a dress provided for her figure.

Annabelle lifted her chin and determined he would not know her discomfort. He would not see her weakness.

"I followed you," she stated flatly.

The muscles in his jaw worked. "As I can see."

She forced herself to hold his gaze until she could no longer stand it. "You lied to me!"

"I protected you!"

"How could you, could you...?" She stammered to a halt. "*What?*"

He made a low sound in his throat, and suddenly his arms were around her. Matthew crushed her against his chest so tightly she could hear the rapid beat of his heart.

"What if you'd been seen? Do you know what they might have done to you?"

She resisted the urge to enjoy his touch, reminding herself he was one of them. She threw her hands up between them and pushed.

He let her go.

She stumbled back and stared at him.

"I've tried to keep you safe," he said with a husky voice. "The less you know, the better." His eyes searched hers, begging her to understand.

She couldn't. "What you meant to do was treason!"

Anger flitted across his face. "We would've gained a bargaining chip from the enemy!"

Enemy. The word slithered over her. She had to remember that she sat on a very dangerous line. Being known as a Southern plantation holder with Northern sympathies would gain her no friends on either side. She swallowed the lump gathering at the back of her throat.

Matthew reached forward as if to touch her cheek but quickly dropped his hand. "I ask again, what did you do?"

She drew her brows together and glared at him.

The muscles in his neck fought against the confines of his shirt collar. "If you found out and somehow managed to warn them…." He shook his head. "I don't trust O'Malley to let your gender stay his hand."

Her insides clenched. Would he really harm her?

Matthew took another step closer. "It's too late for me, but not for you."

Before she could protest, Matthew pulled a stray lock of hair from her cap and rubbed it between his fingers. "Since I failed in shielding you from this, I must now remove you from it."

She craned her neck to look up at him. What did he mean, remove her?

He dropped her hair and gripped both of her shoulders instead. "You can't say a word about this to anyone." He squeezed harder. "Do you hear me, Annabelle?"

She nodded, but still he didn't release her.

"What do we do now?" she asked. She meant the words to come out confident, to prove she was as worthy as any man. Instead, they came out in a squeak.

His brows gathered again. "We get you out of here."

"What about you?"

A sad smile spread on his lips. "I have to find my brother."

"Can't you see this is madness?" Annabelle put her hands on top of his. Surprise flickered across his face. "There's another way." His chest swelled with a deep breath, but Annabelle hurried on before he could answer. "And now that they know, don't you think the next time Lincoln will have someone there to capture you?"

Actually, she was amazed that hadn't happened this time.

He took a step back, shaking his head.

Foolish man and his ridiculous pride! She turned and stalked away. He caught her wrist before she'd made it three paces. She paused but didn't look at him.

"I wish things were different."

She waited, blinking away furious tears.

He heaved a sigh, dropping her hand. "Get back to the house, and be sure no one sees you in men's clothes. I'm taking you to Westerly."

"What makes you think I'll go?"

His face hardened, and part of her regretted the words, though not enough that she wished to call them back. She'd been too soft already, and that gained her nothing.

"You've changed your mind about our deal?"

She clenched her hands to keep them from shaking but managed to keep her words even. "Peggy thinks we should go to New York, to my mother's family."

"What do *you* think?"

She pulled her lower lip through her teeth. If she went north, what would happen to Rosswood? But how could she trust the man in front of her? "And what would I do at Westerly?"

"Stay with my mother," Matthew said quickly. "Heaven knows she could use the company. I will return as soon as I have George free and have kept my word." His eyes bore into hers.

She searched his face. If he took her to Westerly, they wouldn't be here when the law surely came for him. "Very well."

She scurried from the alleyway, and this time he didn't stop her. Breathing heavily, she hurried into the dampened sunlight and toward the stable. Peggy stood on the sidewalk, wringing her hands. As soon as she laid eyes on Annabelle, her face turned from worry to anger. By the time Annabelle reached her side, she felt like a child about to receive a tongue-lashing.

"Where have you been? You done scared me silly!"

"I'm sorry. I... had to speak with Matthew."

Peggy put her hand on top of her head. "Lawd, this here child is gonna be the death of me!"

Annabelle grabbed her arm. "We have to get moving."

Peggy snorted but fell in step beside her. Annabelle released Peggy and stuffed her hands in her pockets, keeping her eyes on her dirty boots. She hoped O'Malley would never discover she'd taken his clothes from the line.

They made it to the back of the boarding house without incident. To her sheer astonishment, Annabelle was back into her own clothes and was reaching for her bedroom door when the men burst into the house, bellowing curses.

Peggy's eyes widened. "What happened to that driver what was gonna take us to New York?" she whispered. "I better go and try to fetch him again."

Annabelle held up a hand to shush her.

"After having everything so finely planned!" a man bellowed. Mr. Surratt, the landlady's son.

Someone hushed him, and their voices lowered. Annabelle grimaced. Mrs. Surratt appeared at the bottom of the stairs, and Annabelle stumbled backward, nearly tripping on her skirts before she got back into her room. She latched the door as quietly as possible. Had the woman seen her?

Peggy's eyes were large and white against her dark face. Footsteps thudded up the stairs and stopped outside the door. Annabelle held her breath and waited for the knock.

When it came, both women still jumped. Annabelle nodded to Peggy to open the door, and she straightened herself as best she could.

"Hello, madam."

"A message arrived for your mistress," Mrs. Surratt said, though she didn't produce anything.

"Oh, do come in," Annabelle said, waving for Peggy to step back.

Mrs. Surratt stepped into the room, looking around as if she expected to find something hidden. "It came when you were out. Seeing the town, I suppose?"

Annabelle forced a vapid smile. "Oh, yes. I'd hoped to. But that terrible mud." She wrinkled her nose. "It makes things so difficult. I'm afraid I didn't get far from the house before I simply couldn't stand it any longer."

The woman looked at her as if she hadn't any wits to spare. Annabelle fluttered her lashes. "You said I had a message?"

The woman fished around in the pocket of her velvet dress and held out a folded paper. "Yes. I'm assuming this letter addressed to *Miss Daniels* is meant for you?"

Annabelle forced a giggle. "Oh, yes, a simple misunder-standing. I said I was traveling with Mr. Daniels. He must have gotten that confused with my name."

"It's interesting how a message would find you here, seeing as how you've been here such a short while."

Annabelle shrugged, not knowing what else to say.

The woman huffed but handed over the paper. They stood there in silence as Annabelle's heart felt like it would gallop out of her chest.

Finally, Mrs. Surratt cleared her throat when it became evident Annabelle wouldn't open the missive in the woman's presence. "Well, I'll leave you to it then."

Peggy closed the door behind the landlady and then leaned hard against it. For several moments, neither of them spoke. Annabelle shoved the message into her pocket and finally released a long breath, offering Peggy a tentative smile.

The look she got in return withered her fragile hope that the woman had bought her act.

Peggy's eyes were alight with fear. "Get your stuff, girl!" she hissed. "That woman knows!"

Thirty-Four

"But to think so fine a plan going astray, and in such a manner! Could he have been warned?"
John H. Surratt

O'Malley paced the floor, his face such an alarming shade of red Matthew feared he would combust.

"How could our plans go awry?"

Matthew offered no reply. Surratt, Booth, and the men they'd brought had left. Matthew suspected O'Malley's anger sprouted nearly as much from being left out of their planning as from not having captured Lincoln. Only Matthew, Harry, and O'Malley remained.

"He should have killed him at the inauguration! He had the chance, the coward!" O'Malley's nostrils flared. Rage seeped from every pore, and the glazed look in his eyes made Matthew question his sanity.

Harry remained eerily calm. The cold detachment equally as disturbing as O'Malley's fire.

Matthew stepped backward to the doorway, keeping his eyes on O'Malley. He had to get Annabelle out of here.

O'Malley quit his pacing and swung his wild gaze onto Matthew. "Where are you going?"

"The plan has failed," Matthew said evenly.

"No! Merely delayed!" O'Malley flung his arms wide. "I will see this through! I *will* see it happen!"

Mrs. Surratt swept into the room in a rustle of black fabric. She eyed Matthew, then swung her calculating gaze to O'Malley. "Do you know where Miss Ross was this afternoon?"

Matthew's pulse quickened. O'Malley glared at her. "Why should I care, woman? Can't you see we are about more important business?"

Unruffled by his briskness, she laced her fingers. "The timing is interesting though, isn't it?" She darted her gaze to Matthew, but he kept his focus on O'Malley.

"Nothing is of interest now, dimwitted woman," O'Malley growled. He pushed past them and out into the hallway, grabbing his hat and coat.

He slammed the front door with enough force to rattle the walls. Harry ducked out and left Matthew with Mrs. Surratt's probing eyes.

"If you will excuse me, please." Matthew made it two steps before her next words stopped him.

"I have quite a few men of influence who find their beds here." She arched a brow. "I'd hate to find that anyone under my roof put my son in danger."

"Of course, madam." Matthew dipped his chin and strode upstairs.

He could hear the women whispering inside Annabelle's third floor room. He rapped on the door.

Silence. Matthew leaned closer. "Annabelle, it's me."

A second later the door flew open. Peggy glared at him.

"I need to speak to Annabelle."

"And I ain't lettin' you."

Annabelle appeared over Peggy's shoulder and gently moved her out of the way. "We're going with him to Westerly."

Matthew gestured for her to lower her voice and stepped into the room without invitation. He closed it behind him and stared at the two women, who seemed to be trying hard to hide their fear. Neither succeeded.

"We need to go."

Peggy pointed her finger at Matthew's chest. "You ain't no master here."

He balked. *What?*

"Peggy, he means to—"

"No! I've been going along with all this. But this time I ain't moving another step without speaking my mind."

Begrudging respect for a slave woman who would dare address him in such a manner blossomed within him. A smirk tugged on his lips, but he knew well enough to suppress it.

"I don't know what you're planning now, but my Belle don't need to go anywhere else with the likes of you."

He held up a hand in protest. "But she'll be safer at—"

"And what's more," Peggy interjected, "you need to know that she's only willing to go with you just so *you* won't be here when the law comes calling!"

"Peggy!" Annabelle gasped. "Hush now!"

"I won't!"

Annabelle's eyes bulged, and she stepped back.

Peggy wagged her finger at Matthew, her tirade clearly unfinished. "She's willing to put herself into more danger just to keep you from getting your due. And besides that, how do we even know you is who you say you is? What if you ain't no man of Westerly? You lied about plenty else."

Matthew clenched his fists. "I'm Matthew Daniels, fourth son of Westerly, and a man of my word. Everything I withheld was only to protect her!"

Annabelle let out a small gasp and plopped down on the bed.

Peggy crossed her arms, tone smug. "Fourth, huh?"

Matthew drew his lips into a hard line and refused to let his gaze snap over to Annabelle.

"Why should she put herself at risk for you? The man who don't even want her?"

"Peggy, no!" Annabelle groaned.

His heart clenched. "What are you talking about?"

"Just 'cause I'm Colored don't make me a fool."

Tears flooded Annabelle's eyes. He snarled at Peggy. "Your skin isn't what makes you a fool. How can you think to speak on my feelings for her? You know nothing of them."

She lifted her brow. "Then why'd you lie about being the brother she was supposed to court?"

Annabelle hung her head, and Matthew's fist clenched. "She deserves better," he growled.

"It ain't 'cause you don't want her?" Peggy pressed.

Matthew stared at the top of Annabelle's head, willing her to look up at him. "It's because I care too much that I wanted her to have what was best for her!"

Peggy smirked, and the pulsing in his temples accelerated. They didn't have time for this! "Get your stuff, woman! We ride while we still can. I care little for how much you hate me. I *will* see her safely to Westerly."

Annabelle rose from the bed but wouldn't look at him. She simply picked up the bag by the footboard and silently walked past them out the door.

Thirty-Five

"Curse it! But for this mishap, the affair could not have failed; and by this time we should have been on the road to Richmond. We shall never again have such a chance."

John H. Surratt

*A*nnabelle could hardly see the stairs for the tears blurring her vision. What would possess Peggy to say such things? Did she think that by exposing Matthew's rejection Annabelle would refuse to go to Westerly?

Annabelle pushed past Mrs. Surratt at the bottom of the stairs and ignored the woman's sputtering.

"Annabelle!" Matthew pounded down the stairs. "Wait!"

She ignored him. Mrs. Surratt said something about exposing them, but the words landed on uncaring ears. She clutched the bulging carpetbag to her chest, flung open the front door, and then scrambled down the outer steps.

Thick mud sucked at her shoes, as sticky as the mess Peggy had put her in. The sun bathed her in warm light but could not chase away the chill that tingled down her spine. She drew in heavy breaths of cold air.

Hold it together!

"Annabelle!" Matthew caught her arm, and she stumbled,

dropping her bag into the mud.

Father's bag! Covered in muck and…and…. She burst into tears.

Matthew pulled her against him and stroked her back. "Hush, dear, it will come clean," he gently said against the top of her head. With his face buried in her uncovered hair, she could almost believe the tender way he spoke to her meant something.

She thrust her hands into his chest and pushed away from him hard enough that she stumbled back, barely catching herself before adding to her humiliation by planting her backside in the dirt. Annabelle ran her sleeve over her eyes, hardly noticing the curious stares of the people passing by. Annabelle kept her focus on Matthew and willed all the venom she could muster into her glare. "Do not think to touch me in such a way, Captain Daniels."

Pain sprang into his eyes for only a second before he inclined his head. He reached down and plucked Father's bag from the ground, attempting to brush it clean with his hand. He smeared the mud further.

Peggy burst out the door, her eyes seeking Annabelle's. Tears welled anew. Annabelle gathered what little dignity she could muster and continued on her way. Surprisingly, neither attempted to speak to her the entire way to the stable.

When she poked her head into the barn, they were both still on her heels.

"May I help you, miss?" the groom asked, dropping his polishing rag and hurrying over to her with a springy gait.

"My horse, please."

"Yes, miss." The boy bounded off.

Annabelle breathed deeply, the scents of horse and hay reminding her of days when her only worry was not to ride too far from Father's side. She lifted her chin and kept her gaze forward. Matthew stepped around her and marched down the barn aisle, likely going after the horses Annabelle hadn't called for.

Peggy touched her arm. "Oh, my sweet girl. I didn't mean to hurt you."

Annabelle swallowed hard and lifted her chin. Peggy wagged her head.

"I'm sorry, Miss Belle. I only meant to get him to say it!"

Annabelle rubbed her hands together. "*Why?*"

"'Cause men's stubborn. He weren't gonna say it unless I made him, and I *had* to be sure before you run off with him again."

She stared at Peggy incredulously. "But *why* get him to say he put me off on his brother? What good could that have possibly done except make things awkward?"

Peggy placed her hands on her hips. "You don't see it, do you?"

Annabelle threw her hands up. "What? Tell me, what don't I see?"

"Humph. You don't see that man loves you, even though it's as plain as day."

"He doesn't...I...I don't want...." she stammered to a halt.

Peggy arched her brows and waited.

Ridiculous! Annabelle searched Peggy's face for any signs of humor but found none. "You must be mistaken. He only wants to be sure I'm safely out of the way."

"Ain't so sure about that," Peggy said, insufferably sure of herself. What did Peggy know about such things anyway? It was just an old woman's imagination running wild. Wasn't it?

Annabelle chewed her lip. Was Matthew merely concerned for her safety, or did his feelings run deeper? By the time Matthew returned with two saddled horses, she was no closer to knowing if she believed Peggy or not.

Where was that groom? He should have had her horse out well before Matthew had time to saddle *two*.

Matthew's boots came to a stop in front of her. She let her gaze drift up the length of him until she finally met his eyes.

What she found there made her heart lurch.

"I'm genuinely sorry, Annabelle," Matthew said, the heaviness in his words making his voice sound deeper than usual.

Annabelle tried to sweep away her pride and offer a gentle smile. "Thank you."

"I was trying—"

She held up her hand to stop him from saying false words meant to soothe. "You don't have to explain."

He furrowed his brow.

"You once allowed me the freedom to bring you my motives and intentions when I was ready," she said. "You didn't press me, and you gave me your trust when I didn't deserve it."

Matthew's nostrils flared and his pupils widened, but his lips remained closed.

"For now, there's only one thing I must know."

Matthew gave a tense nod.

"What are your intentions with David O'Malley?"

"I'm finished," he said through tight lips.

"Completely?"

He stepped close to her. Too close to be proper. She tilted

her chin to keep her eyes on his face. She had to know he was finished with these treasonous games. Whatever happened, she didn't want to see him come to harm. But heaven help him if he lied to her again.

"O'Malley's gone out of his wits. I'll find another way to get George free. Then everything will be set to rights."

"I ain't never liked that man," Peggy interjected.

Matthew's lip twitched as he handed Annabelle the reins, and she suspected he suppressed a smile. Before she had a chance to react, he slipped his hands onto her waist and effortlessly lifted her into the saddle. She flung one leg over and arranged her skirts over the trousers underneath. Strange how sitting astride no longer felt foreign.

The groom cleared his throat, and Annabelle's attention snapped to his red face. When had he come up? The poor boy stood there awkwardly, unsure what to do with the horse he'd fetched, now that she was atop another.

Peggy squeaked as Matthew plopped her into the saddle as well. His words to her were low, but not low enough that Annabelle didn't catch them.

"I'm on to you."

Peggy lifted her chin. "Hmm. I ain't the one you need to be telling stuff to."

Matthew barked a laugh as he handed Peggy the reins. "Just like a woman. Always trying to meddle where she isn't needed." The mirth in his tone belied his words, and a sly smile turned Peggy's lips.

He took the horse from the groom and swung into the saddle. Annabelle couldn't help the smile that tugged on her own lips.

"You gonna bring the horses back today, miss?" the groom asked.

"No. I think not." She looked across the horse's ears at Matthew. "I believe I've had my fill of Washington."

The groom shrugged. "All right then."

They urged the horses out into sunlight that washed over them like a gentle tide. Annabelle looked up, glad that the gloom had been scrubbed from the sky. At her side, Matthew sat tall in the saddle, a look of determination on his face.

He would leave this plan? Because he saw how foolish it was? Or something else? Regardless, she might very well have the information Matthew so desperately desired.

Annabelle let the other two ride on ahead of her as she pulled the paper from underneath her mantle and unfolded it.

One line was scrawled across the middle of the page.

Elmira Prison, New York.

She stuffed it back into her pocket. The last time she'd had secret information, it had landed her squarely in the middle of a dangerous plot. If she shared what she had now, what would it lead her into? Annabelle pulled her lip through her teeth. Westerly might offer quiet safety, but New York held the opportunity to save another man's life.

Annabelle hauled up on the reins, bringing her horse to a stop at the edge of the road.

Peggy glanced over her shoulder and drew up her own horse. "Miss Belle? What's wrong?"

"I think," Annabelle said with a resolute nod, "that we should head to New York."

Matthew wheeled his horse around and came up beside her. "You wish to go to your mother's family?"

She studied him. "If I did?"

Matthew scratched his chin, and his horse sidestepped beneath him as if it were anxious to be on the way. Behind them, the bustle of Washington faded in favor of the gentler sounds of birdsong and whispering winds. "If that's what you must do," he finally said, "then I'll see you escorted there safely."

Her heart warmed. He'd not spoken his feelings with so many words, but the earnest look in his eyes was all she needed. Desperate love for his brother had driven him, and a man who could love like that was one worth hoping for.

A grin split her face. "I know how to save your brother," she said, turning her horse back north. "All we have to do is break him out of Elmira Prison!"

A Dangerous Performance
The Accidental Spy Series Book Two

One

"Always bear in mind that your own resolution to
succeed is more important than any other."
Abraham Lincoln

Elmira, New York
March 14, 1865

To the victor belonged the spoils, but to the defeated
humiliation and despair. Annabelle shivered against the
Northern wind and pulled her wrap tighter. Beside her, Matthew
repeatedly clenched and released his fists as if they were itching
to land a blow. Not that she could blame him. What kind of
people did such things?

She studied the backs of those waiting in line in front of
them. From all appearances, they seemed normal enough.
Nothing about their heavy winter outerwear or their idle chatter
marked them as heartless. But what else could they be?

When had the suffering of one's fellow man become a
means of entertainment?

Annabelle shivered again, and this time not from the biting cold and drizzling rain. The man in front of them took another step forward, moving the line and bringing their little group to the bottom of the wooden staircase leading to the observation platform above.

"This here ain't right." Peggy plopped her hands on her hips, earning more than one raised eyebrow.

Annabelle shot her a warning glance. They didn't need to draw attention. Matthew's piercing gaze—which would have cowed a more timid soul—only made Peggy scowl.

"What?" Peggy lowered her voice. "We're all thinking it."

Matthew stepped closer to Annabelle. "Perhaps your maid should wait for you over there with the others."

Annabelle glanced behind her at the groups of colored folks gathered around hitched carriages and chatting among themselves. "Why don't you wait for us, Peggy?" Peggy opened her mouth to protest, but Annabelle didn't give her the opportunity. She leaned close to Peggy's ear. "Keep your ears open. See what they know."

Peggy hesitated. Ever since the three of them had been on the road, Peggy had clung to Annabelle like a wet shawl. Finally, she grumbled something and stalked toward the carriages.

The man ahead of them paid his fee and walked up the stairs as a well-dressed coupled descended. Annabelle studied the woman's fine furs. Did the wealthy people in this town have nothing better to entertain themselves?

"That'll be ten cents, sir, for you and the lady." The young man held out his hand expectantly.

The muscles in Matthew's jaw tightened and Annabelle slipped her hand into the crook of his arm, giving it a small squeeze. His jaw barely unclenched enough for him to speak. "I was told it cost three cents to visit the observation tower."

The youth shrugged. "Sorry, sir. It's a nickel apiece now. Includes binoculars, though, so don't worry, you'll get your money's worth."

Annabelle could practically feel the anger seeping out of Matthew. "Oh, that's good, isn't it? We'll be able to get a closer look then…." She trailed off, hoping Matthew caught her meaning.

He thrust his hand in his pocket and shoved a dime into the boy's open palm. Unfazed by Matthew's glower, the boy nodded toward the steps. "Got refreshments for purchase, too, case you want to linger."

Disgust bubbled in her stomach. Annabelle drew Matthew up the stairs before the boy found himself at the wrong end of Matthew's ever-growing fury. At the top, they stepped onto a wide platform raised as high into the air as the top floor of Rosswood. It was like standing on a balcony, except this one was disconnected from a building.

The entire structure was a bit unsettling, being so high in the air with nothing more beneath her than some planks and a few poles. Annabelle tried not to think of the open void below and took a place at the railing near several other visitors, careful not to touch the banister. The flimsy thing didn't look as though it would hold her weight.

Out of the corner of her eye, Annabelle watched Matthew snatch a pair of binoculars from a spindly man. Matthew stalked to her side, the veins in his neck bulging with fury. Without a word, he put the looking contraption to his face.

"Excuse me, miss?" The spindly man dangled another pair

of the lenses from a short loop of rope. "You forgot to get yours." When Annabelle hesitated, he wriggled his bushy gray brows. "You'll get to see their punishment much better with these."

Annabelle swallowed her disgust and grabbed the binoculars. He flashed a yellowed grin and continued down the platform to the next waiting group of onlookers. She turned the contraption over in her hand. She'd never used a pair before.

Matthew pressed the glasses to his face and scanned the area below. "I don't see him."

Annabelle put the smaller set of lenses up to her eyes. Immediately, everything in front of her appeared larger, revealing the scene with sickening detail.

Below the platform, a swollen river snaked between the town proper and the massive walls of Elmira prison. Tents lined both sides of the muddy banks. Scattered between the rows of sagging structures, small clusters of men huddled among piles of debris and refuse. With their pitiful clothing hanging loosely on gaunt bodies, they looked like little more than walking bones.

"Why are they out there in tents?" she mumbled to herself. "I thought all the prisoners were kept inside the walls."

"Too many of them now." A middle aged lady to her left pointed below. "Word is they have nigh on ten thousand in there. Too many for the barracks to hold for sure. They stacked them in there until the walls nearly burst."

How would they find George among so many? Most of them didn't have jackets, and some wore clothing so shredded and ragged that it was little more than strips of cloth flapping in the wind. How could the guards not give them proper protection from the elements?

Annabelle tried to cool the anger churning inside her, lest it seep into her words. She lowered the binoculars. "Ten thousand seems like far too many."

The woman lifted her shoulders. "They're letting some of them out, at least. It's a right shame. Traitors or not, no boy should be forced to live like that." The sadness in her voice made Annabelle lean closer, close enough to smell the rosy scent of the lady's soap.

"Letting them out?"

The woman nodded. "But only the ones that sign the allegiance papers, of course."

Annabelle's pulse quickened. Could it be that simple? All George had to do was sign his allegiance to the Union and he would be free to go? Matthew shifted his weight next to her. Was he listening to their conversation?

"I'd think men would be flooding out of there if that's all they need to do."

Matthew grunted. So, he was listening.

The woman solemnly watched the prison walls. "You'd think so, wouldn't you? But it's only one or two every few days."

Annabelle studied her refined profile. "How often do you come here?"

The woman stuffed her hands back into her muff. "I best be off. Good day to you, miss."

Annabelle watched her hurry down the steps. "Well, that was rather odd."

Matthew grunted. Resigned, Annabelle lifted her binoculars again and scanned the tents below. On the breeze, the stench of human waste drifted up to assault her nostrils. She swept her focus up from the tents and onto the tall stone wall peppered with men in blue holding rifles. What of the men inside those walls? Did they fare better than the poor souls at the river?

Rows of squat buildings huddled inside the wall, with scores of men crammed against the sides of them in an effort to escape the wind. Anger burned in her gut. Who was responsible for this place? Annabelle scanned faces until her shoulders cramped and her eyes burned.

Behind them, a man cleared his throat. "Excuse me? It's, uh…getting dark, sir."

Matthew tensed beside her but didn't lower his looking glasses. Annabelle turned to the man, who appeared rather uncomfortable. Good. Someone who peddled misery deserved no less. Though she figured it was more Matthew's imposing presence than the wretches below that had him shifting his weight from one shiny boot to the other.

He extended his hand. "Miss?"

Annabelle tried to force a tense smile but didn't achieve more than a slight raise of her lip as she handed her pair over. Matthew didn't move from his position.

After a few more moments the man reached out as if to touch Matthew's shoulder. Annabelle shook her head, and he let his fingers drop. He might be a weasel, but she couldn't let him unleash Matthew's wrath. Otherwise they would probably never be allowed on the platform again, or worse, would be detained by Elmira lawmen.

The weasel man hesitated only a moment longer and then garnered a pinch of courage. He straightened his shoulders and spoke with more confidence. "I'll have to ask you to hand over the binoculars now, sir. The platform is closing for the evening. You may return tomorrow."

Matthew lowered the glasses and turned his heavy gaze on the spindly little man. They matched stares and Annabelle held her breath. Finally, Matthew reluctantly handed over the lenses. The man scurried away, clearly relieved. Annabelle slipped her hand into Matthew's arm, gently turning him toward the staircase.

Dusk settled, and Annabelle suddenly felt guilty about the warm bed and hot meal she would soon enjoy while George sat out there somewhere, freezing. She gave Matthew's arm a squeeze. He blamed himself for his brother's capture, and Annabelle knew Matthew well enough by now to know that he would hold himself responsible for whatever condition they found George in.

Oh, please, let us find him soon.

Peggy waited for them at the bottom of the steps and fell in behind Annabelle and Matthew. They made their way across the dusty street and away from the abominable observatory deck toward the crowded inn just a few streets away.

Matthew had managed to get them a private room. While Annabelle was glad not to be put into a room she'd have to share with other unmarried females, Peggy had been quite upset about the arrangement. Matthew had adamantly refused to leave Annabelle and Peggy in the room alone, insisting the three of them could share the room just as easily as they had shared a campfire.

Despite Peggy's protests, pleading, and prods at his sense of honor and propriety, Matthew had calmly insisted. Not only were his limited funds from David O'Malley running low, but Matthew had insisted the women would be safer in a room with him. By the end of it, he'd somehow managed to gently bring

Peggy over to his side. He'd treated Peggy with respect and, because of that, he'd gained a deeper level of fondness from Annabelle.

Fondness. That's what she'd call the stirring in her heart.

Inside the inn, warmth and the yeasty scent of bread washed over Annabelle's senses and stirred her hunger. They passed the crowded tables of people already taking their evening meals.

But rather than choosing a table, Matthew stomped up the stairs. Annabelle followed him, Peggy close on her heels. He burst into the room like a bull, the vein in his neck bulging in fury.

"Blasted, dirty Yanks!"

"Shhhh!" Peggy waved a hand at him, unfazed by his seething anger. "You want to let the whole building know you ain't one of them?"

He cast her an annoyed look but clamped his mouth shut. Peggy shook her head and went to start a fire in the hearth.

Matthew paced like a caged bear. "Who pays a fee to watch men suffer and die? What a demented lot."

Peggy struck a match and held it to the kindling until a flame leapt to life. "What you gonna do about it?"

Matthew stopped his pacing and studied her. "What would you have me do, woman? Burn the vile platform down?" He paused, as if considering it. "Would serve them right if the whole town went up."

Annabelle gasped. "Surely you can't mean that."

He drew a long breath and rolled his shoulders. When his eyes turned to her, his features softened. "Forgive me. You shouldn't have to witness my temper. If you'll excuse me, I think I'll go for a walk."

She reached for him as he passed her. "Please, don't do anything rash."

He slipped out from under her touch and stalked out the door.

"That man's wound tighter than a coiled spring," Peggy said, tossing a log onto the fire and prodding it with the poker.

Annabelle plopped onto the bed, which sagged under her weight, and fingered the quilt. "Can you blame him? You didn't see them, Peggy." She shivered. "All those poor men. It's a wonder they've survived such conditions. How could the government could allow something so deplorable?"

"You know war ain't nothing pretty. What you expect to see?"

"I don't know. Not that."

"Seems to me Captain Daniels got plenty of schemes in his head. He'll think of something." Peggy laid the poker beside the hearth and extended her hands toward the fire.

"Perhaps," Annabelle mused, "but I've discovered a simple solution. I'll call on someone in prison affairs first thing in the morning."

"That so?" Peggy left the fire and busied herself spreading out sleeping mats, positioning herself between Matthew's pallet and Annabelle's bed.

She'd suggest they rotate use of the bed, but knowing that both Peggy and Matthew would adamantly refuse, Annabelle didn't bother. "A woman on the platform said they release prisoners who sign allegiance papers."

Peggy scratched her headscarf. "Hmm. Seems to me like they'd get lots of papers signed if that's all it takes for freedom."

Something in the way she said it made Annabelle's heart

ache. They called Lincoln *the liberator*. Maybe if his emancipation papers were signed by the states, then Peggy's people would be free as well. Annabelle gave Peggy a sad smile, which she returned. "I thought so, too. It's entirely too easy. There must be more to it than we know. That's why I need to speak to someone at the prison."

"And you think they'll give you whatever information you want?"

Annabelle shrugged. "Worked last time." Going into the Commissary General's office and asking for help enabled her to find George's location in the first place. She didn't see why doing the same wouldn't help them now.

Peggy smoothed the blankets again and sat on her pallet. "Miss Belle, we need to talk about your plans."

She shifted uncomfortably. "The plan is to get George out of that horrible place."

Peggy rolled her eyes. So much for avoiding the subject of her odd betrothal, which, technically, the groom wasn't even aware of.

"All right, then." Peggy splayed her fingers. "Say you find him, get him outta prison, and ride off free as a summer chicken."

Annabelle crinkled her forehead. What made a summer chicken free? All of Peggy's chickens were kept in a coop. Then they went in the frying pot.

"Then what?" Peggy snorted. "Have you even thought about what's going to happen then? When you have *two* Daniels men to deal with?"

Annabelle scrunched her nose. She *had* thought about it. Every night it kept her awake, and it wiggled into her thoughts at random moments throughout the day. The problem was that no matter how much she thought on it, she still hadn't figured out what to do. "I suppose once we see George freed or escaped, we could go home."

"Escaped? Lawd, child, you—" Peggy shook her head and pointed her finger at Annabelle. "No you don't. We'll talk 'bout that later." She fisted her hands on her hips. "So you think you, me, and them two men is gonna go back to Rosswood?"

Annabelle nodded.

"Hmm." Peggy crossed her arms. "We do still have Andrew to deal with, and your mean ole grandfather, if he's still alive." Annabelle nodded again, unsure where Peggy was going with this. "Yes, ma'am. Even after all this here gallivantin' you've done, we ain't found no solution to the problem that started this here mess."

Annabelle balked. "Gallivanting? Really, Peggy?"

She waved a hand. "What? It's a word I learned from Captain Daniels."

"I'd hardly call what we've been through *gallivanting*. More like running for our lives!"

Peggy shrugged. "I reckon. But we did save the president, and I got high hopes for that man. He's gonna set my people free."

Annabelle grinned. "And if we can do *that*, well then, we can surely save George and Rosswood. Once we have George, then maybe the rest will work itself out."

Peggy's smile faded. "How you gonna tell him about the betrothal?"

Annabelle rose and lit the lantern. She set it down on the small table beside the bed, sending shadows dancing across the quilt. "I was hoping I wouldn't have to."

Peggy lifted her brows. "You decided to tell him the truth?"

Annabelle cut her eyes at Peggy, knowing exactly which *he* she meant. "I've told you, there's nothing to tell."

"Humph. Then what're you talking about?"

Annabelle pressed her fingers into her rumpled skirt. "I'm going to let Matthew and George discuss it. I won't be the one telling George anything." She held up her hand. "And before you say it, there's nothing I need to tell Matthew either. I'll simply let the two of them talk before I go running my mouth."

"Ha! And let them men decide your fate? Since when have you been all right with that?"

Annabelle crossed her arms. "George doesn't know about any of this, and I *don't* want to be the one to tell him."

Peggy's eyes softened and she came to sit by Annabelle on the bed. "You're afraid he's not gonna want you?"

Was she? Or was she more afraid that he *would*... and that Matthew would let him? "I...." She took a deep breath to keep tears from burning her eyes. It was bad enough her heart strained toward one brother who didn't want her. But if George didn't want to marry her so she could regain Rosswood, what would she do? "I'm afraid he won't like the deal Captain Daniels made." She pushed her fingers into her hairline. "Then what? Andrew's probably already seized Rosswood. I'll need an alliance with a strong family in order to get it back."

"There's still hope your Uncle Michael will be able to help."

"Maybe. But it's been so long. Do you truly think he's still alive?"

"Ain't no reason to think otherwise." She patted Annabelle's knee. "You want to know what I think?"

As if her answer mattered. Peggy would tell her anyway.

"I think we still need to get to your momma's family. We're already in New York. Let's see if blood can help you, child. Don't put all your faith in these Daniels men."

Annabelle nodded slowly. Peggy was right. Why leave her fate up to hoping someone would want to marry her? "I don't have any reason to think they'll help, but you're right. We should try."

Peggy wrapped her in a squeeze. "Good girl." They sat there a moment, then Peggy grinned. "And besides, that boy needs to court you proper. It ain't good he thinks he ain't got to woo you."

Annabelle gave Peggy a playful push. "Come now, who *wouldn't* want to court a homely girl with a rundown plantation she can't save? I'm sure I'd be first on George's list of desirable ladies."

Peggy sobered. "Miss Belle, it ain't right you do that. Just because your grandfather was pathetic enough that he needed to put you down in order to make himself feel more important don't mean you should believe him. You're not a plain girl, and you got plenty to offer. Don't go selling yourself short."

Annabelle swallowed the lump in her throat and pulled Peggy into a quick hug. "I was just teasing."

Peggy gave her a squeeze. "Well, I ain't. No more talk like that."

Annabelle stood. "I'm starving. I don't suppose Captain Daniels will return for supper, so why don't we see if we can get us some plates to bring up here? I'd rather we ate alone instead of with the crowd."

A sad expression washed over Peggy's face. "Don't give up

hope yet, girl," she said, not allowing Annabelle to shift the subject. "I still think the captain cares too much to sees you go to anyone else. Brother or not."

Annabelle's heart flipped in her chest, but she forced her features to remain smooth. "Don't be silly. This is simply a matter of convenience."

"Sure it is." Peggy patted her hand and then stepped out the door, leaving Annabelle alone with an ache in her chest she could not ignore.

The story continues in *A Dangerous Performance*,
The Accidental Spy Series Book 2

Historical Notes

The quotes at the top of each chapter are taken from the private journal of John H. Surratt, one of the actual conspirators in the plot to kidnap Lincoln. The diary is on file with the Library of Congress, and is an interesting read. In his diary, Surratt lists March 7th as the date they attempted to take the president. During my research, I found some sources listed this date as March 17th and others as March 20th. I chose to use the date listed in the diary.

While John Surratt and John Wilkes Booth were actual people involved in the plot to kidnap Abraham Lincoln, my characters—Annabelle, Matthew, David O'Malley and friends— are fictional and in no way associated with the historical figures or historical events and outcomes. All words in the book used by Surratt, Booth, and Lincoln are actual historical quotes. (Booth's words at the restaurant prior to the attempted kidnapping are taken from different sources and did not occur in succession.) I did, however, give fictional words to Mary Surratt (John's mother and owner of the boarding house). The boarding house location and description are historically accurate, to the best of my ability.

When Annabelle is in Washington, she sees posters for *Clark in de Boots* playing at Ford's Theatre. While this was a play showing at this location, it was actually featured on February 11, 1865. I took liberties with this for my timeline.

History tells that Lincoln changed his mind and did not

attend the production at the Soldiers' Home and instead went to the National Hotel. I was never able to locate what made him change his mind. My character's involvement is, of course, fictional, as is the driver that Anabelle speaks to and his involvement in thwarting the plot. During my research, I was unable to find any accounts on what happened on the road after the conspirators left the restaurant. The decoy carriage and ensuing chase were products of my imagination.

Rumors abound about the Confederate government being aware of a large group of spies and conspirators that operated throughout the South and had ties to secret government agencies based in Canada. I used this information to expand the reach of the group of historical conspirators associated with the attempted kidnapping. A larger ring of people sharing coded notes with Booth and supporting his activities could have been possible, but are not recorded—at least, not to my knowledge. It simply made a good "what if…" idea for the story.

I attempted to weave together the historical facts and fiction to create an interesting story. Any deviations from actual historical events were purely fictional.

Acknowledgements

A special thanks to Colonel Walt and Miss Jean for allowing me to use their beautiful home as a setting for my story. Rosswood plantation is located in Lorman, Mississippi.

Thank you to Rich Stevens, who helped me check facts in association with army movements and the proper details of a soldier's life. Any historical inaccuracies or misrepresentations are entirely my own. I'd also like to thank Jessica Stevens for her help with concepts and design elements. Thanks to her and my other early readers for helping me make this book possible.

Becky, you are my right-hand lady. Thank you for your help on this and every other project. Emily and Kristen, thank you for your beta read, and, Linda, for your sharp eye on final copy edits. If any typos slipped through, I'm sorry!

Thank you Katie Beth for making a beautiful Annabelle, and Melissa Harper for the photography. Evelyne, your cover is fantastic. Thanks for bringing it to life.

To readers and Faithful Readers Team, you mean so much to me. Thank you for all your efforts in the making and sharing of these stories.

And, of course, thanks to my dear husband and two little boys, who put up with my strange work hours, wild imagination, and obsession with the Old South. I love you three dearly.

Finally, and most importantly, thank you Heavenly Father for the passion to write, for the stories you use to teach me, and the opportunity to share a little of what you give me with the world.

About the Author

Award winning author of Christian historical novels, Stephenia H. McGee writes stories of faith, hope, and healing set in the Deep South. When she's not twirling around in hoop skirts, reading, or sipping sweet tea on the front porch, she's a homeschool mom of two boys, writer, dreamer, and husband spoiler. Visit her at www.StepheniaMcGee.com for books and updates.

Visit her website at www.StepheniaMcGee.com and be sure to sign up for the newsletter to get sneak peeks, behind the scenes fun, the occasional recipe, and special giveaways.
Facebook: Stephenia H. McGee, Christian Fiction Author
Twitter: @StepheniaHMcGee
Pinterest: Stephenia H. McGee